"The author reveals through a vivid, gripping narrative the fear, violence and chaos of that time. Will the assassin's wife have the power to alter the course of history? Read this book and find out."
— Paul Sutherland, Multi-Published Author and Editor

Second Sight is dangerous...

Nan's visions of two noble boys imprisoned in a tower frighten her village priest. The penalty for witchcraft is death.

Despite his warnings, Nan's determination to save these boys launches her on a nightmare journey. As fifteenth-century England teeters on the edge of civil war, her talent as a Seer draws powerful, ambitious people around her.

Not all of them are honourable.

Twists of fate bring her to a ghost-ridden house in Silver Street where she is entrusted with a secret which could destroy a dynasty.

Pursued by the unscrupulous Bishop Stillington, she finds refuge with a gypsy wise-woman, until a chance encounter takes her to Middleham Castle. Here she embarks on a passionate affair with Miles Forrest, the Duke of Gloucester's trusted henchman. But is her lover all he seems?

"...a vivid and visceral journey into the darkest hearts of men during the Wars of the Roses... An incredible, unforgettable story, surely made for the screen. Moonyeen Blakey is a major new talent to watch."
— Sally Spedding, Award-Winning Mystery Author of Cold Remains

ISBN 978-1-61179-218-8
90000

9 781611 792188

A Gripping Tale of Ambition and Betrayal

Second Sight is dangerous...
Nan's visions of two noble boys imprisoned in a tower frighten her village priest.
The penalty for witchcraft is death.

Despite his warnings, Nan's determination to save these boys launches her on a nightmare journey. As fifteenth-century England teeters on the edge of civil war, her talent as a Seer draws powerful, ambitious people around her.
Not all of them are honourable.
Twists of fate bring her to a ghost-ridden house in Silver Street where she is entrusted with a secret which could destroy a dynasty.
Pursued by the unscrupulous Bishop Stillington, she finds refuge with a gypsy wise-woman, until a chance encounter takes her to Middleham Castle. Here she embarks on a passionate affair with Miles Forrest, the Duke of Gloucester's trusted henchman. But is her lover all he seems?

"...a vivid and visceral journey into the darkest hearts of men during the Wars of the Roses...An incredible, unforgettable story, surely made for the screen. Moonyeen Blakey is a major new talent to watch." – Sally Spedding, Award-Winning Author

Winner of the Cornerstones "Wow Factor" Writing Competition

fierce, unforgiving glare. "I thought you understood. You said you'd help me. Why won't people listen? Why don't you believe me?"

"Child, child, I *do* believe you. You have the Sight," he answered, his voice so weary, his kindly face so grave, all my hurt and anger ebbed away. For a moment he studied his ink-stained fingers. Then his eyes flicked towards the statue of the Virgin by the little altar beneath the lancet window where a single candle glowed. He crossed himself.

"But you must ask Our Lady to shelter you from these dark fancies."

"Am I a witch then?" I stared at the plaster face and the blue-painted robes, seeing no warmth or comfort in them. Unwelcome, my mother's face swam into my mind. Her eyes were just as empty.

"No, no." He touched my arm. "You mustn't think such things."

"But I see spirits. My mother says it's wicked. And her friend, Marion— Mistress Weaver, says—"

The candle spluttered, distracting us.

"What happens to the moth that's drawn to the candle-flame?" The priest's eyes focused on the flickering light.

"It gets burned."

"So we must learn to avoid danger." He looked at me intently.

"Am I to tell lies then?" I jerked as if stung. "I didn't think priests were supposed to tell lies." I wanted to hurt him as I'd been hurt, but he answered soft and mellow.

"No lies. But you must guard your tongue. Such talk of spirits frightens people and puts your family in danger. Better to keep silent

dusty cloak. The reassuring kindness of his pale features comforted and I lifted my eyes in gratitude.

He drew a bench from a pile by the wall where an open
press revealed some scrolls, some pots of ink and goose-feather
pens. Across a trestle lay scraps of vellum decorated with loops
and curls and inky finger-marks. I remembered then he taught
the village boys their letters and marvelled at these curious
scratchings like bird-feet in the snow.

He followed my gaze.

"The boys are after practising their writing." A smile
curved his mouth. "Sit down." Plucking a piece of parchment
he held it up for my approval. "Master Palmer has talent. He
may yet prove a scholar—"

The quiver in his voice signalled me to study his face. A
pair of troubled blue eyes met mine and I sensed at once he
guarded a secret of his own.

"Now tell me what you saw." His speech lilted, soft and
liquid. After years among us he still spoke like an outsider.

I closed my eyes, conjuring again the ring of chanting,
spiteful children, inhaling the ferment of pondweed and recoiling from the slap of water against my skin.

"Why did it upset Johanna Nettleship so much?" Sitting
beside me, the hairy fabric of his dark robe brushing my arm,
he put a cup of wine into my hand. Dutifully, I tried to swallow,
but gagged, spewing a stream of bile and pond water across the
flagstones instead.

"No matter." He stooped to wipe away the mess, crouching
beside me, his expression serious. "Was it just a bit of pretending, a bit of making up stories to frighten her? Or were you after seeing shadows on a wall?"

"I saw Will Nettleship as clear as I see you now!" I
clenched my fists, and the church rang hollow with my shouts.
"I told you before, I don't see shadows. I don't make things up.
I see real people like the boys in my dreams who'll be killed if I
don't find them." Impotent rage shook me. I fixed him with a

"She makes up stories. She's just a little girl."

"She told me she'd seen my brother walking by the water-mill. But Will's been dead three months since Easter."

"She's after telling you some tale she's fashioned—"

"Liars should be punished!"

"Yes, but according to their age and by those who understand these matters, not by a mob. Go home now, all of you."

The kindly priest spoke firmly and the group obeyed, but not without some sullen murmurs.

"Can you walk?" He held out a hand.

I nodded, twisting water from a sodden skirt. Green-stained and stinking, I rose trailing slime from tangled hair.

He led me along the dusty, winding track to the yew-shadowed church. Inside its cool, dark walls I stood, uncertain, arms clasped about my shoulders. Looking upward I glimpsed the stone carving of Saint Michael, sword raised high, straddling a crouching demon with curved fangs and scaly tail. Although the grim-faced angel was reputed to protect our village, I felt no reassurance in his stern presence. Gently Brother Brian steered me to the little chapel where he kept his vestments. Dripping and shivering, I waited, transfixed by the flames of Hell leaping up the painted walls, appalled by mocking demons wielding pitchforks, their wide mouths full of pointed teeth.

"Dry yourself." Bundling my ruined shift into a sack, he offered a coarse cloth. "No need to be afraid." He turned me from the sooty demons to wrap me in a

CHAPTER ONE

"Liar!"

"But I did see him! I did!"

Johanna's fist struck me hard across the mouth, splitting my lip.

Sensing blood, boys and girls spilled out of trees and across wasteland. Their voices soared, excitable, unstable. Soon a jostling circle harried us with jeers and shouts.

"Liar! Liar! Liar!"

Johanna seized me by the hair and forced me to my knees. Fleetingly I glimpsed the shifting web of faces hanging over me—mouths spitting spite. And all the while the noise grew louder like the roar of kindling catching fire.

Dragging, shoving, stumbling, they brought me to the pond. Sunlight dappled its lazy, scummy surface. Its poisonous reek tainted the breeze.

Fingers still embedded in my hair, Johanna pushed my face deep into the water. The shock of it was like a bite. No time to scream. No time to breathe. Liquid flooded my mouth and nose.

Wrenched upward for a blessed moment, I snatched at air until she thrust me under. Another rise and gulp, a blast of sound, and then the press, the drag, the pull, the awful, greedy darkness—

"For the love of God!"

I retched among the reeds, noise exploding in my ears.

"Do you want her to drown?" Brother Brian's voice shook with horror and disbelief.

The Assassin's Wife
by
Moonyeen Blakey

How to Order:

You can purchase "The Assassin's Wife" by ordering
it from your local bookseller,

or online from Amazon.co.uk

or you can download it as an e-book on to Kindle,
Nook,
Kobo, Apple (i-Tunes)

ISBN: 978-1-61179-218-8 (paperback)
ISBN: 998-1-61179-219-5 (e-book)

Website: wwwMoonyeenBlakey.com
www.Fireshippress.com

...a secret which could destroy a dynasty.

The Assassin's

Winner of the Cornerstones "Wow Factor" Writing Competition

MOONYEEN BLAKEY

Wife

Do you believe in Fate?

Born into a peasant family in 15th Century England,
Nan has few expectations but...
A dream separates her from family and friends
sparking a dramatic chain of events...
A secret betrothal,
A gypsy's gift,
A binding promise,
And a chance encounter
Will change her life forever...
Follow Nan's quest to save the boys in the Tower
through a country riven by civil war in
Moonyeen Blakey's debut novel
"The Assassin's Wife"
Published by Fireship Press 2012
Now available from Amazon or via your local book shop
ISBN 978-1-61179-218-8
www.MoonyeenBlakey.com

The Assassin's Wife

To Harjinder
Happy Reading!
Love, Moon x.

The Assassin's Wife

by

Moonyeen Blakey

Moonyeen Blakey.

Fireship Press
www.FireshipPress.com

The Assassin's Wife - Copyright © 2012 by Moonyeen Cooper

ISBN-13: 978-1-61179-218-8 (paperback)
978-1-61179-219-5 (e-book)

BISAC Subject Headings:
FIC014000 FICTION / Historical
FIC024000 FICTION / Occult & Supernatural
FIC037000 FICTION / Political

Cover design by Christine Horner

Address all correspondence to:
Fireship Press, LLC
P.O. Box 68412
Tucson, AZ 85737
Or visit our website at:
www.FireshipPress.com

1.0

Dedications

For my parents,
Frederick George and Muriel (nee Higginson) Blakey,
who never stopped believing in me.

And for Eddie, a rock and a haven.
What would I do without you?

Table of Contents

Acknowledgments   i

Prologue   1

Part One: Stanwode, Northamptonshire, 1460   3

Part Two: London, late 1460   41

Part Three: Norwich, 1463   161

Part Four: London, 1464   207

Part Five: Middleham, 1471   243

Part Six: London, 1478   347

Part Seven: Middleham, 1478   369

Part Eight: London, 1484   473

About the Author   511

Acknowledgments

A big thank you to the stalwarts of Yarburgh Writers' Group who endured all the rewrites of *The Assassin's Wife* — especially Tom Beardsley, Sandra Bensley, Lesley Dover, Michelle Elliot, Dave Evardson, Kris Gleeson, Millie Gough, Chris Green, Louise Law, Sylvia Lover, Frank Payton and Jen Ward — whose constructive criticism proved invaluable. And thanks to former Arts Development Officer for Lincolnshire, author Paul Sutherland, Editor of *Dreamcatcher*, who continues to monitor our progress.

Special thanks to authors Sally Spedding and Karen Maitland who have not only lent a sympathetic ear, but offered generous amounts of practical advice. Their continued support and enthusiasm keeps me buoyant!

Thanks, too, to Cleethorpes Library Staff — particularly Jane Coward — and to the Cleethorpes Library Readers' Group, to Michelle Elliot for her photographs, to Edmund Harness for rescuing me from the many and devious schemes of computers, to Kris Gleeson, whose wisdom and friendship remains inspiring and unfailing, and to my patient neighbour, Rhona Emsley, a shoulder to cry on and a tower of strength in matters practical.

And fond memories of absent friends who also played a part in this novel reaching fruition: Joan Hackney, Barbara Harness, David Mordaunt and Heather Sparnon.

Last but not least, my thanks to the staff of Fireship Press, especially my erudite, energetic and patient editor, Jessica Knauss.

Prologue

"It will be a cruel death."

The smooth voice brushes my ear, soft as a caress.

The wood is too green. Only thin trails and wisps of smoke trickle along these damp limbs wrenched from the living tree, spiralling among the intricately-woven basket-work. Caged, the girl stands bound and mute, her head lifted as if to sniff the acrid scent that rises, teasing and prickling the nostrils. Around her the spectators snatch a breath, thrust against each other, tensed for the entertainment that begins now.

Tiny shoots of flame race across the dry sticks some charitable wretch has thrown, licking and sucking at moisture until the black stench becomes a storm-cloud. We are engulfed. Complaining, the worshippers jostle for air and blink away tears.

"I can't see!" The voice is querulous.

The crowd surges forward, open-mouthed, panting with excitement. Bodies press closer as I struggle to escape the crush, the reek of tainted breath, but stout hands hold me. I'm grateful for the mask of fog, though my ears still catch the crackle and the hiss, the roar of burning wood. When the smoke clears, the flames are ragged, gaudy butterflies that leap and plunge, fluttering into ash. The sacrificial figure twists and capers among them, begins to sing. It is an anthem to pain. We gasp and clutch, rank with sweat, straining towards a terrible fulfilment.

"The fire is a demanding lover," insists the voice at my ear. "See how closely it embraces."

I shrink from the heat but the guards' grip is merciless. The song has become a howl, the dance a frenzy.

1

"Nerys! Nerys!" My voice is hoarse, useless. I am shamed.

Through the gamey smell of roasting and the stinking smoke, I watch her features begin to melt and drip like candle-wax. The black strands of her hair ignite and flare like sun-rays, copper-bright around her head, in brief glory.

Sweating, panting, we moan together, shudder and roll upon a spasm of pleasure that peters out into a mere sigh.

Spent and hushed, the crowd separates. The spell is broken.

"You see now what it is to burn a witch." The voice is hard, implacable.

I close my eyes. Tears ooze between my lashes but it is fear, not grief that feeds them.

"I don't want to see," I say. "I don't want to see."

Part One

Stanwode, Northamptonshire
1460

Chapter One

"Liar!"

"But I did see him! I did!"

Johanna's fist struck me hard across the mouth, splitting my lip.

Sensing blood, boys and girls spilled out of trees and across wasteland. Their voices soared, excitable, unstable. Soon a jostling circle harried us with jeers and shouts.

"Liar! Liar! Liar!"

Johanna seized me by the hair and forced me to my knees. Fleetingly I glimpsed the shifting web of faces hanging over me—mouths spitting spite. And all the while the noise grew louder like the roar of kindling catching fire.

Dragging, shoving, stumbling, they brought me to the pond. Sunlight dappled its lazy, scummy surface. Its poisonous reek tainted the breeze.

Fingers still embedded in my hair, Johanna pushed my face deep into the water. The shock of it was like a bite. No time to scream. No time to breathe. Liquid flooded my mouth and nose.

Wrenched upward for a blessed moment, I snatched at air until she thrust me under. Another rise and gulp, a blast of sound, and then the press, the drag, the pull, the awful, greedy darkness—

"For the love of God!"

I retched among the reeds, noise exploding in my ears.

"Do you want her to drown?" Brother Brian's voice shook with horror and disbelief.

"She said she'd seen spirits." Johanna's harsh voice condemned me.

"She makes up stories. She's just a little girl."

"She told me she'd seen my brother walking by the water-mill. But Will's been dead three months since Easter."

"She's after telling you some tale she's fashioned—"

"Liars should be punished!"

"Yes, but according to their age and by those who understand these matters, not by a mob. Go home now, all of you."

The kindly priest spoke firmly and the group obeyed, but not without some sullen murmurs.

"Can you walk?" He held out a hand.

I nodded, twisting water from a sodden skirt. Green-stained and stinking, I rose, trailing slime from tangled hair.

He led me along the dusty, winding track to the yew-shadowed church. Inside its cool, dark walls I stood, uncertain, arms clasped about my shoulders. Looking upward, I glimpsed the stone carving of Saint Michael, sword raised high, straddling a crouching demon with curved fangs and scaly tail. Although the grim-faced angel was reputed to protect our village, I felt no reassurance in his stern presence. Gently Brother Brian steered me to the little chapel where he kept his vestments. Dripping and shivering, I waited, transfixed by the flames of Hell leaping up the painted walls, appalled by mocking demons wielding pitchforks, their wide mouths full of pointed teeth.

"Dry yourself." Bundling my ruined shift into a sack, he offered a coarse cloth. "No need to be afraid." He turned me from the sooty demons to wrap me in a dusty cloak. The reassuring kindness of his pale features comforted and I lifted my eyes in gratitude.

He drew a bench from a pile by the wall where an open press revealed some scrolls, some pots of ink and goose-feather pens. Across a trestle lay scraps of vellum decorated with loops and curls and inky finger-marks. I remembered then he taught the village boys their letters and marvelled at these curious scratchings like bird-feet in the snow.

He followed my gaze.

"The boys are after practising their writing." A smile curved his mouth. "Sit down." Plucking a piece of parchment he held it up for my approval. "Master Palmer has talent. He may yet prove a scholar—"

The quiver in his voice signalled me to study his face. A pair of troubled blue eyes met mine and I sensed at once he guarded a secret of his own.

"Now tell me what you saw." His speech lilted, soft and liquid. After years among us he still spoke like an outsider.

I closed my eyes, conjuring again the ring of chanting, spiteful children, inhaling the ferment of pondweed and recoiling from the slap of water against my skin.

"Why did it upset Johanna Nettleship so much?" Sitting beside me, the hairy fabric of his dark robe brushing my arm, he put a cup of wine into my hand. Dutifully, I tried to swallow, but gagged, spewing a stream of bile and pond water across the flagstones instead.

"No matter." He stooped to wipe away the mess, crouching beside me, his expression serious. "Was it just a bit of pretending, a bit of making up stories to frighten her? Or were you after seeing shadows on a wall?"

"I saw Will Nettleship as clear as I see you now!" I clenched my fists, and the church rang hollow with my shouts. "I told you before, I don't see shadows. I don't make things up. I see real people like the boys in my dreams who'll be killed if I don't find them." Impotent rage shook me. I fixed him with a fierce, unforgiving glare. "I thought you understood. You said you'd help me. Why won't people listen? Why don't you believe me?"

"Child, child, I *do* believe you. You have the Sight," he answered, his voice so weary, his kindly face so grave, all my hurt and anger ebbed away. For a moment he studied his ink-stained fingers. Then his eyes flicked towards the statue of the Virgin by the little altar beneath the lancet window where a single candle glowed. He crossed himself. "But you must ask Our Lady to shelter you from these dark fancies."

"Am I a witch then?" I stared at the plaster face and the blue-painted robes, seeing no warmth or comfort in them. Unwelcome, my mother's face swam into my mind. Her eyes were just as empty.

"No, no." He touched my arm. "You mustn't think such things."

"But I see spirits. My mother says it's wicked. And her friend, Marion— Mistress Weaver, says—"

The candle spluttered, distracting us.

"What happens to the moth that's drawn to the candle-flame?" The priest's eyes focused on the flickering light.

"It gets burned."

"So we must learn to avoid danger." He looked at me intently.

"Am I to tell lies then?" I jerked as if stung. "I didn't think priests were supposed to tell lies."

I wanted to hurt him as I'd been hurt, but he answered soft and mellow.

"No lies. But you must guard your tongue. Such talk of spirits frightens people and puts your family in danger. Better to keep silent than invite undue attention."

"I saw a man in the water."

"What man?"

"In the pond. He floated up towards me. His eyes were open but his face had swollen. Rags of skin were peeling from it."

"A drowned man?"

"Oh yes, but not from here. A nobleman. He said he'd been murdered."

The priest pressed a finger to my lips. "You mustn't speak of this to anyone. I'll talk to your mother and put her mind at rest. No need for fretting."

He took me home under the scrutiny of gossip-hungry villagers on the green, smiling away churlish remarks, rebutting them with cheerful greetings and questions of concern about their families. When we reached the tight fist of houses at its farther edge, the Askew girls stepped from their neighbouring cottage to gawk at me and I clasped his hand tighter.

At our makeshift door my mother waited, holding Tom in her arms. Her eyes accused me, needle-sharp, unkind, but she turned a smiling mouth to Brother Brian and stood aside to welcome him into our home.

"Put this on."

Setting Tom on the floor to play with some little wooden animals my father had carved, she flung a patched shift at me and offered the priest a stool by the hearth.

"I'll wash your cloak," she said, brushing away his murmured deprecation. Wrinkling her nose with distaste, she dropped the sack containing my wet shift into a pail. "Take this outside, Nan, and wait until I call you."

I flashed the priest a glance and caught his smile to comfort me.

"John'll be home soon, Brother Brian. He's helping Noll Wright to mend a cart. Will you take some ale?"

My mother's honeyed words brought fresh bile into my mouth. I dropped the ragged leather flap behind me.

"That's her." Rabbit-toothed Elaine Askew dragged her younger sister to stare at me over their straggling hedge. I pretended interest in a wayward hen which had crept into our garden to forage. "She sends ghosts out in the night."

"Come away!" Her mother's voice rose shrill with anger. "I told you not to speak to her."

"I didn't speak to her. I only told Mattie what Johanna Nettleship says."

"I don't want to hear what Johanna Nettleship says—" Her mother left off feeding squawking chickens to hustle the girls away, glowering at me as if I were to blame for their disobedience.

I stuck my tongue out at her retreating back and shooed the startled hen under the hedge to join its outraged sisters, watching them scatter in a clucking flurry of feathers. Glaring a challenge at other impudent watchers, I hurried off to find my father.

"Trouble's brewing."

Noll Wright's voice, gravel dark and deep, drew me to the forge. Half-sprawled on the ground, he and my father struggled to fix a wheel to a cart. Unnoticed, my nose full of the pungent smells of horse and dung, I crept closer.

"It might be better to choose someone with his wits about him." Noll shook his iron-grey head and grabbed a hammer.

"They're saying in Brafield the Duke of York has his eye on the crown." My father stood and stretched with a luxurious groan. "That's it, Noll, as good as new." He turned. "Here's Nan to fetch me to my supper." His voice held smiles, but something in his eyes warned me he'd already heard about Johanna.

Noll Wright glanced up with a growl of disapproval as I flung my arms about my father. I pressed my face against the soft, faded leather of his jerkin, breathing in the familiar smells of wood-smoke and grease.

"That's a nasty cut." He tipped my chin and touched a finger to my bloodied lip. "Suppose you tell me all about it on the way home."

9

I gripped his hand and began to whisper my story, shutting out the rest of the world, wallowing in the surety of his love.

"There you are!" My mother snatched me inside, her face a white mask of fury. "Didn't I tell you to wait until I called you?" She slapped me hard, tears of anger filling her eyes. "I suppose she told you some garbled tale which you believed." She rounded on my father like a vixen.

"I heard some foolish talk—"

"Talk! The whole village's gossiping about her. Marion says it's got as far as Brafield. I'm frightened, John. It's not just old folk stories now. She's nine—old enough to know what she's saying. Brother Brian had to bring her home—The shame of it! And she still disobeys me—"

Tom whimpered and I crept into a corner while she picked him up and crooned soft words against his cheek. Rigid-backed, she stooped over the hearth stirring the broth for supper.

We ate in silence.

Later as I lay on my pallet, they argued. For the first time in my life, my father's voice grew thunderous. I rolled myself into a ball to shut out the noise. It was as if a great curdling storm cloud had finally burst. Long after the house quieted, I lay awake, listening to the steady drum of rain upon the thatch. The foundations of my world began to slip and slide.

The flicker of the flame woke him. It was no more than a hiss, like a drop of moisture on hot metal, but the sound jolted him awake. His lids opened just as a broad hand reached out to extinguish the candle and the chamber plunged into darkness.

"There's someone in the room, Ned." He pinched the naked flesh beside him. "Are you awake?"

Whispers.

He strained to catch the words, clutched at the prone body beside his, desperate for a protest of complaint, but too afraid to throw back the coverlet or challenge the shadows. He ached for a cherished voice, for a gentle hand on his brow, for the laughter and the pageantry that had once been his. But the isolation and intrigue of this long confinement was blotting out those memories of homage and acclaim.

He held his breath, listened to the waiting silence—heard only the thud of his own heart, a quickening pulse that terrified. The other boy lay warm and still, wrapped in poppy-fed dreams beyond his reach. The doctor had used compassion.

"Who's there?" he dared the watchers. "Is that you, Will?"

The awful press of darkness stifled his voice. Something gathered close, leaned over, hesitated. He caught the breath across his face, smelled the sharp, mingled odours of sweat and fear.

Before the heavy hand seized his shoulder, he rolled away and hunched himself into a tight ball, burrowing down the bed like a hedge-hog. His nails scraped the great, carved corner-post as he twisted himself out and underneath the brocade hangings.

"Blood of Christ!"

The harsh, masculine voice rent the darkness, turned it into a scuffling frenzy. Fists pummelled and probed the mound of blankets. Naked and shivering, he crouched, immobile as a hare in the flare of torches.

"I didn't wake him, Jack, I swear to it."

Something familiar in the flat, northern speech alarmed the child.

"Then make sure of the other one before you rouse the whole stinking place," commanded the first, "and let's put an end to this filthy business."

The shadows shifted. A panicked flailing of limbs above his head set his heart racing, and he bit his knuckles to trap a cry. He held his breath while the fury of Ned's struggles continued. How long before this terrible kicking would stop? Behind his screwed up eyelids, images of pain forced him to cry out. "Please don't hurt me!"

Stillness.

He felt the weight lift from the mattress, heard the men mutter together. His shallow breathing still sounded thunderous in his ears.

"Get the other one, you clumsy oaf. He must be somewhere under the bed. Cut his throat if necessary. There's no time for nicety now. We'll have no other chance after tonight."

This instruction wiped out all reason. What followed was a nightmare of snatching, bruising hands, until, caught by an ankle, he was dragged, flung back brutally amongst the tumbled blankets.

"Got him?"

"Aye, but—"

He clung to the hesitation in the strangled northern voice.

"Then what are you waiting for?— Do it! Do it!"

A taper flared. Even as the fist pressed against his mouth shutting off his wail of recognition, he fought the dark, pushed and heaved and choked—

"Holy Virgin, pray for me. Holy Virgin, help me." I squeezed my eyes tight shut, trying to shut out the boy's face. I refused to listen to his pleas. Instead I buried my face in my threadbare blanket, pressing the fabric over my mouth to stop from screaming —all sweat and gooseflesh at the same time.

But the Virgin remained aloof. She didn't answer my prayers. The boy in the tower chamber stalked my sleep relentlessly. Brother Brian had cheated me. Hadn't he promised Our Lady would take away the nightmares? How much longer could I pretend?

Chapter Two

The following morning while my mother strained over the wash-tub, I amused Tom with blowing soapy bubbles. Stretching fat hands to catch them, he shrieked and crowed as they danced and spun in rainbow colours under the hazy sunlight to burst in foamy splatters.

"Look! Rainbow fairies!"

My mother gave me a sharp look. "Don't fill his head with nonsense." Glancing upward she grimaced at the greying sky. "Help me hang these out."

In spite of the previous day's events, I escaped as soon as I could and ran off towards the woods.

Giggling voices lured me to the pond where Alys and Robin were skittering after dragonflies. A swoop of jewelled wings skimmed the water, arcing and diving in a sudden spear of sunlight.

"Nan!" Alys ran to greet me, her pretty face alight with happiness. "The others are playing war." She flicked a backward glance at the ancient trees which hemmed our village. "Did your mother scold you?"

I shrugged and squatted at the edge, trailing my fingers through the water to send the sticklebacks darting. Alys settled beside me, her shoulder touching mine.

"Can you really see spirits, Nan?" Robin asked carelessly. He scrambled into the willow's drooping limbs and swayed precariously.

"My mother says only witches can see into the future." Alys's eyes shone huge and fearful.

"Sometimes I just know things," I answered, watching her face. "I see pictures in my head. I know you'll marry a rich man. I see his hands pouring gold coins into your lap."

"What about me?" Laughing, Robin dropped from the tree to land beside us in a whip-lash shower of dust and foliage. "Alys promised to marry me. Shall I be rich then?"

"No, you'll be a soldier." The words tumbled out unbidden. "Alys won't marry you."

A shadow crossed his boyish face and for an instant I saw him grow indistinct as if lost in fog, but then the youngest Miller boy came hurtling towards us, his face scarlet, his hair spiked with sweat.

"Quick! Quick! Soldiers have come to the village!"

Without stopping he threw himself into the woodland and we heard him crashing through the bracken. We'd barely gained our feet when an unruly crowd of children bore down on us and swept us up in their excitement. We raced towards the village.

Sure enough, soldiers swaggered on the green—rough-looking men with bristly chins and ragged jerkins. Some of them held pikes. A burly fellow with curiously tufted, mud-coloured hair, bellowed like a bull.

"That traitor, the Duke of York, has rallied his northern troops and is marching towards London. Who'll join the king's army and help destroy this rabble?"

No one spoke. Shifty glances passed among the men-folk. Feet shuffled.

"Will no one fight for King Henry? Will you let these vile northerners slaughter your wives and children?" The leader's eyes raked the listeners, searching out the younger men. "The Duke of Buckingham will pay sixpence a day to any lad brave enough to fight—and food and armour besides."

Shaking off female hands, gangling youths edged forward until a muttering crowd encircled the soldiers.

"Let's show these traitors some southern spirit!" The clever leader urged the jeers while we crept closer, fascinated by the dented armour and the heavy swords.

As it turned out, the Lancastrian army recruited several of our youths. While their sweethearts wept, dry-eyed matrons watched their departure with grim resignation.

"They won't come back," I said.

14

Everyone swivelled toward me, but in that instant cruel fingers twisted my ear and dragged me from amongst my fellows. "There you are! Haven't I been looking everywhere for you? What do you mean by running off?" My mother's sharp white face thrust down at me. Her lips spat venom. "Have you no shame?"

Stumbling home under the fierce pressure of her grip, while men hawked phlegm and matrons brayed their disapproval, I fell, scraping my knees. Before I could rise, she'd hauled me up and shoved me through our doorway.

"How can you say such wicked things? Do you want to see us hanged?"

The blows rained down. Her eyes burned.

It caused uproar in the village. It marked the increase of my folly.

⟨⟩

That afternoon brought the priest scurrying to our door clutching a mysterious, black cloth bag and a string of ebony beads. My father rose and fiddled with his belt clasp while my mother pushed me forward.

"Marion's looking after Tom," she told Brother Brian. Licking her lips nervously, she smoothed the grey folds of her old, worsted gown. "We didn't know what else to do."

"I'm in your hands." The priest smiled indulgently but I sensed his embarrassment.

"She says such things—Tell Brother Brian all that nonsense you've been filling Robin Arrowsmith's head with—that stuff about knights and heads being cut off and boys being murdered in their beds. Mistress Askew said it frightened Elaine to death—"

"It's just a game," I answered. I goaded her with a stubborn stare. "The boys are always playing war." I relished the fact that my defiance annoyed her and wondered if she'd show the priest her temper.

"It's nothing serious, Brother Brian." My father spluttered excuses, twisting at his iron buckle. An awkward grin scarred his mouth. "Giles Arrowsmith was laughing about it earlier. What do you expect when children hear us gossiping about the barons and their squabbles? It's always been the same. When we were lads we played such games ourselves—"

15

"Well I don't think it's a laughing matter when girls make up such horrors." My mother cut him off in exasperated tones, her eyes flashing menace. "And you see how impertinent Nan's grown —" She fixed the priest with a helpless, pleading expression. Its falsehood riled me. "You must cure her, Brother Brian, before she brings more trouble on us. This talk of spirits frightens everyone."

My father laid me on the trestle, nodding and smiling and pressing a calloused finger to his lips. My heart began to pound. Frowning, I watched the priest kneel to light a candle. He opened his book and placed something at my feet. I wanted to look, but my father shook his head. Though his eyes still smiled, he couldn't halt the uncomfortable twitching of his hands and feet, the restless tapping of his tongue against his teeth.

The priest stood at the end of the trestle facing towards me. His lips formed silent words. A censer hung from his hand. He crossed himself. Then the rich melodious swell of his voice filled the chamber.

"In odorem suavitatis. Tu autem effugare, diabole; appropinquabit enim judicium Dei—"

The meaningless murmur was the summer-warm drone of bees. Was I sick that the priest should pray over me? In the shadows his eyes glowed like soft pieces of blue sky. A wisp of white smoke trailed from his fingers scattering fragrance. Its spicy smell conjured the memory of Mass, an echo of chanted prayers and sweet singing—sounds that flew like birds up to the high church rafters so that God and Jesus and the Holy Virgin might hear them. But why? What did it all mean?

Brother Brian dabbed my head, my ears, my nose with a gentle hand, although the strange words beat at me as if demanding answers. But it was my father, whom I loved best of anyone in the world, who repeated the words and said the amens. Once he even called my name. I longed for him to hug me, but he stood distant and clouded, his face fear-frozen and sad. Lines cut deep furrows in his brown skin. By his side my mother pressed her hands over her swollen belly to protect the unborn babe, fright leaping in her hooded eyes. It made me think of the wicked, dancing imps carved above the choir stalls. But there was something else. Anger pulsed about her in choppy waves. What had I done now to make her call the priest?

Dipping his thumb in oil, he traced a cross on my head and shoulders. He called to Jesus and though his face grew grave, his eyes remained kind.

"Exorcizo te, omnis spiritus immunde, in nomine Dei Patris omnipotentis, et nomine Jesu Christi Filii ejus, Domine et Judicis nostri, et in virtute Spiritus Sancti, ut –"

"How will we know?" My father interrupted the spell.

I burned under their fierce scrutiny.

I wanted to ask questions but the priest touched my lips so softly I knew I must keep silent.

"I'm thinking we'd have had some sign by now." He awarded my mother a radiant smile and picking up a flask, scattered some drops of holy water. I felt the waiting like the terrible pause before a thunder-clap, but there was nothing. The priest exhaled a jubilant sigh. "I find no evil in this child."

Afterward he lingered to talk and take a cup of ale while my mother dispatched me to collect Tom. In spite of a thin drizzle, I dawdled along the pathway to the Weavers' cottage, scuffing the dust and pebbles with my toes and puzzling over the strange ritual. In the fields men were penning animals and rounding up stray offspring. The last pennants of sunlight streamed across a smoke-grey sky, and a warm smell of pottage flavoured the breeze.

"It's Nan, Ma—come for Tom."

Fat Marion, a sleepy Tom blinking in her arms, nudged a bevy of pudding-faced sons aside with her bulk, and peered out at me.

"Brother Brian's gone, has he?"

"He's just taking a cup of ale." I studied the doughy rolls of flesh at her chin and neck, the way she chewed at her pink, fat bottom lip like a cow ruminating.

"Can you carry him?" She knitted her brows. "Don't drop him, mind. And tell your mother he's been fed."

I nodded, pressing Tom's soft, round cheek against mine, and my lips to his feathery dark curls.

She laced her arms under pendulous breasts. Splay-footed, she watched from her doorway as I walked away into the long shadows.

By the churchyard I encountered Simon Dobbs and his rabble of ragged henchmen.

"Well here's the witch," he said. He leaned impudently against a grave stone. "Brother Brian's little liar." He smirked at his skulking companions. "Don't look at her lads. They say a witch can lay a curse with just one glance."

"What do you want?" Though wary of their menacing laughter and the way they barred my path, I spoke out boldly and hugged Tom closer like an amulet.

"Ooh! Did she threaten us?" Simon's man-boy's voice cracked. Under his freckles the skin burned red as fire. "Brother Brian likes these odd ones. Alan Palmer's quite a favourite too." He thrust his ugly, bony face into mine. "Can't you weave a spell to bring him here to us, witch? We could show him something."

I stayed quite still while the pack of them raced round me chanting, leering, showering me with insults, until at last, Simon sped across the graveyard towards the dark woodlands beyond the village boundary, whooping like a huntsman with the others at his heels.

Hoisting Tom's weight up a little on my hip, I expelled a long breath. Around me a spatter of stars began to dot the sky and from the fields a faint smell of burning wood drifted on the wind. Unbidden, the memory of the painted demons in the chapel rose up to haunt me and I wondered why, in little more than a day, I'd become such an outsider. A heavy sense of foreboding pressed upon me like a gathering storm.

Chapter Three

Sent to collect kindling early next morning, I wandered in the woods as long as I dared, breathing in the mingled scents of blossom, crawling vetch, leaf mould and spotted fungus as I gathered sticks. I loved the silence of the trees and the sense of freedom the green shadows afforded, but when my bundle grew large and the skies heavy with rain, I knew I must either return home or seek some other shelter.

Beyond the fringe of Herne Woods and far from the pasture encircling the clustered dwellings of our village, stood the lone cottage belonging to Widow Evans. I'd glimpsed her once or twice at the market in Brafield, but mostly she kept to herself, and when people spoke of her they whispered behind their hands and looked sly. Several times I'd overheard Fat Marion tell my mother Mistress Evans was a witch and girls went to her for love potions or ways to rid themselves of babes they didn't want.

Now, hesitating a few yards from her cottage, brushing burrs and dust from my skirt, I wondered if I dare ask the widow's help. If she was a wise-woman, as the priest said, then surely she would understand the Sight? Perhaps she could explain why spirits came to me and what my dreams meant?

Save for a few scrawny hens pecking among the weeds, the Evans' place seemed deserted. Even the birds grew hushed. *Better go home*, I thought, until some instinct told me I was being watched. Turning, I glimpsed a thin, dark girl in a blood-red kirtle standing quite still, just off the path. She held a willow-wand in her hand.

A crow flying suddenly out of the thatch startled both of us. The girl made a noise and gestured at me with her wand. I understood then I should enter the house. Already the door stood ajar.

As I approached, a woman's voice called out. Her strange words alarmed me. Torn between the desire to run and the uncomfortable sensation of the girl close behind, I clutched my sticks to my breast and stepped inside.

A small, dark woman stood kneading bread. She spoke again in a foreign tongue full of musical cadences and laughed at my confusion.

"Come in, girl," she said in English. "Close the door behind you."

I set down my bundle, and with some reluctance shut out the sunlight.

When I was able to see my hostess clearly, I realised she was no ancient wise-woman with a crooked back and blackened teeth as I'd imagined. A woman of middle years whose figure still stood straight and trim, stared back at me. No ragged locks or whiskery chin marred her features.

"Disappointed?"

Had she read my thoughts?

She laughed again but without malice. "Well, what can I do for you?" She wiped dusty hands on her apron. "Did someone send you for a herbal posset or a healing draught?"

I shook my head. The scent of green herbs confused me. "I thought—people say—"

"You thought I was a witch? You've heard people say I can conjure up spirits, put a curse on your enemies, or tell your fortune. Oh, I know all the talk." She paused to look at me kindly then, pushing up a dangling, brown sleeve. "Tell me, little maid, what *you* want to know."

Her black eyes bored into me as she snatched my hands in a powerful grip. Fluttering wings beat in my belly.

"The seasons come and go, and all things have an ending." She stared through and beyond me as if she could see into farthest distance. "There'll be a day when you can look back without weeping. Saddles and horses for you, and a long road to travel. The river will run with blood, but your tears'll dry. You'll travel north, child."

I stood quite still, unable to withdraw my hands, and felt her heave a long, shuddering sigh.

"I can't change destiny, but strong desires lead us on strange pathways." The melodious chant of her dark voice wove its own spell about me. "You walk yet in ignorance but the way has already been shown. You must follow the purpose of your dreams. No one has a liking for rough ground, but there's love and laughter for you too. The rose is a beautiful bud, but it contains the canker. Look to the nun, and beware the man with blood on his hands."

She closed her eyes for a moment and then dropped my hands as if scalded.

"You've no need of me, child. You have the Sight."

"But what does it mean?" I asked, trembling with desire to know more.

"It means you must learn to live without the help of others." Pity shone in her eyes. "Just as we did when Hugh died."

I realised then someone else in the room was watching. By the hearth sat an elfin child, so still she might have been carved out of wood. Yet her hands moved deftly, for she was winding wool. She looked up at me. Perhaps it was a trick of the light, but in that moment flames licked all around her, setting her hair on fire, and I opened my mouth to cry out. But something in her black eyes prevented it. They shone well-deep like her mother's and held the same ancient wisdom.

"There was another girl—"

"Olwyn, my eldest, looking after the sheep."

A long, uncertain silence froze me.

"Your future's written," said Widow Evans. "I can't change it. There's no charm potent enough to turn the tide. Destiny can't be altered to suit us." Her face grew melancholy. "You don't understand half of what I'm saying, do you?"

She glanced up suddenly as if she'd heard something on the roof.

"Storm clouds are gathering. You should go home while you can."

Outside a blackbird sang fiercely, a flood of pure harmony; hens clucked and scratched in the earth; sheep cropped the meadow grass, but there was no sign of the girl with the willow-wand.

With a heart heavier than the burden of kindling I carried, I trudged past the water-mill and the shabby cluster of huts and duck-pens by the little stream, puzzling over the strange fate the widow predicted for me.

Chapter four

"You're in trouble."

I jumped at the reedy voice. Elaine stood up from a huddle of girls playing five-stones at the far edge of the green, away from the houses, but Alys pushed toward me, huge blue eyes blurred with tears.

"Oh Nan, a messenger came this morning and ever since there's been such dreadful talk—"

"But what have I done?" I stared defiantly at the ring of shocked faces, relieved to find Johnanna Nettleship not among them.

"Everyone's talking about a big battle at Northampton." Elaine's eyes gleamed, malicious with secret amusement.

"What's that to do with me?"

"Peter Nettleship's been killed." Alys grasped my hand with painful urgency. "And my mother said the Brewers have lost two sons."

"You said those men wouldn't come back." Elaine's spiteful taunt provoked me. "And now they're all dead. The river's blocked with bodies. One turned up as close as Billing Bridge. You should hear what people are saying about you."

I didn't wait to listen.

Turning back the way I'd come, I skirted round the church. Ignoring the tight knots of women in the lane, I scurried homeward.

The sight of our open door halted me.

"John's a sister in London," I heard my mother say.

"Such a place might prove a grand haven," the priest's mellow tones replied. "But I'm after thinking this will be a warning to her and it may not come to that. She's a powerful imagination, but there's no malice in her—"

"She needs a whipping." Fat Marion growled like a peevish cur. "Jane's been too soft. I'll wager the Nettleships would be glad to see the last of her—not to mention the Heywoods and the Brewers. She's an impudent manner of speaking and it's my belief she likes to frighten folk. Not so long ago she told me I'd lose my lads at harvest time. 'You'll be weeping then,' she said. What kind of child thinks up such wickedness? It's not natural—"

She paused and suddenly pointed through the doorway, reddened cheeks quivering with indignation. "Well, speak of the devil—there she is!" Her eyes darted fury. "See how she creeps about spying on folk—"

She shrugged off the priest's soothing words and stormed out into the road. "Best fetch your washing in, Jane." She held a plump hand upward. "It's starting to rain."

*

Rain.

September brought great floods and swathes of it. It filled the ruts and hollows, swelled the ponds and burst over the fields, greedy as an ogre, consuming everything in its path. Crops barely ripened by a poor summer bowed under the torrents and rotted on the stalk. In an effort to bring in what remained of harvest the men-folk struggled against the elements, until sodden, cold and despairing, we faced the prospect of hunger and starvation.

"Harvest's never easy — Noll says the Nene will flood."

Ignoring my father's words, my mother snatched him out of the winding-sheet of his wet clothes. Muttering, she knelt to rub his mottled flesh into life before our meagre fire. After working in the fields all day he looked bone-weary.

"But this year—I've never seen anything like it."

Shivering, he crouched over the heat, hugging a coarse blanket round him.

The wind drove a sudden rain squall against the house and drops of water hissed among the flames. Stinking smoke rose from smouldering sticks and my father coughed until his eyes streamed.

"Don't sit there choking to death." Impatiently, my mother gathered up discarded garments and thrust them at me. "Eat your supper. I've been trying to keep it hot. I thought you were never coming home."

Dragging the heap of sopping clothes into a pail, I watched him spoon up his pottage so slowly I thought he'd fall asleep over it.

A wretched sense of gloom seemed to settle on the house. Even the sly-lipped goat pressed against the wall, hung its draggled head.

"Giles and Noll are still out there," he said at last, heaving a sigh.

"What? In the dark?" My mother fumed over the trail of wet ash around the hearth, mopping at it with a rag as if her fear and anger goaded her to relentless action.

"They want to finish the top field."

All night wind and rain battered at the house, thrashing the leather door flap, driving in puddles, churning the earth to mud. It rained next morning, too.

And then the sickness came.

Like a gale, it swept into the village, striking down weak and strong without pity. Within days it devoured whole families.

When my father stumbled home early from the fields one dank afternoon, I left off spinning and ran to greet him. Shaking off his draggled cloak, he loitered on the threshold, his face grim.

"Did you hear anything of Roger Miller?" he asked my mother, who was stirring a pot over the fire.

"He died this morning. Marion said his belly swelled up like a great bladder and he raved in agony all night. That's the third one in as many days." She crossed herself and moved toward him. "You're early. What's wrong?" Fear etched deep lines in her face.

"Marion's lad fell in the field just now. He looks bad."

"But Stephen didn't go to work today—Marion said he'd been sick—"

"It's her eldest—Mark." My father's mouth twisted. "Noll and Giles had to carry him home just now. Wait—" He snatched at my mother's arm. "There's nothing you can do, Jane."

"I should go to her—"

"You've your own children to think of."

Defeated, she sank on to a stool by the sodden door flap, her face the colour of bone. "What are we going to do? They say there's

25

no cure for it." She gave me a quick look and bit at a strand of chestnut hair. "Where's it come from, John? What have we done to deserve such a thing?"

It marked the beginning of a time of tears and terror. The burial ground sprouted a crop of new graves and women flocked to buy remedies of Mistress Evans— until rumblings of witchcraft panicked them. Grim faces turned in my direction then. Impudently, I shook off the whispers and nods, but my mother buckled under the shame of it.

"What kind of child are you to heap such sorrow on my head?" she asked.

Chapter five

One raw morning in late September my mother thrust a basin at me. "Go to the woods and pick some berries."

Glad of her curt dismissal, I took refuge among the trees. But I went alone, and before long one of those strange, heavy feelings I couldn't shake off descended on me. It nagged at me like a stitch in the side and I wished I could talk to my father about it. But in spite of the perpetual drizzle, he'd been out in the fields again since daybreak.

In normal times the hedges drooped heavy with fruit, but this year they bloomed with mould. I plucked what whole morsels I could find, my hands stained almost black with juice. I didn't hear the arrival of other foragers.

"Why do you say such terrible things?"

"What *have* I done now?" I rounded fiercely.

A tear-streaked Alys faced me.

"You told my mother her sons would die at harvest time." Alys looked so helpless with her little sister at her side, I grew contrite in a moment.

"I only told her some men would be going away."

"But three of my brothers have died." Her voice trembled. "Oliver was buried only yesterday."

"I'm sorry." Foolishly, I offered the only comfort I knew. "But they'll come back to see you. Don't you remember how I saw Will Nettleship—"

Alys' blue eyes widened. She crossed herself, hugging her sister close.

"You mustn't tell lies!" The flaxen curls shook with horror. "You'll go to hell!"

Friendship melted into silence while other children invaded the grove. They crept up to stand around us, mute and sullen. Glancing from one stark face to another, I caught at last some inkling of the fear I'd conjured in our community.

"My head hurts." The small girl's wail echoed amongst the dripping trees.

Alys dropped her basket to place a hand on the child's brow. "She's burning hot."

Our eyes locked.

"She's got some spots on her neck—" Her frightened whisper provoked a panicked threshing through the bracken. Abandoned, Alys and I clung together, joined again in adversity.

Quarrel forgotten, we carried the sick child from the woods. At Alys' cottage strong arms took up the burden and drew her into the comfort of shared sorrow. But me they shut out, dropping the door flap against my offers of help.

*

No plume of smoke curled from our roof, but a knot of men stood outside. Daft Geoffrey, the miller's feeble-minded son, crooned and swayed on the threshold.

I ran toward them through the spits and spots of rain, but when they recognised me, tension gripped their shoulders, hostility flooded into their eyes. Without a word they stepped aside.

I found my mother hunched over the ashes of a fire, her face blotched with grief. Kneeling by a pallet on the floor, Brother Brian prayed earnestly. Noll Wright, his head lapped in an old, burned cloth, leaned over a huddled figure beneath a heap of threadbare blankets.

My father's face twisted into a frightful grimace, one eye fixed and milky, the other wandering. Like a stone he lay, mumbling strange sounds and drooling like a babe.

"Strong as an ox, John was," said Noll Wright. He rubbed his knuckles over the stubble on his chin. "I've worked with him from dawn to dusk every harvest since we were both young bachelors. I can't believe I'm seeing this."

"Your father fell in the field, Nan." Brother Brian glanced up from his devotions. "Noll, and Giles Arrowsmith carried him home. He's very sick."

The words spilled over me without meaning for I was shocked by the scowl on Noll Wright's face. Never had I seen such hatred in anyone's eyes.

He staggered to his feet to address the priest in surly tones.

"I'll leave you to your prayers, Brother Brian. My work here's done. I'll send my wife to help Jane. Ruth Arrowsmith'll keep the little lad this night." He gave me a hard glance. "The maid must look to herself."

When he was gone I sat beside the priest, listening to the rain drumming on the roof, sensing my world sliding into chaos. I couldn't rouse my mother. She sat by the hearth holding her swollen belly, rocking and moaning. When I touched her shoulder, she turned a savage look on me.

"I blame you for this," she said.

Chapter Six

Throughout the waning autumn, the passing-bell brought many to the churchyard. Daily, hooded women thronged the houses of the bereaved. The drone of loss filled the village like the hum of a busy hive.

But nothing touched me. The Mass, the burial, and the mourning for my father's death sailed like ragged thunder-clouds across my days. Dry-eyed and lonely, I stumbled through my tasks while rotting corpses swelled the burying ground. But when they carried Fat Marion's last son to his grave, the storm of anger broke across my head in all its fury.

"Witch! Witch!"

A clod of earth struck me as I stooped to draw water from the well. I turned in shock. Fat Marion, red-faced and weeping, bore down upon me.

"I'll see you hanged for this!" Shoulders heaving with exertion, she paused to catch her breath. Soil crumbled from her hands. Her shrieks roused neighbours from their houses. Sullen and watchful, they waited on their thresholds.

When she fetched me a cuff around the ear which made me drop my pail, I froze. Around me faces leered, lips drew back exposing jagged teeth, bodies tensed, fist and nail curled in anticipation. I looked into the eyes of strangers, and murder glowered in every one of them.

I ran towards the woodland.

As at a signal, they joined the chase, pelting me with mud and stones. Ahead, the blacksmith stood brandishing a mattock, a giant barring my path, and from all sides, greedy hands snatched and clawed. Like a panicked hare trying to dodge the teeth of the hounds, I ran this way and that—directionless—witless—blinded by fear.

How I reached the church I don't know. Brother Brian stepped through the open door and I fell into his arms.

"That creature's the devil's instrument." Fat Marion panted at my heels. Behind her the feral crowd roared its approval.

"She's only a child," the priest said.

For an instant the snarls abated, held by the power of his words and the church's authority.

"Witches can be any age, Brother Brian." The blacksmith's voice rang fearless. "The devil's in that maid and she's infected all of us. We must burn it out."

The crowd took up the chant. Above the priest's protests, the voices snapped and whined as individual villagers cursed, blaming me for everything, for the battle, the plague, the lost harvest, even for the death of my own father.

Squeezing my eyes tight shut, burying my face in the rough, dusty fabric of his robe, I clung to Brother Brian. Any moment I expected to be torn away and dragged to the stake. I'd heard people talk of witch burning with a strange mixture of glee and horror, and now the crowd's frenzy rose to a screeching, breathless climax —

"Go home!"

The fury of the priest's command brought silence.

"I'm shamed to hear such things. Is it ignorant you are? Have my words meant nothing to you? Have you forgotten how Our Lord was persecuted by an angry mob? And are you after punishing a child? Go home at once and reflect on your sins. I'll hear no more of this."

They slunk away like curs and then he looked at me, his eyes full of tears.

"Child, child, what am I to do with you?" he said.

Chapter Seven

Two days he hid me in the church. I lay in the very heart of the village with my neighbours prowling just outside while the priest kept watch. Alan Palmer carried messages and I listened to their desperate whispered exchanges while pretending to draw ink patterns on scraps of vellum.

"You took the letter?"

"The messenger has it in his pack. He left early. But Master Wright says she must be punished and my father says some of the men plan to fetch Sir Robert from the manor at Houghton—"

"They wouldn't violate the sanctuary of the church." The priest plucked at his mouth and paced the flagstones.

"Her mother won't take her back—"

"The letter was to her aunt. Does anyone know she's here?"

The blond lad shook his head. "I said I'd seen her in the woods and near the Stone on Ford's Hill—"

My heart skipped. Everyone feared the Standing Stone. No one understood the strange designs scratched on it or how it came to be there. Long ago some ancient bones and daggers were discovered buried in the earth nearby, and whispers of pagan sacrifice still circulated. Why had Alan told people he'd seen me there?

"Wait here. I must speak to Martin." The priest snatched up his cloak and gave me a quick glance. He turned back to Alan, his face haggard. "If anything should happen—ring the bell."

An uncomfortable silence settled. I tried to decipher the meaning of their conversation.

"Will they burn me?"

A tremor shook the lad. His beautiful limpid eyes regarded me with horror.

"Brother Brian won't let them."

We didn't speak again. But when the priest returned I knew some irrevocable decision had been made.

"Go home now, Alan. Martin's agreed." The priest crouched beside me, his face strained. "You must eat your supper, Nan, and go to sleep. We've a long journey tomorrow."

⸎

"Quickly now, on to the cart." The carter shoved me mercilessly.

Blind with sleep, I scrabbled up, scraping knees and hands, clawing for purchase amongst the coils of rope and bales of straw.

"Why do we have to go now? It's not even daylight. I wanted to see Tom—"

"Sssh! Do you want to rouse the whole village?" The carter's brutal hiss stung my ear. "You've caused enough trouble—"

Brother Brian sprang to my side and, dropping his bundle, wrapped a protective arm about me. The squeeze of his fingers suggested sympathy, but wasn't it his idea to send me away? I fumed against this restraining grip, but before I could wriggle free, the horse shifted in its harness and the cart lurched forward.

"Steady there—" The carter must have snatched the reins as he climbed into his place. Stamping and snorting, the horse clinked his bit, and I sniffed the moist warmth off him, sensing the quiver of his flanks. Even he seemed anxious.

Save for a peck of stars straddling the black arc of the sky, no lights pierced the dark. Looking back, I distinguished the bulk of the church hunched like a crone over the sleeping village. I held my breath to listen to the night noises—the wind's eerie flap among the trees and the hunting owl's shriek. The smell of damp earth and smoke hung in the air and something sinister, thick with danger gathered in our silence. I realised I no longer belonged in this place.

Smuggled away without a chance to say farewell, cast out and despised, I felt like Joseph in the Bible being sold into slavery in Egypt. But black rebellion burned in my heart. Had Joseph felt like this? Picking a splinter from my thumb, I plotted a childish vengeance. One day they'd all be sorry. But when Robin's contrite face and Alys' reproachful eyes rose up to confront me, I swallowed painful tears.

The cart's sudden pitch plunged us on to the road. Tucking my feet under me, I huddled deep into my cloak, shrinking from the mean tang of autumn on the wind. Eventually, the steady, swaying rhythm lulled me, but every now and then I started up and shivered.

"We'll be at Saint Bede's before dawn." The carter grunted his relief.

"You've done well, Martin. I'm grateful" The priest's words puzzled me. I wondered at his gratitude for such a journey. Although I'd heard talk of Saint Bede's, I'd no notion of where it lay.

Not long after, a worried-looking monk emerged from the black night to beckon us. In the feeble light of his lantern I caught the furtive glint in the carter's eye, the gnawing of a lip, and sensed his eagerness to be gone.

Snatching up his bundle, Brother Brian leapt down while the wheels were still in motion, and before I could think the carter lifted me to join him. Without pause, he hurtled away again into the dark and the monk hurried us inside.

A noxious smell of mould oozed from the flagstones under my feet and a spindly lad in a stained surplice thrust a bowl of porridge into my hands. I tried to swallow the tasteless mess but excitement closed my throat. Instead I stood holding the warmth against my belly trying to decipher the urgent, mumbled conversation between the monk and Brother Brian.

"Quickly, Nan." The priest thrust my bowl at the lad and drove me out after the monk like a recalcitrant goat. Stumbling over the hem of my cloak, I followed the bobbing lantern and came to where two asses waited by a gate, their rumps facing the wind. Another monk helped me swarm up into the saddle, instructing me to cling to the pommel. Once mounted on his own steed, Brother Brian took my ass's reins and turned us back to the road, forcing the animals swiftly into a trot.

"Godspeed!"

The priest acknowledged the blessing with a lift of his hand.

But when the first pale ribbons of dawn began to unfurl across the sky, he pointed out a distant building.

"We can find food and lodging there."

"Will we be in London soon?" My belly rumbled and I'd a pressing need to void my bladder.

Brother Brian laughed. "We must travel several days to reach the city," he answered gently. "But there are many monasteries which will shelter us. And there are good people who'll help us along the way."

So, sick and bruised, I found myself jolted along the London road, only half listening to the priest's voice, and cursing the ill fortune that drove me further and further from home.

My head grew dizzy with the blur of people and places we encountered. Each monastery guest-house brought the same meagre comforts of hard bed, and tasteless food eaten in draughty, prayer-haunted refectories. The faces of the monks all wore the same sorrowful expression as they listened to my piteous tale.

"Nan's been offered a home in her uncle's house in London," Brother Brian told them. "Her father, God rest him, died of the plague just a week or so ago, and her mother's too sick to care for all the children."

This plausible story earned much sympathy. He made no mention of spirits or witchcraft and for that I nursed a grudging respect.

"Do you think I imagined the dreams?"

We stopped to share some bread and cheese by a little, ragged copse.

Brother Brian paused, bread in hand, to stare at me, his blue eyes troubled.

"And did you?"

"No." I returned the stare with a bold tilt of my chin. "And I know they're true. As well as I know Alys Weaver will marry an old man and Robin Arrowsmith will die with a dagger in his throat."

A painful frown cleft the priest's brows.

"I had a brother gifted as you are—"

"A brother? I didn't know priests had families." This information caught my interest.

A smile replaced the frown. "I was born far from here in a country called Ireland beyond the sea. And I lived in a village with my parents and my brothers and sisters—"

"Like me!"

"Well, in a manner of speaking—but in my country people are after believing in seers and wise-women. So when my brother,

Niall, said he could see spirits and the dead returned to speak to him, no one was much alarmed. They thought him chosen for some special purpose."

"What happened to him?"

"He went away to study and learn how to use his gift—" He raised a finger to check any interruption. "But here things are very different. People are frightened by what they think is witchcraft. Your tales are dangerous—"

"But Mistress Evans—"

"The Widow Evans is a good woman who uses her skills with herbs to help others. In Ireland she'd be called a wise-woman."

"She said I had the Sight."

"And so you have. But you mustn't speak of it—except to me." He chewed his bread thoughtfully. "You know, I'm after thinking this might be all for the best, Nan. No one in London knows anything about you. You can begin again."

I looked at him scornfully. How easy he made it sound.

But when dark thoughts kept me awake at night, I repeated this idea like a prayer against evil: *I will begin again.*

Talk of civil war dogged our journey, and the nearer we got to the city, the more the monks warned Brother Brian of the dangers of taking me there.

"There are terrible quarrels among the barons," said one. He shook his world-weary head. "They've turned against King Henry and his queen and stir up anger among the people." He crossed himself. "Many blame the king for the wars with France which made them so poor, and for these plagues and pestilences bringing hunger and suffering—depriving children of their parents." He looked at me with pity in his eyes. "I fear these barons will shortly be murdering each other for the crown. Avoid the city if you can."

Brother Brian grew grave but the monk's gloomy ramblings merely irritated me. What did I care about greedy noblemen? Ever since I could remember, men had boasted of battles with puzzling names like Agincourt and Crecy, and boys had played them. I was sick of war. Hadn't I grown up to the strident blare of its music? But in spite of the monks' warnings I knew there could be no turning back.

The farms and cottages grew fewer. Instead, the roads thronged with carts, horsemen and pilgrims. Brother Brian pointed out riders in liveries of murrey and blue wearing the falcon and fetterlock badge of York. "Those are the Duke's retainers. Many think the Duke of York has more right to rule than King Henry." This sounded different from tales I'd heard in the village.

"But why don't people want King Henry anymore?" I sympathised with the rejected monarch. Hadn't I been turned out too? "Hasn't he anyone to help him? Won't his servants protect him from the Duke of York?"

"The people think the duke will be a better ruler," answered the priest, smiling at my impassioned questions. "King Henry's been foolish—"

With sudden insight I realised I'd been just as foolish. If only I'd kept my mouth shut. The priest was *my* only protector. The advice he'd given hadn't been forced by cowardice. He meant to keep me safe.

A bitter November wind buffeted us next day. Angrily, I pulled my hood over my face so the priest shouldn't see my tears. November was my birth month. At home my father would have cosseted me, hugged me in the warmth of his arms. But now no father would kiss his special girl nor whisper comfort any more. I pretended I didn't care but I wondered if my mother thought of me. I pictured her stooping over the hearth, her face dew-spotted with sweat as she lifted the blackened pot on to the hook, and the memory of Tom's baby-plump hands plucking at her kirtle raised a cruel lump in my throat. I longed then for the smoky fug of the cottage and Tom's soft breath against my cheek.

Perhaps cold or exhaustion sparked the dream that woke me early that last morning before we reached the city. It sent me scurrying through the dark to find the priest. Uncomplaining, he listened to my breathless account.

"I saw three heads grinning down at me from a big arched gateway. There was blood running down the stones—just like the red ribbons Alys got from the fair in Brafield." A bubble of laughter threatened to explode. "Their eyes had been picked out, and there were big black crows flying round and round squawking." I snatched a breath, my heart still hammering with excitement. "And then I was in a frosty field and snow was falling like big goose-feathers—I heard horses galloping. Soldiers raced down a drawbridge carrying banners with that Yorkist badge on them—the one you showed me yesterday. But other men wearing a white swan badge roared out the woods and attacked the ones on horse-back. Soon there were dead bodies everywhere and bloody weapons and horses neighing and screaming—A man shouting orders was dragged off his horse and someone cut his throat." I stopped a moment to catch my breath, the memory of that frothy gurgle still horribly vivid. "And then I saw a boy running away. He had bright golden hair." I paused again to recapture the hideous scene, a knight on horse-back, his face black with fury, raised sword running blood, then the horse snorting and someone stumbling under the hooves and begging for mercy. "An old man tried to escape from a knight chasing him on a big black horse. The boy ran onto a bridge. He hammered on a door but no one would let him in. When the knight grabbed him, I realised he was that boy I always see in my dreams—the one with the murderers—" I stopped, panting with exhaustion, my hands wet with sweat.

"Such a muddle of a dream." The priest hugged me. "And I think you must blame me for it, for haven't I been after talking to you of nothing but fighting? Put it aside now, for today we'll be meeting your aunt and uncle and it wouldn't do to be thinking on such butchery."

We ate in silence. Outside in the mean grey light of morning we shivered, wrapping our cloaks tight about us.

"Will we see the king?"

"I doubt it." His kindly smile touched me. Sorry then for my former anger, I slipped a grateful hand in his to reassure him of my affection.

He lifted me into the saddle and we rode ahead into the wind to join a jogging stream of other travellers. When, at last, the vast city walls rose up to meet us, I cringed from the armed men prowling like hungry dogs at the gates. Were they waiting for someone? A creeping sense of horror kept me from asking any questions.

Part Two

London
late 1460

Chapter Eight

London.

A bewildering hubbub assailed my ears. Narrow streets exuded the rank stench of fish, ordure, and decay. A heaving mass of people lunged and lurched, rumbling carts battered my legs and mangy dogs snapped at my heels. I shrank against the priest clutching at his robe, shocked by the coarse faces, the angry shouts, the storm of rushing bodies.

We reached the city in the late morning when the crowds were at their worst. The long journey had exhausted me. My bones ached from the ass's jarring rhythm. I couldn't shake off the memory of my hideous dream, nor the realisation that I'd soon be left with relations I'd never seen before. I clung to the priest's hand fiercely as he led me through a muddle of stinking alley-ways.

Choking in this fug of unaccustomed smells, my eyes stinging from acrid smoke, I staggered like a drunkard. A horseman trotted by, spattering me with mud, and as I turned in fury, an ill-mannered youth shoved me aside mouthing insults. Separated from Brother Brian, I froze, staring wildly about me. Everyone seemed in such a hurry. Voices yowled like cats fighting, the sounds nothing like speech I understood. I flinched from jabbing elbows and trampling feet until the priest's hand caught me and steered me into a winding lane.

Outside the tall house that teetered over the street and seemed to jostle with its neighbour, our travels ended. An over-powering reek made my stomach heave. I glimpsed some men in stained aprons stirring huge vats in a cobbled yard.

"Your uncle's a tanner," said Brother Brian, pointing. "That's part of his workshop you can see. It's where the hides are cured."

"What's that horrible smell?"

The priest laughed. "The hides have to be kept in vats of special liquor to preserve them. Best not to linger here too long." He led me up towards the living quarters but the stink followed.

A burly, red-haired stranger straddled the threshold. From behind his leather-aproned bulk peered a pale cluster of female faces.

"Welcome to London." The stranger held out his arms.

I huddled against the priest. The booming voice and piercing eyes didn't seem welcoming to me.

"This is your Uncle Will and your Aunt Grace—" The priest nudged me forward.

Aunt Grace murmured, stooping to take my hand. Her smile evoked my father's memory but I clenched my fists and swerved back.

"Don't worry, Brother Brian." From under straggling brows, the red-haired man regarded me with a mixture of suspicion and curiosity. "We'll look after her. You can leave her safe with us."

It sounded a friendly enough dismissal, and perhaps Brother Brian relished the opportunity to be gone, but how could he leave me in the hands of these strangers? Suddenly his kindness along the journey seemed doubly precious. How would I manage without him? I turned to throw myself into his arms and beg him to take me with him, but Uncle Will placed a proprietary arm about my shoulder and steered me into the house.

The bird left off preening its ragged plumage and fixed him with the black glitter of a single eye. It opened its dagger-shaped beak and emitted an ugly squawk that made him flinch, but he didn't give ground. To the right he glimpsed the wide rushing sweep of a wing as its fellow landed with a menacing thump upon the parapet. He heard the scrape of talons on stonework as it strutted toward him, insolent as a rebel courtier, but still he did not yield.

"What are you doing up here?"

A heavy hand gripped his shoulder.

"I wanted to see—"

The hand turned him with a savagery that made him wince, but he didn't cry out.

"You might have fallen." The northern voice contained a mingling of fear and concern.

"No, I can climb better than anyone," the child boasted. "Where's Will? Why can't we go outside anymore?"

"You're nowt but questions, lad."

The statement was made with an attempt at lightness, humour straining against an underlying threat.

Lad. No homage there. Even Will still called him Lord.

"I just wanted to look at the city again."

"No need. Your uncle wants you kept safe. Come down with me now."

The voice was reasonable, kind even, but he followed reluctantly. It was harder to climb down, and he was glad to clamber on the broad shoulders. He put his arms about the man's neck to steady himself, and sensed tension in the strong body. The unkempt hair, black as the ravens' feathers, tickled his nose.

"Why can't we play outside?" he asked when he was set upon his feet again.

The man squatted before him, his shockingly blue eyes level with his own.

"Your uncle won't allow it."

"Haven't you any boys?" the child asked, a mixture of defiance and wistfulness in his plea.

"Aye."

The voice softened. The eyes took on a distant focus as if remembering.

"And would you keep them like prisoners as they do Ned and me?"

"No more questions." The man rose, created a hostile distance between them.

When the child protested, a hand clamped over his mouth and nose, blocking off air. He inhaled the salty, meaty scent of the man's palm and struggled to dislodge the strong fingers, teeth nipping the flesh.

"God's bones! The cub bit me!"

A fist struck the side of his head, sent him spinning into darkness—

I woke sweating and gagging, kicking my feet against the heavy coverlet. The chamber brooded, tomb-dark and still. I hugged the unfamiliar bed-curtains, breathing in their faint scent of lavender, and allowed the dream to fade. As my pulse steadied, I recalled where I lay and what had brought me here.

The high spindly house with its many chambers and fine furniture made me feel shabby. I decided my uncle must be rich, for I'd never seen such a place before. A great wooden table and benches crowded the hall that ran the length of the house, and more stools than I could count. Up in the bedchamber which jutted over the street below, my aunt showed me a carved oak press and linen chest of which she seemed enormously proud. A baize cloth hung from one wall and on another a shelf held a pair of carved candlesticks and a pretty, painted pot. My eyes had widened at the heap of cushions on the two beds the girls' shared in the smaller side chamber and the little shelf where they kept their trinkets and hair ornaments. Even so, the stink of the tannery couldn't be masked entirely by the sweet-smelling rushes and I felt stifled inside the airless building. How I longed to escape it—to fill my lungs with the wide, green scent of soughing trees and hear the secret rustle of bracken under my feet and the blackbird's rattling alarm overhead.

Sleepless now, I listened to the soft breathing of the girl beside me, the curious, night-time creaks of timber, and the far away tolling of a bell. At home the pig snuffled in its pen, foxes yipped and owls shrieked from the woodland.

Home. I mustn't think of it. And yet it drew me with its memories of winding paths and secret hollows, the song of men working in the fields, the shouts and laughter of children playing skittles in the yard by the church. Again I pressed my fingers deep into the springy moss on Stanwode's Standing Stone, hid with Alys amongst hot, dusty cornstalks whose slightest crackle could alert the seekers, yelped at the drunken jab of pollen-laden bees staggering for the hives in summer's long twilight, until the warm, drowsy smell of honey conjured Tom's sticky smile and made my heart ache... I wondered what my mother was doing now. The sight of her cold, hard face as she'd cast me out, returned to taunt me. Tears pricked my eyes like pins. My father couldn't protect me now. Never more would I ride upon his shoulders, nor cling about his neck or shelter in the warmth of his arms when terrible dreams tormented me. My safety had been stolen. Would Tom cry for me? Or would he forget the sister accused of witchcraft? Brother Brian would be safe in his church with its bright painted walls showing

Adam and Eve cast out of Eden by an angel with a flaming sword. But I'd lost my Eden.

At breakfast I faced a storm of questions from my cousins. Aunt Grace, already bustling to and from the kitchen, chuckled.

"Let Nan eat something first," she said. "She'll find things different here from what's she's used to at home."

"Mama said she played in fields and woods when she was a girl and lived in the country," said Sarah who was nearest to me in age. "Did you do that?"

I nodded, refusing to speak for fear of rousing laughter. Last night they'd giggled at my speech until my aunt scolded them and sent us all to bed. I don't think they meant to be unkind but it made me furious. Their speech sounded peculiar to me.

"Well, there's none round here, and even if there were I don't think we'd be allowed to go in them." She spooned up more pottage. "We sometimes play in the streets, but papa doesn't like it."

"It's too dangerous," Judith said. She watched me crumble bread, her keen gaze making me clumsy. "A little girl was crushed by a horse and cart two days ago. It's safer to stay inside." She smoothed the folds of her blue, worsted skirt and smiled. At almost sixteen she seemed very much the young lady. I marvelled at the whiteness of her hands. "Do you know how to sew?"

"Can you play tables?" Meg gave me no time to draw breath.

"Meg's looking for someone else to beat," explained Sarah. "Even Papa can't do it now. But there's a parade through Chepeside this afternoon. Wouldn't you rather see that?"

How could I tell her that the city with its high, crooked houses, and its crowded streets choked me? I longed for the open countryside and the familiar, friendly faces of Alys and Robin. I listened to my cousins pestering Aunt Grace to take them to the parade and tried to look pleased. Hadn't I promised Brother Brian I'd begin again?

Over the next weeks I caught homely Aunt Grace watching me with a puzzled expression. I suppose any other girl would have responded to her affectionate nature, but I brooded, too locked in grief and anger. Each night she kissed my brow as she tucked me into bed, but never once did I fling my arms about her or shed tears. Though I longed for comfort, somehow I couldn't ask it of her. What a hard-hearted, indifferent little wretch I must have seemed.

Worse than the loneliness were the dreams. Now with Brother Brian far away I daren't confide in anyone. Though he'd promised to visit as often as he could, nightly I shared the torment of the boy in the mysterious, dark chamber and woke sweating with fear. It was a blessing Sarah slept so heavily. Each day I searched among the people I met for the boy's face, or listened to their voices for one I might recognise. But no one spoke as beautifully as he did.

New dreams blossomed. In these I ran through shadows from a menacing figure with cruel, yellow eyes. It dragged me towards an enormous bonfire, the heat searing my eye-balls, and thrust me into the blazing heart. I woke then with the stench of smoke and singed flesh in my nostrils; the pitiless roar of flames and howling laughter still ringing in my ears.

Gradually though I grew accustomed to the new order and began asking my patient aunt a deal of questions about the city. Eager to make me feel at home, she did her best to acquaint me with the place, taking me first inside the great church of St Martin le Grand to light a candle for my father. Later she took me to the markets, threading through the busy streets crowded with shops and taverns, and showed me the high archways and bridges across the river, pointing out the houses of the nobility and the palaces with pride.

"What's that place?" I asked one day, drawn unwillingly to a striking building with lofty, white-painted towers and liveried guards about the gates.

"Why, that's the Tower of London. It belongs to King Henry and is where he sometimes holds his court."

"Are there any boys there?"

"What a strange child you are!" My aunt laughed, putting an arm about my rigid shoulders. "I daresay there are several belonging to the guards and servants who live there, but King Henry's son isn't old enough to go to court yet."

Her answer puzzled. The Tower haunted me. That night I dreamed of entering its massive portals, not as a guest, but as a searcher lost among winding passageways Whatever I sought evaporated as swiftly as morning mist when I opened my eyes, and my nocturnal ramblings left me with a throbbing head-ache. It was the first of many dreams I had concerning the place, although I told no one.

∽

Cold winds buffeted the year towards its end, but driving sleet and shadowy days couldn't suppress the swelling excitement in the house above the tannery. Daily the girls clamoured to watch the pageants in the streets, chattered of Mummers, dancing fools and carolling at St Pauls, pestering my uncle for coins to buy sweetmeats until the poor man clapped his hands over his ears and fled into his workshop.

"He doesn't mean it," Meg told me, her cheeks flushed with teasing. "He likes to see us merry."

"Just wait until we deck the house with greenery," said Judith. Her hazel eyes flashed like spangles on the players' jewelled costumes we'd seen so recently in the Chepe.

"Christmas is the best time of all," said Sarah, twirling before the fire like a mischievous imp.

Watching their easy pleasure, a knot of anticipation formed deep in my belly. But it wasn't excitement. It was fear.

Chapter Nine

That first Christmas above the tannery certainly proved a grand affair. Never had I seen such extravagance, yet I soon discovered my aunt and uncle always kept this feast with tremendous merriment. Their house, festooned with garlands of holly, bay and ivy, rang with laughter. Numerous guests thronged the table, gorging on scalding soups and richly crusted pies, hot roasted capons and enormous hams glazed with honey. My cousins drew me into games and dancing, cosseted me with sweetmeats, welcoming me into the giggling circle of their friendship. As if released from shadow I grew bolder, daring at last to think myself a member of the family.

"Who's the grey-haired lady in the velvet gown?"

My flustered aunt looked up as I trotted down into the kitchen. It was the feast for Christ's nativity and the hall rang with noise. Between the courses, my uncle sent me up to the bed chamber to fetch a shawl for one of his aged cousins.

"What lady's that?" My aunt lifted a vast steaming pudding stuffed with raisins, dates and almonds from the fire. Plainly she didn't trust Betsy, the frivolous kitchen maid, with such a precious burden. Having set down the heavy dish, she stood back to heave a sigh and pat a wisp of stray hair from her damp brow with the back of her hand. Her pink face shone with sweat. Evidently pleased by the delicious aroma that filled the kitchen, she rewarded me with a vague smile.

"The one who went into the girls' room, just now." I gestured with the shawl. "I met her on the stairs. She asked me to tell you how glad she is to see you all so happy together."

The smile vanished. "What did you say?" All attention now, the piercing light in her eye unnerved me.

51

A tremor of unease prickled my neck. "She's about your build." I feigned boldness although my fluting voice betrayed me. "Her gown's dark blue and she's wearing a silver necklet with little blue stones in it. She said, 'Find my Gracie and tell her I'm come to share the feast.'"

"Sweet Lord!" She put her fingers to her lips, then crossed herself, her eyes filling with tears. "How could you—?"

A draught carried in a sudden gale of conversation. Stooping under the lintel my uncle rose to tower over us, his flame red hair all awry, teeth gleaming through the tangle of his beard in a tipsy grin.

"The guests are calling for the pudding, Grace." Ale swelled the hearty voice. He turned to me, eyes a-twinkle. "And you, little maid, should be with your cousins, not sneaking in the kitchen to beg the first tasty morsel." He winked at giggling Betsy as he bore me away.

In the early hours when the first grey glimmerings of light trickled through the shutters, I overheard my aunt and uncle talking. Creeping from bed, I pressed an ear against the thin plastered wall of their adjoining bed-chamber.

"Don't encourage her." My uncle grumbled sleepily.

"But, Will, she described my mother as she was in life. Right down to the necklace she always wore at Christmas. Just ask my cousin, Joan. That child sees things, and says things she couldn't possibly know about—"

"Ignore it. Remember why she's here. Keep her busy and let's have no more superstitious nonsense."

They drifted back to sleep, but this episode served as a warning. Though I joined in the Christmas revels, listened eagerly to the boisterous guests who stirred up the household with their comings and goings, and learned to play at tables with Meg, I said nothing more of the woman who regularly met me on the stairs or watched our games. Seeing spirits caused trouble and I was determined nothing should spoil my new content.

But the fortune-telling proved my undoing, though my cousins pressed me to it. It was the day before Twelfth Night and we gathered together in the little chamber off the hall which my aunt liked to call her "parlour," much to my uncle's amusement.

"Mama and Papa are going out to dine." Judith tossed her head, raising her chin in a superior manner. "I'm to take care of you all. Betsy's been told to prepare something special for supper and we can wait up until they come home."

"I wish we could go to the Kingsfords'." Meg looked up from her embroidery with a dreamy expression on her pretty face.

"Only because you want to make sheep's eyes at Matthew," Judith accused her with a teasing smile.

"No I don't! The Kingsfords always have lots of interesting guests and—"

"Their son Matthew is the handsomest young lawyer in the city!" Judith finished with a flourish.

Meg threw down her needlework and gave chase round the chamber. Shrieking, Judith raced away from her sister's grasping fingers, upsetting the checker-board by the hearth where Sarah and I were playing, scattering trinkets from the shelf.

"I wonder what Tom Proudley would say if he could see you romping like a tavern wench?" Meg panted for breath and leaned against the settle.

Judith collapsed on to a stool, red-faced and hoarse with laughter. "No more than Harry Mercer if he could see you now."

"And I wonder what Mama and Papa would say if they knew you were breaking the house down instead of looking after us." Sarah tried to look prim and shocked as we picked up the fallen trinkets.

"And I suppose you intend to tell, do you?" Judith stood up, pretending to be cross. "Then I shall tell them that you've been talking to the goldsmith's apprentice—"

"You wouldn't—?"

"*And* you let the butcher's lad hold your hand," Meg joined in the teasing.

"He was helping me over the step," said Sarah. "Anyway, Nan likes that little lad with the yellow curls who brought the medicine for Mama." She tugged at my gown while I stammered fierce protests.

"What!" Meg pinched me, cheeks pink with mirth. "You mean the apothecary's apprentice?"

A storm of laughter drove us to the casement to watch the people hurrying to and fro in the street far below, their cloaks flapping in the wind like the wings of giant birds. We pointed out any whom we knew, my uncle's wealthy customers, ladies we admired, the swaggering youths and tipsy messengers.

After an early supper we grouped about the fire. The drowsy afternoon darkened. Tired of nibbling sweetmeats and playing merrills, our idle chatter turned once more to marriage and young men.

"Betsy told me a way to discover the name of your sweetheart." Judith twisted a strand of her dark red hair about her finger, her hazel eyes dancing with mischief. Her full lips pursed as if to suppress a secret jest.

Meg was captured in an instant. "How?"

"It's a game." Judith sprang to her feet, eager as a young hind. "We'll need a bowl of water and some greenery."

"I'll fetch the water." Pert, little Sarah already by the door, hopped from one foot to the other with excitement. "I'll ask Betsy to put some in a bowl."

While she scampered off to the kitchen, Judith handed Meg and me one of the green branches from the garland over the fireplace. Already the leaves were dry and curling.

"Break off the leaves and flower petals," she said. "But try to keep them whole."

By the time Sarah returned, I'd filled my lap with leaf dust.

Solemnly, Judith set the basin of water on a stool. "Now, we must sit round it and be very quiet." She threw Sarah a warning glance. "Each will take a turn. You must take some of the leaves and petals and throw them into the water. Betsy says if you ask Green Jenny, she'll show you the first letter of your true love's name amongst them."

"Who's Green Jenny?" Sarah's lips already twitched with laughter.

"Sssh!" Judith put a finger to her lips. "She's a water spirit."

Though her eyes sparkled, the gravity of her words alarmed me. Hadn't I promised Brother Brian not to speak of spirits? But how could I gainsay my elder cousin?

We gathered about the bowl, kneeling among the rushes, quivering with guilty anticipation. Our eyes fastened on Judith.

"I'll go first." She spoke in a breathless whisper. She picked up some broken greenery. "Green Jenny, Green Jenny, show me please, the name of my true love. I cast these leaves into the water and call on you to reveal the secret. Green Jenny, Green Jenny, show me please, the name of my true love."

Tension kept me rigid. The twirling leaves and petals bumped and spiralled in the cloudy water. Gradually they stilled. A tingling sensation coursed through my limbs, heightening my awareness. Imperceptibly, the room grew colder. A curious vibrancy filled it, subtly altering its usual cheeriness to an eerie, watchful atmosphere. Smoky darkness thickened about the shivering candle-flames. We leaned close over the bowl, shoulders touching.

"It looks like a J," whispered Meg. "Or perhaps a T." A nervous giggle trembled in her voice. I knew Judith was betrothed to someone named Tom Proudley and supposed Meg teased her.

"Sssh!" Judith's hissed warning set the leaves bobbing. The pattern changed. But I no longer saw leaves or petals. Instead, I saw a long stretch of flat, furrowed land, and a man with a team of stout horses. Beyond the hedgerows I heard the melancholy low of cattle.

"What else? What else can you see?" Judith's voice seemed urgent, fearful. The chamber pulsed with energy. I must have spoken out loud.

"Inside the house there's a baby in a cradle—a little boy with hair the colour of a fox's coat—and there's a woman sewing by the fire—"

"Me next!" Meg scooped the leaves from the water and threw in some petals of her own. Vaguely, I realised she must have selected these before the game began. In a shaking voice, she invoked Green Jenny's aid, while I watched the pictures begin to form beyond the foolish scatter of dried roses.

"Trays and trays of loaves," I said. "The place is as hot as a forge but I can smell new bread. There's a young man carrying a sack of flour on his shoulders. He has brown hair and a scar on his left cheek—"

"Harry!"

A scuffle and a giggle followed. Amidst some stifled protests, Sarah dipped her head, stretched out a hand to remove the petals —but before she could take her turn, I gasped. The girls froze.

"What is it?" Judith's voice yelped.

Too engrossed in watching a face form in the water, I didn't answer. A dark masculine face stared out at me—a strong, rugged face with shockingly blue eyes. Surely I'd seen this face before? It seemed so familiar I couldn't tear myself away. A secret grin curved his mouth. But when he opened it to speak, I screamed.

55

Shouts and footsteps on the stairs scattered us, knocking over the stool; the slop of spilled water mingled with an unpleasant, spinning sensation. I must have fainted.

When I came to, my aunt bent over me holding a lavender soaked cloth under my nose. A scared Betsy gaped. One of the girls sobbed as my uncle's growl punished all of us with questions.

He sent us to bed in disgrace. His harsh, unjust words rang in my ears.

"I'm not sleeping with Nan," snivelled Sarah. "She frightens me."

"You can snuggle up with us." Judith wrapped a comforting arm about her.

"I'll not have anyone conjuring spirits under my roof," my uncle raved. His fiery beard and hair cast sparks about the darkened room. "What did I tell you, Grace? You and all this so-called fortune-telling? I warned you about encouraging her! This maid will bring shame on all of us! She puts our house in danger!"

No one listened to me. I lay alone in my bed planning a tearful revenge. If only I could turn time back and avoid that foolish game so that everyone still loved me!

Chapter Ten

In the bleak chill of a winter's morning Aunt Grace rushed me through the winding streets to the Chepe where the busy market stalls and shops touted their wares. I suppose she was too frightened to defy my uncle, but it seemed as if she couldn't wait to be rid of me. How I despised her weakness!

On the corner of Bread Street, always warm and fragrant with fresh baking, we stopped at a big shop. Aunt Grace pushed me inside.

"Is this the maid?" The stout woman in the bleached linen apron turned to stare. From the open bake-house door wafted a mouth-watering smell of new bread, and the sight of heaped loaves and pastries on the shelves caught my greedy eyes.

"Aye, this is Nan."

Aunt Grace nudged me forward like a horse for inspection.

"How would you like to help me in the bake-house?" the woman asked. She regarded me shrewdly. "I could use an extra pair of hands." Ignoring my sullen silence, she nodded to my aunt. "She can sleep in Philippa's chamber."

This news alarmed me. Was I to be a servant now? Who was Philippa?

Still smarting with the injustice of my exile, I feigned indifference. As their punishment, Uncle Will denied my cousins the royal procession, but he sent me away to work. It wasn't fair. But then a little, niggling doubt sprouted like a weed. Suppose I *was* to blame for all the things that had happened? Suppose I was a witch? What should I tell Brother Brian when he came to visit?

A dusty young man with a scar on his cheek appeared from the bake-house.

"Take Nan to your father," Mistress Mercer said. "He's expecting her."

The sight of the bake-house immediately brought back the vivid pictures I'd seen for Meg. Motes of flour floated in the air, and a blast of heat as if from a great furnace enveloped me. Out of searing mist appeared Big Hal, Mistress Mercer's husband, a giant in a straw-coloured jerkin, his face powdered thick and white like a spectre's. Nodding and smiling, he scraped out crumbs and ashes from the ovens with huge, dust-dried hands, while Harry, the sturdy, brown-haired youth with the kindly face, lifted trays heavy with hot loaves on to a trestle just as I saw in my vision.

Wiping floury hands upon his apron and inky-coloured hose, Harry gave me a friendly wink. "These will be delivered to the rich houses in the city. My father bakes the finest bread in London. No one has a reputation to match his. Mercer's bread is famous."

Scorched by the breath of the ovens, I watched Harry's strong hands kneading and shaping dough. The lad's cheerful manner put me at ease and I listened hungrily as he confided to me the secrets of Mercer's famous bread. Though the big man with the powerful shoulders said little, his eyes twinkled with good humour. I felt an immediate desire to earn his approval. Perhaps, Brother Brian was right about things happening for the best. Here, in the heart of the pie shop, I'd learn new skills and meet new people.

But I learned quickly that Mercer's pie-shop wasn't just famous for its delicious breads and dainties. It bubbled with juicy morsels of gossip in a city teeming with rumour, and throughout my first week the shop buzzed with talk of a fearful battle in the north in which the Duke of York had been killed.

"They stuck his head on Micklegate Bar in York so he could over-look the city," a talkative matron said, twitching at her brown hood. She opened her eyes wide in pretended horror. "And his son's too."

Astonished, I listened avidly. Had Brother Brian heard this tale? And would he think of me?

In these early days, clever Margaret Mercer made no attempt to win my confidence. She kept me busy and asked no questions. But bit by bit she lured me into the circle of her affection. Though Aunt Grace came to see me often, sometimes bringing a sheepish Sarah with her, I greeted her with grudging courtesy, listening behind the bakery door and gloating when she wept: " I'd have her back at the house, Margaret, but Will—I treated her like one of my own and she was just beginning to settle when—"

"There, there," Margaret Mercer would say, "She'll come round in time. She's doing well, and Hal enjoys her company—and as for Harry—She's an uncommon child. Just leave her be a while. Let her grow used to us. It's not been easy for her."

Clever Margaret Mercer—I think she knew I listened but I didn't care. I was still a novice in the art of dissembling. No one had considered my feelings before. I'd not come here willingly, but now I determined to stay. Harry had won my heart.

It was easy to love the homely youth who treated me with simple kindness. He entertained me with stories about the city and in his leisure time let me watch him carving animals from bits of wood. The little, knock-kneed horse he gave me became my greatest treasure. I hung on his words and followed after him, longing to confide my secrets. But mindful of the priest's solemn counsel to ask the Virgin to take away my "dark fancies," I said my prayers and struggled on alone.

Harry first took me through the warren of streets in the Chepe and taught me about the city. Gradually the sights and sounds grew familiar. Delivering baskets of succulent, golden pies, and honey-glazed pastries allowed me opportunities to see the market traders at their stalls, and explore the lanes bustling with shops. The tangy stink of the fishmongers, the pungent butcher's stall, and the aromatic scent of leather from the shoe-maker's filled my nostrils. I revelled in the sharp odour of resin from the carpenter's shop and learned to distinguish the mingled smells of beeswax, honey and wine. By degrees I grew proud to belong to this family of tradesmen. I loved to watch the milling people. Peddlers, hawkers, pilgrims, ragged vagrants begging for alms, raucous apprentice boys with impudent faces, blousy women in draggled skirts accosting burghers, painted players, cut-purses and jugglers formed only a part of the throng which filled my daily life with colour and noise.

On one of these occasions I met Maud Attemore, the cutler's wife, who kept the shop in Forster Lane.

"You've a new helper, Harry?"

The woman's handsome, weather-roughened face smiled down at me. Harry grinned back as if sharing a joke.

"This is Nan, Mistress Attemore. She's learning her way round the city so she can make deliveries on her own soon."

"She's a lucky maid then." Mistress Attemore, a striking figure in a garnet gown with mole-hued sleeves, picked coins from a worn leather purse. "She's got the best of guides." She winked as she counted the money into Harry's dusty palm. "What do you think of London, Nan?"

The bright expression encouraged confidence but I wouldn't answer.

"Shy, is she?" Mistress Attemore darted a bold glance at Harry. "She's a bonny, little thing. Lovely grey eyes—just like wood-smoke."

"She's from the country," said Harry. He dropped the pennies into a cloth bag and tied it fast. "It's a bit strange to her here, but she's learning fast. Shall I put these pies on the shelf?"

"Aye, there's a good man." She craned her neck to watch people passing in the street—a habit I got to know well, for Maud Attemore never missed a thing.

"Well, look at that!" She smiled with satisfaction. "See that fine lady just outside, Nan –the one in the rose-coloured gown?"

She turned me by the shoulder and pointed to a stately figure in velvet standing by a jeweller's shop across the way.

I nodded, holding my breath with wonder. The woman stood straight and slender, her hair hidden beneath gold nets decorated with pearls on each side of her face, exposing the white sweep of her brow and finely arched eyebrows. On the top of her head sat a fantastical heart-shaped cap draped with a gauzy veil in palest rose. The gown itself hung in shimmering folds, the wide sleeves cut into points that almost swept the ground. Below the skirt I glimpsed purple leather shoes with high wooden soles and heels.

"One of the queen's ladies." Maud laughed at my amazement. "See the two men-servants in blue livery? No noblewoman goes out without someone to protect her. There's always something going on in the city, Nan. You'll soon learn to love it as we do."

Harry lurked at my elbow, eager to be gone.

"Wait," said Mistress Attemore, disappearing into the shop.

She was back in a moment and holding a reddish ball under my nose.

"Take it," she said, with a wink at Harry. "A pomegranate. A welcome gift."

"What is it?" I trotted after Harry like an obedient puppy.

His laughter warmed me.

"Maud Attemore's the biggest gossip in the city," he said. "If you want to know anything, just ask her." He took the pomegranate. "And this is a fruit." He tore back the thin, leathery skin to reveal the ruby flesh of the seeds.

"Like jewels," I said, dazzled by this new wonder.

"Sweet," said Harry, "all the way from Spain."

We shared Maud Attemore's treasure as we finished the rounds, and I raced Harry back to the shop.

Chapter Eleven

My life took a new turn. Days flew by so swiftly, I'd little time to brood. At night I dropped into a heavy, dreamless sleep from complete exhaustion.

We rose early, for the bread must be in the ovens before dawn streaked the sky, and I went out with deliveries while it was still warm. The day's business so occupied me I ceased to think of the visions, and if spirits roamed among the throng in the streets I didn't recognise them. Instead I glimpsed the wealthy ladies carried upon litters, goggled at jewel-encrusted gowns and elaborate head-dresses, and admired the noblemen astride brightly caparisoned horses.

Harry made me a regular visitor to my uncle's house, sending me with tokens for Meg. Both families approved this burgeoning love affair, and with three daughters to be wed, poor Uncle Will's mind buzzed over the next months. Scarcely had Judith celebrated her marriage in far off Lincolnshire, than Meg was planning hers.

Philippa and I chattered of it incessantly as we lay in the comfortable seclusion of our little chamber high above the bakery.

Philippa turned out to be a handsome, bold-eyed wench of fourteen or so, who helped in the shop and sometimes took baskets of bread and pies to special patrons. She treated me like a younger sister and delighted in teaching me all the feminine arts. Her knowledge of the latest fashions and city scandals soon won my admiration. I longed to have her easy manner with the customers and secretly coveted the golden hair that tumbled down her back like liquid gold.

"Why do you always braid it?" she asked one night, watching me brushing my own hair before bed. "You should wear it loose." Taking the brush, she made long, sweeping strokes through the curling mass which hung to my waist, humming with satisfaction as it crackled under her fingers. "See how thick it is!"

"But it's dark," I said with a dissatisfied pout, "not fashionable. I wish it were fair like yours."

She shook her golden mane, laughing as she ran her hands through the silky locks. "But mine's nowhere near as thick as yours. Yours has such a sheen. See how it gleams red under the light. It's a shame to hide such curls."

She arranged it loosely about my shoulders, stepping back to admire her handiwork. "See! It makes those lovely eyes of yours look huge! There's many a lad in London would be glad to woo a wench with such wonderful dark hair!"

I blushed, making her giggle. Philippa had a liking for young men, and Mistress Mercer teased her about the swaggering young swains who hung about the premises in the hope of a glimpse or a word, but while she chattered and tossed her wayward locks at all of them, Ralph Fowler won her favour. Sometimes, lying in the dark, she told me about him, whispering of their trysts and her hopes of marriage.

"But suppose his parents won't let him marry you?" I asked, excited by the daring tales she told.

"Pooh!" she said, wrinkling up her nose as if at a bad smell, "they couldn't stop him. I know how to make him want me so badly, he can't think of anything else!" Her eyes sparkled as she confided the latest intimacy she'd allowed him, laughing at my ignorance. "I thought country girls knew all about the natural needs of men." She raised her eyebrows knowingly.

Sometimes Philippa questioned me about my country home. When I spoke of it, I realised how small my village really was. But that didn't stop me yearning for its green fields and shadowed woodlands. How different did the tiny thatched cottages seem after the teetering city houses with their lofty wooden frames and painted walls, how little the squat-towered church— and yet I craved the earthy smell of the byre, the comforting hiss and fizzle of the forge, the familiar discord of the blacksmith's clanging music. I understood then how Brother Brian felt about his home across the sea.

"Why did you come to London?" Philippa leaned on her elbow, all curiosity.

"My father died, and my aunt and uncle took me in." I fidgeted, uncomfortable with the memories this stirred.

"But you don't live with them now." She eyed me closely. "Betsy told me they sent you away for conjuring—"

"The fortune-telling got me into trouble," I answered, incensed by the serving maid's tittle-tattle. "I wasn't really to blame. Betsy first suggested it anyway. It was around Twelfth Night and my aunt and uncle had gone out. Judith wanted us to play this game she'd had of Betsy—she said if you threw petals or leaves into a bowl of water, a spirit would show you the letters of your future husband's name."

"What happened?" Philippa's eyes gleamed with excitement.

"I don't really know. I'd never played it before, but I saw pictures in the water and it frightened them. A face appeared and I screamed. There was a great commotion because my aunt and uncle returned early and I fainted. My uncle was furious and accused me of conjuring spirits."

"But what made you scream?" Her voice fell to an awed whisper.

"I'd seen that face before in my dreams."

She waited for more but I didn't tell her I'd know it anywhere by the piercing brightness of its blue eyes and the sensual curve of its mouth.

During the turbulent events of my eleventh year, however, my new dreams set Philippa complaining.

"She wakes me with nightmares." She adopted a pained expression. "How can I sleep when she's always talking about murderers or being chased by monsters with yellow eyes, or setting people on fire? It scares me."

Harry laughed at her grumbles but Mistress Mercer's watchful glances put me on edge. I grew clumsy and distracted, spilling flour and dropping loaves, until Big Hal turned me out of the bake-house and sent me on various errands in the city.

Here, the bustling streets and alley-ways buzzed with rumours of new plots to seize the crown. Tired of weak government, the Londoners insulted King Henry openly now, and nick-named his wife "the she-wolf." Every day I heard more lewd remarks about her. Fat Marion's bawdy gossip now made sense. People called Queen Margaret's prince a bastard but they praised the late Duke of York's eldest son.

"Edward of York's the handsomest lad in the world," Philippa said. Her eyes grew dreamy.

"What, handsomer than Ralph Fowler?" Harry feigned shock.

Philippa flounced out of the bake-house into the shop, and we listened to her regaling Mistress Mercer with lurid tales about this golden youth. Big Hal shook his head. His eyes twinkled down at me.

"I daresay you wenches are all in love with this popinjay. But he's barely eighteen. A king needs more than fine features."

"Oh Meg told me Nan favoured the apothecary's lad." Harry laughed. "But now I hear she's fond of lads with black hair. I've seen her looking—"

It was true I'd told Philippa I'd a fancy for dark-haired men but I never thought she'd betray this confidence to Harry. My cheeks burned with embarrassment and rage. This amused Harry and his father all the more and drove me out of the bake-house too.

Maybe the unrest in the city generated my new nightmares. Several times I dreamt of men skulking on a shadowy staircase, carrying a bundle lapped in a bloody counterpane, and the man with black hair and vivid blue eyes dragged me onto a dun-coloured horse and rode off with me into wild, open countryside. One February morning I woke just as the horse stumbled over a rocky ledge dazzled by a huge sun-burst—

Philippa stood by the casement, shivering in her shift. Outside all the bells were ringing. Shouts and hurrying footsteps from the street below shattered the remnants of my dream.

"What is it?" Flinging on a robe, I leaned out to shout down to a skinny lad in the alley-way. "What's happening?"

"Edward of March, York's eldest son, has defeated the king and is marching towards London!"

Philippa hugged me. Squealing with excitement, we raced downstairs to celebrate the news.

The Mercers plied their customers with ale that day. Although no one thought the saintly king would really be overthrown, they didn't want to miss a chance of revelry. Besides, the gossips hailed this victory as a kind of miracle.

Maud Attemore, robust in a bilious green gown with mottled sleeves, had a great crowd about her the following morning when Harry and I walked through the Chepe.

"Three suns shone clear in the heavens on the morning of the battle," she said. She held up a hand as if to point them out. The listeners stood impressed, goggle-eyed and open-mouthed.

"Three suns indeed!" A jeering voice broke the spell. "What piss! How does a poxy drab know about miracles?"

We turned to confront the beef-faced heckler, a corpulent fellow in a soiled grey doublet bearing a Lancastrian device upon the sleeve.

"Let wenches follow after York's bastard spawn with the pretty face. He's not fit to lick Royal Harry's boots. Didn't you all swear allegiance to the House of Lancaster? Where's your loyalty now, eh? Since when did bawds champion kings?"

Shouts of support fragmented the crowd. Maud's listeners grew troublesome, trading insults, their ranks swaying menacingly. Harry's brows knitted together. He pushed me through the ugly press of bystanders.

Though I thought Maud's tale more extravagant than usual, she obviously believed it. Her bold leer taunted the heckler. "Young Edward of March knelt down before his soldiers and begged God for guidance." She shouted above the noise, crossing herself elaborately. "Isn't that proof of the lad's piety? I tell you, he's been chosen for great things." She threw back her head as if to challenge all disbelievers.

"Come on, Nan." Harry's arm circled my shoulder protectively, steering me unwillingly from the roars of outrage. "We'll be late with the deliveries."

"One minute people shouted for King Henry and the next for Edward of York." I spilled my news to Big Hal that afternoon, breathless with excitement.

His eyes twinkled at my enthusiasm. "Don't pay too much heed. Maud Attemore likes to amuse folk with these stories. But what does it matter? Whoever's in charge, the poor will still be poor." He tugged my long braid mischievously. "And the nobles will ride rough-shod over all of us as usual!"

But by March, this Edward was being hailed as king and I was afraid to go to sleep.

Chapter Twelve

"What's wrong, Nan?" Harry watched me load my basket with warm loaves. "You're not yourself these days. You've lost your smile and you look tired and pale."

I kept my head down. "I'm not sleeping well." I ached to confide and wondered how much he really knew of my history.

"Why's that?"

"Sometimes I wonder what's going to happen to me." I trailed over the words and scuffed my feet in the dust. "Now Judith and Meg are settled, Aunt Grace's discussing suitors for Sarah." I didn't mention my lack of dowry. Girls without dowries ended up as servants or nuns. I didn't want to be a nun, but Mistress Evans's warning, "Beware the nun," haunted me.

Harry laughed. "Oh, some handsome tradesman will sweep you off your feet! Is that what you're worried about? You maids are all the same." He tweaked my nose. "My mother says you'll make an excellent wife and you're pretty as a princess."

I smiled wanly but I didn't dare ask him who'd want a penniless maid? Nor did I mention I'd overheard them saying my mother planned to remarry.

"That's better. When you smile you melt people's hearts." He grinned. "Then they put money in my father's purse. We need your smiles, Mistress Nan."

How could I stop myself from returning the grin? Harry knew how much I loved him. I didn't want to think about my mother or who she might marry. He and his parents were my family now.

"Is this an arrow-graze?" I touched the puckered skin on his cheek, just below the bone, my heart beating fast.

"It is. How did you know that?" His eyes glinted. Dusting crumbs from his russet tunic, he drew himself up proudly. "When I was twelve, I was sent to help my Uncle Robert at his tavern in St Albans, and got caught up in a skirmish between the Duke of Warwick's men and the Duke of Somerset—"

"The inn sign has a castle painted on it," I said. My head filled with a rush of images. "Soldiers crash through the streets and some are tearing down the houses. There's an abbey and a barricade. Archers rain arrows and you drop your basket of pies. They burst open like ripe pods and a skinny cat licks up the gravy. Someone shouts for the king and men hammer on the inn door. A knight appears brandishing a sword and four rogues fall under his attack. But another knight in a scarlet tunic with the badge of a bear on it lifts an axe and fells him. Blood spurts from his throat—"

Astonished by this great welter of words, Harry grasped my hand. "My mother mentioned fortune-telling," he breathed. "But I never thought—"

"I hate it," I replied fiercely. The pictures splintered like shattered glass.

Harry's eyes filled with questions reminding me suddenly of Brother Brian. Tears stung, forcing me to turn away.

"Why, Nan, what is it?" Harry slid a brotherly arm about my shoulders—a gesture which completely broke my control. Sobbing against his chest, I confessed the frightful nightmares that had followed me from home.

"I'll be sent away."

He held me tight. "No, you won't. I won't let them. I promise." He smeared away my tears with his thumb, and I looked deep into his eyes, reassured. "I won't say a word. And don't worry what Philippa says." Wrapping me in my ash-coloured cloak, he gave me a quick hug to send me on my way. "I know you like her but she's not always honest. We're used to her tale-bearing."

Harry's promise became my talisman. When Mistress Mercer told me Brother Brian was coming to London the following week, I sang through my chores and Big Hal joined me in the choruses.

"The Mercers speak highly of you, Nan," said the priest when the Mercers left us alone together in the little chamber off the hall where Big Hal sometimes met rich patrons. "You're happy here, I'm thinking?"

"I don't want to leave." A sudden warning chill made me clench my fists.

"Of course not. But Mistress Mercer worries about your troublesome dreams." Questions filled the priest's eyes.

"I didn't have them for a long time, but—"

"Now they're back?"

I nodded, biting my lip. "And worse than before." I struggled to explain. "The faces are clearer. The one I saw in the water at my uncle's house I've seen lots of times in dreams. It's the man who guards the boys."

"And these boys, would you be after knowing more of them now?"

"I've only seen one properly. But I'd know him anywhere."

Brother Brian set down his goblet and stared into the flames. "Perhaps, in time, these fragments will make a whole. Then we may make some sense of them."

Deep lines etched his face now. I wondered what new trouble had put them there. "Who's Michael?"

The priest's face blanched. "Dear God," he said crossing himself. "Who told you about Michael?"

"No one," I said. The flash of terror in his eyes shocked me. "I just heard someone calling that name."

He touched my hand gently, his eyes veiled. "It was a long time ago."

"Does Tom remember me?"

"Of course." His voice grew warmer. "He loves watching the blacksmith at work. And your new brother grows just like you in looks."

"Does my mother ever ask about me?"

The priest shook his head with embarrassment. "Everyone's busy with match-making," he said cheerfully. "Your friend, Alys, and young Robin Arrowsmith seem very fond of one another."

We're growing up, I thought, with a pang of regret for the days of play. I imagined my former companions flirting with the rowdy boys at whom we'd once sneered. A happy picture of Alys and Robin holding hands under trees garlanded with May blossom flooded me with envy. What chance had I of such a settled future? But then I saw the aged hand reach out for Alys to drag her away—

"Several of my scholars have begun working," said Brother Brian. "Simon Dobbs is apprenticed to the dyer in Brafield. I must admit to feeling relieved. I found him troublesome."

"And Alan Palmer? Will he be a scribe?"

The priest's mouth trembled. "It's what brings me so soon to London. He's expressed a wish to enter Holy Orders." His eyes grew soft with longing. "Even now I left him at the Priory of Saint John. He'll study there and, if he finds the work to his liking, he'll take his vows when he's old enough. St John's is famous for its illustrated manuscripts."

"So you'll have cause to visit London more often?"

"I may indeed." He patted my hand. Though he smiled encouragement, his thoughts roamed elsewhere. It troubled me.

Philippa's clumsy scuffling woke me that night. I watched her struggle into her clothes, but as she tip-toed away she must have sensed I'd woken.

"You'll not tell anyone?"

She fidgeted by the door, face sharp with suspicion in the moonlight, impatient to be gone.

I shook my head and pulled the bed-covers about my shoulders. The little chamber felt chilly at this hour.

"I promised Ralph I'd meet him outside the bake-house," she said, "just for a moment. His mother's sick and he can't get away during the day—"

I knew she was lying by the way she stammered and fiddled with her shawl. Besides, it wasn't the first time she'd sneaked out of the cramped room we shared above the shop. I'd pretended sleep before. Once she was gone so long I worried about her safety. Mistress Mercer often spoke of the rogues who prowled the muddle of narrow streets at night.

"You shouldn't be out after curfew."

She laughed nervously. "Ralph'll look after me." She twisted her fingers through the tangled web of the honey-gold hair I so admired. "Go back to sleep, Nan. You'll understand when you've a sweetheart of your own."

As she tiptoed down the stairs, I imagined her furtive passage through the shop into the bake-house. Outside it would be icy cold. Was it worth creeping about like a cut-purse to venture into that raw, inhospitable dark to spend an hour in a lover's arms? Philippa was wrong if she thought I knew nothing of such things. Since my last birthday the black-haired stranger with the fierce eyes came oftener into my dreams, and his presence aroused in me the most shocking desires. For a long time I wondered if all girls had such impulses and what the priest might say if I confessed them.

Lying alone in the dark, I imagined meeting this lover and persuading him to help me find the boys in the Tower. My thoughts drifted sleepily to marriages and how Margaret Mercer and my Aunt Grace seemed as eager as rats at corn to have Meg and Harry's solemnised. The prospect of the wedding feast lulled me, so I didn't hear Philippa crawl back into bed.

Instead I dreamed of snow. It swallowed up a vast sweep of rugged countryside, flooding fields, hedges, ditches and rutted lanes like an endless white wave. Icy flakes settled on my eye-lids, stinging me into blindness.

Out of the blizzard stumbled a troop of ragged soldiers weighed down by weapons. They slipped and slid, frozen fingers clawing for hand-holds as they sank to their knees in treacherous gullies. Ghost-white faces stared at me.

I followed the petals of blood until a great bay horse rose up before me, its hooves pawing the air. I flinched from the wild roll of its eyes and grinding foam-flecked teeth, the hot stench of its breath soiling my face. As its feet plunged down I looked up into the eyes of a huge, golden knight brandishing a sword like a shaft of sun-light. He was bare-headed, shouting and laughing, his hair a flame of red-gold, his features dazzlingly handsome, like a painting from an old romance. He rose upright in the stirrups, careless of the arrows falling about him, the shower of blood. "Swear to be faithful—"

The hooves crashed down again, crushing heaped mounds of broken corpses. Far into the snow-bound distance they stretched, blood-bathed and frost stiffened. Their sightless eyes spoke of countless grief and loss. But the youth held out his hand, his hazel eyes still bright with laughter, and a voice called "Nan! Nan!"

"Wake up, slug-abed," Philippa dug me in the side with her elbow. Groaning, I shielded my eyes from the harsh morning light creeping through the shutters. "Don't you know there's to be a grand procession today? Mistress Mercer says we'll be busier than we've ever been before. Everyone in the city will be celebrating King Edward's arrival."

Although he hadn't been crowned, Edward of York styled himself king from the moment he rode into London. Crowds flocked to catch a glimpse of the handsome young man about whom the ballad-mongers were devising glorious songs—songs that urged the people to walk "in a new vineyard" and accept the sovereignty of the "fair white rose." Hearing them for the first time, I thought about poor, dull-witted King Henry. But Philippa proved right about the vast numbers of customers who patronised the shop during these hectic days. While Big Hal sweated in the kitchens baking extra loaves and pies, Philippa and I were rushed off our feet assisting Mistress Mercer in the serving of them, and poor Harry staggered alone through the bustling streets with all the deliveries.

"Well, I won't complain about the good business the new king's brought us." A dazed Mistress Mercer closed the shop-door behind the last customer. It was long after curfew. Smiling broadly, she poured us all goblets of sweet wine. "I think we've earned this," she said. We raised our cups to the new king. In spite of our exhaustion, we laughed and gossiped late into the night.

"They say he's the handsomest prince in Christendom," said Philippa, swallowing a greedy mouthful of wine. "I wish we'd been able to see him." Rosy colour stained her cheeks. She brushed some drops from the tight bosom of her bronze gown. The shameless sparkle in her eyes infected all of us with excitement.

But Edward lingered only a short time in the city, staying at Baynard's Castle, the York family's turreted house by the Thames. Then, in bitter weather, he rode north to meet his clever cousin, Warwick, and face the Lancastrian army.

"That French queen isn't going to yield the throne, even if the king's no fighter," said Harry. He stuffed loaves into baskets for deliveries.

"Well, what mother would want to see her son disinherited?" Margaret Mercer answered, shivering in spite of a heavy walnut-coloured shawl about her shoulders. "You can't blame her."

I'd forgotten the queen's son. Prince Edward of Lancaster was just a boy, younger than me. Could he be the boy whose face I saw in my dreams? With a jolt I remembered how I'd vowed to save that boy from a dreadful fate.

Throughout the bleak days leading up to Holy Week, anticipation simmered in the city. The cutler's shop became the busiest in the Chepe, for buxom Maud with her saucy tales of the new king drew customers from far and wide. But when groups of armed men began skulking about the streets looking for quarrels and rumours of an imminent battle reached boiling point, Big Hal kept me in the bakery until it was over.

Edward's victory at some place called Towton ignited wild celebrations in the city for days, and jubilant strangers hugged me in the streets. But later, learning of the terrible slaughter he'd meted out to his enemies, the laughter died away. I slept badly that night.

"What's the matter with you?" hissed Philippa. "You're as restless as a colt." She seized the bedclothes, and with an ill-tempered grunt, turned her back on me.

"I've got terrible belly-cramps."

She sighed. "Is it your courses?" I detected a note of sympathy. "Mistress Mercer keeps a herbal remedy in the kitchen press. Just take a sip of that."

I lay a moment longer, hoping she would find it for me, but when I felt her huddle down into sleep, I crawled reluctantly from the bed and wrapped my night-robe about me. Tip-toeing down the stairs, trying to avoid the treacherous creaks, I groped my way into the kitchen. My hands fumbled in the press, found the little flask—

Darkness curdled about me. Unable to move another step, I listened to the swish of heavy robes across stone, the barely perceptible foot-falls. My flesh crawled. Behind me something paused and waited. A cool breeze fanned my ear, lifting the stray wisps of hair across my cheek. Rigid with fear, I held my breath, heard a sigh, a whisper, a sinister chuckle—

At once the chamber relaxed as if something had passed out of it. With trembling fingers I drew the stopper from the flask and swallowed the few drops of vile liquid within. Sweat cooled on my body. I shivered.

Climbing the steps, I glimpsed the swirl of a gold-encrusted hem, the gleam of polished leather shoes above me on the landing. Heart stuttering, I sidled towards the open door of the bed-chamber, hands slithering over the rough plastered wall for comfort.

"Ugh! You're cold as ice," complained Philippa. I snuggled up against her, trembling.

"I saw someone on the stairs," I whispered. "And there was someone in the kitchen."

Philippa's body stiffened. "What do you mean?" Fear strangled her words.

"It was walking about the kitchen and it came up behind me. I heard it laugh—"

"Stop it! I thought you meant a thief. Now you're seeing spirits. I don't want to hear your horrible stories." Behind the anger, terror stalked. She pulled the covers over her head, buried herself beyond my reach.

Saint Paul's bells tolled five times before I slept.

Chapter Thirteen

"Here." Mistress Mercer, still clad in her plum-coloured night robe, pressed some coins into my hand. The bleak morning light accentuated her wrinkled brow and pursed lips. "It'll cost a shilling or two. But you look as if you need it, Nan. You're as pale as ash."

Gritty-eyed with lack of sleep, I picked up the basket of warm loaves.

"Go before you start your deliveries. Just ask for Nell Waters in Butcher Lane." Mistress Mercer, handed me the little flask. "She lives above the basket-maker's, third house on the left—the one with the iron boss on the door. If she's not there, you'll find her in The Crown tavern. She's well-known about the place—There's not a woman in the city hasn't sought her skills some time or other."

I found the house easily enough but the basket-maker's assistant gave me a sly wink as I mounted the steps. About half-way up I encountered a girl on her way down. Though she clasped her dark, woollen cloak about her with whitened fingers, the hood part fell from her head, revealing a luscious fall of flaxen hair. I caught a brief glimpse of a pretty, tear-stained face as we passed. Dismayed, I watched her pause to retch and called out to offer her assistance, but she snatched up the trailing hem of her russet gown and fled, snivelling. With some misgivings I continued upward to tap on the door.

There was nothing of Mistress Evans in the hard-faced woman who urged me into the shadowy room, but the familiar scent of dried herbs perfumed the air. Bundles of lavender and tansy flowers hung from the beams, and on the dresser-shelves crowded an array of dusty, earthen jars and curious bowls. Other containers clustered before the fire, dishes filled with blossom-heads, seeds, nuts, and fragments of aromatic wood. From a hook above the flames, a cauldron bubbled. Inhaling the steam, I identified the distinctive, pungent odours of sage, rosemary and crushed ginger —an expensive spice much favoured by Big Hal in the kitchen—but another strange, underlying smoky fragrance made my head spin.

The sum she asked to refill the little flask seemed enormous. *I could have bought a new woollen cloak for that*, I thought, counting out coins.

"It's costly, I'll agree," she said, as if she'd read my mind. Rapaciously, she thrust the money into her purse and plugged the flask with a rag. "But these herbs are from the Indies." She examined my face. "Are you interested in the making of healing remedies?"

"As a child I visited the village wise-woman. People spoke highly of her."

"I've an idea you've a talent for such skills yourself." She waited a moment as if expecting some answer and I clenched my fists, aware of a growing tension in the room which set my heart drumming. She shrugged, her thin lips twisted in a knowing smile. "There's something to cure all ailments." Her shrewd appraisal suggested other abilities. I wondered if she had the Sight. "It's women-folk who mainly seek me out but it's men who make the troubles they bring." A glitter of crafty humour sparked in her eye. "There's many a lass who needs a tincture for her courses like you, but others need mightier remedies to ease them. Did you meet that foolish wench in the blue cloak on the stairs?"

I nodded, disturbed by the piercing, unblinking gaze. Nell Waters possessed the owl's fearless scrutiny.

"I might have helped her if she'd sought me earlier. I've a tisane to bring on a woman's courses and expel any little problems but timing's important in these matters." She took a jar from a shelf and removed the stopper so I might sniff the contents. "There's extract of hibiscus in there and in here—" From another she extracted some dried white flower heads and a long, green, shrivelled pod like a bean. She proffered her palm to me. The aroma it exuded was curiously warm and rich. "Something very special. The taste, they tell me, is unpleasant, but if a drastic cure's needed a woman must accept the consequences." Her eyes met mine. "You'll find what you seek but not without difficulty. You think you're settled, but you've many journeys ahead of you. Loyalty can be a dangerous thing, but a woman's hand will lead you northward. You guard your secret well but the man of God will betray you at the last." Cupping her palm she poured the strange fruit and flower heads back into the jar. When she looked at me again, it was as if the shutters closed. "I wish you good day," she said.

"A messenger came just after you left," said Margaret Mercer, when I returned to the bakery. "Your priest will be here on Friday and he'll meet you at St Martin's. You can walk home from there together and join us for dinner."

Cheered by this news I hung up my cloak and hastily extracted some coins from my purse. "This is the change from Mistress Waters. The flask's in the basket with the bag of bread money—"

"Feeling better?" Margaret Mercer cocked her head on one side to survey my face. "Philippa tells me you saw something on the stairs when you went down in the night—something which frightened you—" Her eyes probed mine.

"I only told her I *thought* I saw someone—" I answered in a low, hesitant voice. "I was sleepy, so I probably imagined it—"

"What was it like?" She wasn't to be fobbed off so easily.

"I thought it was a man in rich robes," I said, truthfully. "But it can't have been, can it? The bakery's locked up at night. So I must have been dreaming—"

She eyed me suspiciously but said no more. The memory jangled my nerves and kept me wakeful. Then Nell Waters' words played over in my head like a repetitive, irritating tune—"you've many journeys ahead."

On Friday I waited for Brother Brian in the church of St Martin-le-Grand after my morning work. Shivering in the nave's vast cavern, I lit a candle for my father. Watching my breath spiral upward like smoke, I hoped my prayers would be carried heavenward with such ease. Guiltily, I realised a year in London had already dimmed my father's face.

"Forgive me, Nan." The familiar voice turned me from the votive candles. "I was delayed at St John's."

"Are you sick?" Brother Brian's gaunt, white face shocked me. The flesh had fallen from his bones. I clasped his hands, flinching at the feverish tremble of his dry fingers against my palms, alarmed by his troubled smile.

"No, no—"

"Mistress Mercer's preparing dinner." I urged him into the street and pulled my hood over my head. "How's Master Palmer?"

"Nan, I've disturbing news."

I halted by a locksmith's swinging sign, braving the stinging sleet to face the priest. His eyes burned with shame. "Your mother's after marrying again."

"Who?"

"The smith. He's a good man, and the boys are happy. He lost his wife of the sweat and has a daughter—"

"You told me Tom was enchanted by the forge." I laughed bitterly, remembering the smith armed with a mattock, barring my path as I fled the mob. "The smith called me a witch and drove me from the village. He and my mother will be well suited."

"Nan—" The priest laid a gentle hand on my arm but I shook it off.

"My mother never cared for me." My voice hardened into sneering resentment. "She'll be glad to have a proper daughter to help her now."

Turning into Bread Street the smell of new-baked bread welcomed us.

"Come in out of the cold." Margaret Mercer ushered us in from the street and led us into the little chamber off the hall.

We shrugged off our sodden cloaks to wallow in the fire's welcome glow.

"Everyone else's eaten." She bustled us to the table, the sopping garments over her arm. "So I thought you'd like to dine here and be cosy together."

Swallowing the gobbet of malice in my throat, I set about the stew hungrily, refusing to let my mother's new marriage spoil my appetite. Presently however, an uneasy silence drew me from my food to glance at the priest. Brother Brian sat crumbling bread into dust, his haggard face immobile and absorbed.

"What's wrong?" I set down my knife, unnerved by his strange manner. "This has something to do with Master Palmer, hasn't it?"

The frightened flare in the priest's blue eyes indicated my question had found its mark.

"I fear I'm not the virtuous man you think." He studied his hands. "You remember Simon Dobbs?"

"How could I forget such a bully?" I spat the words, recalling Simon's uncanny ability to scent weakness in others and how he'd revelled in tormenting me. "What's he done now?"

A moment's pause—then the priest drew in a shuddering breath. "He made certain remarks about my interest in Alan Palmer to his master in Brafield."

Danger fluttered in this whispered confession. Hadn't the village boys made similar taunts? I found myself tongue-tied.

"There's since been some unpleasant talk in the village—some questions—"

"He likes to spread evil gossip." I recalled the many, spiteful ways Dobbs had urged others to goad the kindly priest. I laid a hand across the tightly-laced fingers. "Everyone knows Alan Palmer was the best scholar in your class. You encouraged him to pursue his studies. No one can fault you for that."

"But I *am* perhaps over-fond of Master Palmer." His voice shook. "But I'd never harm anyone placed in my trust—"

"I know that." Impetuously I squeezed his hands, touched by the embarrassment of this painful admission. "Haven't I always brought my troubles to you? Don't worry. Dobbs can't hurt you with lies."

But when the priest left I thought long and hard on what he'd told me, the delicate face of Alan Palmer sharp in my mind. Simon Dobbs' sly insinuations made sense at last. I was no longer the innocent village girl. Since coming to London I'd learned a deal from Maud Attemore concerning the ways of men. She'd delighted in pointing out the painted catamites who hung about the streets ready to accost certain noblemen, explaining their practises to my astonished ears. Was it possible the gentle priest was enamoured of the clever lad in his care? Was it this that brought him so often to the city? I marvelled at my lack of revulsion, for weren't the pretty boys who sold themselves in the dingy alley-ways abhorrent to me? I couldn't consider the priest's devotion in such wise, but I feared we hadn't heard the last of this business.

Chapter Fourteen

Sweet-scented May burst upon us at last— brilliant with sunshine, jubilant birdsong and blossom-decked trees—fitting auspices for Harry's wedding day. Philippa and I were sent to supervise the final preparations for the celebration meal. One of the Mercers' wealthy patrons loaned his house for this feast, and when we arrived troops of servants were already laying the tables and decorating the dining-hall with flowers.

"You're needed in the kitchens." The spry, bustling steward sent us scampering.

"Mmm," I groaned, "just smell that!" I rubbed my belly extravagantly and licked my lips as we passed the cook's men toiling at the ovens among the mingled flavours of honey-glazed meat and fruit-stuffed pastry.

"My mouth's watering already." Philippa oohed, eyes half-closed in ecstasy. "Mistress Mercer and Big Hal prepared lots of these dishes. I can't wait to taste them."

"Take those platters quickly or no one will taste anything." The good-humoured cook brandished a ladle, his plump face puce and shining with sweat.

Lit by a hundred candles, the wood-panelled hall with its long trestles draped in linen cloths festooned with sprays of blossom and greenery, silver spoons, and goblets of sparkling Venetian glass, gleamed mellow and warm. Fragrant herbs and posies of flowers scattered amongst the rushes, and in the gallery, musicians hired to entertain, tuned their instruments.

"There'll be dancing afterwards." Philippa giggled, her eyes sparkling. She wore her best gown with its blackberry-coloured kirtle that accentuated her curves and set off her pale complexion. "I hope some of Harry's friends will be here."

"I love to dance." I smoothed the soft fabric of my own gown—a dark green that had belonged to Judith once and gave my eyes a smoky gleam. My feet tapped to the snatches of old tunes they played. "In my village there was always dancing on May Day. The games and the merrymaking went on till dawn. All the lads sang raucous songs—"

"I'll wager they were bawdy songs too." Philippa smirked with delight and thrust a stack of damask napkins in my hands.

"They were." I laughed at the memory of the bolder striplings trying to out-do each other in ribaldry. "It makes me blush just thinking about them! The prettiest girls wore their finest gowns and dressed their hair with flower-garlands. Everyone wanted to be chosen as May Queen." I smiled wistfully as I placed the napkins. Alys would be queen this year. I saw her surrounded by giggling attendants and adoring swains. Would she and Robin Arrowsmith creep away with the other couples to plight their troth? "It's a country custom for young men and women to sneak off into the forest to pledge their vows to one another on May Eve," I told Philippa.

"Did you ever do that?" Her eyes danced with mischief.

"No, you jade." I laughed, pinching her arm. "I left long before."

"I'm glad to see you in such a cheerful mood, Nan." My Uncle Will waited by the door. I rushed to welcome him and Aunt Grace, and for a moment we stood together at the back of the great hall, admiring the servants' handiwork.

"You were such a sad-eyed, angry little wench when you first came to London." Uncle Will's brown eyes teased. "Margaret Mercer's wrought a miracle since she took you into the shop."

I'd no time to reply. Behind them pressed other guests and the jostle for places began. Amidst laughter and shouting the newly-wed couple were escorted to the high table, and the chamber soon echoed with cheers, the tinkle of glass, and roars of merriment. Servants scurried to pour wine, others to carve and serve platters of smoking meats—haunches of wine-drenched beef, clove-studded pork, lamb redolent with rosemary, huge pigeon pies, succulent capons crisp and bronze-breasted, fat ducks and apricot-stuffed geese.

Philippa's jaw dropped open when a great coffin of golden pastry spilled open to reveal an enormous ham. As its hot savoury flavour wafted deliciously under our noses, she laughed aloud. "No noble wedding could rival this." She nibbled a fistful of raisins and almonds, relishing each crunch. Although placed far from the high table, the array of wealthy merchants and their finely dressed wives dazzled us. It was my first wedding feast, and looking back I think it was the best I ever attended.

"Meg's gown must have cost a fortune!" Philippa goggled at the heavy brocade embroidered with false pearls. I thought it as exquisite as any I'd seen on a noblewoman, and Meg's pale complexion glowed rosy in the candle-light. Beside her, homely Harry in his blue doublet seemed handsome as a prince. The loving glances that passed between them brought tears to my eyes. Would I, one day, enjoy such happiness?

A burst of applause interrupted this day-dream. Servants appeared bearing a subtlety upon a silver platter. Two turtle doves carved out of pastry and gilded with gold were set down upon the high table. In their beaks they held a single knotted ribbon signifying the bond of marriage. It seemed a shame to watch this magnificent confectionery broken and distributed amongst the guests, but I devoured my morsel stuffed with sweet marchpane as eagerly as the rest.

The trestles were cleared at last and the finely furnished hall rang with praises.

"Hal Mercer's paid for this feast and refurbished chambers above his shop for the young ones." A merchant's wife with painted eyebrows confided this piece of information gleefully. "It must have cost a pretty penny. And you won't believe the ample dower the bride's brought young Harry."

"Aye," nodded her heavy-jowled husband, "her folk have lavished them with a feather bed and bolsters, linen sheets and embroidered coverlets, as well as—" He began counting on his fingers, "an oaken chest and carved chairs, bowls, basins, and goblets of ruby glass—"

Music struck up, interrupting his extravagant list, and muttering swift excuses, Philippa and I scuttled away to join the dancing.

The revels continued long into the night and finally I plunged into bed, giddy with giggles, my feet sore and my head spinning.

In the kitchen next morning, however, my temples pulsed painfully from the effects of unaccustomed wine. Big Hal shielded his eyes against the light and rubbed his head ruefully, muttering something about getting back to normal life. Smiling grimly, I gathered together my basket of loaves and pies and ventured out into the already busy streets. The shouts of the vendors jarred in my ears and the greasy smells of cooking meat churned my stomach, but somehow I managed to make my rounds. Nevertheless, when inquisitive Maud Attemore tried to engage me in conversation, I cut her short. "I'll tell you about the wedding later." I yawned, screwing up my eyes with pain.

"Oooh! Sore head, is it?"

The throb of drums prevented a response. Flocks of ragged girls and boys collected along the street as the rhythmic beat grew louder.

"What's happening? Is there a procession today?" My head rang with the noise. Maud shouted to her serving wench to look after the shop, and dragged me into the boisterous crowd already swelling on the corner.

"Warwick's on his way to speak to the king." A stout butcher's wife in a tan kirtle joined us. Maud craned her neck for a better view. A buzz of excitement travelled through the throng. Shouts and cheers heralded the arrival of the first foot soldiers in their bright red livery emblazoned with the bear and ragged staff. Some of the bolder wenches threw flowers. Behind these troops came the drummers, and at their heels the trotting horse-men, proud and upright in polished leather saddles, their woollen cloaks billowing behind them.

Maud yelled and pointed but the pulse of the drums was too loud. Following the line of her arm, I saw a tall figure in an armoured breast-plate mounted on a huge, dappled horse, caparisoned in crimson. Bare-headed, this handsome nobleman carried a burnished helmet under his arm, one hand gripping the reins, the other resting on the pommel of his sword. As he passed, I studied the arrogant lift of his brow, the fierce, aquiline features, and the sheen of honey-gold hair. The mouth expressed grim purpose but the blue-green eyes blazed with triumph.

Behind him marched the other ranks. Men and women waved and roared as these disciplined lines swept by, for it was a brave display clearly designed to impress.

A shock of black hair caught my attention. Standing on tip-toe, I strained to catch a closer look at the tall, muscular figure among the soldiers. The familiar face made me catch my breath. I waved a hand, and for an instant a pair of startling blue eyes locked on mine. I couldn't tear my gaze away nor control the lurch in my belly when he smiled back, but his fellows roared about him, thrusting him onward and my blue-eyed man strode away too fast.

"What do you think of the Kingmaker, then?" Maud Attemore turned on me eagerly when the drum-beats faded and the last horsemen disappeared.

"He seems very sure of himself." My attention fixed on empty distance.

Maud grinned, pushing me back through the babbling people, a bustling bumble-bee of a woman in her black and tawny gown. "And well he might be. Since he returned from France he's more popular than ever. They say his men will follow him anywhere. And what magnificent fellows they are, eh? I saw you looking! How do you fancy being a soldier's wife, eh, Nan?"

"What! And have him march off to war and be carried back with an arrow in his throat?" I was still stirred by the sight of the black-haired man. Foolishly romantic now, I'd already fallen in love with the man of my visions. Had I really just seen him in Warwick's army? The memory of his impudent smile stayed with me as I sauntered home. How could I find him? A fanciful idea of somehow meeting him in earnest banished my headache and set me smiling. Several swains shouted bawdy remarks as I passed them.

"Will you take a stroll with me, sweeting?" A youth with tousled brown hair called to me from a tavern door. "I'll wager you've been admiring Warwick's men today—but I'll be here tomorrow, and the day after, not marching off to war. I'd be glad to keep you company!"

I tossed my head the way I'd seen Philippa do. The approving glances this won from men of all ages delighted me. Perhaps I'd make a match after all!

At supper I entertained Big Hal with Warwick's parade.

"More trouble." He shook his head. "These barons and their quarrels will be the ruination of the country."

"But Mistress Attemore's a great admirer of the Earl of Warwick." I tried to stifle a yawn. "She says he's very generous to the poor."

"A mighty clever man," replied Big Hal, "but don't listen too much to Maud Attemore. Gossips like her thrive on hearsay. We've no need to worry about him and his schemes. The bakery's what matters. People always need bread." He laughed at my yawns. "Get yourself to bed, Nan. It's been a long day."

Philippa showed no desire to talk. Closing my eyes, I nestled down in the bed, recalling with pleasure the comments I'd roused amongst the youths in the streets. If only I could find my black-haired man—

My dream drove me through endless, winding corridors where stones oozed damp and flickering torches smoked. A reedy river smell clung about the place, and sounds grew distant, muffled by barred windows and stout walls.

"Don't hurt me!"

Sudden fear filled the chamber like the frantic beat of black wings. A child's white face pierced the gloom, its mouth stuffed with feathers, and then the walls unravelled. Stone by stone the dark descended and pressed and pressed—

"Jesu! What a noise!"

Philippa was squealing like a sow in farrow while Mistress Mercer panted up the narrow stairs.

Drenched in sweat, my arms tangled in the bed-clothes, my voice hoarse with shouting, I glared at Philippa cowering in a corner, crossing herself and whimpering.

"What's the matter?" Margaret Mercer's voice betrayed alarm.

"She woke me with her screaming," began Philippa at a furious pace. "She has these terrible dreams and it frightens me. She tells horrible tales of murder—and she sees spirits. I can't stand it anymore."

"Get dressed and go down to the bake-house," Mistress Mercer told the hysterical girl. "Hal's there already, raking out the ovens. Ask Harry or Meg to give you something to eat. If you start work early, you'll not have time to dwell on nonsense."

"I'll not stay another night with her." Philippa threw on her clothes. "She's a witch." Her voice shook with a passion which made me wince but I noticed Margaret Mercer didn't scold her. Instead she fixed me with a wary glance.

"Now, Nan," she said, when Philippa was gone, "what am I to do with you?"

"It was just a dream." My heart still thumped with fright. "But it was so real—It was all muddled up. I didn't mean to shout—"

Margaret Mercer's eyes pierced mine. "Just a dream, eh? These dreams of yours cause a deal of trouble." She sat down heavily on the edge of the bed. "Your Aunt Grace was very disturbed by your tales and some fortune-telling episode frightened your Uncle Will out of his wits. And now Philippa—What are we going to do?"

Speechless, I stared into her face, realizing she intended to send me away. The thought of leaving Harry and the comforts of this place I thought of as home, horrified me. Hadn't I tried to suppress the Sight? Mounting rage forced me to confront the future. Why must I be different from other girls? Would I be sent from house to house for the rest of my life, a victim of this curse, forced to see the future and yet unable to prevent it? It didn't matter what I did, I always ended up in trouble. What were these spirits? Was I truly a witch?

"I don't want to send you away." Mistress Mercer lifted up my chin with her finger and thumb so she could scan my face. The kindness in her homely features broke my resolve. Folding me into her stout arms, she kissed away my tears, stroking my hair, murmuring soothing words as though I were her daughter. "Shush, we'll think of something. I'll send for that priest of yours. In the meantime, you shall have a room of your own." She kissed me on the nose, smiling at this notion. "I'll get Hal to sort it."

They put me in the little store-room. Between them, the men converted it into a tiny chamber, bringing in a pallet and making it snug. Harry fixed up a shelf for my little horse and promised he'd make another to match it. Afterwards, I avoided Philippa, but if we met on the stairs she shrank away as if I had the plague. How trusting I'd been. I wondered what she might tell Maud. I didn't want to be the subject of the latest city gossip. The Londoners relished witch hunts, and flocked to executions at Smithfield—suppose someone pointed me out?

Chapter Fifteen

Brother Brian arrived in late August but he didn't come to the bakery. Instead Margaret Mercer sent me to meet him at St John's.

"I think he'd rather speak to you privately." She gave me a half-hearted smile and squeezed my hand, but she didn't meet my eyes.

Over-joyed at having the chance to talk to someone who understood me better than anyone else, I shrugged off her odd manner and raced through the streets, heedless of the curious stares and cries for caution.

The small chamber at the Priory of Saint John gleamed mellow in the candle-light. Brother Brian crouched over a desk strewn with scrolls, but his face lit up at my entrance.

"Mistress Mercer asked me to talk to you." He returned my impulsive hug and set aside his writing implements. "And the prior is after loaning us the use of his private chamber for it."

Smiling encouragement, he indicated a stool by the hearth. A tiny fire danced, shedding its glow upon the shelves of books and papers, illuminating the faded arras on the wall.

"Did Mistress Mercer tell you about the dream?"

"It caused a bit of an uproar, I'm thinking?" Listening to my version, his eyes clouded. "The reoccurrence of these visions reminds us of the need to discover their meaning. Niall spent much time interpreting dreams—for they were prophecies—and so we must pursue the purpose of yours." He took my hands in his own, squeezing them gently, and smiled at me. "You've surely been chosen for a special task. Between us, we must solve the riddle."

"But I frighten people. Even the Mercers are scared."

"The Mercers are good people. They speak of you with great affection. Indeed, they're loath to part with you—" He looked at me with such gravity then, my heart skipped a beat. "Nan, for your own safety we think it's best to find employment for you elsewhere —at least for now. I've been making enquiries about a young widow who requires a maid-servant—"

"They're sending me away."

Betrayed, disappointed, angry, I shrank from his solicitude.

"Listen to me Nan." His voice shook. I guessed then the Mercers had elected him to break the news. "This widow's husband was killed fighting for King Henry in one of the foolish quarrels amongst the barons—She's presently renting a house in the city while she petitions for the restoration of the estates that were confiscated on her husband's death. And because she's only few of her old servants with her, she's after hiring others. We thought—"

"To be rid of me."

It was a cruel judgement born of self-pity. But the gentle priest offered no recrimination. Instead he tried to soften the blow. "It's safer to find you another place while that wench, Philippa, remains in the shop. Her accusations rouse gossip. Witchcraft's a dangerous matter." His blue eyes flashed a warning.

"But Harry's my friend — and I don't want to go to new people—"

"It's just for a little while—until the gossip dies down."

"But what about the dreams?"

A wary expression entered his eyes. "Say nothing to arouse curiosity. Who knows, but working in a new place might drive them away for a while—as they did when you first came to the Mercers—"

"But I need to find the boys."

The priest looked at me steadily. "There are no child prisoners in the Tower, Nan. I made enquiries."

"But—"

"Perhaps the time is not yet come." He took my hand and spoke slowly, almost tenderly. "Niall taught us that such prophecies can't be hurried. You must be patient a little longer."

I snatched my hand away. "People will talk about my sudden dismissal from the Mercers." How petulant my words sounded.

"I'm sure we can tell them something plausible." But his argument failed to convince. I knew Maud would gossip. There was only one way to prevent it. I must lie. I'd tell her the Mercers had given me a marvellous opportunity to work in a noble household. That would quash any of Philippa's malicious tales.

"There's something else." I glared at the priest so his eyes seemed to slide away from me. "Something you haven't told me yet."

A sudden image of Alys filled my head. Golden coins lay in her lap but her eyes streamed tears. "Something about Alys."

The priest flinched, his face full of shadows. "She's to be married."

"But not to Robin."

He averted his glance to stare into the fire. "Young Robin's joined the army—to mend a broken heart, I fear."

"I told you Alys would marry an old man and Robin will die in battle."

The priest shuddered and crossed himself. "The reeve's not so old—"

"Old and rich. Poor Alys!"

"It'll be a prosperous marriage."

"But she loves Robin!"

"Sometimes we can't choose the things we most desire." The priest smiled wryly, gazing into long, painful distance. I wondered then what demons troubled him and fine-featured Alan Palmer flashed across my mind.

"Is there anything else you're wanting to tell me now?" His sombre blue gaze fastened on me once more.

Bile rose in my throat. Dare I speak of the black-haired stranger with the fierce blue eyes whom I welcomed with wanton delight in my dreaming and whose presence I looked for daily in the scores of men who patronised Mercers' pie-shop?

A muted squawk distracted us. I spotted a hunched black bird in a domed cage of osiers hanging from a beam in the corner. It winked a bright eye.

"Nothing else," I lied, accepting the bird's warning.

⁂

By autumn they'd condemned me to be this Dame Eleanor Butler's new maid-servant.

"Shall I come with you?" asked Harry.

I picked up my basket to make my last bread delivery. "No, I promised to see Maud." My cold answer kindled a dark flush in his cheeks.

"It won't be for long," he said with an unaccustomed stammer. "You'll be back before you know it."

I flashed him an accusing glance. "You promised I wouldn't be sent away."

I turned on my heel then, ignoring the honest youth's blustering protests. I left the little horse on the shelf in my chamber. I hoped it hurt when he found it there.

Maud left off serving a talkative matron in a stained, rusty-coloured gown to greet me. "You're early." She took her loaves with a quizzical look, pressing them against a plump, linen bodice edged with damson ribbons. "Are you in a hurry? I suppose you know the latest news?"

I glanced from her to the stout customer. A bubbling excitement simmered between them. They watched me eagerly like dogs who've caught the scent, but I just shook my head and shrugged.

"That bold-eyed wench who works in that shop of yours has been jilted by the Fowlers' lad," Maud said. Her companion nodded smugly, arms folded across her ample bosom. They awaited my signal of approval or astonishment, their eyes bright with expectation.

"I didn't know."

"Oh aye." Maud plumped herself up like a pigeon. "We were just talking about it."

"The Fowlers have fine plans for their son," the stout woman said. She wobbled her head from side to side for emphasis.

Maud winked at her. "They say that lass's no better than she should be." She lowered her voice, inviting me into their confidence. "I expect she told you a thing or two about her trysts with Ralph, eh?"

"Philippa doesn't tell me anything—"

"Well, talk is she's been to Nell Waters—"

"I don't know and I don't care." My snapped response outraged the gawping matron. "I came to tell you this is my last day at the shop. I'm going to a new place in Silver Street where I'm to serve Dame Eleanor Butler." I waited a beat, allowing them time to take this in. "Her father was Lord Talbot, a great hero in the French wars, and her husband was Thomas Butler, Lord Sudeley. I expect you've heard of them."

Awe-struck, bold eyes bulging, Maud spluttered her astonishment. But she recovered her composure quickly. "Well, it's not far away, so don't forget your old friends now you've risen so fine." A calculating glint entered her eye. "Come back and tell me all about your new mistress."

I left her with the inquisitive matron, their heads locked together, evidently much impressed. Though ashamed of my lies, I knew they'd give Maud something to feast on, but would they keep me safe?

Chapter Sixteen

Joan, the plump cook-maid with the frizzled hair, met me at the kitchen door of the shabby, aristocratic house in Silver Street, and ushered me inside just as the first flakes of snow fell from a livid sky. She'd been appointed to show me round, and after a fleeting introduction to a shy kitchen wench with a scarred face, and an impish scullion, whisked me away through a maze of dark, twisting passages.

"Of course Sir Thomas was much older than the mistress." She indicated a portrait hanging in the draughty corridor outside Dame Eleanor's chamber and I noted the haughty features of a sumptuously dressed man. "He was a wealthy gentleman and we lived in luxury at Sudeley. It's a pity he didn't think to make sure my lady was well provided for after his death though." The sigh and the sadness in her eyes plainly expressed regret for a much-loved home as well as concern for the widowed Eleanor.

Lowering her taper and dropping her voice to a whisper, Joan confided, "Dame Eleanor's been left with few means. Her manors are all forfeit to the crown." She nodded to where the greedy shadows swallowed up the inscrutable face. "It was a foolish oversight on Sir Thomas's part and has brought shocking changes on the household. She's barely enough to pay us, let alone run this place—but you'll find her a kindly mistress."

Joan spoke fondly. I was struck by her loyalty to the Butlers in spite of their fallen fortunes. "You might think her rather giddy at first." A flush of embarrassment stained her cheeks. "She's inclined to sudden whims and can be rash in her affections—but she's still a young woman. She hasn't been used to shoulder responsibilities—"

She darted a sudden glance over her shoulder, plainly ill at ease. Looking along the gloomy corridor, I experienced a curious prickle of dread.

"This house—?"

"Belongs to my lady's cousin." Joan grimaced with distaste. "It's a damp, old building. I suppose it was once a grand place, but there's something about it—I don't know—I can't explain. I daresay it's because we were so happy at Sudeley. But it's convenient for the city and suits my lady's present purpose—"

Joan's unreasonable dislike of the house came as no surprise. A familiar tingling sensation alerted me to the presence of an unquiet spirit. Involuntarily, I turned to gaze along the shadowy corridor.

"This way." Joan placed a hand on my arm. I jumped like a startled hare.

"Are you nervous?" She feigned a laugh, apprising me of her own poorly concealed fright. Shivers ran down my spine. "But perhaps you're trembling from cold? This is a cheerless house and I'll be mighty glad to quit it. It gives me—well I've never felt at home here. Every day, I pray my lady's petition will bring success and return us to our rightful place. But since we've some leisure I'll show you the rest of the chambers." Her eyes darted unwillingly towards the steep oak staircase. "We don't use the upper part of the house much."

As we crossed the chilly passageway I wondered at these cryptic words. Already I sensed danger. A smell of mould and decay pervaded a deserted chamber with its shrouded furniture and I flinched from the sinister, grim-faced portraits whose eyes followed our progress back to the kitchen. Here, at least, a meagre fire burned, and stringy-haired Alison with the pock-marked face smiled up at me from toiling over dishes. Gratefully, I hugged the hearth while Joan issued brusque instructions regarding food and little Jack pulled faces at her as he turned the spit.

Presently, Lionel, another of the remaining Sudeley servants, staggered in under the weight of fresh logs. "It's freezing out there," he said. He awarded me a welcome nod. Dropping his burden by the fireside, he shook himself like a dog, scattering droplets of moisture from sandy hair and eyebrows and stamped thin, sodden boots. "I reckon we'll have a blanket of snow on us by morning if this goes on."

"You'd better fetch more wood for my lady before that happens." Joan flashed him an impudent smirk. "We'll soon use this lot up."

Lionel blew on his hands and winked at Jack. "You're a hard-hearted wench, Joan, condemning a man to such a cruel task." Joan puffed out her cheeks in mock exasperation. "If I don't return within the hour, I trust you'll send someone to look for me." Assuming an expression of martyrdom, he stepped outside, allowing a vicious blast to swirl snow into the kitchen. Joan shrieked at him to close the door. The affectionate banter between them spoke of long familiarity.

Joan caught me watching and left off whipping eggs to take platters from the dresser. "This *is* a cheerless house." She grumbled with an exaggerated shiver, knotting an earth-tinted, wool cloth about her shoulders. "I'll wager all the wood in Christendom wouldn't make a fire strong enough to warm us. I don't know about the rest of you, but I'm chilled to the marrow. And it's barely October! We're doomed for a long winter, I'll be bound." Her eye lit on me hunched over the heat then. "Go tell my Lady it's time to dine."

Reluctantly, I threaded through that draughty corridor to where Dame Eleanor sat reading before the blaze in her own chamber, a great swathe of furs about her. How feebly the flames fluttered, even here, in spite of the generous heaping of logs. Gloom seemed to quench the candles in their sconces. Momentarily I quailed at the grotesque shadows thrown on the thread-bare tapestries decorating the oak panelled walls.

"Dinner's ready, madam." I executed a clumsy curtsey.

"I've little appetite," she answered, glancing up at me. Then she threw down her book and made a swift study of my appearance. "Stay and talk," she said with a smile. "Sitting here alone the strangest thoughts seem to come into my head. I fear— " She flinched suddenly, as if aware of some noise in the upper storey. "What do you think of this house Nan? Don't you think it odd?" She gazed round the shadowy chamber then, her eyes large and liquid in the dim candle-light. "I'm sure it's haunted." She shuddered. "Often in the night I hear footsteps outside my chamber door but when I look there's no-one. Have you noticed anything yet?"

Wary about what she might have heard about me, I feigned nonchalance. "These old buildings tend to creak and groan," I answered, remembering Joan's nervous laughter. "When tree-branches flap against the shutters it sometimes sounds like footsteps."

She giggled at this fanciful explanation. "Come and sit by the fire and tell me about yourself. Your priest thinks highly of you." She spoke pleasantly as if to draw me out. "He told me about your misfortunes and the need for you to make a new beginning."

I wondered then exactly what Brother Brian *had* said of me. If she'd known I'd been driven away by my family for suspected witchcraft, would she have been so cordial?

At close quarters, I estimated her to be in her early twenties. Her gown, caught high under her bodice, fell in exquisite rosy folds. I studied her fair face and luminous brown eyes, admiring the pale yellow hair she wore in elaborate coils fastened with jewelled pins. A delicacy about her features suggested modesty but the full lips promised carnal pleasures. I knew instantly she'd no desire to remain a widow.

As she chafed my chilly fingers with her own extraordinary slender ones—a gesture I found embarrassing from one of noble birth—I pretended interest in the discarded volume by the hearth. I didn't want to acknowledge the spectral nun who stood behind her in the shadows and silently invoked Brother Brian's prayers of protection against evil spirits.

"Can you read, Nan?"

I shook my head, ashamed at my ignorance. Her brown eyes shone warm with sympathy but I realised she longed for a companion with whom she might share her interests. I imagined her older husband had cosseted her. Now loneliness drove her to seek new means to fill her empty days, but I puzzled at this eagerness to befriend servants.

"Has Dame Eleanor no family to help her regain her property?"

Later that evening Joan and I hugged the kitchen fire, sharing sweet-meats.

Joan cast nut-shells into the flames, chuckling as they popped. "She's a wealthy sister in Norfolk—married to a duke. This sister and she were always very close, but he's too wary of jeopardising his position in the new order to help us."

"But why doesn't King Henry do something for her?"

"Lionel says King Henry's no power since Warwick set the Duke of York's eldest son on the throne."

"How can he do that? We can't have two kings, can we?" All the wrangling amongst the barons muddled me, although mention of Warwick reminded me of the parade in which I'd glimpsed my black-haired lover. Would I ever see him again? This exciting thought quickly distracted me from Dame Eleanor's problems.

Joan shrugged, her mouth crammed with filberts. "I can't understand what's going on in this country anymore. None of it makes any sense to me, nor am I very interested!" She laughed then, spitting nut-crumbs. "I don't suppose it matters much who's king as far as you and I are concerned, Nan. If you're so keen, you'll have to ask Lionel about it."

As it turned out I'd no need.

One wet afternoon when Joan scurried off to the butcher's and Dame Eleanor took instruction with Brother Thomas, her chaplain, Lionel returned from the tavern in a particularly good humour. Breathing ale fumes, he gathered us around to share the latest jests and repeat one of many lurid stories about the baron's squabbles.

"Great gobs of blood ran down the steps and all the gawping people in the market place were frozen with horror," he began. Little Jack's eyes started from their sockets and his mouth dropped open. Lionel continued his gory tale, his voice low and full of menace, and I thought at once of Robin Arrowsmith scaring us with similar stuff. "That night, when everyone had crept away to their homes, a mad woman came and picked up the head." He crouched before the hearth, picking up a log to demonstrate, cradling it in his arms. "She washed the blood from it and she kissed the open eyes." He paused as Jack gulped. "Then she combed the blood-soaked hair, and kissed it. She sang to it, and she fetched candles and lit them all around. It sat there on the steps staring into space. Soon there were hundreds of lights shining and flickering. It looked as if the eyes and the lips were moving, as if the head was still alive—"

The door opened suddenly. Shrieking, we clutched at each other.

"Whatever's the matter?" Joan bustled in with a basket of dead rabbits and slammed them down on the table. The sight of the bloody animals thrust so glaringly into our midst sent Alison jumping away and Jack made an unpleasant gurgling sound in his throat. Alarmed, Joan looked at me. "What is it? You look as if you've seen a ghost."

Laughing uproariously, Lionel said, "I've been telling them about Owen Tudor's execution."

"And who's this Owen Tudor?" Joan jabbed a finger in his chest, plainly infuriated by his teasing manner.

"He was married to mad King Harry's mother." Lionel loved to win Joan's attention for whatever reason. "He and his son—the king's half-brother—joined the Lancastrian army—the one beaten by Edward of York at Mortimer's Cross last February—"

"Never heard of it," said Joan, dismissively. She picked up a knife.

Lionel winked at us. "Well, it wasn't that long ago, Joan. Have you been asleep? Never mind, listen— when Owen Tudor was sentenced to be executed, he didn't believe it could happen— because of his royal *connections*. It was only when he saw the block, and they ripped off his collar, he realised they were actually going to kill him."

Lionel guffawed again but Joan's face grew stony.

"So you think that's funny, do you? Chopping men's heads off is a joke to you men, is it?"

"A mad woman came and kissed his head after it was cut off." Jack's horrified whisper silenced everyone.

Appalled, Joan crossed herself. "What terrible things have you been saying to this child? Have you no sense? Do you want to frighten him out of his wits with your play-acting?"

"But it's true, Joan." Lionel held up his hands as if to emphasise his innocence. "I have it on the best authority."

"Aye." She busied herself with the rabbits, lips pursed. "From some alehouse, I'll be bound." She looked up from slitting the soft underbelly of one of the beasts to point her bloody knife at him. "Have you nothing better to do than scare children? There's wood to be chopped."

"I shall perform my duties without fail." He sketched a mock bow. "But when murderous soldiers come battering at the door, Joan, I've no doubt you'll sing a different tune. You'll run to me for protection then, not drive me away with endless wearisome tasks." He twisted his face into an amusing expression of mock suffering.

"Get away, you rogue," said Joan, shaking with suppressed laughter. "There'll be no soldiers coming here—murderous or otherwise. Anyway, you shouldn't speak so disrespectfully. You know my lady's husband was a staunch supporter of King Henry." She paused in her gutting, her plump face serious as if she felt guilty for her earlier mirth. She lowered her voice. "The butcher's wife told me the poor soul spends all his time in prayer and fasting. This Edward's an upstart the Kingmaker's set on the throne for his own ends."

"That may be true," said Lionel, winding his old red chaperon about his shoulders. "But young York has a better claim to the throne than ever daft Harry did."

Joan shook her bloody fingers at him. "Pish-posh! I'm tired of all this nonsense! Edward of March will end up like his father, crowned with paper and his head stuck on the city gates for his pains. And Warwick with him! Just you wait, Lionel Hillers!"

Joan's words reminded me uncomfortably of the three severed heads I'd once revelled in telling Brother Brian about. I didn't care to think too long about such horrors now.

At Mass that Sunday, Brother Thomas preached of miracles. For me, these stories of Jesus brought back childhood memories and the comfort of Brother Brian's familiar, kindly face as he told them. But when the young chaplain spoke of what he called the "miracle" at Mortimer's Cross, I recalled Maud's fanciful tale which had so incensed the Lancastrian supporters and the strange dream I'd had that very morning.

Joan nudged me. Glancing round surreptitiously to where the men sat together at the back, we noticed Lionel, muscular arms folded across his broad chest, looking very smug. He nodded and smirked.

The chaplain paused. Someone—probably Jack—farted. This produced a sudden convulsion of stifled sniggers and shaking shoulders among the men-folk. We turned back swiftly, hanging our heads to avoid the priest's reproachful stare. Joan's plump cheeks burned bright as fire, and I barely managed to suppress the bubbling giggles which threatened. Fortunately, Dame Eleanor was too enraptured by the sermon to notice anything.

"I never heard such nonsense," said Joan. Back in the kitchen, a vast linen apron tied about her waist, she set about stirring sauce. "Brother Thomas's young and gullible, but he shouldn't repeat such tattle. As for you—" She gave Jack a cuff around the ear which sent him scuttling. "I never felt such shame." She turned back to her tasks, lifting fish on to a platter, tutting with exasperation. "These stories are made up by the Yorkists to fool honest folk into believing their champion's the rightful king. Three suns indeed! How can a priest speak so foolishly of divine approval and heavenly signs? Has he forgotten King Henry was anointed before God?"

"But perhaps it's true." Alison's scarred face glowed bright with excitement, for the sermon *had* been a stirring one. "Can't there be miracles today just like the ones in the Bible?"

Lionel and Joan soon reached logger-heads concerning the nature of miracles.

"It's the Earl of Warwick who's to blame!" Jack's boyish treble halted their squabble. "He changed all the rules and put a new king on the throne. That's why he's called "the Kingmaker". King Henry's mad but Edward of York's clever and a brave fighter —"

"And they say he's ever so handsome—" Alison's cheeks bloomed hot pink.

"And I suppose my lady will have to present her petition to this stripling now?" Clearly irritated by the scullery-maid's ardour for the usurper, Joan splashed wine into a goblet. "Kingmaker indeed! Warwick wants to watch his step or he'll be ending up with his head on the block like that Owen Tudor you love to talk about. There've been too many changes this year and some people are easily swayed by fair faces and fair words —"

The bantering continued as I drifted into a day-dream. In it, I watched my golden knight ride towards me, the sun's rays about his head streaming like a bright halo. But his smile soon twisted into a snarl. Drawing a dagger, he leapt from his horse to strike an unarmed youth kneeling at his feet. In horror, I cried out—

"Nan! Whatever's the matter?" Joan dropped the bread knife, scattering crumbs.

"You're very pale." Stalwart Lionel drew me gently to a stool and chafed my hands.

"Just a bit faint." How feeble the excuse sounded. Looking into Lionel's puzzled, brown eyes I wondered what I'd said to cause such consternation. "I'm sorry. Did I frighten you?"

"You looked as if you'd seen a ghost." Joan's perturbed expression flustered me.

"You were just staring into space," Alison said. She looked impressed. "I thought you were going to have a fit. I had a sister like that. She used to—"

"Too much excitement." Joan flashed Alison a warning. The girl stooped to retrieve the fallen knife, but didn't hide her knowing smirk. I opened my mouth to speak but Joan held up a hand, cutting off any inquiry. "It's enough to upset anyone."

Joan was certainly right about changes. Hadn't my visions become more urgent and confusing? This latest menacing development disturbed everyone. My head swam as I stumbled to Dame Eleanor's chamber. Something wrong about this house affected all of us— something which encouraged my premonitions. I wished Brother Brian back in the city. I badly needed his advice.

Chapter Seventeen

As Joan feared, bleak October brought bitter weather. Trees sprouted whitened buds and every branch sparkled with frost. Great globules of ice hung from the eaves and birds fell dead, their feathers stiff and sharp as daggers. At night I shivered listening to the wind's moan and the creak of timbers, dreading the moment I must rise and dress. The treacherous slide across the courtyard to the water butts brought daily misery. Lionel broke the thick panes of ice sealing their surfaces to reach the freezing liquid, but that didn't stop us grumbling. Stung by pellets of hail or drenched in sleet, we scuttled about unwelcome tasks, hands and heels red with chilblains, snapping at each other like bad-tempered terriers. Small wonder my lady bewailed her loss of land and comfort in this inhospitable atmosphere.

Daily she sought an audience with the king. But who was king? Was it mad Harry who spent more time telling his beads than considering matters of state, or was it proud Ned of York, the Rose of Rouen, whose burnished hair made ladies sigh—at least according to the ballad-mongers who sang so ardently of his gallant deeds? The city seethed, rife with gossip. *Maud would revel in these rumours*, I thought grimly every time I rose to face another cheerless day.

"Nan, I want you to sleep on the truckle bed in my chamber tonight."

Surprised, I leapt up from storing linen in the carved oak chest just outside Dame Eleanor's chamber. "I thought Gerta—"

"Gerta grunts and snores." She giggled, pressing a hand to her mouth like a young girl.

Gerta, a big-boned, bland-faced Fleming, had been hired to attend upon Dame Eleanor's wardrobe. She rarely ventured into the kitchen because Lionel mocked her guttural speech and Joan proclaimed loudly before her, "I can't understand a word that wench says!" She kept mostly to her small chamber close to Dame Eleanor's, ready to help her dress or run errands.

"There are so many strange noises in this house at night I don't like being alone." There was no laughter in this confession. She twisted the rings on her fingers and nibbled her lower lip, her eyes flicking towards the stairs.

I dropped a curtsey. "I hope I'll prove a quiet sleeper, my Lady."

Quitting the easy company of Joan and Alison in our shared bed-chamber was hard, but Eleanor showed me many favours. She allowed me to look at the lovely illustrations in her Book of Hours and even attempted to teach me to read. But her giddy nature prevented perseverance. Her mind flitted like a butterfly unable to settle for long on one flower and too often frivolous gossip fuelled her imagination.

"Tell me about your home in the country," she said one night. She wrapped her night-robe round her, shaking out the tangle of her pale hair, while I folded away her garments.

I began describing the tiny cottages, the painted manor house, the great windmill spreading its sails over us like a sentinel, the men toiling in the fields, the blacksmith sweating at the forge, Noll Wright carving wood and Fat Marion brewing ale. The words brought back poignant pictures of a life that now seemed so far away. I tried to imagine my brothers playing on the green or racing by the water-mill to dangle their toes in the pond just as I'd once done—

"Did you ever see King Henry and his queen?"

Although I'd learned quickly Eleanor rarely gave anything more than superficial attention, this abrupt question startled me.

"My Aunt Grace once took me to watch a procession." I left off combing her hair then, frowning to recover this memory. "I was newly arrived in London and amazed by the bold way people leaned out from the casements, cheering and waving." I laughed, recalling the noisy crush in the stinking street and the excitement dancing inside me. "I almost fell over when the crowd pressed forward and then a workman lifted me on his shoulders so I could watch in safety." Fondly I pictured again the rough-haired man with the calloused hands and unintelligible speech. "Queen Margaret was so beautiful," I said, sweeping a brush over Eleanor's pale tresses. "Her black hair shone like silk and flowed over her shoulders right down to her waist. And she was dressed in gorgeous vermillion and gold robes." Vividly, I saw again the "she-wolf" as a creature made of flames, her eyes flashing dark fire.

"What about the king?" Eleanor's face looked strangely sad in the candle-light. For a moment, with her pale hair hanging about her shoulders and her hands pressed together as if in prayer, I thought her a penitent seeking absolution.

"He didn't wear a crown. His robes were really drab, just like a monk's. I was so disappointed." I paused, the brush in my hand, visualising the frail, lean figure with the childish face. "Poor King Henry! He had wispy brown hair and darting eyes—he put me in mind of a starling. But I was very young. I'd imagined a king would be strong and proud—someone who'd wear magnificent robes emblazoned with precious jewels. I suppose I'd listened to too many old tales about handsome swains and daring knights!"

Alison's description of King Edward flashed into mind. My golden knight was reputedly setting the latest fashions at court and outraging the wealthy citizens with his extravagance.

During the long hours of these winter nights I often lay sleepless. I listened to the restless steps along the corridors and whisperings from the stairs. Twice I heard an owl hoot at dawn, an omen country folk always thought to presage some catastrophe, but I didn't mention it to Eleanor. Her feverish imagination conjured too many superstitious fantasies concerning the house as it was. Sometimes she woke me saying she heard whispering outside the door. She clutched my arm with icy fingers, a nervous laugh bubbling in her throat, eyes wide like those of a panicked deer. I did my best to soothe her, but too often she sought to engage me in ghostly tales and mysteries—tales that plainly exercised a powerful fascination for her. Worse, she sent me for a cup of warm wine to bring her sleep. Then I left the drowsy warmth of my bed to cross the corridor, walk down to the kitchen, heat the wine and return, carrying only a flickering candle to keep away those prowling shadows.

This journey to and from the kitchen terrified me. Here I'd first sensed the malign presence that made Joan so uneasy, but I daren't speak of it to Eleanor.

"Nan, are you awake?"

How I dreaded these words! Could I deny the hand shaking my shoulder?

"I can't sleep. I've been lying awake for hours."

Shivering, I donned my robe, fumbled for the candle. The flame's soft glow illuminated briefly the dark hollows of her eyes, the hunched posture, the apologetic plea.

The corridor uncoiled before me black with menace. Sucking in a breath, I pattered across it on bare feet, focussing my eyes on the dancing flame in my hand, intent on shutting out those lurking depths beyond its beam. A few more steps brought me to the safety of the kitchen and the comfort of its fading heat. I closed my ears against the seething dark that seemed to press so eagerly behind me until I crossed the threshold.

Among the ashes of the fire lingered a few glowing embers. A little wood might yet stir them into life. While I warmed my hands, I breathed through my teeth, shuddering. Until the wine heated I refused to contemplate the return. I thought of Brother Brian and muttered the childish prayers against evil he'd taught me long ago. Already I'd seen too many ghostly apparitions in this place.

Holding the cup against me and armed with the candle, at last I forced myself to confront the pool of waiting shadow. Now it crouched like a snake ready to strike and swallow me up.

Alert to every creak and sigh in the fabric of the building, I crept back along that dreadful corridor, careful to avoid the cavernous spaces far beyond my feeble lantern's glow. But a few paces from Dame Eleanor's door the candle flame grew eerily tall, became a thin, poised, bluish finger. A chill, crawling sensation forced me to a halt. My scalp tingled. About me swarmed those hungry shadows, greedy for my attention. I heard the whisper of silk across the stones. Far away a high treble voice began to sing. The tune quivered, melancholy, faintly familiar, the words indistinct. Motionless, but for a feverish trembling, I listened unwillingly to the plaintive rise and fall of notes—until the candle went out—suddenly plunging me into deepest black. In that very moment a tiny hand touched my face.

"Help me." A child's voice fanned my ear like a cold breeze. The crawling dark engulfed me—

Did I scream? If I did, no one spoke of it. I must have dropped the candle in blundering through the door. Wine spilled over my feet but nothing would induce me to go back for more or retrieve the candle.

"What happened?" Eleanor's voice shook, breathy with horror.

"I thought I heard a noise upstairs—" My own voice cracked. "It was probably just a rat or something, but it startled me. I'm sorry about the wine."

Cold and shaking, I handed her the cup, fending off her questions with plausible excuses while my ears strained for sounds. But the house lay silent as a sleeping beast. Crouched in my bed, I recited Brother Brian's prayers until menacing darkness engulfed me.

I stood in a vast courtyard. A melancholy white face pressed against the upper window of a huge tower wreathed in shadows. Its lips moved and I struggled to make out the words.

"Watch me, Will!"

The familiar voice summoned me to a sunlit green where the merry lad with red-gold curls shot arrows at the butts.

A huge bear of a man, rough-haired and black-bearded, shambled across the grass, beating a great paw upon his thigh as a bolt thudded home. The sound echoed ominously and from the corner of my eye I glimpsed a body drop from a scaffold. Before I could scream, a raven swooped across the sun to settle on the battlements. It squawked at me mockingly, flirting black feathers, its single eye like a shining nail hot from the forge.

"Master Slaughter!"

The giant turned, his eyes filling with sudden fear. A green stone set in a silver ring flashed in the sunlight as a hand reached for the boy.

"Help me!"

The raven launched itself, scattering dark plumage across my vision, just as the hand pressed against the boy's mouth. In a stairwell, two hooded figures dragged him into that stifling bedchamber where the shivering candle-flame invited me to witness murder—

Waking suddenly in a tangle of bed-clothes, I sat upright, sweating with fear. In the dark chamber, the soft rise and fall of Eleanor's breathing continued undisturbed. I cursed the house and its ghosts while I tried to piece together the fragments of my dream. Who was Will Slaughter, the attendant with the inauspicious name? Could there truly be such a person? And who'd snatched the boy away? Something about the figures on the stairs seemed horribly familiar. Who were those boys in the Tower whose plight still filled me with futile rage? When would I save them as Brother Brian had promised? Hadn't I been patient long enough? Surely I should have had some sign by now. And how would I find the black-haired man while trapped in this horrible house?

Next morning I avoided Eleanor's questions. The memory of the ghostly little hand on my face haunted me too vividly. I didn't want to walk down that corridor at night ever again. Even in daylight, the others avoided it or pretended they needed someone to help them with their errands to escape being alone in that part of the house. Little Jack raced through it and once I met Lionel pale and trembling, though he wouldn't say why.

I blamed the house for raising my old terrors. Once I dreamed I was back in my village being chased by men with staves. Seeking refuge in the church, I found Alan weeping by the altar. On the village green, girls wove coloured ribbons round a maypole, while Alys, crowned with white blossom, danced with a stripling in blue and murrey livery.

"Robin?" I reached out to touch his shoulder. Turning to greet me, his throat spouted blood—

Fortunately Eleanor slept soundly.

⁂

At the beginning of a harsh November, Brother Brian stopped on his way to the little Priory of St John to deliver messages. I was certain these included a visit to Alan. I ushered him out of a fierce sleet storm into the kitchen.

"Dame Eleanor's gone to present her petition."

"It's a bitter day." The priest shivered, his coarse robes steaming from the heat of our kitchen fire. "The roads are almost impassable."

Lionel poured him a generous measure of warm ale. "Some wise woman said this cruel weather promises more trouble." He grinned at Joan's impatient hiss. "I don't know much about fortune-telling, Brother Brian, but common sense tells me there'll be more fighting. There's still plenty of support for the old king—" He flashed Joan a teasing glance. "Though I daresay the wenches would be sorry to lose their golden Edward."

"We're not all taken in by fine appearances. But what chance does Dame Eleanor have of regaining her stolen estates with this stupid squabbling going on?" Kind-hearted Joan wrapped a warm mantle about the priest's shoulders. "Alison, give Brother Brian a bowl of pottage."

"I can't see any petitions being granted with matters amongst the barons so unsettled, that's certain." For once Lionel looked serious.

"Is there any news of King Henry?" Everyone clustered about the priest pestering him with questions like children seeking entertainment.

"I'll be at St John's just for a few days," he said. He rose reluctantly from his stool by the fire and handed Alison his empty bowl. "I'm sorry not to have seen Dame Eleanor, but with the weather so inclement I daren't linger."

I followed him to the door, desperate for a word.

"Ask permission to come to St John's," he said, and squeezed my hand in absent-minded farewell. With impotent rage and frustration I watched him disappear behind a veil of falling snow.

Not long after Dame Eleanor returned, rosy-cheeked and breathless, excited as a maid with a new gown. She handed me her sodden, woollen cloak with its concy fur-trimmed hood and asked Joan to send some warm wine to her chamber.

"Do you think that upstart's actually granted her petition?"

"She certainly looks happy." I gave Joan a pewter goblet from the press.

"Please God, Lionel's wrong and we'll be back in Sudeley this summer!" Joan chuckled, humming a merry little tune as she poured the wine.

I found my Lady just as elated, dancing about her chamber as if practising for a ball.

"Ah, Nan, you should've seen him!" She clasped her hands together like a coy maid and executed a giggling twirl. "Such a handsome young man and so tall. He's the very flower of courtesy." She snatched the goblet, the ecstatic gleam in her eyes sending a jolt of alarm through me. She hardly listened to my request to visit Brother Brian. Instead she drained her wine and prattled of the many compliments the king had lavished upon her.

"But did he grant your petition, my Lady?" I grew disturbed by her frantic manner.

"He promised to give it his personal attention." She giggled. "He said fair damsels shouldn't be troubled by heavy business matters."

When I relayed this news to ever practical Joan, she looked dubious. "I'll wager this young man makes clever promises but he's little intention of keeping them. I hope my Lady isn't fooled by pretty words."

"But if the king's given a promise—" Alison looked puzzled and disappointed.

"The king relies on his charm to dazzle all the ladies," said Lionel. He glanced up from heaving logs on the fire. "His ambitions are far more important to him than keeping his word." He grinned at Joan. "Some of us keep our promises though, don't we?"

Joan's flush and downcast eyes cheered me but I couldn't help thinking how gullible Eleanor seemed. Loneliness made her highly susceptible to flattery. Her frivolous chatter continued to alarm me.

Chapter Eighteen

"The king's here!" Jack rushed into the kitchen wild with excitement.

From outside came the clatter of hooves and Lionel's startled voice raised in greeting.

Barely a week since Eleanor's visit, Edward Plantagenet arrived at the house accompanied by two noble companions and a mere handful of retainers.

"What are we going to do?" A flustered Joan clutched at her throat and ran about the kitchen clucking like a startled hen. "We've very little wine—there's a meat pie—"

"But where are we going to put them?" I shook her arm, conscious of the approaching hum of male voices. "Alison, run and tell Gerta to prepare my Lady. Tell her the king's here—and hurry!" I addressed the bright-faced scullion next. "Jack, go and help Lionel with the horses and try to buy us some time—"

"We're not ready for visitors." Joan babbled, plucking at her apron, tugging at strands of wayward hair. "We can't put them in that chamber Dame Eleanor calls the parlour—It's not been used for months. How can we strew fresh rushes now? Even without that fusty smell we've little enough wood for fires—"

I'd never seen Joan in such a flutter. Fleetingly I thought of my aunt with her pretended parlour-chamber and how my uncle winked at me whenever she mentioned it. "Then where?" I feared our guests would enter at any moment. "Most of the chambers are damp and mildewed from lack of use. There's nowhere else. What are we going to do?"

"Gerta must take him to my Lady," a goggle-eyed Joan replied. "And the rest must come in here."

We staged a frantic attempt to tidy the place, and then, smoothing our hair and gowns, sank to our knees just as Lionel ushered in our royal guest.

While the king parleyed privately with Eleanor, we entertained our illustrious visitors in the kitchen, plying them with what meagre provisions we could muster.

The gentlemen sprawled by the hearth, the common servants by the trestle. All drank our ale at an alarming rate and made ribald remarks which scandalised Joan and sent us into peals of laughter. A rich odour of spice and male sweat, a rustle of opulent fabric and a dazzle of jewels, overwhelmed the familiar shabbiness of our surroundings. It seemed as if we'd been invaded by a gaggle of exotic birds in brilliant plumage.

A pair of huge, smelly dogs with muddy paws panted and drooled before the fire. Little Jack, cheeks scarlet with delight, revelled in the privilege of attending on them, and a dizzy, dreamy-eyed Alison fawned upon the men-folk, spilling ale and simpering excuses. Unwillingly, I found myself distracted by provocative comments and kindling glances. The heady atmosphere transformed even sedate Joan into a scatterbrain. Recalling how Eleanor's first meeting with the young king had similarly turned her head, I despised myself for being so foolish. Nevertheless the opportunity of seeing the king and his friends at close quarters proved irresistibly fascinating. Amazed, I found myself conversing with them in an easy manner.

"What do you think, Will?" asked Lord Hastings of Lord Herbert. They lounged by the fire, supping their ale. Hastings lifted a rakish eyebrow.

The other gentleman gave a cryptic smile. He tapped his finely polished nails on his leather boots. "A castle that speaks and a woman that will hear, they will be gotten both," he replied.

Hastings smirked, licking the red slash of his mouth.

"Ned has a way with words," he said, warmly. His eyes slid over me. "What do *you* think of the king, fair damsel?"

"His Grace is well-favoured, sir," I answered honestly. Seen close, the shining knight of my visions proved a golden giant with long, loose limbs and a smile as radiant as an angel's. In a moment people fell under the spell of his easy charm. I noted how readily Lionel yielded when the king placed a friendly hand on his shoulder and requested him to take care of the horses, just as if speaking to an old friend rather than as master to servant.

"Aye, Ned's a comely lad. He finds much favour with the ladies." Hastings flicked a speck of dirt from his velvet sleeve. "But there are others who can dance as merrily, I assure you." My cheeks burned under his candid scrutiny. Fortunately Gerta's arrival broke this interlude.

Flustered, Joan watched the buxom Fleming set down the tray of empty wine cups. "Does my lady require more wine?"

Plainly Gerta misunderstood. She shrugged, slumping down heavily on an old settle.

"Nan, see if she needs anything," Joan whispered. "I can never get any sense out of that lumpish wench."

From Dame Eleanor's chamber the king's hearty laughter echoed through the corridors. The trill response of her giggles unnerved me. Twice I lifted my hand to knock and twice my courage failed. The conversation dropped to a low caressing murmur. How could I interrupt? A strange intoxicating silence lurked beyond that portal. I knew in an instant an irrevocable step —one with far-reaching consequences—had already been taken. Yet I grasped the door-handle—

Without warning, a subtle change pervaded the atmosphere. I froze, yielding to the spell of creeping solitude, the uncanny silence permeating the passageway. An irrational terror prickled my scalp sending tingles of unease down my spine. Unwillingly, my eyes shifted towards the great oak staircase. Among its crawling shadows something stirred. For a moment I thought I glimpsed a hooded figure looking down at me.

Fleeing to the safety of the kitchen, I discovered Hastings had turned his attentions upon a moon-struck Gerta. I stood uncertainly amidst the noise and merriment.

"Why aren't you with Dame Eleanor?" A bewildered Joan confronted me.

"I daren't interrupt." My voice rasped, hoarse with tension, and Lord Herbert caught my eye.

"You mean she's still alone with the king?" Joan's eyes darted from me to the waiting gentlemen, a scarlet, shameful flush staining her neck and cheeks. She squeezed my hand, pressing her lips together as I whispered in her ear. Lord Herbert's sardonic smile mocked our subterfuge.

"Have you no more to do than to lollop there like a great heifer?" Joan turned on Gerta impatiently. Before the baffled Fleming could respond, the dogs rose barking with excitement and the king entered in a gleam of blue satin and gold. Whining slavishly, the animals fell upon him, leaping up to lick his hands and face, scattering gobbets of drool on his amethyst-coloured hose. Good-humoured as ever, he stooped to fondle them. Then he turned as if to draw us all into the wide embrace of his smile.

"We thank you for your hospitality." He rose to his full height. This stately courtesy so impressed, we knelt in homage. The firelight caught the gold collar of suns and roses about his shoulders creating a tawny halo about his head and my recent terror ebbed away.

Outside Lionel shouted for horses. Hooves sparked over frozen cobbles and stormed away into the darkness leaving us shivering by the door, hands raised in farewell. An anxious Joan soon bustled us back inside issuing a string of breathless orders. Then she turned on me with a thousand questions in her eyes.

"Best to say nothing," I said, with a warning look. I noted Jack's interest as he crouched by the hearth pretending the business of cleaning.

Undressing for bed, Eleanor's incessant chatter set my teeth on edge. The hectic flush in her cheeks and the feverish light in her doe-eyes betrayed complete infatuation with the young king. Sick with foreboding, I folded away her discarded garments.

"We must be careful not to expect too much of the king's promises," I said.

She preened before her glass, running restless hands through the falling tangle of her pale hair. "But isn't he incredibly handsome, Nan?" She giggled, scattering jewelled pins, swivelling this way and that, admiring her figure in the glass.

"Incredibly." I gathered up the pins and dropped them into the little enamelled casket on the shelf. "But he's very clever with words."

She tumbled into bed and lay smiling up at the faded curtains, her eyes full of secrets. She said nothing at all about her petition.

Chapter Nineteen

The king kept Christmas at court, and from what we heard, celebrated it with much pomp and luxury. He sent gifts to Eleanor, including a great haunch of venison, sweetmeats and costly delicacies, but the bearer of them brought no message for her beyond that of "good cheer."

Eleanor, on the other hand, being pious, kept Christmas with unexpected austerity. At midnight we celebrated the Mass, a solemn occasion in which Brother Thomas urged us to reflect on the gift of the Saviour's Birth. As he intoned the prayers in his soft voice, my eyelids drooped. At the end of a raw, arduous day, I longed for sleep. But barely had I lain down before Eleanor roused me again.

"I like to keep the Angel Mass," she said. She opened the shutters and I blinked in the cruel light of dawn. "Will you join me?"

I helped her dress, my fingers clumsy with cold, but she paid scant attention. "Do you know this special service marks the actual birth of the Holy Child?" Her shining eyes pierced my guilt. What did I care for such matters?

Bone-weary, I stood again in the little, draughty chapel and endured more of the priest's irritating drone. Eleanor's face lit up as if with ecstasy, so that in her dark gown she might have been a nun enjoying a holy vision. Bright as the sweep of a sword's blade, a sudden image of mad King Henry at his prayers flashed through my head, startling me into wakefulness.

The vision tormented me all the way back to the bed-chamber but I said nothing. Eleanor remained abstracted while I stripped off her garments and then slipped silently into her bed. Snuffing out the candle, I lay down and closed my eyes, my mind still spinning with disturbing images.

A fierce pounding snatched me from the very edge of sleep.

"What is it?" Eleanor's voice seemed to call me back from a great distance.

Before I could reply, the singing began. It was the same voice as before, but when it broke off, such a profound silence enveloped the house that neither of us dared move. Then a chilling, hollow laugh rippled along the walls of the corridor. Something so maleficent in its tenor caused the hairs on my arms to rise like hackles on a cornered hound. It petered out at last into a desperate fading sobbing, during which Eleanor began muttering repetitive prayers begging it to depart and I sank into an unpleasant, drowning sleep. In the fragmented dreams which followed, white-coifed nuns processed through icy cloisters singing plaintive anthems.

"What do you think it was?" Eleanor's morning question stirred a profound unease.

"We were tired, my Lady. The noise was probably someone in the streets."

Keen to avoid any talk of spirits, I slipped to the kitchen to assist with the preparation of breakfast.

After the feast I'd enjoyed at my uncle's house, the frugal fare in Silver Street surprised me. We began Christmas Day with frumenty. At dinner Joan presented us with a rabbit broth flavoured with almond milk and spiced with cloves, nutmeg and ginger, followed by a roasted capon in pepper sauce, a tart of eggs and ground pork with pine nuts, wafers with cheese, and a platter of dates, figs, pomegranates, raisins and nuts. As Lionel toasted the season with festive ale brewed with apples and honey, I couldn't help but compare this meal with the vast amount of delicious courses Aunt Grace offered.

Later we followed Dame Eleanor to the chapel for the High Mass. Afterward she dismissed me to "Take some leisure with the rest of the household" while she spent time in prayer and contemplation. As she bent her head over her book, I shuddered at her nun-like appearance and intensity.

"Is it always Dame Eleanor's custom to mark the season in this way?"

I discovered Joan in her best, blue, kersey gown and Lionel in a dark, worsted tunic trimmed with sheepskin, sharing ale and gossip by a roaring fire fragrant with pine cones in the "parlour." Noticing Alison and little Jack playing merrills, I recalled my lively cousins in the congenial house above the tannery. "Won't there be any merry-making at Twelfth Night?"

"Things were different when Sir Thomas was alive." Joan's sigh sounded wistful.

"We feasted well at Sudely then." Lionel smacked his lips over his ale, his eyes brimming with laughter. "He liked to entertain friends and was always a generous host. There were minstrels and mummers and dancing until dawn—none of this over-pious foolery—" Joan made an impatient, disapproving noise. "I'm as respectful as the next man, Joan, but my Lady's over-fond of prayer if you ask me. Did she have you up at dawn, Nan?"

My rueful nod stirred sympathetic laughter.

"No wonder you look tired." He sprawled back against the settle. "I'm thankful she didn't wake me."

"It's a wonder you didn't hear the noise."

"What noise?" Joan's guarded manner piqued my curiosity.

"Oh, a hammering at the door and some laughing and singing," I answered, feigning carelessness.

"It's always rowdy in the streets at Christmas," said Lionel. "The Watch is lax during holidays. But I've grown used to it. I slept like a log."

"You snored like a hog too," remarked Jack, with an impish smirk. His jest provoked much laughter.

"Christmas was lovely when I worked for Mistress Proctor," said Alison. "We always played games and made special cakes."

"Perhaps I'll make a cake for Twelfth Night." Joan's remark fuelled whole-hearted applause. "Dame Eleanor may be pious but she won't begrudge us some pleasure."

An impulsive visit from the king on a wild January afternoon filled the house with sudden tumult as if a great storm had entered the building. Once again he arrived without warning. Lord Hastings, Lord Herbert and some other gentlemen accompanied him, but this time we proved better prepared. Having opened up the "parlour" for the festive season, we entertained our noble guests in more suitable fashion.

The king looked at Eleanor with kindling eyes and she gazed back at him like a maid in love for the first time. Her doe-eyes shone with devotion. This ardour reminded me unpleasantly of Philippa's infatuation with Ralph Fowler.

But once again the spell of the young king's charm proved irresistible. He enchanted us all with his witty conversation, his playful impersonations of noted courtiers, his naughty tales of dull banquets, and the inclement weather that imprisoned him when he'd rather have been out hunting. His handsome face glowed under our approval. Like a gaudy peacock, he preened himself, conscious of every admiring glance—for he was dressed in a striking emerald doublet edged with red fox fur and elegant silken hose that displayed his long limbs to advantage. No lady could ignore such a figure and even the men-folk seemed impressed.

"Elizabeth Lucy must have lost her charms." Lionel winked. "The king's always looking for new pastimes to amuse his leisure hours." He slipped an affectionate arm about Joan's shoulders. "He quickly tires of his ladies."

"Get away with you, you rogue." She tried half-heartedly to shake him off, laughter bubbling behind compressed lips. "We need more ale from the cellar."

"You should be thankful for my attentions, Joan." Lionel maintained his hold, his grin broadening. "He's not a faithful swain like me!" He gave her a little nudge that brought the dimples in her cheeks. Smiling to myself, I listened to her humming snatches of a popular ballad as she carried dishes to and fro, delighted the king's presence could create such an affectionate atmosphere in the gloomy old house. But I wished it might blow away the boiling storm-cloud which I sensed and couldn't shrug off.

With an apologetic bob, I handed the king a cup of indifferent wine. "Truly," he said, acknowledging me with a brilliant smile, "I'd have rather spent Christmas here than with those greybeards at court." He turned to beam at little Jack. "Sing something for us, lad."

The boy executed a merry ballad of Robin Hood in a sweet high treble that at first reminded me of the ghostly singer, but the lively tune quickly dispelled any melancholy thoughts and set my feet tapping. Besides, the king's careless words planted an idea in my head. Could I devise a way for Eleanor to lure him to Sudeley? Although I longed to return to the Mercers, a chance to see this manor whose praises Joan sang constantly offered a welcome interlude. If only the king would grant Eleanor's petition for its restoration, perhaps all would be well.

Chapter Twenty

By February, the king's frequent visits to Silver Street roused some salacious gossip in the city. According to Lionel, Dame Eleanor became the subject of much speculation. Dispatched to the Chepe upon an unexpected errand, I seized the opportunity to stop at St John's.

"I must see Brother Brian!" My panicked request earned a curt response from the fleshy-nosed monk who admitted me. Sniffing his disapproval, he ushered me to the tiny guest house and abandoned me by the door, shuffling away like some dusty beetle into the shadows.

In the stupidity of haste I tapped and entered.

Alan Palmer and Brother Brian sprang apart. Afterward I couldn't swear to it, but I thought I saw Alan snatch his hand away from the priest's. Whatever had passed between them, the atmosphere throbbed with tension and I felt like an intruder. Overcome with shame, I hovered in the doorway until young Alan fled, murmuring excuses.

"Gerta was supposed to be collecting some gloves that needed mending. But she's sick with a belly-ache from eating too much eel-pie."

This trivial information spilled in a rush of embarrassment.

"I've been asking permission to see you for days, but Dame Eleanor keeps making excuses—This is the only chance I've had—and I need to do something before it's too late—"

I sat down abruptly on the edge of the hard pallet nearest the door. Distracted by Alan's hurried departure, the priest stood looking bewildered.

"Why all this haste?"

Wary of others who might enter the guest house at this hour, I lowered my voice. "Since my lady pleaded for her estates, the king's visited her in Silver Street several times. It's supposed on the pretext of considering her petition but these occasions are so secretive—and she's quite infatuated with him—" I paused, hoping the priest would grasp my implications. "Ever since I set foot in that house my dreams have become so strange. Unless I take action something terrible's going to happen—"

"What have your dreams to do with Dame Eleanor and the king?" Brother Brian seemed more perplexed than ever.

"The boy in the dreams looks very much like the king." Increasing anxiety drove my speech. "And the place is certainly the Tower. Perhaps the king's in danger—I feel I should warn him— He's very easy to talk to—"

"No!" Brother Brian's eyes widened with fear. "Have you forgotten what happened in the village? Witchcraft's an ugly word and rouses much antipathy. Even Mistress Evans has suffered recent accusations."

"But I must do something— I can't just stand by and watch—"

The bell tolled the hour, startling me to my feet.

"I have to go." But still I hesitated. "I'm frightened of what's happening in that house. I feel so helpless—I wish I were back in the pie shop." The meaningless babble tumbled from my lips.

"That may be possible when Dame Eleanor leaves London." The priest evidently tried to make some sense of it and hurried after me into the street. Loath to let me go, he grabbed at my hand. "Mistress Mercer tells me Philippa's betrothed now to the chandler's assistant."

"What use is that to me?" I turned on him angrily. "Dame Eleanor's petition hasn't been granted yet. And what use are visions if I can't do anything about them?" His bafflement spurred me to greater vehemence. "Dame Eleanor's in danger—And I'm sick of being a bystander—I must *do* something—" Conscious of the hour yet torn by my desire to stay, I hovered uncertainly. "Be careful of yourself." I planted an impulsive kiss on his cheek. "I *must* go now—"

"We'll speak soon," he promised, but I tore my hand away.

"Soon," I said, wondering at the bright gleam of tears in his eyes. Reluctantly I rushed off to the glover's in Wood Lane. I meant to keep my promise. But as I feared, events decided otherwise.

"The king's been here again." A flustered Joan met me at the door. "I'm worried about the mistress' reputation. Lionel says the king's a great lecher and has already fathered several bastards—Speak to her Nan. She listens to you."

I wished I could confide in Joan. I valued her judgement. She'd a practical way of looking at things, a common-sense attitude which might have proved useful had I dared voice my own misgivings.

"If we get her back to Sudeley she'll forget this flirtation—I'm sure it's nothing more." I patted her arm reassuringly, picking up the embroidery silks Alison had purchased, trying to believe in my own lies and despising myself for telling them.

❦

I found Eleanor at her glass, her eyes full of dreaming.

"The king admired my blue damask," she said.

I didn't answer, but put the silks into her embroidery basket and her gloves into the press.

"He said the court ladies are wearing their hair up under tall hennins now." She loosened hers from its pins and stared at her reflection.

"The king's an eye for pretty ladies but I expect he'll be considering marriage soon," I dared to say as I began combing the primrose fall of her silken hair. "He'll have the pick of Europe's princesses for his bride."

A secret smile curved her full lips. "Ah, but he's promised to marry no one but me."

I almost dropped the comb. Radiant eyes met mine through the glass.

"A jest surely, my Lady?" My strained laugh bordered on hysteria. "I don't think kings choose for themselves—"

"You know nothing of love, Nan. Love may do anything." Tossing her head, she stormed away, fighting tears.

A sudden movement in the glass halted me. A shadowy figure in a cape stood by a hearth, the flicker of flames illuminating the jewel-encrusted hem. My sharp gasp startled Eleanor.

"What is it?"

The figure turned. Never had I seen such malevolence than in those yellow eyes. But when the figure raised a severed head dripping blood, I cried out.

"Did you see—?" I pointed at the glass.

Eleanor snatched my hands, her face blanched with fear.

"What? What is it?"

The glass stood empty save for the commonplace reflections of the chamber, the oak panelled walls, the mulberry hangings, the settle's arm, the corner of a silken cushion—I laughed without mirth then, pressing a hand to my mouth to suppress the staccato stutter. "Forgive me, my Lady, I thought I saw—" I shook my head. "Imagination. A trick of light. I'm sorry I alarmed you."

"I swear this house is haunted." Her widened eyes betrayed unease. "I told the king—"

"You should ask the king to grant the return of your estates immediately, my Lady," I said, gathering control. "Then you could leave this horrible place."

"But I can't leave yet. His Grace has promised me marriage." Her shining eyes rebuked my doubt. "You mustn't say anything to the others." She pressed a finger to her lips as if to stifle laughter. "We must keep it secret a little longer."

How could she believe such a practised liar? I almost wept with rage. Everyone in the city knew Edward of York would tell a wench anything to get her favours. Eleanor Butler behaved as foolishly as Philippa in her lovelorn trysts with Ralph Fowler. I'd wasted energy on vain attempts to divert her. Sudeley no longer enchanted. Her every thought fixed on the fickle youth who'd snatched the crown.

That night ugly dreams of the boys in the Tower plagued me yet again. This time, not only did I share the terror of the child pursued by the assassin, but the elder boy, crazed with fear, shrieked for his Uncle Antony. His melancholy face, framed with pale gold hair, haunted me long after I woke. He looked about twelve and his voice wobbled with that curious timbre between child and manhood. I knew no more of this Uncle Antony than I did the mysterious Will Slaughter. How could I find out? Clenching my fists, I fumed with impatience, desperate to speak to Brother Brian or even Harry.

Chapter Twenty-One

"I didn't expect to meet you here." Lionel's jovial brown face creased into a smile. I pushed through the boisterous crowd round Maud's shop to greet him.

"Gerta misunderstood Dame Eleanor's instructions so I'm going to Hosier Lane to exchange some items." I raised my voice above the hubbub but didn't mention my delight at the opportunities this errand offered. "Mistress Allemore seems to be on form today."

"Oh aye, she's got some juicy court gossip." Lionel winked at the handsome figure in the purple mantle and ornate linen head covering. "And as usual she's making the most of it."

"Elizabeth Lucy's given the king a son." A coarse-looking woman offered us this nugget of information. At the same moment, the crowd roared with laughter.

"I thought you said the king had tired of her." I threw Lionel a teasing look. The coarse woman sniggered with her neighbour and other bystanders shouted bawdy remarks.

"Well, I daresay they were very close for a while—" Lionel raised his eyebrows to a rakish angle. "But only last week in the Black Bull they were saying he'd found himself a more pleasing mistress—"

"Were any names mentioned?"

"None that we'd know." Lionel cast me a pertinent glance.

"Well, I must hurry. I want to drop by St John's to see if my old priest's there."

But I didn't find Brother Brian, so I visited the Mercers instead.

Their cheerful welcome enveloped me like a fine woollen cloak. I felt as if I'd returned home after long absence and lingered as long as I could in the hope of seeing Harry.

"He's gone to talk business with a wealthy patron." Big Hal squinted at me through the heat haze in the bake-house. "He'll be sorry to have missed you."

Twilight fell as I turned into Silver Street. After the noise and bustle of the bakery the place lay strangely silent, the houses crouched like watchful beasts eager for prey. A pale sickle of a moon sailed the sky. Glancing at the upper storey of our dwelling I glimpsed a white, boyish face pressed against the window.

Joan waited at the kitchen door, plainly ill at ease, twisting the strings of her apron and fiddling with her hair. "You're very late."

"I'm sorry." I unpacked my purchases clumsily. "Brother Brian's left St John's. I went to the bakery."

"Lionel said he'd seen you in the Chepe where the Attemore wench was spouting the latest court gossip." The old anxiety lurked in Joan's eyes.

"Maud's famous for her stories but they need taking with a pinch of salt."

"So it's not true about the king fathering a child by that Lucy woman?"

"Oh, that's true enough. She's been the king's mistress for some time. The boy's to be called Arthur like the story-tale hero."

"I wonder what my lady'll say when she hears that? She's mighty taken with the king herself." Joan gave me a hard look.

"It's no use telling Dame Eleanor anything unsavoury about the king. She's besotted with his charms."

Alison and Jack sniggered but Joan's frown deepened. "I wish the rogue would grant her petition and have done with visiting. How long can it take to consider a petition anyway? I've a bad feeling about all this—"

Again I wished I could share my own concerns with Joan. The brooding sensation of a gathering storm still troubled me. I'd experienced such premonitions before and my father's sudden death returned as a reminder. I fretted then over Eleanor's shared secret, certain her love-sick folly would drag us with her into ignominy.

"What's that?" Jack pointed to the large, still-warm pie I set on the trestle.

"Mistress Mercer sent us it to share. Her pies are famous."

The succulent smell of meat pervaded the kitchen. Little Jack and Alison swarmed round the trestle, smiling at one another and licking their lips.

"No doubt you told her we keep a poor table here." Joan tapped her feet and eyed the crisp, golden crust with grudging admiration.

"Not at all. But Mistress Mercer thought to save you time and labour by this gift."

Little Jack sniffed appreciatively. "Mmm—It smells heavenly."

"Finish your chores or you'll not have a crumb of it." Joan placed the pie on a platter as if it were a crown. Then she whisked Alison back to scouring dishes and set to peeling parsnips.

Taking a bowl from the dresser I began slicing a pile of leeks into it. "Jack— were you upstairs when I came in?"

Three pairs of eyes goggled at me.

"Me?" Jack shuddered and pulled a face. "I wouldn't go up there. Alison says it's haunted—"

"That's enough," snapped Joan. She turned to me with an anxious frown.

"I thought I saw a boy at the window," I said, returning her stare.

"One boy's enough in this house." Joan swerved away to concentrate on the parsnips and an uncomfortable silence flooded the kitchen.

"Nan, can you help me fetch some water?" Something in Alison's plain, pock-marked face alerted me. Recognizing this pretext for private speech, I glanced at Joan preoccupied in preparing supper, and put a finger to my lips. Signalling a curious Jack to keep silent, we slipped outside.

"Did you really see a boy at the window?"

"I did. And it's not the first time I've seen spectres in this house." We struggled with the pails. "You know something of its history—"

Alison shivered. "Joan's forbidden me to talk about it for fear of frightening Jack but he knows anyway."

"You've been together a long time, haven't you?"

"Since his mother died." She set down her pail as if she'd made her mind up about something, fumbling with the fraying edge of her threadbare, blue sleeve. "His mother wasn't from round here.

She was a pretty girl—no older than you are now. Mistress Proctor said she'd have to go when she found out about the expected babe. Kezzy—Jack's mother—said his father was noble-born, but Mistress Proctor always swore he was just some tinker passing through the city. I don't know. I was only about five or six. My mother persuaded Mistress Proctor to let Kezzy stay till she had her babe. She wasn't a bad mistress. Anyway, they stayed until Jack was about three and then Kezzy got sick and died. She took the pox. My mother and sister and I took it too. I was the only one who survived." The girl's eyes gleamed moist, but the smile that twisted her lips wrenched my heart. "Mistress Proctor said I'd never find a husband with a face like this. Then she turned me and Jack out the house. My aunt promised she'd look after us but she took us to a church one morning and never came back. We've stayed together ever since and we've worked in lots of places, but this house—" She glanced at the upper storey with a shudder. "Dame Eleanor shouldn't stay here. There's no luck in this place—" She stared into my eyes. "You know that."

"Will you go with her to Sudeley?" I asked. The girl's intuition chilled me.

"If she'll have us." She picked up her pail. The weary acceptance in Alison's shadowed face filled me with an aching pity, but how could I share my secrets with her?

Chapter Twenty-Two

One mellow April afternoon, the king cantered over to Silver Street accompanied by Lord Herbert and two men-servants. Something furtive and hasty in his manner spoke of danger. With barely a brusque acknowledgement, he stormed past us to Dame Eleanor's chamber.

"You'd better take some wine." Joan looked alarmed by the manner of this sudden intrusion. "That Flemish trollop has gone to Paternoster Row for some book or other my lady wanted. I wonder what's brought the king here in such a temper?"

She drove me out of the kitchen and sent Jack to wait on Lord Herbert who lingered outside in the gardens.

Raised voices issued from my lady's apartment.

"You treat me no better than a harlot." Eleanor's unaccustomed anger surprised me.

Though I couldn't decipher the king's murmured response, I suspected he was soothing her with his usual practised charm.

"Welcome! Welcome!" He greeted my hesitant entrance with honeyed laughter, no sign of displeasure spoiling his handsome features.

Rosy-faced Eleanor, eyes fever-bright, leapt from his side, but the king sprawled on the settle. Indolently, he watched me pour the wine, but beyond this feigned repose, I sensed how he waited, lithe as a cat poised to spring.

When I made to depart he rose swiftly. Seizing my arm, he drew me so close, I noted the golden hairs on his chin the barber had missed, and smelled the scent of wine on his breath. His hazel eyes glinted. I wondered if he was already drunk.

"Stay a moment."

My face burned with embarrassment. Turning to Eleanor with a wide sweep of his saffron-coloured sleeve, he pretended astonishment. "Your waiting woman trembles in awe of me. What dreadful tales have you been telling her, Nell?" He drained a cup of wine at a single draught. "I'm sure she's some inkling of the reason for my visits. Eh, wench?"

Eleanor squirmed while the king's brows knitted together. I wanted to laugh, knowing he liked his play-acting to be applauded. Peevishly, he poured more wine. Swallowing this with a flourish, he retrieved his heavy, miniver-lined cloak from the settle, flinging it round his shoulders like an actor in a pageant.

"I fear I must bid you farewell." He performed a courteous bow.

For the first time, I noted the flinty look, the cruel line of his mouth. Behind the façade of cordiality lurked a dangerous enmity. Something I must remember.

"But you promised—" Eleanor stammered, bewildered by this sudden change.

"And will make that promise good." In two strides he took her in his arms. "Do you doubt me? Before your waiting woman, I swear my pledge of true devotion—I will marry you!"

Time stopped.

Pressed against the panelled wall by the door, I tried to steady my quickening heart-beat—

"No word of this to anyone." The king thrust his face close to mine, his mouth grim. "This must be a secret. Understand?"

I fled at once and for a moment I halted in the passageway, stunned by what I'd just witnessed. Had I really heard the king offer Eleanor marriage?

In a daze I wandered out into the orchard and discovered Lord Herbert.

"Is the king ready to depart?" Rising from his seat beneath the almond tree, this elegant gentleman brushed dust and insects from his hose with a fastidious hand. I dithered while he called the slumbering attendants.

"Summon the grooms to bring the horses, girl." I jumped at this command, flushing under the accusing stare of mingled impatience and exasperation. I ran at once to the stables and found the king already there with Lionel, sharing some jest.

"No need for ceremony," he said, laughing at my clumsy curtsey. His lips quirked with amusement. "I'm sure your mistress needs your assistance more than I do." He stared deep into my eyes. Draping an arm about Lionel's shoulders, he said, "Let's take the horses to Lord Herbert, my friend."

"Oh Nan!" Eleanor flew at me like a swallow as soon as I returned to her chamber. "Is it true? Did you witness the king promise me marriage?

"Yes, Madam." Breathless with running I struggled to speak. "But—"

A restless excitement bordering on hysteria set her pacing up and down, nervous fingers clasping and unclasping the delicate fabric of her gown. The ecstatic light in her eyes unnerved me.

"We must keep it secret, Madam," I reminded her.

"Oh Nan, I must be dreaming. How could the king choose me above all others?"

How indeed? What about Lady Lucy and the rest? I knew King Edward possessed no sense of fidelity.

"Surely, a king must yield to the wishes of his council when it comes to choosing a wife?"

She stopped suddenly, fixing me with a wide-eyed stare. "But you were witness to our contract. A betrothal's binding, isn't it? Fetch Brother Thomas. I must tell him at once."

"Brother Thomas? But we're sworn to secrecy."

"There are no secrets before God," she answered.

Chapter Twenty-Three

May came in hot and sunny that year. Tensions ran high in Silver Street. All of us watched Eleanor. Giddy as a maid with her first sweetheart, she talked of nothing but the king's next visit. She dispatched Gerta to purchase costly fabrics, ornaments and jewellery. When she commissioned sewing women to make new, fashionable gowns, I warned Joan about the mounting debts.

"How will she ever pay for all this?" Joan gestured to the heap of fabrics delivered that morning.

"She wants me to fetch the shoemaker this afternoon," I said, fuming at this foolish extravagance.

Overwrought and skittish, Eleanor ran us all ragged with her errands.

"It's like living in a tinder-box," I said at the end of a frantic week. "What will she do next?"

"Anything to impress the king." Joan stared at me, hands on hips, as if she knew my secret.

"And he delights in making mischief."

I thought back to the king's impassioned promise. Would he stand by it? I knew a betrothal couldn't be broken but Edward of York flouted rules. Everyone talked of his headstrong nature and the way he charmed his courtiers into doing what he wanted. Even his arrogant cousin, Warwick, couldn't curb him, although Lionel said he tried hard enough.

"The young king's like a wayward horse." Lionel grinned at us and shrugged his shoulders. "He's a will that can't be broken."

But would he break his oath? I wondered.

In the quiet hours before sleep, I slipped outside into the drowsy summer garden. Daylight was fading, but the sultry heat grew heavy on me like a coverlet. Trees loomed soft-edged and indistinct; dainty, spindle-legged flies danced upon the air; doves throbbed and cooed in hidden leafy bowers; a hazy quietude hung over everything like an enchantment.

"I don't like what's happening in this house, Nan." Joan's voice startled me. She was sitting so still on the stone steps, I hadn't noticed her. "It needs no scholar to fathom the secret matters here, but I'm shamed to think our good name will be draggled in the mire." She sighed, plucking bay leaves from a flourishing shrub in the nearby urn. "Dame Eleanor's enamoured of the king, that much is certain, and that he's robbed her of her virtue, I don't doubt. Oh it's an old tale oft sung and the chorus of it is tears."

"But things won't go on like this for ever." I thought her words remarkably apt. "When Dame Eleanor complained of the heat today I suggested we might go to Sudeley so the king could enjoy the hunting there."

"I hope she listened to you."

I'd expected Joan to show enthusiasm but her plump face remained grave. Her gaze travelled over the garden.

"This place has such an unquiet air. Alison tells me its history isn't a happy one, and amongst the neighbours there are some odd tales—but there, I'm beginning to sound like young Jack with his nonsense about ghosts."

"Have you ever thought of marriage, Joan?" I was always eager to avoid the subject of restless spirits.

She laughed. "Who would wed me now? What was considered homely at fourteen is surely past distinction at four and twenty."

"Don't be so sure about that." I gave her a playful pinch. "A certain gentleman with a talent for telling tall tales is mighty fond of you! I know you'll wear a wedding band on your finger yet."

I thought to amuse her, knowing she harboured soft feelings for Lionel, but her smiles faded.

"You should be careful of your prophecies." Her brown eyes grew serious. "There are those who've been hanged for less. Maud Attemore tells some strange tales about you. She told Lionel some lass named Philippa had a hand in banishing you from Mercer's pie-shop."

"Philippa?" I adopted a careless manner. "Has she accused me of sorcery? I shared a room with her and disturbed her once with a nightmare. Ever since, she's been embellishing the tale."

"Be careful, Nan." Joan placed a warning hand upon my arm. "Even a jest about such matters can be dangerous. I don't want to lose your friendship."

A tardy blackbird began to sing.

"Tell me about Sudeley," I said to distract her.

Joan turned her head to search for the late songster among the tracery of the trees. "We were happy there," she began. "And if you speak of sorcery, why then, that place wove its spell upon me, for I never saw anywhere so lovely."

✍

Towards the end of the month the king's visits ceased quite suddenly.

"I told you, young Ned's a lad for the ladies." Lionel cocked his head and winked, a wide smirk curving his mouth. "He's probably found a more willing wench than our prim little widow."

I wasn't so sure Eleanor was prim, but the king's absence certainly troubled her. She grew melancholy, slept poorly and ate so sparingly her slender form grew wasted. Hour after hour she sat idle in the garden, forlorn face pinched, eyes distant, slender hands resting on the pages of an unread book. It drove me to distraction.

"The king must be busy with affairs of state," I said, although I knew full well he spent his days hunting. "You should remind him you're desperate to get away from this gloomy old place." I leaned over the bench, forcing her to give me her attention. "We could be at Sudeley now. I thought the king had your welfare at heart?"

Her eyes brimmed with tears but I refused to be diverted. I swung under the lowest branch of the cherry tree, shaking off the heavy blossom in fragrant clouds. "Joan says there's no better place in the whole countryside and Lionel's always boasting of the fine entertainments and the charming neighbours. It sounds so exciting I wish I could see it for myself. Wouldn't it be wonderful if we could all go this summer?" I glanced at her through a lattice of pale blooms. "Why don't you go to Westminster?" I feigned a teasing tone. "I'm sure the king would be pleased. It must be tedious to be burdened with state business instead of sitting among friends. If you like, I could accompany you?" I added the last part with a wistful look as if expressing a girlish longing to visit such a place, but she merely shook her head and averted her eyes.

♊

"I hear the king's found a new paramour."

Eleanor's plaintive tone caught my attention as we prepared for bed that night. I halted in unpinning my hair.

"She's called Elizabeth Lucy and they say she's very beautiful."

"Oh, my Lady!" I pretended stifled laughter as I picked up soiled linen. "Who's been feeding you such nonsense? That frowsty jade's little more than a courtesan!" As if amused, I stooped to whisper secrets in her ear. "She's said to have had so many lovers, she's lost count."

"But the king—"

"Has no interest in her now. Oh, it's true she was a great beauty but flowers once plucked and often handled soon lose their bloom." I pursed my lips and affected shock.

Blushing, she lowered her voice. "They say the court ladies are very liberal with their favours and the entertainments there are scandalous—"

"Ah, you must have been listening to Mistress Attemore." I giggled, dismissing with mere hints further timid questions about the lewd games and fashions being devised for Edward's particular pleasure. The seed of a new idea began to germinate. I lifted a hank of her hair, expressing admiration for its silky lustre.

"My mother had such hair—the Beauchamp women are famous for it," she said with a nervous laugh. "And my Neville cousins are all fair too—but Meg—my sister—is dark like the Talbots. People say the king prefers maids who are fair, but—" Tears choked off her words.

"You've nothing to fear from these over-blown court beauties, my Lady. Put on your finest gown and let me dress your hair in its most fetching manner. Then we'll go to court." I began to arrange it loosely, humming under my breath, lifting it high above her slender neck in a tumbling cascade. "The king will have eyes for no one else. And once your petition's granted, who knows?" I giggled, peeping at her in the glass. "Surely you haven't forgotten that special promise the king made?"

Poor Eleanor! I wondered what Brother Brian would think of my browbeating her in this fashion. Without doubt my falsehoods would grieve him. I could almost hear him saying, "Lies can't be used for good purposes." Guiltily I thanked my lucky stars that he hadn't heard me. Nevertheless his continued absence began to irk. Each day I felt him grow more distant. In my dreams he vanished into a swamp of darkness. The sensation terrified.

All through that night I heard a baby crying. I squirmed so restlessly I woke Eleanor.

"What's wrong, Nan? Are you sick?"

"Don't you hear it? That babe crying?"

The house lay silent as a tomb.

"I can't hear anything. Perhaps it's a cat outside."

I must have dozed at last because I woke with a start at dawn just as a babe's wail was cut off short somewhere close by.

"Please God the king grant your petition, my Lady," Joan said. She bobbed a curtsy as we departed for the palace. In the clear light of day my confidence deserted me. Instead, a dull throb of fear gnawed deep in my belly.

Chapter Twenty-four

An overpowering stench rose from the river. In spite of the heat, I pulled my cloak over my mouth and nose to block out the worst of this frightful odour. The burly boatman chuckled and spat into the oily water.

"I warned you, Nan," Dame Eleanor said, with a grimace, "travel by river is a dirty, unpleasant pastime."

Grunting, rubbing his hands on a greasy doublet, the leering boat-man tried to catch my eye. Swallowing hard, I turned from his sour-smelling breath to look back towards the untidy cluster of buildings hanging tipsily over the bank. Ravens and kites scavenged among vast heaps of rubbish squawking and flapping their ugly wings, while troops of children smeared with river-dung waved at passing boats. Raising my hand, I wondered if they envied us our journey. Standing on this grimy barge, breathing in the rank miasma from the water and the corruption of the middens wafted from those straggling houses a sudden swell of irrational excitement drowned my fear.

As the boat turned a magnificent building seemed to rise from out the waves. All intricate turrets and pinnacles, Westminster loomed before us like a painting from an old romance. Graceful, carved curves swooped over my head; towering stonework gleamed mellow in the sunlight; latticed windows and gilded metal took my breath away. Never had I imagined a royal palace so vast or grand.

When the boat docked the boatman handed Dame Eleanor out first, doffing his soiled crimson cap. Daintily she crossed the wet stones and turned to wait for me. I took the sweaty hand with reluctance but the boat shifted dangerously against the bank-side. Lifting me in a powerful grip, the boatman set me down safely.

Feeling ungracious for my former manner, I rewarded him with a smile.

He touched his cap and winked. "I'll look for you on your return," he said, exposing yellow, broken teeth in a grin.

Giggling, I tried to amuse Eleanor by whispering to her of this attempt at gallantry. "Keep close, Nan." Nervously she picked her way up slippery steps. "The cobbles here are slimy and there'll be a press of people to see the king."

Within minutes, a colourful crowd clamouring outside the great, armoured doors swallowed us up. Though I stayed at Eleanor's side, I couldn't help staring. I gawped at the dazzling, peacock-coloured clothes of the nobility as they strutted to and fro, the ladies in tall, elaborate head-dresses, the gentlemen flaunting elegant sleeves and fantastical footwear.

Eleanor hesitated. A lean figure in swooping ecclesiastical robes bore down upon her.

"Dame Butler?" The voice rang out resonant and solicitous.

Startled, she looked up. "My Lord Stillington." She stretched her lips into a smile. The eminent churchman inclined his sleek head. His eyes, yellow as a hawk's, flicked over us with the shrewd appraisal of the hunter.

A sudden faintness overwhelmed me. The horror of a severed head, lips pulled back in a fearful grin, filled my mind with awful clarity. Here stood the churchman I'd seen in the glass at Silver Street! I clenched my fists, fighting long buried memories that surfaced like a shocking pageant, recognising in this prelate the sinister incarnation of childhood nightmares.

"Doubtless you still seek the restitution of your property?" The slight rise of his voice tailed off, as though he thought his question presumptuous but his scrutiny burned fierce as a flame.

Dame Eleanor tinkled laughter, her own nervous glance darting from side to side. "His Grace has promised to consider my petition most carefully, and I—" She clutched at words as she slipped off her azure, velvet cloak and handed it to me. The astute cleric, sensing her discomfiture, blinked his compelling eyes and offered her a life-line. "Permit me, Madam, to accompany you into the Palace."

Gratefully, she took his arm. The full sleeve swept down like a wing. For a moment, in her pale silk, she seemed like a fragile dove enfolded by a huge bird of prey.

142

"It's no easy matter for a lady among such a throng," the cleric said. He inclined his shapely head toward the crowd as if in acknowledgement of its power. The smile painted on Eleanor's lips trembled.

A first glimpse of the palace interior took my breath away. The magnificent richly painted roof caught my eye at once. Craning my neck towards this lofty ceiling, I discerned carved beams ornately decorated with angels, swans, and recumbent harts beneath twisted trees. All about the chamber hung brilliant-coloured tapestries and sumptuous cloth of gold. Light danced through jewelled glass and gilded every polished surface, creating such a sense of grandeur I believed I'd stepped into a world from an old tale of King Arthur and his Knights.

We joined an assortment of splendidly dressed noblemen and women hoping to present their own petitions to the king. Several of them nodded to our ecclesiastical companion. Others smiled when they saw Dame Eleanor. Something in these sly looks and whispered exchanges made my cheeks burn.

Stillington regarded her then with a mixture of curiosity and contempt. "You must forgive me if I leave you now but important matters call upon my time. His Grace will shortly send someone to attend upon you." Again the gentle bobbing of the head and the quick, predatory glance in my direction before he turned to leave. "I trust your perseverance will be rewarded, madam." The final remark slid silky as a knife-blade into flesh and Eleanor winced. The colour drained from her cheeks as the prelate swept boldly through the mass of people, no doubt relishing the effect of his words.

In spite of the heat in the hall, I shivered, filled again with a strange sense of foreboding. I *recognised* Stillington. Those hooded yellow eyes haunted me. At last I confronted my pursuer, the voice that whispered when I woke in breathless darkness, the menacing shape that lurked by the cottage doorway on moonlit nights, the demon of the dreams I'd babbled to my anxious father. Destiny had brought me here. I'd meet Stillington again. Momentarily the glamour of the court faded and I wished for the safety of the kitchen with homely Alison and Joan.

A rustle of excitement startled everyone. Trumpets blared. Dismayed, Eleanor pressed a hand to her throat as Edward Plantagenet and his noisy entourage entered the chamber. They swept by so close I could have reached out to touch his silken sleeve. We sank to our knees in homage but he showed not a flicker of recognition, though he must have seen us. Instead, his lips curled into a sneer. "I declare there are more and more of these beggars with their endless petitions today, Malyn."

The stocky gentleman in the crimson doublet held out a scroll but the king flicked a dismissive hand, alarming the brindled hound fawning at his heels. "Get up, get up," he said impatiently. In a moment, however, he recovered his famous good humour and placed an arm about Malyn's shoulder. "You read the names, Malyn. Or better still, choose the ones I should hear today." His hazel eyes flirted over us mischievously. "Choose only the pretty ones, Malyn!"

The courtiers laughed.

Leaping to his throne with the skill of an athlete, he draped his arms carelessly allowing the candle-light to dance on his jewelled fingers. He threw back his golden head with the sinuous grace of a stretching cat, and thrust out his long legs, loosely crossing the ankles, permitting us to marvel at his appearance. The velvet doublet with its purple dagged sleeves proclaimed the height of fashion. It was cut daringly short as to expose the lithe, shapely limbs in their fine, emerald hose. The bright gold and enamelled collar of white roses about his shoulders dazzled the eye. By his side crouched his fool, a tiny, wizened rogue with a face like a walnut. This fellow grinned up at him with impudent admiration. *His* eyes, however, lingered on the low-cut gowns and moist parted lips of the beautiful court ladies clustered about him.

"Be comfortable," he said. He sipped from a silver-chased goblet proffered by a kneeling page, his eyes scanning us in amusement over its rim. Like a cat toying with a mouse, he watched us intently—all feigned pretence—even the long deliberation while he fondled the silky ears of the hound lolling against his thigh.

The attendant addressed as Marlyn unfurled his scroll. As he stooped to whisper into the royal ear, the royal eyebrows lifted, the royal lips tilted upward. We held our breath, waiting to be summoned. Though impossible for us to hear, evidently the king's witty comments and gestures amused his courtiers. Giggles, snorts, and raucous laughter followed each exchange. Had I been a petitioner myself, I'd have fumed at this delay, but the magnificent garments and studied manners of these noble men and women fascinated me. How they aped the king's mood! Plainly, a clever courtier might earn favours by pleasing his sovereign. I speculated on the tales I'd tell Joan and Alison that night. Never had I seen such costly gowns, or such outrageous designs. Never had I witnessed such play-acting.

"Dame Butler." A bold-looking fellow bowed before us with elaborate courtesy. "His Grace craves your pardon, but he cannot consider your petition today. Pressing affairs of state command his attention." He plainly gloated on delivering this message and I longed to strike the smug expression from his sallow visage. Instead, I spoke up. "My lady is troubled by this delay in her affairs." I hoped the king heard me. Certainly, I caused a screech of consternation from the nearest listeners.

"I can assure you," the messenger replied, barely able to conceal his fury, "His Grace will give the matter just as much study as it needs."

"Forgive me, I'm unwell." Dame Eleanor's trembling voice prevented me from further argument. Alarmed by the tears on her cheeks, I took her arm, whisking her through the press of curious faces toward the chamber doors. Whispers and sniggers pursued us but I held my head high. I wondered if Canon Stillington watched this shameful departure. How could Edward Plantagenet treat Eleanor so cruelly? I all but turned to remind him I'd witnessed his promise to marry her only a few weeks ago. What would those posturing courtiers have said then?

Outside, a swarm of beggars hovered. A ragged old woman accosted us. Seeing Eleanor's face, however, she fell back.

"Lady, have a care," she croaked, crossing herself. "Those won with fine words fall fast from favour."

I urged Eleanor towards the river while the crone called after us, "Secrets can't be hidden behind stone walls or in stair wells."

Those cryptic words plagued me ever after.

Chapter Twenty-five

Just as we were about to sit down to supper the following evening, someone hammered at the door. Gerta admitted a messenger in fine blue and silver livery and accepted a document bearing the royal seal. Amidst a burst of questions she bore it off to Eleanor, and while Lionel stood chatting to the messenger in the doorway, the rest of us simmered with curiosity.

"Perhaps Dame Eleanor's summoned back to the palace?" whispered Alison.

"She'll never—"

Joan didn't finish, for Dame Eleanor herself burst into the kitchen.

"Convey my heartfelt thanks to the king," she told the man in livery. She dismissed him with a coin and turned to us with a radiant smile. "My estates have been restored to me. We must depart for Sudeley at once!"

Immediate commotion set us whirling. Lionel almost overturned the trestle as he darted towards her, his face florid with good humour.

"Joan and I could go ahead to make the house ready," he said.

"I could begin packing after supper." Joan laughed, tugging at her frizzled hair.

"Tomorrow—we'll begin tomorrow." Dame Eleanor's eyes sparkled. "But fetch some wine, Joan, and let's drink now to the king's health."

Perhaps this excitement and my visit to Edward's licentious court with its heady atmosphere of sensuous magnificence kindled the powerful dream that disturbed my sleep that night.

Trembling with anticipation, I waited on the stairs in a great, draughty castle. I wore a fine dress of pale grey worsted cloth, the sheen on it like silk. Wide sleeves edged with coney fur hung down, a girdle of plaited leather encircled my waist and a velvet hood hid my hair. Tremors of excitement and danger shook me. In the sconce on the stone wall a torch cast mysterious, flickering shadows.

Footsteps descended from above. Caught in a pair of strong arms, I responded to a sensual embrace, pressing my lips feverishly against those of my lover. Equally ardent, he carried me to a tiny, turret chamber where he covered my face and throat with kisses. Looking into his shockingly blue eyes, desire leapt in me like a flame. We sank together upon the great bed, caressing each other, murmuring endearments. Freed from the confines of its hood, my hair spilled its pins and he buried his face in its tumbling fall. Languorously we shed our garments, stroking and crooning, until our mutual urgency demanded other, fiercer pleasures. When his mouth slid down towards my breast, my limbs melted. A delicious hunger flooded through me. Naked and wanton in his arms, I pressed my body against his taut, eager flesh, thrilled to his hardening need. Savouring the sultry heat emanating from his skin, I teased him towards ecstasy with tiny bites. As my hands caressed the tangle of his black hair, lazily gliding down the muscular arch of his back to grasp the tensed buttocks, I ground my body voluptuously against his. We groaned together luxuriously, until, throwing back my head, I glimpsed the jewelled edge of an ecclesiastical gown in the doorway, and froze—

Heart thudding violently, I shot upright in the first grey haze of morning, my body slick with sweat. Eleanor's bed-curtains remained drawn although one pale hand drooped toward the floor. I imagined the careless scatter of her soft hair across the bolster, the delicate parted lips—and wondered if she dreamed too. What night-time adventures did she enjoy? Did she meet with the king? Or was she reunited with her late husband at Sudeley?

"Oh, Nan, what am I to do?" She sprang from her bed, anxiety distorting her fine features. She snatched up an azure gown and ran to the glass, holding the garment against her body. Something in her demeanour made me shudder. Struggling into my own gown, I remembered she'd worn the dress when the king had first called on her.

"Suppose the king forgets me?"

"How could he do that, Madam, after the promise he made?"

"Call Gerta." Skittish as a colt, she flung open the cedar chest in which she kept her garments. "We must pack my gowns." A faint aroma of lavender and verbena filled the room. Sun-light streamed now through the mullioned windows, mellow and warm, gilding her pale hair. A hectic flush bloomed in her cheeks as she dragged out skirts and sleeves while the inscrutable Gerta knelt to fold linen kirtles.

Perturbed, I watched Eleanor grow playful, casting garments over her shoulders and laughing as they floated down into a tangled pile, some on the bed and some on the floor. "Take these away," she ordered the Fleming, kicking a pile of discarded gowns. "Nan can help me with the rest."

She pranced before her glass holding up one garment after another, laughing immoderately, and then threw herself among the ravelled sleeves, hose and kirtles on the bed.

"Will Gerta accompany you to Sudeley?" I folded and replaced items into the chest.

Absently, Eleanor stroked a silver tissue sleeve. Her eyes grew huge, lit by brilliance—her face dreamy, as if she looked into far distance. "Oh no," she answered, her expression indifferent. "She was hired here in London and has no desire for country living." Her head on one side, she held the sleeve out fondly. "Do you remember how much the king admired me in this?"

"I do, indeed." I took it from her to fold alongside its partner. "And I've no doubt it will be admired again at Sudeley."

Crushing my hand in a fierce grip that made me cry out, she cried passionately, "Come with me!"

"I promised to return to the Mercers."

"But you said you wanted to see the place." She fixed me with a wounded look.

"And so I should, but, like Gerta, I belong in the city. It's a great honour you should ask me, my Lady, but—I've matters that detain me in London." I thought then quite unexpectedly of the stark, white fortress of the Tower and the blue-eyed man who haunted my dreams.

"Is it your priest?" One restless hand twisted the golden chain about her throat, the other plucked at her skirt. Her mounting agitation alarmed me. I'd seen her overwrought before but this nervous state bordered on hysteria.

"I'd like to see Brother Brian again but there are others I wish to contact—" How could I tell her about my visions? What would she say if I told her I sought a black-haired man and two noble boys whose lives were in such danger?

"If you were with me, Nan, I think I could bear this separation from the king more easily," she said. Her doe-eyes stared, full of pleading. "Promise you'll stay until he sends for me."

I wanted to scream. I knew the king meant to wriggle out of the promise he'd made. The restoration of her estates merely provided a means to be rid of her. But what would happen to me?

I ran to the stables almost weeping with frustration. "How shall I ever escape?" I leaned against the chestnut mare's warm flanks for comfort. Gently, she nudged me, her lips nibbling my sleeve, her dark, liquid eyes hopeful. I stroked her glossy neck. "One day, I'll be free of all this trouble." I rubbed away angry tears. "I'll have a home of my own and sit dozing by the fire with my grand-children. All these secrets will be forgotten—and then the king may go hang himself, for all I care!"

Chapter Twenty-Six

Inexorably, the year rode on like a faithful pilgrim towards a shrine, but I wasn't so patient or so purposeful. By mid-June Eleanor's dithering drove us all to distraction, and I snatched the first opportunity I could to escape the stifling atmosphere of the house. Anxiety drove me to St John's. Hearing nothing of Brother Brian since that fateful day in February, my anxiety nagged incessantly like a rotting tooth.

On the way I stopped briefly at Maud's shop.

"She's gone to her sister's in Barnet," called her garrulous neighbour. She heaved her ponderous bulk after me into the street. I paused a moment and she caught me by the sleeve, panting breath shaking an enormous bosom. "She's missed all the scandal about Shore's wife and King Edward." Her heavy, mottled face quivered with the effort of running but her little sow's eyes glinted spitefully. "Aren't you the fortune-telling wench who used to work at Mercers' Pie Shop?"

I wrenched my arm away babbling excuses. "I'm late—I'm sorry I can't stop to talk now—" and left her staring after me.

In a fever of impatience I rang the bell outside St John's. "Is Brother Brian here?" I asked the elderly monk who finally unlocked the door. He peered at me through screwed up eyes. "Have you any news of him?" His evasive manner annoyed me. "I hoped to find him here. It's been almost four months—Do you expect him soon?"

"I fear Brother Brian is unlikely to stay at St John's again," he answered gravely. He bowed his head over his tightly laced fingers.

Alarmed, I clutched at his sleeve. "Why? What about his pupil, Alan?" Sudden fear strangled my voice. "May I speak to him? It's a matter of utmost—"

His rheumy eyes rolled upwards. "Master Alan is no longer with us." Appalled, he stepped back a pace. "He's gone to Ely."

"And Brother Brian? Where's he?"

"I've no information concerning Brother Brian." He blinked nervously. "I think you must leave now."

I remember little of what happened after except the heavy door closed in my face and I ran to Bread Street.

"Is something wrong?" Meg stared, arms full of loaves.

"No, not at all," I lied, panting hard. Something prevented me from confiding in her. "I'd an errand to run for my mistress and thought I'd drop in to see you. It's been an age since I was able to leave the house."

"Why's that?" She handed me a warm, sweet pastry.

"Dame Eleanor's busy packing." I noticed Philippa listening intently so I chewed my pastry with slow pretended pleasure, licking crumbs from my fingers.

Meg gave me a sharp look and snorted with exasperation. "Well, we thought she'd be gone by now, unless— There's some odd tale going about— But we could do with you back in the shop." She stroked the proud curve of her belly. "Harry'll need help when this babe arrives and Philippa leaves. You know she's betrothed?"

"Who?"

"Why, Philippa, of course." Meg shook her head at my dizzy manner.

Fortunately customers flooded the shop and curtailed further conversation.

"Is Harry on deliveries?" I hovered in the doorway. "I might meet him on my way home."

"Not unless you're passing the Tower." Meg's eyes danced with mischief.

"The Tower!"

"Even the king has a taste for our pies!" Meg's words delighted her customers, especially as I gawped. "No! Not quite!" she added, laughing. "But Harry's gone to take bread to the guards and their families. We have their patronage now. It's been a great boon for business." Swiftly, she wrapped a large meat pie in a cloth. "Take this home. It's a new receipt. Tell me what you think of it next time you're here. And don't make that too long!"

I'd little desire to return to Silver Street. The tension in that accursed house tightened like a noose about my throat. Meg's cryptic remarks about Eleanor stirred my unease. Where was Brother Brian now? I wished I could run to ask Mistress Evans for some help. A vague recollection of the priest's words about the wise woman disturbed me. And where was Ely? The throb of a headache beat above my brow as I dawdled among the muddle of women bargaining for basins and jugs from a stall in Honey Lane.

Outside All Hallows Church I caught a glimpse of a golden-haired boy in a blue velvet doublet. As I pushed my way through the frowsy press of thick-bodied matrons, he slipped inside the building. But when I turned into the shadowy portal I found the place quite empty. A chill sense of menace breathed among the crouch of pews and watchful statues. Light barely trickled through the lancet windows, but in its haze dust floated and scurrying insects crept into crevices. In a dark niche a single candle quivered. I stood a moment, soaking in the silence, cold seeping into my bones.

"Help me."

The child's voice called out clearly, sending icy shivers coursing through my blood. My flesh crawled.

Escaping, I brushed against a hooded figure, but nothing would induce me to look back. Entering the hot roar of the street, I stumbled blindly in the sunlight.

"Watch where you're going!" A black-clad lawyer in fur-collared robe glared at me.

"Nan!" Lionel grabbed my basket and steered me away, leaving the affronted fellow gathering up his scattered documents. "Joan asked me to find you." Agitation beaded his reddened face with sweat. "I've been searching everywhere. Dame Eleanor's sick and rambling about a marriage celebration."

"A celebration?" I pressed a hand to my temple, struck by sudden foreboding.

Lionel's eyes bored into mine. "We thought you'd understand. She mentioned our royal visitor a lot. Nan, what do you really know about her relationship with the king?"

This day marked the beginning of an uncertain time.

"Please God, it's not the sweat." An anxious Joan brewed possets and nourishing stews, fretted throughout the day and slept so little her ill-temper sent us scuttling like rabbits.

"There's talk of plague in the city." Lionel's bass voice rang with doom, though his eyes danced with mischief. "Some wise woman in the Fleet's saying there'll be a great pestilence throughout the country this summer on account of wicked lechery in high places."

"Leave off, you rogue!" Joan tapped his arm with a ladle but the blow was half-hearted. "Instead of frightening us you could lend a hand by sweeping out the kitchen. Jack, run and fetch a broom from the store, and Nan help Alison put those dishes away while I warm some wine and honey for my Lady."

"Do you know where Ely is?" I asked, reaching up to open the press.

"A long way from here," said Lionel. "It's in the Fens."

"Why would you want to go there?" Joan looked up from pouring wine.

"Oh, I don't want to go there, but—"

Jack stood by the door, his face white as milk.

My gasp of shock alerted the others.

"What's wrong with you, lad? Where's that broom?" Lionel chafed the child with good humour.

"I'm not going back. There's a ghost in the passageway."

"Nonsense! Go back and fetch a besom at once!" Joan spat with exasperation but a fearful shadow lurked deep in her eyes.

"I swear on my mother's soul I saw something on the stairs!"

Joan's threats proved useless. Touched by the child's genuine fright, I persuaded him to accompany me in this task. Though I pretended courage, I sensed immediately the malign presence that troubled the house and wondered if Eleanor's sickness had roused it. As we emerged from the store-room, something warned me not to look up. From the corner of my eye I glimpsed a white shape hanging from the beams. Huddling Jack close, I hurried away, my heart yammering with fright. I made a game of my haste to distract the boy, telling him a giant hound was at our heels so that by the time we reached the kitchen we were both breathless with nervous laughter.

Chapter Twenty-Seven

In late June, when blossom lay in deep drifts and the last tiny flakes danced like moths around the wind-wracked trees, Eleanor finally rallied.

"Now, perhaps we'll get away." Joan, busy with her chores, muttered to herself. But the unexpected arrival of a strange noblewoman in a sable hooded cloak interrupted our final preparations.

Just before noon, she swept into the house without warning, accompanied by a lofty fellow in the blue and murrey livery of York. Her icy command to be taken to Dame Butler stunned us. We froze like guilty children caught misbehaving. Strangely, stolid Gerta, spurred into action by the woman's haughty manner, bore her off along the draughty corridors without any questions as to her identity or errand.

Alison peered through the shutters into the courtyard. "She must be very important. There's a whole troop of men outside."

We all gawked at our unexpected visitors—some on horseback, others milling about, and all bantering loudly.

"Who is she?" asked Jack when the Fleming returned much agitated.

"I wouldn't be surprised if it isn't—" A fierce knocking on the door interrupted Lionel's speculation.

Before anyone could open it, a sudden rain squall drove several members of the entourage into the house. A burly fellow in a fine woollen cape issued orders for the care of the horses and demanded the whereabouts of his mistress.

A panicked Joan hustled Lionel off to the stables, instructed Gerta to take the men to Dame Eleanor's chamber and ordered

Alison to the cellar to fetch some ale. Then in a ferment of indecision she set about wiping up the damp trail our intruders' cloaks left behind.

"Try to find out who that noblewoman is." I whispered to Jack, sneaking him outside while Joan wasn't looking. I'd a bad feeling about our mysterious visitor which I couldn't shake off.

"I'd like to know what's going on," Joan said. She wrung out her cloth in a pail and flashed me a nervous look, her eyes full of disquiet.

"I think we're in for more upheaval."

Jack burst in then, his cheeks poppy-red with excitement. "It's the king's mother, the Duchess of York. One of the men told me she'd quarrelled with the king. Do you suppose she's come to fetch Dame Butler to the palace?" His eyes shone with innocence. "The man said—" But at that point the inner door swung open and the Duchess of York herself confronted us.

We sank to our knees. Imperiously, she subjected us to a full and pointed inspection. Flanked by her attendants, she stood splendid and tall in her sombre velvet cloak, the fur-trimmed hood now thrown back to reveal a high white forehead and exquisite features. Though past her youth, she retained an astounding beauty. No wonder people called her "The Rose of Raby". She's discovered the secret betrothal, I thought with sudden shock as her cold eyes fastened on me.

Her silent disdain belittled all of us. Then, in a shimmering whirl of raven-black, she turned on her heel and swept away.

A rain-spattering wind rushed into the room almost extinguishing the fire. The outer doors hurled wide, startling us with their sudden, explosive noise. Jack ran at once to close them behind the last attendant. Abruptly, this big, broad-shouldered man spun round on the boy and drew a dagger. Transfixed by this unexpected attack, we froze, while Jack stood trembling with either cold or fright, the wild wind rampaging about the kitchen like a mischievous elf. A pan crashed to the floor and several knives skittered across the trestle. Grinning wolfishly, the knave threw back his hood, revealing a tangled mass of black hair. He turned upon us next like a predator assessing a flock of sheep.

A shiver that owed nothing to the cold passed through me. The piercing blue eyes blazed as dangerous and as irresistible as lightning. Caught in their power, I burned with sudden, outrageous desire. Afterwards I shuddered at the wanton nature of my response. But I knew him instantly. Hadn't he stared at me in this same bold fashion from out the water-bowl at my cousins' house three years ago? And hadn't I seen him again in the city streets—not to mention in my lurid dreams? Fascinated, I watched him sheathe his blade and run a careless hand through his ravelled hair. He smiled at me enigmatically, stirring a singular quiver in the pit of my belly, then vanished into the rain without a word.

"Well!" said Alison. "Who's that arrogant rogue? Nan—?"

I rushed outside, ignoring the sudden clamour of startled voices. The duchess's entourage already seemed a distant blur in the gauzy rain-fall but a familiar voice hailed me from the stable.

"Looking for me?"

He leaned in the doorway, his hair slick about his face in oily tendrils, his eyes smouldering.

Without a moment's hesitation I ran into the shelter of his cloak.

"So, you're here at last." Warm, triumphant laughter welcomed me into a firm embrace. "And haven't I waited long enough?" Caged in his arms, the heat of his body overwhelmed my senses. Dizzy with desire, I melted into the enchantment of those stormy blue eyes, my hands pressed against his chest. What magic made me so bold? Drops of rain fell on my face as he bent his head, his mouth at last seeking mine. Was this the passion I'd dreamed of for so long? The kiss roused a sweet, wild hunger and we clung together as if drowning.

"Come with me, lass."

In an instant I was lost—all thoughts of duty, all concept of loyalty or integrity swallowed up in that one delicious moment.

He mounted a silver-dappled horse and stooped to swing me up into the saddle before him when a guttural voice called out.

"Nan, my lady is sick. She asks for you." Gerta, her heavy face paler than usual, dragged at my arm.

Torn— one hand on the horse's neck, yet forced to pity by the desperate pleading in Gerta's eyes— I dithered in the damp dung stench of the stable-yard.

"You can find me at the Boar's Head." My lover pressed my palm to his lips, his eyes full of warning sparks. "Your mistress will be gone from the city in a day or so. I'll wait for you there."

He spurred away into the bone-chilling drizzle, and like a sleep-walker I followed Gerta back into the house.

I found Eleanor stooped at the privy. When she'd done with retching and could rise from her knees, I helped her to her chamber.

"I suppose you know who our visitor was?" She crouched on the settle like a wounded animal, eyes dull as agate, face white and drawn. Tendrils of sweat-soaked, yellow hair clung to her neck and shoulders.

"Jack said it was the Duchess of York." I draped a shawl about her, distressed by the shocking deterioration in her appearance and conscious of the damp seeping through to my skin.

"She told me to stop bothering the king! Can you believe that?" She plucked at the fabric of her skirts. "He's very young and over-rash with his favours," she said. "And like all young men, his ardour burns hot for a little while but then—" She struggled to deny the rising sobs. "But he loves me! You heard him promise—so how can she tear us apart?"

What could I say? Could kings break oaths? If only I could ask Brother Brian's advice—

"She ordered me to leave for Sudeley at once. But how can I go, like this—?" Without warning, she sprang to her feet, casting aside the shawl, her eyes rolling. Up and down the chamber she paced, twisting her hands—a familiar sign of growing agitation.

"Is there no one who might help you?" This frantic pacing set my teeth on edge. My own thoughts span, plotting ways I might follow after my black-haired lover. Anything to get away from that wretched house!

"Do you think I should go to the king?"

"No!" The rising hysteria in her voice terrified. "He'll surely send for you—"

Why did I lie? I knew, despite his promise, Edward of March would never send for her again.

"Joan says you've a sister in Norfolk—"

The wild look in her eyes reminded me of a trapped deer but the sudden eerie sound of her laughter made my hair stand on end. In the grey winter light, her face gleamed corpse-pale, the pearls about her neck like a rope. "Ned asked me to keep our betrothal secret, but secrets will out. One day I'll have revenge for this perfidy—"

She laughed again, a chilling, discordant trill. "Tell Joan and Lionel to make ready for departure. They must go on to Sudeley this day. You and I leave for Norfolk at first light."

Eleanor didn't bother to bid Joan and Lionel farewell. She shut herself in her bed-chamber while the rest of us helped the carter and his lad heap the baggage high. Joan and I parted with tears and foolish promises.

"I don't know why I'm crying." She gripped me in a fierce hug. "You'll soon be joining us at Sudeley."

A misty-eyed Lionel lifted her on to the cart and we watched them trot away on the first part of their long journey.

How empty the house seemed without them! I set Alison and Jack to prepare supper while Gerta and I packed for the journey to Norfolk.

Engrossed in wrapping my lady's precious Book of Hours in soft cloth, I turned suddenly to find Little Jack standing in the chamber doorway looking frightened.

"Canon Stillington's serving-man's taken the chaplain away."

"What?"

"He asked me to take him to Brother Thomas. He was very angry."

"Why?" I shook the boy by the shoulders, annoyed by his confusion. "Oh you stupid boy! Why didn't you come to me? What have you done?"

"He said Canon Stillington wanted to speak to him upon a very important matter." Jack gulped back tears. "And Gerta said Dame Butler mustn't be disturbed. So I took him to the chapel. Did I do wrong?"

"It was a mistake." I swallowed my rage with difficulty. "Gerta should have consulted me. It's not your fault. Forget about it now."

Next morning Eleanor handed the keys of the house to Gerta and dispatched her to return them to her cousin in Barnet. Without another word she allowed the carter to help her up while I comforted a sorrowful Alison in the street.

"Go to the Mercer's shop in Bread Street," I said, ignoring Eleanor's calls for haste. "Speak to Harry. Tell him I sent you." I dropped a kiss on little Jack's tousled head before climbing on to the cart. "They'll give you work."

As the horse jolted forward, I held up a hand in farewell. Alison draped her arm about Jack's shoulders and he looked up piteously, his nose drivelling snot from weeping. A heavy sense of foreboding fell upon me as the cart rolled towards Norfolk.

Part Three

Norwich
1463

Chapter Twenty-Eight

Eleanor's arrival caused uproar.

"Your mistress has caused no end of trouble." The Duchess of Norfolk's russet-haired serving-maid collapsed into infectious giggles.

Outraged, the haughty pack of household servants in the hall stared down their elegant noses as if they smelt something unsavoury.

"Drink your ale," the maid said. She clamped her hand over her mouth to smother further mirth. Her eyes danced. "I've something to show you."

Cleverly, she drew me away from the prying eyes. No doubt they talked of me over dinner while we hid together in an alcove on the magnificent manor's great oak staircase. "You should have heard them quarrelling," she said, clutching at my arm, tears of laughter brimming in her eyes. "I've never seen the Duke in such a passion, and now he's ridden off to his estate at Framlington. Oh, this will provide gossip for days and days!"

"But what did he say?"

I'd some inkling of what might have hatched the raised voices and the slamming doors but I wanted to discover how much the rest of the household actually knew.

"Why, that Dame Butler's played the harlot, and even if she *is* his wife's sister, he'll not let her bring dishonour on his family." Her amber eyes sparkled. "Oh you should've heard him rail!"

"But my lady's no harlot." Now the secret was out I felt compassion for poor, jilted Eleanor. It was too late for anger.

"No?" The maid's impertinent grin widened. "But she didn't get herself with child without she danced the bed-chamber jig with some knave, did she?"

"No knave," I replied hotly. "My lady's no wanton."

"Then you know who the child's father is?" The amber eyes grew round with curiosity, the pert face pink with excitement.

"No," I lied.

Throwing back her russet curls, the flighty wench uttered an earthy, full-throated gurgle. "You must know something otherwise you wouldn't look so guilty." She gave me a sly look.

"I know nothing to speak of." The bloom in my cheeks betrayed me. I feared she'd see into my mind where the king's golden image roamed, vivid as the knight in the huge arras hanging on the wall behind us.

But she laughed again without rancour. "Of course not," she said artfully.

When I made some feeble excuse and fled down the stairs, she hung over the banister to call after me, "But why is it such a secret?" Her trills of mischievous laughter taunted me all the way back to the servants' quarters.

"The Duke's banished Dame Butler from his house." A bold-eyed kitchen wench plainly relished muttering this information as she passed me in the corridor. The loftier servants eyed me suspiciously, flicking furtive signals to one another until I grew so uncomfortable I sought refuge in the chilly, sun-lit gardens. While I wandered up and down the avenues of wind-whipped trees, shivering in my thin cloak, Eleanor's troubled sister persuaded her to enter a convent.

It seemed a simple, heartless, solution. Clinging to the belief that the king would still send for her, Eleanor agreed. But she wouldn't part with me.

"Without your aid how can I bear it?" Her eyes clouded, stormy with grief. "Stay with me, Nan, at least until September."

"Until September," I said, steeling myself to endure further servitude.

I imagined the convent to be something like the monasteries in which I'd stayed on my journey to London with Brother Brian almost four years before. My mind recoiled from the memory of those meagre lodgings, the bone-gnawing cold and the sad-faced monks, the melancholy tolling of the bells, the eerie chanting and perpetual twilight.

"The Sisters at Norwich are Carmelites." The Duchess patiently explained matters to her sister. "Their lives are sheltered, dedicated to prayer and contemplation. I'm sure you'll find it a comfort at this difficult time and as a tertiary you may receive visitors."

Sitting mouse-small and still in a shadowy corner of her grand and gilded parlour, I listened as she counselled Eleanor to be strong. Having witnessed Eleanor's past piety, I thought she'd find little hardship in such a mode of living but I quailed for myself.

"The Sisters eschew vanity. They embrace poverty and chastity." The Duchess's sombre words fell upon me like drenching rain. How would I endure it? The memory of my black-haired lover tormented me. I didn't even know his name! How long would he wait?

Outside the convent's lofty, ivy draggled walls, I looked back toward the river, watched the rippling sunlight dancing on its surface, and glanced up to follow the graceful, arcing flight of a swan, silver against the blue-washed sky. I'm bidding farewell to freedom, I thought, as the great gates swallowed us up.

"Welcome." An elderly woman with a white mantle over her brown habit glided toward us. Eleanor's face lit up with a serenity that terrified, but an overwhelming urge to run clutched me in its vice. My panicked gaze flicked at the high, encircling walls, the crouching buildings, the arching cloisters and the long, long rows of inhospitable stone. Would my black-haired lover keep looking for me at the Boar's Head tavern? September suddenly seemed a long time away.

On the second day of our confinement Stillington appeared, black-clad and sleek, demanding speech with Eleanor. Had the Duke sent him? What did it matter? Eleanor's fate was sealed. What business could Stillington have with her now?

Surprisingly, he sought me out. "Ah, yes, the serving maid." His head bobbed. "We met at Westminster." The yellow eyes gleamed savage, unflinching.

"Do you love your mistress, girl?"

I swallowed hard, my mouth so dust-dry I couldn't speak.

"You wouldn't want any harm to come to her?" He waited, his murderous smile an ominous caress, allowing me time to digest the implication of these words. "You've no memory of her *encounters* with King Edward?"

I flinched at the menacing stress. I knew Ned Plantagenet had cast Eleanor off as carelessly as he cast off his gorgeous robes at the end of the day. He wouldn't be sending for her. If he thought of her at all, it would be as a mere dalliance. But now I recognised Stillington meant to silence both of us.

"Some matters are best hidden." The silken voice drove shivers through me. "Dame Butler will be safe within these convent walls. It wouldn't be wise to trouble others with our secrets. I think you understand me?"

"I do sir." I tipped up my chin, returning stare for stare. Silent rage throbbed through my body. I clenched my fists.

"Ah, but you are so young and impatient." He smiled indulgently. "No doubt you long for marriage and children?" He studied the ebony crucifix nailed to the bleak stone wall of our tiny chamber. "Few of us can make such sacrifice."

Sacrifice? What was he talking about? I wouldn't stay here. I'd find my black-haired man. He formed the link between me and those boys whose lives I must save. I lowered my eyes so he couldn't read the schemes festering in my mind. I refused to be intimidated by these veiled threats. I'd no intention of surrendering my freedom.

Chapter Twenty-Nine

But the Blessed Sisters had other ideas. Each passing day they subjected me to patient servitude, demanding I follow the wearying routine of convent life along with my mistress. They extolled the virtue of their calling, tempting me with its promise of heavenly merit and tranquil sanctuary from a sinful world. Dutifully I traipsed after Eleanor but I refused to be persuaded.

"We will bring you to God."

Sister Ursula's voice grated like the scrape of flint. Her smile, a gash in a face bleached almost to whiteness by lack of sunlight, challenged me.

"But I don't want to be a nun." I lowered my head in respect, keeping my voice neutral. From the chapel drifted the monotonous chant of early morning prayers. A breeze whipped through the desolate cloister, flapping angrily at Sister Ursula's sombre robes.

"Many shun the quiet of the convent at first." Behind the terrible smile she held hostility in check. "But in its shelter, a woman may discover the true nature of fulfilment."

I refused to answer. Sister Ursula's pretence of persuasion only made me more determined to escape. I fisted my hands, keeping my gaze fixed on the flagstones.

"Well, if prayer can't offer solace, you may help Sister Agnes in the bakery."

The calculated cruelty of these words snatched my attention. I looked up.

The dreadful smile still carved her face. I thought instantly of the stone gargoyle in the chapel. Her answering gaze struck me with a coldness which sickened me to my stomach. She knew I loathed Sister Agnes. "Perhaps some day you'll follow your mistress' example," she said smoothly. Her eyes stung, sharp as slivers of metal. "She finds much consolation in her devotions."

"My mistress clings to her faith." I gazed fascinated by the extreme ugliness of her jutting jaw and thought what little else Eleanor had to lean on until September brought us both release. Inwardly I railed against the impetuous pledge I'd made. "But I must admit a longing for the things of the world." I forced a smile. "Of course I admire those who possess such piety." A delicious memory of a passionate, rain-blessed kiss coursed through me. My black-haired lover was no longer a figment of dreams. He was real and I meant to find him.

Feigning obedience, I trudged towards the bake-house, my every step under the chilly, disapproving eyes. But Sister Ursula couldn't read my thoughts. I would never surrender my liberty. Even Brother Brian wouldn't have asked that of me.

The bakery's welcome blast reminded me of the Mercers but Sister Agnes' acerbic tongue spoiled my pleasure.

"Not yet ready to discard vanity?" She peered at my gown with frank disapproval. I'd refused to don the brown habit favoured by the Carmelite community, though Dame Eleanor adopted it willingly along with the curious cloth known as the scapular, worn over the chest and back, fashioned by one of their saints who declared the Virgin delivered it to him in a vision. Such piety alarmed me.

Joining Sister Clement kneading dough, I cooled my simmering rage by wrestling the uncooked mass beneath my fingers. Timid Clement nodded fearfully. Sister Agnes had crushed her spirit.

"I understand Dame Butler kept an easy-going house in London." Aware the comment was designed to goad, I didn't answer. I'd learned quickly this malicious nun's appearance, as well as the gentle name she'd adopted, belied her true nature. The wren-like stature and soft, pink lips suggested gentleness but she burned with a fierce energy, and her beady eyes constantly probed for secrets.

"Indulgence is a grave mistake." She pursed prim lips. "Without discipline, servants are apt to grow dishonest or even wanton. Is it true the king was a frequent visitor?"

She can't know, I thought, my heart racing. Surely she can't know!

"His Grace called once or twice regarding the restoration of my Lady's estate," I answered steadily.

"They say he's very handsome." Dreamy-eyed Clement carried a tray of loaves to the oven, clumsily knocking an earthen jug to the floor in passing.

"Slovenliness is a sign of an unclean mind," Sister Agnes snapped.

Tearful Clement stooped to gather the shattered pieces.

"This world is awash with uncleanness," Sister Agnes continued. She thrust the loaves into the hot dark well of the oven with a malice bordering on joy. "They say our handsome sovereign keeps a lascivious court, where lust and covetousness are cultivated like precious flowers, and virtue is ridiculed."

She fixed her nasty, little eyes upon me.

"I can't say for I was never at court," I replied, shovelling the unwieldy dough into the moulds. In spite of Brother Brian's early teaching, I lied to the nuns without compunction. I wouldn't share the memory of the noise and extravagance of Westminster with them. These cold virgins savoured no joy. Discipline etched lines into their faces. It stiffened the soft curves of their bodies, dowsed the light in their eyes. They subdued pleasures of the flesh with rigorous fasting, mind-numbing tasks and constant prayer. I despised the way they shuffled through the cloisters, eyes bent modestly toward the dry dust to which they would return, seeing nothing of heaven's reflection in the busy heat of life. Secretly, I delighted in the knowledge that Eleanor had enjoyed at least a moment of pleasure.

"A king is known by the company he keeps. King Henry was a saintly man and kept about him devout men and women." Sister Agnes wiped her virtuous hands on her linen apron.

"Sister Ursula told us King Henry spent so much time in prayer, at the Eucharist he was blessed with visions of Our Lord." Sister Clement's piety earned a rare nod of approval. I fumed at this naïveté, recalling the damage poor Henry's madness had inflicted on the country.

"Dame Butler's husband was killed in battle, wasn't he?" Clement threw me a shy glance.

"He was," I replied. "Although I wasn't in service at Sudeley then. I didn't have the good fortune to meet Sir Thomas."

"You surprise me." Sister Agnes" sharp voice intruded. "From your closeness to Dame Butler, I thought you to be one of the old family servants. He must have been dead some time then?"

I cursed my careless tongue.

"For a child not to know its father is so sad." Sister Clement's plaintive interruption saved me a reply. "Did you know, King Henry's father died when he was only a few months old?"

"Any fool knows that. Fortunately Dame Butler has the quiet of the convent to comfort her. Here she may bring her child into the world without arousing undue attention." Again, Sister Agnes fixed her sharp eyes on me. Heat flooded my cheeks. I longed to slap the self-satisfaction from her smug face.

"She seems so very melancholy." Ingenuously, Sister Clement voiced my own disquiet.

"She's encountered much adversity." I pictured the king's faithless, heart-stealing smile. "She misses her family and her old friends. When she returns to Sudeley, I'm sure she'll—"

"Sister Clement!" Sister Agnes jolted me from my reverie. The slack-faced Clement flapped like a bewildered goose. "Can't you smell the bread's burning?"

Chapter Thirty

Every afternoon before Vespers Eleanor and I hunched in our sparse, little room sewing garments for the poor. The dreary silence of the convent and the steady drip of rain from the eaves lulled me into a kind of trance, so that my fingers hemmed of their own volition allowing my mind to travel. It carried me across a wide expanse of moorland. Rolling hills opened out before me and huge crags like ancient monuments reached skyward. Streams cascaded amongst stones, sunlight painting them with sparkling rainbow hues, while skirling birds wheeled over pasture-land teeming with grey-faced sheep sporting curling horns. Slate-coloured clouds scudded across a vast, wind-scrubbed sky.

"There," said a familiar northern voice. "That's it."

I followed the line of my lover's outstretched arm to where the magnificent castle walls rose up—

"My cousin, Gournay, and his wife will take the babe when he's born." Eleanor's voice startled me.

She'd not spoken of the expected babe before. Her shame-faced sister apprised me of the situation in Norfolk although I'd already guessed at it in Silver Street. The Duchess swore me to secrecy. I wondered if Stillington knew.

Secrets—so many secrets—Whenever I heard the word, I thought of Mistress Evans and wondered what else her prophecies held in store. I'd already travelled north. And hadn't she told me to "look to the nun"? But which one of them deserved my special attention? My mind leaped to the final part of her prediction: "Beware the man with blood upon his hands." A pair of fierce blue eyes filled me with the shameless heat of desire. But Mistress Evans' prophecies had a way of turning out quite unlike what one expected.

"Won't you keep the babe, madam?" Drawn back into the harsh present, an unpleasant thought struck me with all the suddenness of an arrow-bolt. Suppose Eleanor chose to remain in the convent after the birth? My mind raced with the implications.

A tear fell on the coarse fabric. "Canon Stillington said it would be best—" Her words choked into incoherence.

Stillington! Even his name had power to chill me.

Eleanor's muffled weeping forced me back into the bleak reality of the little chamber. Shadows crept across the floor blurring my vision.

"Shall I light a candle, madam?"

"Aye, light a candle for me, child. I've need of prayer."

Involuntarily, I jumped, dropping my needle. Something about Eleanor's hunched shape and odd manner of speech recalled mad King Harry. Hadn't he bidden his captors pray for him? Sister Clement's innocent words darted shockingly into my mind. I half rose. Eleanor pinched my arm.

"Ask Brother Thomas to come to me." Her eyes stared wide and trusting as young hind's.

"Madam, we're at Norwich."

"Norwich?" Fear leaped into her puzzled gaze.

I crouched beside her, speaking soft and slow. "Brother Thomas isn't with us anymore. Don't you remember leaving Silver Street? Canon Stillington sent for Brother Thomas the night before we left."

Eleanor stared blankly, her fingers fumbling at her crumpled needlework.

"Jack told me and I meant to find out what happened to Brother Thomas but—"

The memory of the missing priest flooded me with guilt. What had become of him? Suppose Stillington had arrested him too?

Eleanor's whimper stopped me from screaming. She pressed her hands against her belly, her sewing sliding to the floor.

"Help me," she said. Her delicate features distorted with pain and fear. "Fetch Joan."

Chapter Thirty-One

Eleanor's child was a boy as she'd predicted—a tiny, frail infant with a fuzz of golden hair, born on a mellow September afternoon as the bells tolled the Angelus. Holding him in my arms I experienced a tremendous rush of love. How could she think of parting with him?

"Would you like to hold the babe, madam?" When I tried to lower the child in her arms she shrank away, averting her head. "He's a lovely boy." I knelt beside her, cajoling in my most persuasive manner. "Look at his little hands. He's a strong grip already." She shuddered with distaste.

Pale and silent, she sat gazing into the hearth while the wet-nurse suckled him, and I ached with desire. *If he were mine*, I thought, *I'd walk through flames to keep him.*

"The Duchess of Norfolk has been informed." Sister Ursula hovered in the doorway. I wondered how long she'd been watching us. She pursed her lips, her wintry eyes fixed on Eleanor's back. "How long has she been like this?"

The wet-nurse shrugged.

"Since the babe was born," I said. "She's said nothing for days now."

A flicker of unease crossed the nun's face. "Better she doesn't become attached," she muttered. "See that she eats something." She addressed me in a cold, imperious tone. "And keep her occupied. Her sister will take the child shortly."

Although I craved the Duchess's visit which would release me, I couldn't believe she really meant to take the child away and hide him among strangers. But as the warm days drifted by, I grew increasingly impatient.

One late October morning, a young novice arrived to fetch Eleanor.

"What does Sister Ursula want?" I asked, puzzled by the vagueness of the message she delivered.

"She didn't say." The girl darted frightened glances about her.

"You'll need to keep a careful watch." I helped Eleanor to her feet. "Dame Butler doesn't always remember where she is."

I watched Eleanor led away like a sleep-walker and had barely turned back before the Duchess of Norfolk swept into the chamber and dismissed the wet-nurse.

We stood together awkwardly, looking at the child in his plain wooden cradle.

"Dame Eleanor's been called away—"

"I've already seen her." The Duchess sounded embarrassed. She twisted the rings on her index finger. "No doubt you've heard of the king's marriage."

"Marriage, Your Grace? But surely—"

"He married a widow named Wydeville at Grafton on the first of May and kept it secret for months." Her voice trembled, breathless, embarrassed. "The Earl of Warwick was furious because he was negotiating a French match. But London ran wild with excitement. Exaggerated stories are still circulating." She paused as if wilting under my scrutiny. I imagined Maud entertaining a feverish crowd. "They made it sound like a tale from an old romance, with a moonlit meeting in a forest and a mother reputed to be a powerful witch—" She crossed herself elaborately.

An icy chill shook me. I clutched at my gown. "But how could the king wed another while troth-plight to my lady?"

"But he *has* married." Her face froze, rigid as a mask. "And the stability of the realm depends upon our silence. "Canon Stillington's anxious no gossip should sully the king's marriage celebrations."

Stillington! What power the prelate wielded!

Shocked by her willingness to conceal the truth, I opened my mouth to protest.

"Some things are best kept secret." The duchess echoed Stillington's warning. "No harm can come to those who guard their tongues." She flashed a pointed look. "You've knowledge of a situation it wouldn't be wise to share."

"But how can you condone your sister's betrayal?"

The child's cries interrupted.

"My sister's been foolish," said the Duchess. Restraint tightened her voice. She looked down at the child. "She was always giddy and profligate with her affections. This boy's to be named Thomas after her husband and educated in the Gournay household as befits a gentleman. We needn't speak of him again."

The harsh, careless words horrified. "And will my lady take the veil?"

The duchess's delicately arched eyebrows drew together in an ugly frown. "It would be best she remain at Norwich."

"And what's to become of me?" A frightening possibility struck me like a fist. Could Stillington have found the perfect solution? "Sweet Jesu! He means to shut me up!" The Duchess's face blanched as I turned on her in fury. "I can't live like this forever! I can't bear it! How dare you condemn me to this?"

"Of course no one can force you." She backed away, the stammer in her voice betraying fear. She couldn't meet my eyes. "The good sisters wouldn't keep you here against your will."

"Then take me with you!"

Like a thief, she snatched up the howling babe and ran toward the door. "I've no authority—You must speak to—"

"Stillington?" I demanded, white-hot with rage. As she turned the handle, I grabbed at her arm. "You can't leave me here!"

But she wrenched herself away, wrestling me off with all the fury of an ale-wife, and fled with the frightened babe shrieking in her arms.

Eleanor didn't seem to notice. She never asked for him. *He might never have been born*, I thought, watching her wandering up and down the chamber, a strange, ecstatic expression on her face. But she wouldn't let me leave her. Though I tried to explain my need to return to London, she clung to me, weeping so fiercely, Sister Ursula admonished me for heartlessness. "Surely you don't grudge your mistress a few more days of your company?"

Alone in the dark I shed many tears for the little boy who must be raised in secret and would never know his parentage.

"Poor little mite," said the carter's wench. We stood together in the cruel light of early morning. "The sisters said his father was killed in battle and his mother died when he was born." She crossed herself. "Did you see him?"

"Little Thomas? Oh yes—a bonny little boy," I answered, with a wistful smile. "I believe his cousins intend to raise him."

"But he's called Giles." She grinned at my ignorance. "I remember because it's my father's name. Fancy you forgetting!"

Since that terrible day, Eleanor's life seemed frozen in the barren walls of Norwich and mine with it. She never spoke of Sudeley again. Instead she drifted in a twilight world between prayers and sleep, and day by day withdrew a little more.

A life of prayer and contemplation—How often the Duchess's words returned to torture me. Daily I passed the monstrous painting of Elijah in the desert, before whose image the patient nuns paused to genuflect.

"This holy prophet taught us the value of poverty and solitude," Sister Ursula said. Grim satisfaction twisted her mouth. "The Lord lives, in whose Sight I stand." She reverently read out the black script, while I stood with lowered eyes trying to hide my hatred of the bearded, robed figure who'd stolen my liberty.

At two, before the birds began their morning chorus or the sun rose from its sleeping place, the stern-faced Sisterhood rose for Matins. Rebelliously, I listened to the virtuous shuffle of their sandaled feet outside my door, praying Eleanor wouldn't spring up and urge me to go with her to the chapel. At Prime, I squirmed on my hard seat, stomach growling over the breakfast bread and ale, forced to sit in silence listening to Bible readings in the Chapter House. Work followed Terce—needlework for those whose skilful fingers embroidered fine vestments or created elaborate hangings woven with gold and silver threads—for the rest, spinning or weaving, or copying manuscripts, while the lowly lay sisters tilled the fields or drudged over laundry. After Sext we ate—simple foods, pottage, bread and broth, poorly prepared and served in unappetising, meagre portions. How often I longed for the Mercers' luxurious feasts then! Until Vespers the Sisters returned then to their tasks and after supper came Compline and rest. I pondered on the nature of their thoughts as they shuffled through the cloisters or bowed over their labours. Did they yearn for the world which boiled and bubbled beyond those stout, grim walls? Did they think of loved ones now lost to them? Did they long for words of affection, for laughter, for a baby's cry?

Hours of regimented silence punctuated by bells and prayers stretched out before me and I cursed King Edward for putting me in this place. The good Sisters had no intention of releasing me.

Daily I plotted how I might escape the convent. If I could contact Brother Brian, I knew he'd rescue me. But where was the priest?

Chapter Thirty-Two

"Pretty, isn't it?" Sister Absalom moved soft as a cat even though the ground lay winter-hard. She stood at my shoulder, our breath blowing like smoke into the breaking dawn. Beyond us stretched the gardens gleaming with the painted rime of hoar-frost like a spectral fairy-land. "I rise early too."

"The carter's daughter tells me King Edward's queen expects a child," I answered.

"Ah, you are greedy for news of the world." Sister Absalom smiled. "I thought as much when I saw you here. You've no desire to remain here with your mistress?"

I shook my head, my eyes still focussed on the trees' white skeletons, the naked, frozen flower-heads by the wall.

"Such a life can be rewarding." She laughed at my hiss of contempt. "Come with me to the library. Let me show you the precious volumes I'm entrusted to guard."

"I can't read."

"I could teach you."

I followed her into the building with reluctance. But when she revealed a manuscript she was working on, an alchemy of blackest spikes embellished with drops of gold, I thought instantly of Alan Palmer and wondered if he'd become a scribe at Ely. The words of the elderly monk at the priory still troubled me. Something shameful had occurred between Brother Brian and Master Palmer. Why else had my old priest been so ignominiously dismissed?

"Will you teach me to write?"

Sister Absalom proved a patient teacher as well as a skilled calligrapher. At last, I learned to unravel the secrets of those sounds and signs I'd watched Brother Brian teaching the boys in the village church all those years ago. Within a month I'd mastered the skill.

"How will you fare when your mistress takes her vows?" Sister Absalom's eyes examined me carefully as I perused the books.

"If I believed my lady's faith had drawn her here—" I watched my ghostly wisps of exhaled breath float away like spider-webs for it was always chilly in the library. "Once she was a noble lady destined for another kind of life, but adversity hasn't dealt kindly with her."

"Few choose their own pathway." Sister Absalom's words reminded me at once of Mistress Evans. "Does it trouble you that she should become a vowess?"

"I fear she's unwell."

I didn't mention Eleanor's increasing strangeness or that now she seemed as enamoured of her prayers as ever she was of Ned Plantagenet but I knew Sister Absalom understood.

The sonorous bells tolled for Prime.

"I want to write a letter."

Sister Absalom waited. Over the weeks I'd worked with her she'd induced me to tell her much of my history. She possessed a clever way of drawing out information without obvious probing and I realised how easily one might fall into this trap.

"I'd like to write to Brother Brian, my village priest."

"To what end?"

I thought the inquiry sharp and must have looked startled, for Sister Absalom smiled as if caught out and spoke swiftly as if to soothe my suspicions. "I meant to say, what news could a priest be desirous to receive of you? Are you anxious to learn something of your family?"

"I'd like to thank him for his kindness." Something in her change of manner put me on guard. "Beware the nun." I heard Mistress Evans' words as clearly as when she'd first spoken them. Did Sister Absalom act on instruction from someone else?

She slithered away to fetch writing materials. "Will you return to your family when your mistress takes her vows?"

"Oh no, my brothers will be young men now." With longing I thought of Tom as a little boy clambering upon my knee, of my father's loving arms, of Alys and Robin teasing me, even Fat Marion's scolding—How far away village life seemed. But the memories brought Brother Brian's presence nearer. Our shared secrets bound us.

She handed me pen and ink. "Let's write to your old priest and tell him of your employment here. I'm sure he'll be pleased to know you've learned your letters." She gushed encouragement.

While I scratched, puzzling over elusive words that ran from me like hares across stubbled corn, I pondered too on Sister Absalom. Had I been deceived by her former guise of friendship? Had she worked all this while as an instrument to learn my secrets? Even while I wrote she plied me with eager questions, mopping up ink, ignoring the sweaty finger-marks that marred my copy.

"Will you continue as a lay sister?" Her friendly manner rang false now.

"I'd rather find employment in the village. You know I lack faith for the religious life."

"Don't tell your priest such heresy. He'd be disappointed to discover his instruction has proved so feeble."

"Oh I attended Mass and listened to his lessons. Brother Brian knows all my sins. I'd trust him with my life."

Later, in the chapel I watched Eleanor from a pool of shadow by the pillar. Her hands trembled as she lit a candle. A drop of wax fell like a single tear upon her robe. Kneeling before the painted figure of the Virgin, she placed her offering amidst the other flickering votive-lights. Slender fingers sketched the cross, lips moved in whispered prayer. I felt ashamed to intrude upon such devotion.

"My Lady, Sister Ursula asked me to summon you to the refectory. It's time to eat."

"To eat?" She repeated the words emptily. "No, I may not dine today until Ned's here."

"We mustn't keep the Sisters waiting." I cajoled like a beggar— angry to be reduced to such occupation.

"He promised. He promised."

This was one of her bad days. But, truly he *had* promised. I'd heard him. I wondered if gorgeous, golden Edward of York ever thought of Eleanor. Did he wake sweating in the darkness and tremble at what he'd done? Did he pause at the hunt, or halt in the dance, or sicken at the feast when he remembered Eleanor?

The chill of the chapel seeped into my bones like water. I tried to draw Eleanor to her feet.

"My sweet Ned promised he would visit today. I must make ready." She rose, momentarily resolute and proud as if in the old London days, and then she loosed her hair from the nun's coif. Once the yellow cascade would have spilled almost to her knees, but now I could have wept to see the pale stubble about her head. Like a child in her mother's old cloak she looked down at the coarse habit of the Carmelites. "Why am I dressed in this?" Her eyes widened. "I can't receive my sweet Ned in these garments."

"Lady," I reached out a hand, "we're at Norwich."

"At Norwich?"

"The House of the Carmelites. There's no Lord Ned."

"No Lord Ned!" The stricken eyes turned on me, the pupils shrunk to pin-pricks. I could have bitten out my tongue.

"I mean, Lord Ned is England's king. He can't dine with us today." My fingers grazed her robe, but the white figure slipped like smoke back to the statue of the Virgin where myriad candles winked and guttered.

Softly she began to laugh, an eerie ripple of sound that made the hairs upon my neck rise.

"My Lady, you must be calm."

Eleanor's head tilted back, one hand at her mouth, her eyes fixed on the statue. Awful laughter bubbled from her mouth, the uncontrollable laughter of the mad.

"Lady Eleanor! Lady Eleanor!" I called in vain. The wild creature laughed and wept and shook its yellow head so it seemed a living candle dancing before the Holy Virgin.

"My sweet Ned is King of England!"

"You mustn't speak so loud. It's a secret. Remember your promise? It's a secret."

In the refectory Sister Agatha read from the scriptures. Her nasal tones droned among clanking jaws and slurping mouths. The warm stench of gathered womankind filled the chamber. No one looked up but Sister Ursula's eyes followed me as we slid into our places. I chewed on gristle, trying not to inhale the greasy smell from the bowl. Opposite, Eleanor sat silent at last. Her translucent hand toyed with food but nothing touched the rose-bud mouth. Beside me Sister Theresa's stomach rumbled and I kept my eyes hooded to shut out the jellied wobble of her whiskered jowls. Rebellious as ever I prayed for a miracle to bring escape.

"You must guard her more carefully." Sister Ursula's eyes fixed me with stony disapproval.

"I try. But sometimes she slips away from me."

"You must watch her at all times. She's becoming more and more—" She paused to watch the sisters file out of the refectory, "distracted. Her behaviour causes comment, particularly among the younger sisters. You understand my meaning?"

"Yes, Sister Ursula." I forced an acquiescent tone. What use to argue?

Eleanor was quite mad. She spoke rarely, but when she did, she hinted at an intimacy with the king that provoked scandalised speculation amongst the nuns; she danced and laughed during prayers; she screamed in the night and ran after shadows. And I'd assumed a gaoler's role.

Of course I watched her, followed her, attempted to contain her in her cell, but she regularly eluded me. Sometimes I left her with Sister Matthew in the infirmary to steal moments of solitude.

Leaving the refectory I walked with Eleanor in the convent-grounds. How beautiful the gardens appeared in the sunlight. All the nuns returned to their cells for the hour of private contemplation.

Sitting on the bench, I pointed out to Eleanor a pair of brilliant butterflies flirting among the foxgloves. How I envied them their freedom. What did it matter they only lived for a day? One day of utter joy was better than years spent in this prison. Wistfully, I thought of the man who haunted my dreams and whose blue eyes regarded me with obvious desire. What might I give for one hour in his arms?

Secrets, I thought closing my eyes for a moment against the sun's rays, are all I have left of the world outside the convent walls. Throats have been cut for speaking ill of the king, and doubtless Brother Thomas paid dearly for knowing too much. Did he dare to speak out? I'm the only other guardian of that secret, I thought. The realisation startled me awake.

When Eleanor's dead I'll leave this place. But weak, sickly Eleanor could live years and years. Overcome with guilt, I looked for my charge. The gardens lay empty. Eleanor had gone.

Outside the chapel door, I hesitated, suddenly faint and nauseous. Perhaps I'd taken a fever from sitting in the sun? Leaning on the warm stonework, I closed my eyes against a spinning sensation, swallowing hard. Then drawing a deep breath,

I pushed against the door and stepped inside. The chapel beckoned cool and empty. Before the Virgin the candles flickered. The scent of incense hung upon the air.

As my eyes adjusted to the darkness I raised my head at last and saw the horror. Eleanor's body swung from a beam above the Virgin's image. She'd hanged herself with her girdle.

Chapter Thirty-Three

Shock drove me to sudden, reckless flight.

"You've got to help me."

Sister Clement's body writhed but I pressed my hand hard over her mouth. Her teeth nibbled against my palm. Her left arm flailed but when I thrust the dagger to her throat, hissing into her ear, "Don't struggle. I'll cut you if I have to," she stopped. Pressing the blade so the point bit into soft flesh— just enough to draw a bead of blood— I gloated with my own power. Tension fluttered in her like a trapped bird, the pent-up scream desperate for release. Sweat trickled between my breasts. Until I knew she wouldn't make a sound I kept the pressure on her mouth.

"You've got to help me escape."

The eyes pleaded. Bird-like whistles wheezed in her throat. Her lips mumbled against my hand.

"No noise." I touched the point of the dagger to her cheek so from the corner of her eye she might catch a glimpse of it. "I need to get away. Something terrible's happened."

She struggled to shake her head from side to side.

"Keep still. Listen and remember what I say. What'll happen if they find out you sneaked off from your prayers to sleep in here?" Fear made her rigid. "Believe me, I'll tell them if they catch me. Now, I'm going to let go, but if you utter one squeak I'll kill you. Do you understand?"

She nodded, blinking tears.

Trembling in every limb, I stood upright, relaxing my grip. "Now come with me."

Paralysed with fear, her eyes followed the dagger, but I grabbed her wrist, pulling her into the empty corridor. Around us, the whispered breathing of the sisterhood at prayer continued. Nothing must disturb their devotions. My hold upon her arm grew vicious.

Once outside the building, Clement found her voice. "What have you done?"

Poor Clement. She possessed a timid, kindly nature and I meant to use this weakness to my own advantage. I couldn't have been more fortunate to find her sleeping in the kitchen when she should have been at prayer in her cell.

"Who has the keys to the cemetery gate?"

"Sister Ursula." Clement's eyes rolled wild with fear.

"No one else?"

"I think Sister Theresa has some keys."

"You must get them for me."

"How?"

"Don't whimper. Go and ask her for them after prayers. Say the carter's daughter's arrived to collect refuse. Tell her anything as long as you get those keys. I'll hide in the cemetery—I can hardly go out the main gates, can I?"

"Suppose she comes with me?"

"She won't," I said, with a confidence I didn't feel. Sister Theresa, a garrulous old busy-body, would welcome an opportunity to gossip. "Tell her the carter's daughter said there's plague in the town. That'll keep her away. Now go, and try to look confused."

The last instruction proved unnecessary for Clement rarely looked anything else. She'd a reputation for stupidity which fuelled much teasing among the spiteful sisterhood.

I watched her scuttle back into the building and then ran towards the burial ground. Crouching among the tombs, I prayed, not for the speeding of the departed souls to heaven, but for the saving of my own.

⁂

An hour or so before Matins the birds began calling to one another.

Dew-drenched, I shivered beneath the hedge peering into the cobalt shadows of the new day. Thin streaks of light appeared between earth and sky. Sister Anthony called the morning chorus a "magnificent anthem to our Lord," but at this moment, it sounded like a cacophony that would rouse the hunters and direct them to my hiding place.

I'd spent an uncomfortable night huddled up against this prickly tangle. Though exhausted I couldn't soothe my restless mind. Every creak jerked me into wakefulness. Now, as I continued on my journey, my temples pounded with a thousand hammers. My eyes seemed full of grit as if I'd stood too close at the forge.

Dear Clement—she'd not only acquired the keys but she'd thought to bring me an old cloak, and the bread I'd eaten last night. I hoped Sister Ursula wouldn't punish her too harshly.

A cart rumbled alongside.

"Where are you bound for, young mistress?" Watery blue eyes squinted in the sunlight. "You seem to be in an almighty hurry."

"I'm looking for the London road." I replied, panting for breath.

The wheels creaked to a stop and the occupants of the cart, a grizzled farmer and his mousy family, helped me aboard. Gratefully, I settled myself between the flabby-bodied wife and two goggle-eyed boys.

"We can set you on your way a piece." The wife eyed my old-fashioned dress. "It's not safe to wander abroad alone in these unsettled times. Have you family in the city?" She smiled as if encouraging confidence.

"I can offer you nothing but thanks." I decided to risk a blunt approach. "I'm in a hurry. I've run away from my master and want to get as far away as I can."

The farmer gasped, swivelling his head like an owl's. The squat wife raised her eyebrows.

"He was cruel to me," I said before they could ask. "He beat me often."

I drew back my sleeves to show some old bruises. How plausible I sounded! "But when he tried to—" Darting a nod at the two young boys, I eyed the woman as if to share some dreadful secret.

"You poor child." She reached out a moist, friendly hand. "How you've suffered."

The farmer sniffed and I wondered if I should further embellish my tale.

"Where's your home?"

I shook my head, compressing my lips as if distressed. "My father's dead." Genuine tears welled up. The wife's ugly features melted with pity. "And my mother's re-married." At least that part was true, I thought, ashamed at gulling honest folk. "Her new husband threw me out and my sweetheart's forsaken me. I've an aunt in London."

"It's a mighty way to London." The woman and her two boys stared at me, mouths slack with wonder. She looked inquiringly at her husband, but he shook his head.

"I can take you to the London Road a piece." He rubbed his fist against his nose as if embarrassed. "Maybe you'll find someone to take you onward when we get to the cross-roads."

Thanking them for their kindness, I wondered what they'd say if they knew I'd just escaped from a convent. Guiltily, I remembered how I'd prayed for a miracle to release me from the place. Had I caused Eleanor's death? Fat Marion once told us as children to be careful of our wishes. But I couldn't regret my freedom.

*

The track wound on, rough and dusty. For weeks no rain had fallen. Vegetation rose parched and spindly. A heavy, clinging scent of pollen sucked away the air. My stomach gurgled. I'd eaten little since yesterday. Licking my lips I tasted salt. The day promised to be hot. I must find water.

Intense and glowing as if just taken from the forge, the sky took on the colour of shimmering steel. Not far off the road I found a shallow pool. Scooping up the brackish water greedily, I drank my fill, then casting some over my head, allowed it to trickle through my hair and down my neck. The fierce heat made me drowsy. Crawling into the shade of a huge tree, I bundled up my cloak and lay down. Around me stillness gathered. No breeze stirred the leaves; no bird sang; no insect hummed. I closed my eyes against the fractured glare that pierced the branches.

A clap of thunder woke me to awful darkness. A brooding tension, taut as a bowstring, quivered in the air. Ominous thunder rolled. Momentarily, I shrank against the tree-trunk pressing my face into its bark but the uncanny atmosphere drove me to action.

Wrapping my cloak around my head and shoulders, I ran towards the road, desperate for some sign of human life. Lightning tore across the clouds in a jagged cut briefly illuminating the countryside in silver. Forced to a standstill, I cowered under another ear-bursting crack. Its echo scarce died away before another shaft of lightning blinded me.

Fat drops of rain began to fall. Plopping and bouncing, increasing in speed and strength, the deluge quickly turned me into a sodden creature. Blundering ahead, I barely made out the wagons clustered like circled sheep against the road-side. Some stocky horses huddled against a hedge, draggled heads hung in stubborn misery.

Boldly, I approached the wagons.

Faces loomed before me; faces young and old; faces neither friendly nor hostile; dark, foreign faces, openly curious.

An old woman leaned down. Her eyes gleamed smoky-dark, her smile enigmatic. She seemed somehow familiar. When she reached out a scrawny arm, I took it without a second thought. For her years she proved surprisingly strong. She hoisted me up into the wagon and those around her drew back a little to allow me space. I sat a moment, dripping and panting while the dark faces watched as if I were a rare wild beast which might at any moment spring upon one of them and tear him to pieces.

Lightning flashed. Under the wagon, an old, grey dog, crouched against the wheel, began to whine. I murmured my thanks, but the woman touched my arm so softly the words died into silence. So we sat, mute and immobile, while the rain fell in long needles and pools of water gathered in the grass.

"I've been waiting for you," she said at last. "Welcome."

Behind her, I heard a collective sigh and knew some important step had just been taken.

Chapter Thirty-four

How did Mara recognise in me the strange ability Brother Brian called the Sight? I hadn't been an hour in her company before she asked me about it. While rain tumbled from an angry sky I sat in the shelter of the wagon recalling the days of my childhood, telling her how I'd come to realise I was different from others, an outsider in my own village. And Mara listened. Something in her silence encouraged confidence and I saw myself back in the chapel after Mass and eight years old again.

"My mother sent me to the priest for telling lies. But they weren't lies. I saw spirits ever since I can remember. I thought everyone saw them. Only Brother Brian believed me, and he told me I'd been chosen for some special purpose—" Tears choked off my words for I'd had no news of the priest since I'd written my letter. In my mind I saw suddenly the dust kicked by cantering hooves, the jouncing leather saddle-bag by the rider's heels.

Mara's hand touched my wrist, light as the brush of a leaf. "The messenger travels a long road," she said, as if she could see my thoughts. "But there are many stopping places and many hands exchange the contents of his pouch. There are eyes greedy to read, but take heart, for the letter will reach its destination."

"But how will he find me?" I cried out. "How will he know where I am?"

"How does the bird know the way to fly home?" Her eyes stared deep into mine, so my fright ebbed away under their calm, liquid scrutiny. "Trust is the key to understanding. Now you must trust me to show you the way to interpret your Sight. We'll begin tomorrow."

ഔ

At Mara's feet, the candle-flame cast a flickering light over the smooth surface of the crystal. In it, darts of fire trembled blue, green and purple. I screwed up my eyes in an effort to search its core. For a while it seemed shadows moved, but when I realised this was only a trick of reflected light I shook my head in frustration.

"It's not the way I see."

Mara laughed huskily. Looking up, her dark eyes sparkled with amusement as if watching a babe trying to stand for the first time.

"There's no way better than another," she said in her deep voice. "In time you'll learn to see this way."

"Is it important?" Her lazy reaction to my failure puzzled me.

She shrugged her shoulders, implying no cause for concern.

"Why should I *need* to learn other ways?"

Mara smiled so the deep wrinkles about her eyes gaped like cracks in the dry earth. Leaning back, she regarded me with patient tolerance. "Your natural skill is a thing unpolished." She waved her hands as if to catch an explanation. "It's like rough stone. If you want to learn to control such a gift, you must look deeper. The true drabardi must interpret the meaning of what she sees. You've a good inner eye, but things come to you as—" She waved her hands again. "They happen without warning. I can teach you how to catch the pictures and open the door to that inner world where true wisdom lies waiting."

Her strangely accented words flowed over me like the sonorous voice of a river. Captured by her promise to teach me to understand what it meant to be a seer, I turned again to look into the crystal.

"No more today." She wrapped black fabric around it. Seeing my disappointment, she laughed again and patted my hand. "Tomorrow we'll look again and I'll teach you how to use the cards. You must learn quickly, for our time together will be brief."

Taking my face in one gnarled, brown hand, she smoothed back my hair with the other. Her black eyes probed deep into mine. "You've a long road to travel, child," she said. "Sometimes the way will be hard. There'll be heavy burdens to carry and promises to keep. You'll have joys too, but like the wings of the swallow, they move swiftly, and can't be held captive. When the stones cause you to stumble, remember the path has already been chosen. The inner voice will guide your steps. Many will seek your help, for you'll be a keeper of secrets."

I opened my mouth in shock—Hadn't Mistress Evans told me this too? I began to tell Mara how I came to be travelling alone, the events that prompted my flight, but she placed a finger on my lips in the old signal for silence. "No need," she said, nodding her head sagely. For a moment our eyes locked and I felt as if she'd looked into me and read all there was to know.

"You think me a crazy old woman, but you'll remember my words one day and know I've spoken truth. You must learn the ways of the Roma, for among my people those who walk with the spirits have an honoured place. We are just travellers, and you must join us on the journey a while. With my people you'll be safe. By the time we reach the city you'll have made some important decisions and be ready to move on to the next stage of pilgrimage. Sleep now."

She blew out the candle and the shelter plunged into darkness. As I hugged my blanket around me, I made out the distant glow of the camp-fire. For the first time in months I no longer felt alone. Perhaps this sense of kinship arose because these people were outsiders too. They owned no dwelling place, bore no allegiance to anyone outside their own tribe. Noisy, lively and quarrelsome, they delighted in danger and scorned those in authority. Though I'd feared arrest for vagrancy, they showed no such anxiety. They were accustomed to persecution.

Certainly they aroused curiosity wherever they went for their ways and customs were very different from ours.

"We are the Roma," Luri said as we sat by the camp-fire. Pride shone in his swarthy face. "We have our own laws, our own rules. We are family. We keep together and defend our own people. We stay apart from the gaujo."

"Gaujo?"

Luri laughed showing white teeth. "You are gaujo," he said. It's the name for people who are not Roma."

My acceptance within their community I owed to Mara, for whilst Luri was their leader, she enjoyed the status of an elder. I felt surprised, and strangely moved that she had chosen to train me, as one might an apprentice, in the ancient arts.

"Mara is the Puri Dye, the old mother," Luri told me. "Very special. Listen to her wisdom."

"Wolfsbane," Shangula said, thrusting the flame-coloured flowers so close to my face I flinched. She grinned mischievously. "For bruises," she explained, dropping the daisy-like blooms into the cloth bag she carried around her waist. Mara had entrusted her to teach me the various uses of plants and herbs. Beyond us, at the edge of the woodland, Akasha gathered the leaves of a tall dark plant, smiling as if mulling over a secret.

"What's this?" I knew the woolly, hoof-shaped leaves for coltsfoot and the Roma used them to soothe coughs and diseases of the chest but I tried anxiously to distract Shangula. The two young women could not long be together without enmity. Shangula provoked Akasha for she thought her a rival. Both possessed a fiery beauty, but Shangula's sharpest weapon proved her quick-witted malice.

"Coltsfoot." She spat the answer. No one fooled her easily. Sly amusement danced in her black eyes. "Yon skinny crow will need a potent brew if she wants to keep Dev's attention for much longer." She nodded in Akasha's direction.

I rolled the coltsfoot leaves without speaking. Dev, Akasha's man, was well-noted for his roving eye. As he moved around the camp, Akasha watched him closely, her vigilance betraying her anxiety, reminding me of poor Eleanor's devotion to the king.

Dev seemed much taken with Duka, Luri's daughter, a shy fawn of a girl, no more than fifteen, but with a delicate quality that drew men to her. Every evening Dev lingered by her father's cart, and though he feigned interest in Luri's words, all the womenfolk saw how his eyes followed Duka.

"Duka's young and pretty. Yesterday I saw Dev helping her gather firewood,"

Shangula said just loud enough for Akasha to hear.

"It's a shame you've no man to fetch and carry for you, Shangula," Akasha said. She threw back her raven hair, her lovely features distorted by a sneer. "Then you wouldn't be so envious of others."

"Why choose one when many wait in attendance? It's the timid creature that fears to walk alone." Shangula taunted with a wicked smile. "The tamed hinds herd together, while the stag seeks out the youngest and most beautiful from those just out of reach."

"Mara asked me to find some borage. Can you help me?" I moved close to Akasha. The pain in her eyes told me Shangula's spiteful comments had found their mark.

"I'll show you where it grows."

As we moved away under the shadow of the trees, Shangula called after us. "If it's something to ease the heart that's needed, I've some lovage."

Amongst the Roma, this herb is made into a love potion to arouse the affections of any man who has lost interest in his lover.

"Perhaps you should keep it for yourself, Shangula," I said ingenuously, "for I think Mara has no longer any desire for a lover."

Shangula's laughter rang scornful but I knew she wouldn't bear me a lasting grudge. I had Mara's protection and goodwill.

∽∾

"Everyone must work, no matter their age," Mara told me, when I returned with the herbs. She pointed to the women and children weaving baskets from osiers, the men carving and fashioning tools. "We'll sell these at markets to buy food or things we need. Any money left is given to me for safe keeping."

"How did you become travellers?" I watched her divide the herbs into smaller bags.

"Travelling is the Roma way of life," she replied, sniffing the borage. "We rarely stay more than a few days in one place. The stories say we left our homeland in search of a lost dream of peace. We follow the way of the wind, and are carried like leaves from place to place. We harm no one and return at last to the earth, just as old leaves fall and make way for new."

"Outsiders call us Egyptians," said Shangula. She sat beside us braiding her shining hair. "No one knows if this is where our people truly began."

"I've travelled many roads." Mara handed me some acorns. "Even as a baby I travelled. I saw many places, France, Italy, Spain —And I was taught respect for nature, to take only what is needed. The herbs and plants you've gathered today will make medicines and charms. The Roma believe the earth offers her fruit to everyone."

Each morning we took to the road on foot or in carts drawn by stout horses, and at nightfall built camps at the roadside or in the woodland. Mara showed me how to make a fire, while the men built dome-shaped shelters from twisted hazel branches which they covered with blankets for the night.

In the villages, the men entertained with displays of tumbling while the women, flamboyant in their long coloured skirts and tinkling jewellery, danced with a wild stamping and clapping that made the heart race. Their dark-skinned, "foreign" appearance and colourful, strangely fashioned garments always attracted much attention. Though the villagers often stood in hostile clusters, clearly under an unwilling enchantment, they gaped curiously at these brightly dressed strangers who spoke in an outlandish tongue. It brought some interest to their dull, plodding lives. Only the children would gather eagerly to devour the spectacle of tumblers and dancers leaping and twisting in a whirl of rainbow magic.

Once, when Praba stooped to gather the scattered coins and bow his thanks, the watchers drew back and crossed themselves, frightened by the white smile in his dark face. Fascinated by his garish clothes, a tiny girl crept forward. When she reached out a hand to touch him, her mother snatched her away.

"Tell your fortune, lady?" Mara asked in her husky voice.

The woman shrank back, holding the child against her.

"Want to know about the man with only one hand?"

Gasping, the woman crossed herself.

"No need to be afraid, lady," said Mara gently. "The miller don't forget his promise to you—"

Stifling a sob, the woman picked up the child and ran, while around Mara the other villagers stood open-mouthed.

"How did you know about Seb's hand?" asked a greasy woman.

Mara smiled impishly. "Same way I know about the baby boy you lost in autumn." She stared directly into the woman's frightened eyes.

"Tell me what you see for me," a rough male voice commanded.

Mara turned slowly holding out her hand. "Give me a coin, then, sir," she answered in a wheedling tone. "I'll tell you what you most desire to know."

This first time I saw Mara use her gift to tell fortunes, I marvelled at her skill and audacity.

"Don't you fear being accused of witchcraft?"

"I do this to earn a few coins now I can no longer lift my skirts in the dance," she answered with a laugh. "It's just nonsense to entertain the needy ones. It needs no skill such as you and I possess."

"But they understand you. And they'll tell tales. Aren't you afraid of punishment? And are all the fortunes you tell mere nonsense?"

Mara's eyes grew misty with remembering. "Once on Astwith Gorse, I saw a special one. Oh, but she was a fine lady, not like these peasants. I'll not meet with such a one again."

"Who was this maid? What did you see for her?"

"She was no maid," Mara's dark eyes gleamed. "She was a woman men would die for."

Something in her black eyes puzzled me.

"Tell me more."

Laughing softly, Mara took my hand. "I told her she'd wed a royal prince. Destiny had chosen her for greatness."

"Did she believe you?"

"It pleased her much. I remember she turned to her friends with such pride they treated her with mock homage. It was sport to them but not for her. She believed it. I saw it in her face."

"But was there more?"

I knew it, for Mara's eyes shone bleak.

"I told her she would know grief beyond all imagining. Oh, I saw her recoil then like a little bird from the shadow of the hawk's beak. I knew by that she'd already chosen her path. I saw darkness in her and I was afraid."

"What did you see?" I asked in a whisper, my flesh crawling.

"Terrible, unspeakable things. How could I reveal them? 'Troubles dire will fall upon your head,' I told her. It was enough." Mara trembled. She'd forgotten my presence in re-living the past. "She steeled herself as if for a blow. I couldn't stop. "Your beauty and your fame will continue beyond death," I said, "for bone of your bone will join three great houses in one."

"Who was she?"

"You've no need to ask." I shivered then under the scrutiny of her ancient eyes. "You can uncover such secrets yourself. Besides, you must remind her of the message one day. I'll be with you when you speak to her."

She wouldn't say more of this though I asked often. "Soon enough when the time comes, child."

Chapter Thirty-five

"Great changes." Mara turned over the card. I leaned forward to study the image of a wheel rolling with outlandish figures clinging to its rim. Seated upon a kind of pedestal, a crowned, winged creature clutched a sword. "The wheel of fortune," she said in her husky tones. "Our lives turn within it. Our destinies are carried in the spokes. All is ordained. As the wheel moves, so our lives change. One moment we rise, in another we fall. As light and dark, so fortune and misfortune are linked."

With bated breath, I watched her take up the next card from the pile I'd shuffled, according to her instructions. This time, her face assumed a puzzled expression as she laid the card crosswise upon the first. I leaned forward, too eager to remain silent.

"What is it?" I studied the play of light and shade across her features in the mysterious candle-light.

A man in a curious hat stood behind a table on which lay several objects, a knife, a cup, coins and dice. "The juggler." Mara pointed to the rod he held. "The wand is power but he turns his face away. Before him lie the instruments of his greatness, but he doesn't notice them. Many things are within his grasp but he looks without seeing and so wastes his talent." She raised her eyes to look at me gravely. Shaken, I sensed the importance of this moment. It was as if she has seen into the core of me and found a void. "Such gifts as you possess should not be wasted. You must be bold. The way is hazardous, but you've the skill to take it. The juggler's a master of disguise. You, too, must wear a mask for your enterprise is couched in secrecy."

The third card revealed the faded picture of a monkish figure holding a lamp, as if he embarked upon a pilgrimage. "Brother

Brian," I said involuntarily, and Mara's glance grew piercing sharp.

"The hermit travels through darkness, but see how his face turns towards the past. He is alone and has learned wisdom through harsh experience. You must learn, child, to turn away from the past, and look to the future. Like the hermit, you've walked alone but you've yet to reach true understanding. The past is gone, but the future waits. You have a promise to fulfil. You must meet it with fortitude."

Over the weeks we travelled together, I became familiar with these strange devices—swords, pentacles, wands and cups. In the faint candle light, I studied again the pictures that seemed to dance as if within some stately promenade. The Hanged Man grinned at me as he swung from his gibbet; the Devil leered and twisted the chained slaves at his feet; the Hermit shuffled into the unknown, and beyond the ring of light, other images pointed toward the mystery of the future. But the past clamoured for my attention, and I listened, spell-bound, as Mara unravelled it, her dark voice probing secrets that had long lain hidden. The moments spilled like coloured beads, and I saw events painted in fresh, vibrant colours as if I stood amidst them for the first time. The Knave of Swords stared up at me lasciviously and I felt a lurch of desire in the pit of my belly. Close by, the King of Cups looked beyond earthly matters with a world-weary gaze that brought tears stinging behind my eyes.

"You must look forward," Mara reminded me. "The experiences of the past are but lessons to prepare us for the future. You have an important task to fulfil."

I thought then of the boys who'd haunted my dreams since childhood.

"The child is precious," said Mara, as if she'd read my thoughts. "You must save him."

When I opened my mouth to ask more, she pressed her finger to it. "Not yet," she said. "You must find the father first."

❧

"Among the Rom it is called dukkering."

Mara's husky voice growled warm and mellow, in the dregs of the day. We sat with our backs against the cart, luxuriating in drowsy companionship as the last tatters of sunlight faded. Tracing the fine lines across my palm, she instructed me to note their names—life, head, heart, fate—pointing to where they met or crossed like spider threads. "Each hand is different." I peered at the tiny marks. What mystery lurked in this delicate tracery? Was it really possible to read a life from such a fractured pattern?

Mara grasped both my wrists and nodded, as she thrust the upturned palms towards my face. "Left hand is for the fate chosen at birth, and right for the ways in which you meet it."

"Can I change my fate?"

Mara laughed her familiar husky laugh. "No man can change his fate. Each man meets his destiny according to his own choice."

"That doesn't make sense. If we can choose, then we can alter our fate as we wish."

"No." Mara's face grew sombre. "Our fates are written. No matter where we run, whatever path we take, however far we travel, wherever we may hide, our destiny leads us willingly or unwillingly to the same end. There's no escape."

"Then what are we to do? Do we just sit and wait for things to happen?"

"No, we are travellers and must face the hazards of the journey with a purpose."

She called Akasha from feeding twigs into a pile of brushwood being built for the evening cooking fire. The young woman crouched at her feet.

"Give Nan your hand." Without a word Akasha placed it, palm upward into mine. I allowed the lines to take me on their intricate journey and found myself unfolding Akasha's past with growing confidence. The pictures spun me forward—I chased them eagerly until—

A gasp of horror forced me to confront Akasha's expectant gaze. A bruise, like a purple flower, bloomed upon her cheekbone, and another angry weal lurked at the corner of her swollen mouth. More shocking than these ugly wounds gleamed the look of acceptance in her eyes.

"Akasha knows," Mara said. "Nothing you say can hurt her more."

"But she can't, mustn't—" Emotion strangled my voice.

"No man or woman can escape destiny."

Akasha smiled up at me with such tender resignation I felt shamed.

Death by sudden violence, death at the hands of strangers, early death and a child left lonely by the roadside. How could she accept such a future with a smile?

"Shangula will take the child," I said. "He'll be a joy and consolation to her in her solitude." Gratitude shone in her eyes. "He'll grow up strong, a man of worth among his people. He'll be loved. His children will be many."

Through the shimmer of her unshed tears, I read relief and satisfaction.

"Akasha was stoned yesterday in the village." Mara gestured to the bruises. "The Rom are not always welcome visitors."

I stared at my own hands as if afraid to read what lay ahead.

"Sometimes we must conceal what we see, for some are not strong enough to face the fate. As you grow older, you'll learn what to open and what to wrap in darkness. Many will call upon your wisdom to guide their steps. You must guard your tongue lest it leads you into grave danger." Mara closed my fingers and took my fists in her own strong grip. "You've such a long road to travel, child. Already you have a purpose. Be sure to see it to its end."

༄

Thin fingers of light stretched across the black arch of the sky when we heard the mewling cry of the child.

"Kamala's babe is born!"

Shangula's voice broke the tension. We rose at once, chattering like jays. Someone passed me a cup and I drank the hot spicy liquid, scalding my mouth. I coughed until tears filled my eyes.

Mara melted away into the shadows. I knew she would go back to her charts. We'd awaited this birth anxiously for it was Kamala's first child.

Pulling my shawl around me, I stamped my feet against the cold. Stars still hung like twinkling jewels above us. I tried to make out the constellations Mara had taken such pains to point out to me and wondered what the future might hold for the new baby.

"Our fortunes are written in the heavens," Mara told me. She stretched out her bony fingers to the smattering of stars across the

200

skies. "The pattern changes with the seasons. Each constellation has its reign, just as a king rules his people for a span, and those born under such and such a star, will share its spirit."

"I can't see how the rising of a star might have any bearing on a human life. You told me our fates were written in the lines on our hands, and now you tell me the pattern of the stars shapes our destinies."

"Oh child," murmured Mara, laughing and squeezing my hand, "what wondrous doubts you have. How I love the way you mock me with your unbelief. But I'll show you how the stars form their own pathways across the heavens, pathways that echo the fate that lies in the lines of every hand."

She taught me names and told stories of the lights that speckle the night sky. Then she showed me how to plot the charts of a nativity. "Each chart must be carefully prepared. At the very moment of conception, fate is written in the position of the stars in the heavens. Each birth chart is quite different, for no two men are alike in every detail. The time and place of birth is also most important, for at the first cry, the first gulp of air an infant takes, its fate is sealed within a cosmic moment." She looked deep into my eyes. "One day, you'll remember my words, as you hold a new-born in your arms."

"It's a boy," said Kamala's mother-in-law. Her black eyes sparkled with pride. A boy was the best gift of all, for a boy ensured the continuation of the tribe. One by one we knelt like worshippers to admire the new-born. Shangula lifted one of the spidery hands and sighed as the tiny fingers curled about her own. This sigh was echoed by the other women. Again I felt that surge of love. How I envied Kamala her babe. Homage made, I crept away into the ghostly grey of the morning to where Mara sat hunched over her chart.

"So, what destiny map have the stars drawn for Kamala's babe?" I asked, eager to learn the skill that I would one day use, myself.

⁀ℐ⌒

Greedy flames licked the woodwork. The crackle and fall of burning timber, the whoosh of scattered ash and the plaintive song of the young men haunted us, as we stood in huddled groups watching the pyre. It seemed to me the sob and wail of the mourners increased as the hungry fire became a roar, engulfing the cart in vermillion splendour. In spite of the heat, I shivered. Mara handed me a cup, and I gulped the hot liquid gratefully. It burned in my throat bringing tears to my eyes. The familiar taste reminded me of the morning we'd celebrated the birth of Kamala's child just a month before. This time we drank to Keshav's passing.

Shama began to howl as the men broke the cooking vessels and destroyed Keshav's belongings. Dev cut the dog's throat swiftly, while the horses stamped, their eyes rolling white, their nostrils quivering at the smell of fire and death. Mara touched my arm. We withdrew, leaving the white-clad mourners to join in the crescendo of grief as the last pieces of Keshav's life were eliminated.

"Why did Dev kill the dog?"

"The Rom believe the dead have need of their possessions upon the spirit path. In life, a dog is a guard and a protector. In death, it may walk with its master and be a guide."

"Do you believe this?"

"Have you learned so little of my beliefs, child? All this time I've taught you how to unlock the secrets of the spirit world, and you ask me such a question! The dead may speak to us in dreams or visions; they may walk with us on our journeys; they may depart into the distant realms of light and dark; they may return in newer forms to walk the earth. There are many pathways they may choose."

"But I don't understand why you mustn't speak a person's name after he's dead," I persisted. "To wipe someone from memory seems cruel and wrong."

"No one is ever wiped from the memory. Those we love are locked forever in our hearts, but to speak out a name is to call back one who has departed, and that too may be unkind. Only the drabardi may call out to the dead, and only then when it is absolutely necessary." Again she looked at me long and hard. "One day you'll be forced to call upon the spirits to bring you guidance. They'll hear you. The wise man's love may cross between the two worlds. The sacrifice will seek vengeance. But such events are uncommon. The dead return as and when they must. You know this. It's not for us to disturb them."

She put a finger on my lips to silence me. "Yours is a thorny road, but love is never wasted or forgotten. You'll dance at a wedding."

I wanted to speak of the black-haired stranger then, but she put her finger to her own lips. "Don't ask," she said.

"But I dream of him constantly." The admission brought the hot blood into my cheeks. "I want to find him."

"He also dreams," she answered.

She bade me lay out the cards, imperious as an ancient queen. Darkness spiralled like smoke around the tall arrow-head of the candle-flame. Taut as the hare on the edge of a danger it cannot flee, I crouched over the painted images.

"When the strong man takes you upon a new journey, you'll begin to understand your dreams at last. I see a sword, and the naked blade is turned against two children. A terrible order is given. The parchment is signed and sealed by a woman's hand. Because of it much blood will flow and there'll be great weeping. Such deeds cannot remain hidden. When the sun stands in the noontime of the year there'll be a reckoning. Other innocents will be sacrificed. She who sows tears, will harvest sorrow."

A terrible premonition of my own part in this great catastrophe flooded my mind. Darkness threatened to engulf me. "But I've set the wheel in motion," I cried out.

"No!" Mara was implacable. "The wheel turns of its own volition. Those who remain in its pathway are merely caught up in its spokes. Sometimes you can do nothing but watch. This is the seer's burden. I told you it wouldn't be easy."

"But how then can I save the children?" I cried out in desperation, terrified by the seeming futility of my actions.

"Follow your purpose," replied Mara without hesitation. "Trust the visions and do what you must. Even the assassin requires love. Rejoice that you've been shown the way. Learn from both success and failure. Above all, remember that birth and death are written and unalterable. Nothing is ever left to chance."

"I don't understand," I said, my head aching with confusion.

Mara's hand touched my brow, cool and soothing. "Be patient," she said softly. "Learn all you can, daughter, for you'll need all the skills you can muster. This is why I share my wisdom with you. Sometimes the seer is merely the messenger. But you're more than this. Though your purpose is clear, warnings may often be disregarded—even our own desires may be thwarted—remember this when the widow rejects your service." Though I begged her to explain, she'd say no more. We were within days of London. Mara called young Durga into the wagon to meet me.

"You'll never find all those lost children," Durga said, her tight serious little face fixed upon mine.

"Lost children? What lost children?"

"The little boys," she said, with a hint of scorn.

"The boys? Where are they? How can I find them? I must help them."

She muttered something to Mara in her own tongue.

"She says they're not yet born," answered Mara.

The girl watched me with the intensity of a stoat. At no more than seven summers, Durga already had the seer's gift. Mara had singled her out from among the children to train in the arts of "dukkering." Already she'd learned to scry using a shallow dish of inky water.

"Durga says you'll touch upon a special child one day. Such children are precious gifts given only for a short space for us to cherish so we may glimpse perfection."

"The least wanted in the great house will command the direction of your foot-steps and the black-haired man waits in the shadows," said Durga. "Save one child and lose all."

I wanted to ask her more, but Mara put a hand upon my arm.

"You mustn't look for answers now," she said. "Durga has dreamed of swallows. She tells me we must soon leave this place. The cold wind begins to blow and it'll be unwise to linger."

Puzzled, I stared at her. Could a child's dreaming change important plans in a moment? "Luri said you'd stay in the city throughout the winter."

The child ignored us, engrossed in laying out the pack of painted cards.

"I know, but dreams must be heeded." Mara watched the girl deftly weaving the mysterious pictures into a pattern of her own devising. "They bring portents the seer must interpret. Durga's had the same dream three times and now she's sure of its meaning."

"And that is to travel?"

Mara nodded, her attention fixed on the fall of the cards.

"But what if you choose to ignore her advice?"

"To do so would be foolish."

I snorted with exasperation.

She smiled, shaking her head at me in that indulgent fashion I'd come to know so well. "Ever the doubter, and yet I've taught you to search your own dreams for instruction. Durga wouldn't bid us travel on during the hardest of all seasons if she didn't believe it necessary. What she lacks in years, she makes up for in understanding. You'll see."

Durga held up the Knight of Wands.

"What does this mean?" she asked suddenly, her manner shockingly un-childlike.

"Sudden flight and separation," answered Mara.

The child laid the card in my lap. "I give this to you," she said, her gaze pitiless. Then she began to sing in her shrill child's voice. The words were alien, but the plaintive melody spoke to me of loneliness and exile.

Mara pointed ahead. "Look where the city towers rise up before us. By nightfall we'll be in London."

Part four

London
1464

Chapter Thirty-Six

"Go now!"

Shangula thrust me back so I couldn't see Mara. When I tried to approach, she snarled, cursing in the language of the Rom so savagely, spittle flew from her mouth.

"I want to help!"

Around us, stunned bystanders watched and I sensed their anticipation. They lusted for further bloodshed.

I knelt in the filth where Mara struggled to rise. A scarlet thread ran from a corner of her mouth. She clutched at her chest. Even while Shangula tried to drag me away, the old woman pushed something into my hands.

"We don't need your help." Shangula wrenched at my arms. "Don't you see what your people do to us? Leave us alone!"

Through her pain, Mara smiled and nodded. "Go, child— Remember, find the black-haired man and he'll lead you to the children—Go now—"

This instruction spurred me to action. Blind with tears, I burst through the array of stubborn ruffians. Someone threw a clod but I dodged into a coiling alley-way.

Finding myself in quieter streets at last, I pulled my shawl over my head to disguise my dishevelled appearance, and after climbing some steep steps, hid briefly in the shadowy peace of a church. As the hammering of my heart stilled, I saw again and again the terrible pictures of the day's events.

Three days we'd stayed in London. Three days we'd enjoyed the patronage of the crowds.

"Egyptians!"

The word buzzed through the city, drawing people to us like eager moths.

They marvelled as we danced, whirling bright colours, and sang strange, rhythmic music. Scarlet and gold, vermillion, ochre, amber, and sapphire, the shocking garments dazzled and bewitched. The drums pulsed. As Luri plucked the strings of the strange bulb-shaped instrument, the wailing sound pleaded like unfulfilled desire. Caught like insects in the spider's gossamer, the spectators sighed and groaned, held by the magic of the music, the kaleidoscope of colour.

And while they gazed, Mara and Durga and I moved among them, cajoling coins in exchange for words of wonder, telling secrets of the past and future, while Shangula sold them packages of herbs to cure the ague or to capture the heart.

Three days we entertained them, spun them tales of exotic lands and peoples, but on the fourth—

"Thief!"

A red-faced, bull of a man seized Akasha by the hair. She screamed, twisting to shake free, but he wrenched her head back so cruelly I thought he'd snap her neck.

"I felt her hand upon my purse!" he roared at the fascinated crowd. "Now it's gone. I'll wager she has it about her somewhere!"

He fumbled at her breasts, ripping at her clothes. The crowd surged forward. Above the clamour, I heard the ribald jests.

Dev fought his way through the press of bodies. Behind him Luri howled. The crowd became a mob that battered and trampled. Jabbed aside, I snatched at figures in a struggle to maintain my balance, and met with elbows, fists and nails. Briefly, I glimpsed the torn face of Akasha. Her eyes gleamed wild, the whites turned upward like those of a maddened horse.

Someone threw stones. I shrank from the whistle and thud, the high shrieks of pain. Pitiless in my desire to escape, I thrust myself against all those who obstructed me, forcing them to give way.

Someone tugged at my arm.

"Mara!"

Durga's bloody face confronted me. Her eyes glowed like tempered steel. She dragged me to where Shangula knelt by the old woman. Shangula, tangled hair about her face like a lion's mane, roared curses.

Shangula drove me away. I knew then there could be no turning back. No longer part of the Rom, I must travel alone as Mara had taught me. I quickened my pace and the city streets grew familiar. Soon I stood in Forster Lane with its shops full of bright Venetian glass. Purposefully, I walked towards the Chepe.

⁂

Standing by the steps, the open bake-house door wafting its familiar mouth-watering fragrances, Margaret Mercer, smaller than I remembered in a charcoal, woollen gown, eyed me with a quizzical expression.

"Well, I never expected to see you!"

Surprised by the wariness of her manner, I hesitated.

"You'd best come in."

She moved back a step as if to allow me passage to the living quarters above the shop but the lack of warmth in this welcome made me awkward. I stood smiling uncertainly, conscious of the hum of voices from below.

"I couldn't wait to get here," I said at last.

"You've certainly kept us talking these last months." Her keen gaze travelled over my gaudy, thread-bare garments. "I don't know where you've been, but we've had no end of folk enquiring after you."

"People asking after me?"

Her shrewd appraisal unnerved me almost as much as her words.

"Aye, men from Bishop Stillington's household—saying he was anxious to speak to you. Hal told them you were still in the Butler wench's employ as far as we knew, and that we'd heard she'd gone to Norfolk."

"*Bishop* Stillington?"

"Aye, Bishop of Bath and Wells. King Edward appointed him so just after the Wydeville wench was proclaimed queen. Where've you been hiding, Nan? Didn't you hear any news?"

She waited then, her eyes steady on my face.

"We heard little in Norwich," I answered, vague with shock. "The sisters have turned their backs on the world—" A wave of unease passed through me with sudden violence. Why had King

Edward shown Stillington such a mark of favour? Conscious then of Margaret Mercer's relentless gaze, I began to bluster. "But why would Bishop Stillington want to speak to me?" Feigning astonishment, I tried to hide the stab of fear that set my belly lurching. "When he knew I was with Dame Eleanor?"

"Why, indeed." Time had whitened much of her hair and etched more lines into her face, but her mind moved as astute as ever. Her unblinking eyes probed mine. "Only last week another came hunting you—telling us you'd disappeared. We were so worried then—"

"I thought I knew that voice!" Someone seized me from behind and caught me in a warm, flour-dusty embrace. "I was just finishing in the bake-house—How long have you been here?"

Grateful for the interruption, and remembering how I'd parted from Harry in anger, I hugged him hard. "I'm sorry I—"

"No tears." He squeezed my shoulders and steered me up towards the living quarters. "We're overjoyed to have you back, aren't we, Mother?"

"I was telling her, we began to think we shouldn't see her again," Mistress Mercer wheezed, plodding behind us on the stairs.

Settled by a cheerful fire, I fed my listeners with a tortuous tale of my travels, although I took care not to mention the Roma.

"Fancy Dame Eleanor taking the veil!" Meg gasped. "And then to die so young!"

"She took a fever." I swallowed sweet wine, hoping they wouldn't ask too many questions. The news of Stillington's advancement still rankled. "They wanted to make a nun of me too," I said with a shudder. "But I told Sister Ursula I'd family in London." Looking round at their homely faces, I smiled in genuine pleasure. "I couldn't wait to see you all again."

"And there are more of us to meet now." Big Hal beamed. "Meg and Harry named their little girl Nancy for you." He turned to include his wife in this delightful piece of news but her wrinkled face remained inscrutable. I wondered then how much she believed of my story and what had made her so suspicious of me.

At supper I met my namesake, a winsome child with russet curls, who took a great fancy to me. While Meg chattered of Aunt Grace selling the tannery after Uncle Will's death and moving to Dorset to be with Sarah and Walt, Nancy sat on my lap stealing morsels of food from my dish—an indulgence which made Margaret Mercer raise her bushy eyebrows in mock reproof.

"And Judith?"

"Has a little boy—with red hair just as you predicted."

Meg's careless words sparked a sudden, uncomfortable silence. The fortune-telling incident returned to taunt me then, and I wondered how much she'd told the Mercers.

"Has anyone seen Brother Brian?" My innocent query produced another strange effect.

Big Hal coughed. "A friar came looking for you, not long after you'd gone to Norfolk." He avoided my eyes, his awkward delivery suggesting embarrassment. He cast sheepish glances at the others. "He told us your priest had gone into a monastery up north." Again he paused to clear his throat. "There's some scandal about him and a young scholar getting over-fond of one another."

"I hope you won't mind sleeping in the attic." Mistress Mercer's strained voice cut short the conversation. With a nod at Harry, she ushered me upstairs to the old chamber I'd once shared with Philippa. Fidgeting uncomfortably, I pretended interest in the furnishings, the newly painted walls and velvet hangings.

"Remember this?" Harry picked up a wooden creature from the shelf.

"My little horse! Oh thank you, Harry!" I flung my arms about him. "What a crosspatch I was for leaving him behind."

"And here's the companion I promised." Blushing, he indicated another, more skilfully executed.

Mistress Mercer eyed me pertinently. "No one likes this chamber much," she said. "Marian complained she had bad dreams and wouldn't sleep in it after she saw something on the stairs just outside—"

My cheeks flamed. "Perhaps she heard some tale from Philippa," I answered, arranging my little horses on the shelf in an attempt to divert her.

"You can help with the deliveries tomorrow," said Harry, without consulting his mother.

Still breathing hard from the steep climb upstairs, the stout matron gave him a sharp look. "Aye, I've no doubt she's anxious to acquaint herself with the city again."

Outside in the street next morning, he tipped me a sly wink. "You've not told us much about your time in Norwich, Nan.

There's some secret or other about that affair, I'm certain. You've never been much good at lying. Mother's got the scent of it, I warn you!"

Wary of listeners, I glanced about me. "I've good reason to keep quiet," I answered. "There are some things I can't tell you—at least, not yet. But I truly need your help. I'm looking for someone and it's very important I find him soon. He's in the Duchess of York's household."

"Ah, it's a he, is it?" Harry's eyes twinkled. He drew me round the corner. "I thought as much. And in a noble house, eh?"

"You must promise, first, to say nothing to anyone—not even Meg."

Dear Harry. Swearing loyalty, he listened with patient humour as I described the man I must find.

"You saw him in Silver Street among the Duchess's men? And he asked you to meet him in the Boar's Head? But you didn't bother to ask his name?" Harry looked at me in amazement. "Well, I wonder why you're so very keen to find him—" His teasing brought colour to my cheeks. "Tall, black-haired, blue eyes, muscular, strong-looking, northern speech—A fine man for a maid, eh? But it's not much to go on, is it?"

My urgency halted his laughter. "I'd know him anywhere. I must find him, Harry. He's connected with a dream I've had since childhood." I tried to cover my confusion by glancing at the stalls and passing customers. How could I tell him I'd been on the verge of running off with this man and still blushed at the memories he roused?

A solemn Harry confronted me. "Mother says you've Second Sight. She and Aunt Grace gossiped of it often enough. You women are all alike when it comes to spells and potions and fortune telling —can't get enough of it. But it's a dangerous thing—"

"It's not a gift I'd wish on others."

"But this dream—Is it so important you'd risk your life for it?" His unaccustomed gravity alarmed me. "There was a witch hanged in the city only last month—"

Shutting my ears to his warning, I spilled something of my secret. "The lives of two noble boys are in danger. Somehow I have to save them. Don't look like that! It may sound silly, but Brother Brian believes me."

At the mention of the priest's name Harry winced.

"Whatever people think, I trust him absolutely. It's why I wrote to him from Norwich." A group of nuns passed us, reminding me unpleasantly of Sister Absalom. "I wish I knew how to find him. Perhaps I should write to Alan Palmer in Ely?"

His shoulders rigid with anxiety, Harry gave me a hard look. "Perhaps you should." His expression reminded me of his mother then. "And why's this Bishop Stillington so desperate to find you?"

I shook my head vehemently. "Better you know nothing of him," I answered, the memory of the hawk-faced prelate causing my heart to race. "If I can find those boys, I know I can outwit him, too."

"I promise I'll do all I can to help you." Harry made this pledge with such solemnity tears stung my eyes, forcing me to turn away from him.

"I thought Maud might know something—but we'd have to be discreet," I said, adopting a lighter tone. "I don't want her prying —"

"Well, that's a challenge in itself!" He handed me one of his baskets, a mischievous grin back on his face. "No time like the present. Are you ready to face the notorious Mistress Attemore? I'm sure she'll be more than happy to see you and share the latest scandal!"

Though we pretended nonchalance about this enterprise, a sense of dread, like a chilling fog, enveloped me as we headed into the market.

Chapter Thirty-Seven

Though Harry and I searched high and low over the next weeks, we discovered no trace of my black-haired man. Harry tried the Boar's Head in Knightriders Street and even went to Baynard's Castle, the Duchess of York's London residence.

"I spoke to one of the men at arms, but he said the duchess's attendants come and go all the time."

During this turbulent period the Yorkist troops moved constantly. It made enquiries difficult. Of course, when Maud discovered my quest, she teased me mercilessly, reminding me of my pretended disinterest in Warwick's men when we'd watched the parade all those years ago.

"And now you're looking for some knave you glimpsed just for a moment." She gave Harry a bold wink. "It's time we got this wench a husband. How old are you now, Nan? Fifteen? What do you think of the butcher's apprentice for her? When she's a pair of brats to feed, she won't have time to go searching after mysterious black-haired lovers!" Her coarsened features creased with mirth. I was glad when she turned her attention on Harry, for she drew other matrons into her banter and I loathed being the butt of their ribald jokes. "How's that wife of yours?" she asked him. "Her babe must be due any time now?"

"The sooner the better, for her temper's very short these days." Harry assumed a pained expression. "How I suffer for it!"

The inquisitive matrons clucked their sympathy but humour sparkled in their eyes. Maud began some tale of a mild-tempered woman who'd turned into a shrew every time she bore a child. "Ten times her husband had to endure her terrible wrath," she teased. "You've only begun your trials, Master Mercer!"

But the new babe turned out to be a healthy boy, born in the early hours of a bright spring morning and named Will for Meg's father. Big Hal poured us generous measures of fine wine. "Let's drink to the health of a new baker!" He raised his goblet high.

〆

Somewhere close by a horse screamed. Between the ribbons of fog I caught a glimpse of plunging hooves and blood-flecked flanks. Far away, the muffled blare of trumpets signalled danger. But the white web drifted across my eyes, blurring the shifting shapes. Nothing in this landscape seemed familiar. A loathsome sense of isolation overwhelmed me.

Shockingly, unpredictably, arrows fell, whistling and thudding. Staggering blindly about the field I blundered into a savage group of men fighting hand to hand. My head rang with the hollow sound of clanging metal.

"The queen's used her witchcraft." A familiar voice whispered in my ear, insidious, gloating.

I turned to confront its owner but was caught among shadowy figures brandishing murderous weapons—sword, knife, bludgeoning mace.

Groans echoed. Something in their eerie timbre captured my imagination. I knelt in awe while the infernal fog billowed over me, inexorable as waves washing up a beach.

From out the eerie twilight a giant loomed. He rode a monstrous horse and wielded a battle-axe. Nothing could withstand him. Like a human battering ram, he trampled down his enemies. Through his visor I saw the spark of green bale-fire, and knew I was trapped among the damned.

Nearby, a soldier fell. Blood gurgled in his throat. A hand reached out.

"Alys—"

Robin Arrowsmith's tortured face looked up at me. "The Earl of Warwick will be destroyed by witchcraft," he whispered, as if imparting a great secret. "On Easter Sunday the world moves toward destruction. Find Miles—Find Miles—"

〆

That night I woke the household with my shouts. Margaret Mercer drove the others back to their beds and brought me a soothing drink.

"One of your bad dreams?" She hugged her heavy, brocade night-robe about her, sitting close by me on the bed.

Exhausted by my vision, I struggled to speak. "There was a battle. I felt I was in it—lost in fog—and then I saw someone I knew—"

Her face pinched with anxiety, she leaned over me. "What did you see?"

"A great battle at Easter and a hard reckoning—the standard of the bear and ragged staff lying in the mud."

"Warwick." She crossed herself and shivered, her frown growing deeper.

"Events are spinning fast towards an end that will bring a new beginning—" I struggled to remember the things I'd seen, pressing my palms against my eyelids to recapture the ugly pictures. "When green buds burst men will wade in blood. And many flowers must fall. Where men look for sanctuary they'll find none, and the last hope of a great house will be trampled into dust. Two battles in two months and the petals of the red rose scattered on the wind—"

"The badge of Lancaster."

"The battles *will* happen. It'll mark a change in all our fortunes." I looked into her face.

Her own gaze hardened but I knew she believed me. "You've a fine way of telling these visions."

"I met an old wise woman as I travelled from Norfolk." Mara's wrinkled brown face flashed into my mind. I heard her husky laughter. "She taught me how to see clearer, and to interpret the symbols."

"Did she give you the cards?"

Too shocked to speak, I could only stare at her.

"Nancy found them. We were playing a game. She hid her doll in the oak chest where you keep your clothes. She found the cards hidden among your garments. The pictures fascinated her—Don't worry, I wrapped them up and put them back. I told her they weren't playthings."

"The wise woman taught me how to use them to tell fortunes. They were her last gift."

"Fortune-telling's a dangerous pastime." These warning words set me shuddering.

"You're cold," she said, tucking the coverlet about me. "Put these terrible things out of your mind. Such dreams can do no good to anyone."

Heaving herself to her feet, she picked up her taper and shuffled towards the door. Stifling a yawn, she asked, "Tell me, who's Miles? You were calling his name."

∽

"Miles—" a sleep-starved Harry sighed, when I told him next morning on deliveries. "Well, it's a start, I suppose." He'd recently struck up an acquaintanceship with one of the duchess's men in a tavern by Fish Lane. "I'll see what I can find out from Edgar."

I fumed and fretted all day.

"I stopped to see a friend at the The Waterman's Tavern," he said, arriving late for supper. Kissing Nancy, his eyes signalled success.

"Ed says there *was* a Miles Forrest answering your description, but he left to follow Warwick." While Meg put Nancy to bed, Harry joined me in the bake-house, cutting the last of the loaves to divide among the beggars in the morning. "This Forrest's a mercenary of some kind—soldiered in the Low Countries from being a lad—and has a name for being something of a brawler—"

"And?" I knew Harry was keeping something back.

"It seems he has a reputation amongst the ladies too—Ed asked if it was some lass wanting to know his whereabouts—"

"Where's Warwick now?"

"That's a question I can't answer." Harry gave me a rueful grin. "Warwick's quarrelled with King Edward and left London—He's probably gone back north to Middleham."

"Middleham." I rolled the word around, savouring the strange familiarity of the name. "Where's that?"

"Yorkshire." Harry laughed then, stifling his yawns. "I'm not likely to be going there in a hurry, Nan, and nor are you. You'll have to wait until Warwick returns!"

Chapter Thirty-Eight

Under Margaret Mercer's watchful scrutiny, my days fell into a regular pattern, but tension kept me on edge. Once or twice she mentioned Stillington or asked questions about Eleanor that tripped me up. Though she made no reference to the extraordinary dream I'd shared with her or to the fortune-telling cards, I sensed her anxiety. Only out in the streets when I was free of her vigilance, could I speak openly to Harry about my quest, but even he cautioned secrecy.

"The city's not safe these days," he said, as we passed a knot of rogues arguing outside a tavern in Newgate. "You never know who's listening."

On the first day of October, it seemed his warning would prove true. A flood of excited people choked the streets surrounding the Chepe, and several men accosted us with tales of treachery, bloodshed and disaster.

Alarmed, we hurried back to Bread Street, forcing our way into a shop full of rowdy, gesticulating customers.

"What on earth's happening?" Mistress Mercer shouted over their heads. "It's been like this all morning—What's all this about Warwick putting King Henry back on the throne?"

Surrounded by impatient tradesmen, Harry tried to catch his breath. "Well, news in the city has King Edward fleeing to Burgundy yesterday without a penny on him—"

Sudden as a falling axe, the racket ceased. Every face turned on us.

"Maud Attemore's telling a tale of how he had to pay his passage with a marten-fur cloak." I said, breaking the shocked silence. A memory of the handsome king flinging this very cloak about his shoulders brought a vivid image of Eleanor into my mind.

When a wealthy looking man began pestering Harry for information about threatened trade, the babble restarted with increased vigour.

"The French are already dancing in the streets, they say—celebrating the Lancastrian victory."

"Aye, and no doubt King Edward will drag us into a war with them." A florid Big Hal hefted a sack of flour through the door.

"Well, Burgundy's certain to help him get his throne back!" Harry's thoughtless remark to his father roused further consternation.

"But what about the queen? She expects another child at the end of the year. Surely the king didn't leave her behind?"

A tradesman's lewd reply set the men-folk sniggering.

"I blame that Wydeville wench and her greedy family for this trouble," he said. "Ever since the king married her she's had her fingers in his purse!"

"Aye," said a straggle-haired wench, "and what use is that? Nothing but daughters she's whelped, in spite of her French mother using witchcraft to lure him into her bed."

Wincing at the mention of witchcraft, I pushed my way towards the living-quarters.

"No, it's Warwick who's too ambitious." said a richly dressed burgher. "There's been dissent ever since he married his daughter to the king's brother, George."

"Aye, the king forbade that marriage but they went ahead with it—"

"I blame George of Clarence for stirring up this quarrel—"

"There'll be more bloodshed yet—"

The cacophony of male voices followed me up the stairs.

⁓

For days news about Warwick raised feverish commotion throughout the city.

"I can't believe he's joined Queen Margaret," said Harry, arriving home one evening. "Why, he called the woman a "she-wolf"! But I just heard there's a public reception for King Henry and a grand parade through the streets to St Paul's tomorrow."

Big Hal shook his head. "I can't see that poor, feeble-minded soul rousing much sympathy."

"Never mind that," said Mistress Mercer. "Supper'll be on the table in a moment. Is there no bread left?"

While she and Meg fussed over food, I followed Harry down to the bake-house.

"So Warwick's back in London."

Startled, he looked up from the trestle. "You made me jump." Then, handing me a misshapen loaf, he gave me an impish look. "I suppose you want to see the parade?"

"I'm sure Nancy would love to see the king," I answered with a smirk.

⁓

Big Hal proved wrong about King Henry. Plainly determined to impress, Warwick soon had the gullible citizens eating out of his hand with a cunning spectacle. For once the old king abandoned his monkish dress to wear robes of state and a crown, but even in this finery, he made a pitiful figure when compared to his golden predecessor.

At the cathedral, where we joined a restless, heaving crowd, the Kingmaker himself carried the royal train, and people shouted, "God save King Henry!"

Recognizing Warwick's clever piece of strategy, I fretted at their disloyalty. "Not so long ago, these same people cheered for King Edward."

"But King Henry has a son, Nan."

Harry lifted Nancy from his shoulders and we wandered through the streets thronged with merrymakers. "If Edward had married a French princess as Warwick wanted, things might have been very different. Elizabeth Wydeville and that secret marriage provoked this disaster. Warwick detests her and all her family."

The mention of secret marriage brought Eleanor into mind again, and I wondered if I dared tell Harry about it. Perhaps it was well that Nancy interrupted.

Tilting her chin in a manner reminiscent of her grandmother, she said, "I love that story."

"What story?"

Shaking her russet curls, she opened her blue eyes wide as if exasperated by my ignorance. "Why, about how the king met the queen in Whittlebury Forest. Tell Nan, papa."

Obligingly, Harry recounted the amazing tale with its moonlit, forest meeting, the beauteous widow and her witch mother, reminding me of the time I'd first heard it from the Duchess of Norfolk. Harry's version sounded far more magical, but when he described Elizabeth Wydeville standing beneath the oak tree holding her two little boys by the hand, waiting for King Edward to return from hunting, my heart missed a beat. Two little boys!

"Are you alright, Nan?" asked Harry. "You've gone very pale."

"I was thinking," I said, lowering my voice. "Suppose Queen Elizabeth's boys are the ones I must save?"

"Well, there's no sign of your mysterious man among the soldiers," began Harry. He frowned. "Perhaps—"

"What will happen if Queen Elizabeth's new baby's a prince, papa?" Nancy tugged Harry's sleeve, her smile revealing enchanting dimples in her cheeks.

"I don't know." Harry grimaced at me. "She's living in the Sanctuary at Westminster—"

"Why did the king run away?" Nancy looked cross. "Jack Green ran away and left us, didn't he, papa? Grandma Mercer says he went off with knaves. I shan't ever run away. I shall work in the bake-house when I'm grown."

With a tinge of sadness I smiled at this childish assurance. Margaret Mercer's news about Alison and Jack had proved a sorry piece of business. Alison's cough worsened and she died during that first winter with the Mercers, and not long after Jack vanished into the secret corners of the city.

But the day's merry mood so delighted Nancy, we lingered in the streets bustling with peddlers and entertainers. Outside a busy inn, we stopped to listen to a minstrel with a lute and Harry plied us with sweetmeats.

"They've caught the Butcher! They're taking him to Temple Bar!"

This infectious cry passed swiftly among the spectators. Victims to the whim of a mob who'd shortly cheered King Henry, we found ourselves swept along like so much flotsam.

"Where are we going?" Nancy squealed in alarm when I shouted to her to hold fast to her father's hand. "I don't like this. I want to go home."

A laughing, wild-haired woman threw back her head revealing the blackened stumps of her teeth. "No man who loves his country will go home today," she said. "The best is yet to come! Tiptoft's arrested! You'll see the Butcher of England's head taken off!"

"Why are we going to the butcher's?" The stricken child cried out amidst guffaws of mirth.

Buffeted into alleyways surrounding the Fleet, Harry managed to shake off the main body of the press and escape into a little-used lane.

"You can let go of my sleeves now, but mind where you put your feet!"

Down the centre of the lane ran a stinking sewer full of refuse and ordure. Nancy wrinkled her nose. "Who's Tiptoft, papa?"

"A wicked nobleman who's been caught and will be punished. But don't let it spoil your day, sweeting. You've so much to tell Grandma about the king's parade."

Picking our way through this muddle of streets and squalid houses, we turned into Rood Lane at last, and encountered a rabble spilling out of a tavern.

"Did you hear the news, mistress?" A drunken fellow wearing a soiled livery embellished with the bear and ragged staff accosted me amiably. "John Tiptoft's to be chopped tomorrow!" Lurching forward, he made as if to embrace me. Outraged, I recoiled from his reeking breath, provoking a gale of laughter from his fellows.

"Are you the Earl of Warwick's men?" Harry stepped forward to take my arm, Nancy held protectively by his other hand.

"What's it to you? Are you for Lancaster or for York?" Rubbing his misshapen nose, a hulking youth squared up to Harry.

"We're the king's true subjects," Harry answered without hesitation. I admired the way he could speak so calmly in the face of this rowdy, unpredictable group.

"Then, come and drink with us." The stripling turned to smile at me lasciviously. "And bring your lovely wife with you."

"No more drinking here tonight, my lads." The landlord's muscular figure appeared in the inn doorway. "The curfew bell's ringing. Away to your lodgings."

He nodded to us as we watched the melee weaving about the street, following a raucous voice urging them to The Golden Lion.

"I hear the Butcher's lodged in the Fleet." He picked up a pewter pot from the steps. "Will you go and see him dispatched tomorrow?"

Harry shook his head. "I've no stomach for it."

"What about you little one?" The landlord squatted to address Nancy, but she hid her face. "Hey, look where you're going!" He rose at once to face another storm of ruffians charging down the street.

I cried out when one of them knocked me off balance.

"Your pardon, mistress." The culprit executed a tipsy bow, while I struggled to my knees.

"Never mind the ladies, Jack," said one of his companions. "There's some serious drinking to be done. Time enough for courtship later."

"Let me help you."

The voice rang boldly, delivered in the flat manner of the north. A firm hand gripped my elbow.

"Thank you, I can manage." Wrenching my arm away, I confronted my assailant with the intent of giving him a piece of my mind.

"Nan?" Harry called anxiously. "Are you alright?"

I stood rooted to the spot, my heart pounding. Even in the shadows I'd have known those piercing blue eyes. The familiar swarthy features creased in a smile that lured me with its promise. Spell-bound, I grasped the proffered hand just as another crowd of merry-makers swept around the corner. They barged between us. Unwillingly, our hands separated and I floundered amongst the mob, trying to scan the whirl of faces, until Harry dragged me away. With Nancy under his other arm, he ran without stopping until we reached Bread Street. Behind us drunken laughter roared and bottles thudded among the cobbles.

"Was that someone you knew?" Setting Nancy down, Harry leaned against the wall to catch his breath. "You seemed—"

Even Nancy stared at me.

"Jesu!" The colour drained from Harry's face. "Was it him?"

I nodded, the blood burning in my cheeks.

"He was wearing Gloucester's device—Remember that."

An excited Nancy hammered on the bake-house door. Before we could say any more Mistress Mercer snatched us into the house, gathering the bewildered child into the safety of her embrace.

"We've been out of our minds with worry. There've been dreadful noises and drunken rogues dashing up and down the streets all night."

"A bad man's having his head cut off." Nancy imparted this shocking news with a child's gravity. "And a man with blue eyes tried to take Nan away."

Alarmed, Margaret Mercer glanced first at me and then at Harry.

I made a poor attempt at laughter. "I thought he was someone I knew."

"It was just one of Gloucester's men who'd drunk too much ale." Harry's lie made both of us look sheepish. "Let's get Nancy to bed. She's had a busy day."

In the living quarters Meg soothed a fractious Will. "Marian said the crowds had turned violent." A little pulse twitched by her mouth. "Is it true about Tiptoft?"

Sleep eluded me for a long time, but when it came I was sucked into a whirlpool of vivid dreams in which an unseen enemy hunted me down. I raced through endless, dark streets to avoid my pursuers, but as I turned into an alleyway, the blue-eyed man snatched me in his arms and carried me into a rowdy tavern. I didn't struggle. In fact, I allowed him such licence and took such delight in it that I awoke with a flush of mingled shame and pleasure.

Chapter Thirty-Nine

On the last day of December a hooded figure startled Mistress Mercer as she raised the shutters at first light. Big Hal, down in the bake-house, heard her scream, but by the time he arrived in the shop the rogue sped away into the frosty darkness.

"He asked for you," she said, recounting her tale at breakfast.

Four pairs of eyes turned to accuse me.

Heart thumping, I rose from my place. "Me? Why?"

"Was it that Bishop Stillington's man again?" asked Meg.

"Was it a tall, dark, muscular fellow?" Harry asked before she'd finished.

For a moment hope made me bold. "Was it Miles?"

"It was dark," she answered, shaking her head irritably. "But not so dark I couldn't see it was a lean, young rogue."

"But why would he want Nan?" Harry flashed me a warning glance.

"This is happening too often," said Big Hal. "It upsets your mother."

"He spoke like a nobleman," Mistress Mercer interrupted, frowning as if to recall the memory. "But there was something about him that seemed familiar."

For days after this event, a nervous, edgy atmosphere persisted, making us jump at any unusual event and balk at strangers.

⁀⁊⁊

Twelve nights in succession a flaming star appeared in the January sky. Maud Attemore, bold eyes flashing, promised terrible disasters for 1471, and even the priests urged us to Mass. While Meg pointed at the night sky, her face painted with horror and excitement, I thought poignantly of Eleanor's youthful chaplain, Brother Thomas, with his tale of the miraculous three suns.

"Don't let such sights alarm you," said Big Hal. "I remember seeing a star like that in 1456 when I was still an apprentice. It had a tail like a sabre and the Pope pronounced it the devil's agent which would bring disaster. The only disaster that happened that year was that I met Margaret!"

"Hold your noise, you rogue." Laughing, Mistress Mercer gave him a dig in the ribs. She was still beaming when she turned to me. "How would you like to come with me to Dowgate tomorrow? Sir Robert plans to give a banquet and I'll need all the help I can get."

This wealthy patron regularly asked for her services. Captured by her enthusiasm and the opportunity to see his fine property, I readily agreed.

"Meg and Marian can manage in the shop. There'll be plenty of other maids there for you to gossip with and if Master Rowland takes a fancy to you, you could find regular employment. It's time you met others of your own age." She gave Meg a conspiratorial wink which left me wondering if Meg had arranged this, or if she'd finally devised a way to hide me.

"Master Rowland's Sir Robert's steward," she told me. "He's strict with servants but you'll find him fair enough."

Next morning she packed two huge baskets of provisions and by the time we arrived at the stately mansion-house a feverish turmoil already bubbled. Men and maids dashed and wove between us in the narrow corridors to and from the kitchen, forcing her to grip my arm to prevent me stumbling.

"By God, girl, get a move on!" Master Rowland's sharp reprimand startled me. He gave one of the rosy-faced maids a hearty push. "The guests will be in the house and the meal not ready. There's no time for gossiping now."

The impudent, blonde wench stuck out her tongue at his haughty back, and the ensuing sniggers swivelled the steward into a sharp turn, forcing the scullion to smother his laughter with an elaborate cough.

"You see, Mistress Mercer, we've a truculent set of rascals today," said the steward. He glowered at the giggling maids. "I advise you to use a firm hand."

By late afternoon sweat bathed my body. My cheeks burned as I stooped over trestles laden with row on row of golden-glazed pies fragrant with the scent of spice and meat. Steam wafted from beneath flaking crusts and a great clove-studded haunch of venison smoked on a platter. Roasting meats cooked to rags with pungent herbs and warm spiced sauces mingled in a rich aroma of flavours which made my head spin. Soups, capons basted with hippocras, pork glazed with honey, baked carp, vast puddings stuffed with raisins, dates and almonds, custard dowcets, marchpane and sweetmeats waited to be served.

"Is that pottage ready, Nan?" Margaret Mercer glanced up from stirring a bowl of eggs and cream. "Sir Robert doesn't like to keep his guests waiting."

Bustling to and fro, men-servants staggered under the weight of huge dishes, their plum-coloured faces strained and beaded with moisture, and as one course followed another, the volume of noise rose to such a hubbub I grew dizzy.

"You'll get used to it." Margaret Mercer chuckled, stifling a yawn, as we trailed back to Bread Street swaying with fatigue, feet swollen, backs and legs aching, under a pale dawn sky.

Called back to Dowgate within a week, I embraced my new employment eagerly even though it meant sharing an attic room with several others. Though I missed the Mercers, Dowgate offered many opportunities for meeting new people. The house proved far grander than Silver Street and sheltered no malign spirits, although it stormed with activity of a different kind. Distinguished guests regularly gathered under its roof, and listening to their effusive servants, I stored snippets of information which might prove useful. I'd not forgotten those noble boys or the black-haired lover who would lead me to them.

At the busy day's end I lay on my pallet drinking in the girls' gossip and eavesdropping as they traded secrets, quickly warming to impudent, fearless Kate, pretty Cecily, who dreamed of marriage, and kind-hearted Dorothy. With them I laughed at Fat Rosamund's frequent squabbles with peevish Jennet.

"Are you a relation of the Mercers?" asked this Jennet, her mean eyes probing my face.

"I feel as if I am," I answered. I thought with pleasure of the family who treated me with kindred warmth. "But Mistress

Mercer's just a friend of my aunt's and offered me work when I first came to London."

In April, when the Earl of Warwick died in a battle at Barnet, struck down by King Edward's victorious army, shockingly superstitious tales circulated—tales of sorcery, treachery and malign spirits with the Wydeville queen at the centre of them like a cunning spider in a web. The attic buzzed with excitement.

"I'm glad King Edward's back." Cecily smiled, starry-eyed and tender. "He'll be able to see his baby son now."

"But he's made King Henry a prisoner." Jennet's face gleamed sharp in the rush-light. "At least he's not married to a witch. And what about *his* son?"

"Warwick's the one who said the queen was a witch." Rosamund stared at Jennet belligerently, plump cheeks wobbling. "And he was the king's best friend before *she* came along."

The girls fell into the usual animated quarrel.

Closing my eyes, I thought back to my vision of the two battles. Clever, unscrupulous Warwick's cruel death had roused much speculation. Big Hal saw it as the fall of the old nobility. What next? I wondered, remembering the hard aspect of Edward's character I'd glimpsed at Silver Street. I shuddered at the callous way he'd abandoned Warwick. Who else would fall victim to his enmity?

A month later, a distraught Master Rowland strode into the hot clamour of the kitchen cutting off Margaret Mercer's busy instructions.

"King Henry's son's been killed at Tewkesbury."

Eyes fixed on our tasks, we listened to his dreadful tale of murder and betrayal.

"This is the end of an era. King Henry remains a poor prisoner in the Tower. I doubt we shall hear much of him again." He crossed himself in an exaggerated pious fashion, his pale, fishy eyes melancholy. "This house has always favoured York's claim to the crown, as you know, and the king's brother is a close friend of Sir Robert. But I'm grieved to hear of the wicked deeds perpetrated in his name. Let us pray there'll be no more bloodshed."

During an embarrassed, uncomfortable silence, Margaret Mercer flashed me an odd, satisfied look. "Your prophecies concerning two battles in two months have come true, Nan," she said, when the steward quit the kitchen and the astonished murmurs began. "I've no idea where Tewkesbury is, and I doubt any of these," she indicated the whispering servants, "care much who wears the crown, but I'm certain we'll see some drastic changes when the Wydevilles take charge again."

I didn't answer. An image of the frail Lancastrian king kneeling by a little altar in a turret chamber burst into my inner vision like a shooting star. His up-turned face gleamed white and ethereal in the flickering light of a single candle, while over him loomed a monstrous shadow, black as a raven's wing. A wave of nausea set me sweating. Around me voices echoed hollow as bells while figures blurred and span—

"Nan?"

Someone brought a stool. A wet cloth pressed against my brow, and a hand pushed a cup to my lips.

"The heat—"

Kindly Dorothy steered me away.

⌁

"My Ralph says the queen used evil spells to have him murdered." Kate's voice on the stairs startled me from sleep.

"Do you feel better, Nan?" Dorothy's rush-light drove the dusty shadows away, while the others spilled, chattering, into the chamber.

"I don't believe such silly stuff." Cecily flounced onto her bed, loosening her red curls from her cap. "How can the queen be a witch?"

"She learned from her mother," Jennet said. "The Duchess of Bedford's French—"

"But that doesn't make her a witch," said Rosamund. "The French—"

"Are perfidious, evil-minded villains." Jennet's spiteful tones finished for her. "Everyone knows the stories of that French witch who called on demons and rode into battle dressed as a man."

My flesh crawled at the memory of Simon Dobbs stabbing his finger and laughingly designating me to play this role in one of our old war games.

"Do you think it's possible?" Kate interrupted the brewing quarrel. "I mean, I know there are wise women who can read the future and make potions to cure ailments, but can they really cast spells to make people do terrible things?"

"Why not?" Fat Rosamund's face quivered with horrified pleasure. "My mother knew a woman who could make any man fall in love with her."

"A pity you didn't learn how to do that!" Jennet's sneering laughter whipped a hot bloom into Rosamund's plump cheeks.

"Oh I'm sure there are some who can look into the future." I spoke softly. "I knew an old woman who possessed the Sight and she taught me to use her special cards—"

Four pairs of eyes fixed on me.

"Would you like to see them?" In a moment of pure recklessness I slid the bundle from my pack of belongings and offered to tell their fortunes. It wasn't the time to be boasting of such matters but I wanted to see if I still had the skill. Besides, Mara had been on my mind ever since I'd heard about Tewkesbury. Now her wry smile and the wise twinkle of her black eyes teased me, as if she urged me to this daring act.

"How can you know that?" Cecily's amazement at my vivid description of her grandmother's house clearly impressed. "You've never been there, and she's been dead fifteen years."

"Tell me if I'll marry," begged fat Rosamund, snatching the cards. The others sniggered and made cruel faces behind her back.

Even shy Dorothy demanded to know her fate.

"How did you learn such tricks?" Sallow-faced Jennet examined the curious images with a suspicious frown.

I shook my head. "No trickery."

"Witch-craft's a hanging offence."

"It's just a game," said Kate carelessly, but Jennet's vindictive glare put me in mind of Johanna Nettleship and the ducking she'd given me in the village pond.

"I told you, an old woman gave them to me. She taught me their meanings."

"You didn't tell Anne's fortune." Cecily indicated a thin, quiet girl on the corner bed. Green eyes brilliant in the rush-light, she huddled against the wall as if ready to ward off a blow. She'd only recently joined our company and so far no one had heard her say a word.

"I'm sure she's not right in the head." Kate whispered in my ear as we turned to face the newcomer.

"She's in shock," I replied without thinking. "Mistress Mercer told me she lost her father recently and one of her relations begged Sir Robert to take her in."

"She has very fine hands." Dorothy's words turned our attention to the refined quality of the girl's appearance in spite of her coarse clothes.

"Would you like me to read your fortune?"

She stared at me with such anguish, a lump of pain formed in my throat.

"You have to shuffle and make a wish." Rosamund thrust the cards at her with an air of superior knowledge.

She took them as one might a dish hot from the oven, staring at them for a long time.

"Go on, shuffle them," Rosamund said.

With mounting apprehension, I laid out the familiar pattern.

"Well?" Kate asked impatiently. "What wondrous future lies in store for Mistress Anne?"

"Too much noise up there!" We jumped apart. "Who's wasting light?"

"Master Rowland!" Cecily leaped into the bed she shared with Dorothy. "Put out the light, for God's sake or he'll be up here!" She pulled the coverlet over her head and someone speedily extinguished the light. Kate muttered a curse on all troublesome stewards. Amidst a general scrambling into sleeping places, a shuffling and arranging of bed-linen, I found myself abandoned trying to retrieve the dropped cards.

"What did you see?" The fierce whisper shocked me. Icy fingers seized my wrist.

"A crown," I answered, amazed by the strength of those delicate hands.

She uttered a hard laugh that made my scalp prickle.

"What's that?"

"Ssssh! Go to sleep. You'll have old yellow-breeches up here."

In the anonymous dark the girls shrugged down into their mattresses with a shift of limbs, a flap of coverlets, a sigh and settling of breath.

"Lady," I said to my companion in an undertone, "you have many secrets. You're not what you seem."

In the glitter of her eyes, slanted and green as a cat's, shone an astonishing rage. I knew instantly some terrible injustice had put it there. Clearly there was more to this strange girl than the shock and fear I'd first noticed.

"If you two don't stop whispering, old Rowland will punish all of us." Jennet's peevish tone hissed a warning.

"Your destiny lies in the north lands, lady, for in the south there's danger. And in spite of all, the crown will be yours."

Jennet snapped another caution and I slunk to my bed. Fat Rosamund already snored and grumbled. But long after the others slept, I lay shivering beneath the coverlet.

You'll take me with you, lady, I thought. Your destiny and mine arc intertwined, but why do I have such awful premonitions concerning the outcome?

Chapter forty

When Master Rowland assigned our morning tasks, a sour expression distorted Jennet's features. "Why can't Anne go to the fishmonger's?"

"If she went with you to fetch the fish," said fat Rosamund, "I could go with Nan to the market." Her moon-shaped face beamed in pretended innocence

Jennet rewarded Rosamund with one of her particularly spiteful glares. "You could take Anne to the fishmonger's just as well as me. Then *I* could go to the market. Why should I always have to go for the fish?"

"Because you're so much better at dealing with slippery things." Rosamund's sweetly spat venom made us gasp.

"My dear young ladies!" Master Rowland pressed his index finger against the corner of his mouth as if perplexed, although he knew perfectly well none of us relished the stink of Billingsgate's fish market. "I'm amazed at these displays of ill-temper." With a martyred sigh, he explained our duties again as if addressing simpletons. "Dorothy has tooth-ache and Mistress Anne will go nowhere." He glared at a truculent Jennet. "Her family requested she remain in the house until stronger."

His fishy-pale eyes followed us as Jennet flung on a shawl, and Rosamund lumbered off to collect her basket.

"Who is this Anne?" Jennet asked. "Why should she merit special treatment? Anyone would think she was royalty the way Master Rowland talks."

We spilled into the street.

"Mistress Mercer said her father died recently. Perhaps he was killed in the fighting at Tewkesbury," said Cecily.

The appearance of the carpenter's apprentice, a handsome lad with an abundance of auburn curls and a winning smile, quickly diverted our attention.

"Good morning to you, ladies," he called out jauntily. His eyes appraised Rosamund's voluptuous curves with amusement.

She simpered coyly, plump cheeks wobbling, and while he and Jennet fell into the sparring conversation of young men and women who find one another interesting, she stood gazing with calf-like eyes. Cheerful Cecily scampered off towards Smithfield and I headed to the Chepe.

A strange quiver of unease passed through me as soon as I entered the market. I lingered amongst the press of matrons by a pie stall, aware of a dark-clad figure lurking at the edge of my vision. Heart thumping, I turned carefully and caught the stranger melting into the milling crowds. Feeling foolish, I moved among the stalls pausing to make purchases and exchange pleasantries with familiar traders. Eventually, however, I realised the hooded stripling followed my every step. He paced with stealth and purpose, steadily closing the gap between us. My heart quickened its beat. I tried to keep my gait unhurried whilst pretending interest in the stalls, but my mind teemed with thoughts of escape.

Unease finally gave way to panic. I almost fell as I slipped into the narrow darkness of Cutter's Lane. Sunlight rarely penetrated this passageway and the cobbles lay slick with slime. Turning sharply, my basket struck against the corner with such force several objects leapt out and rolled away.

I daren't stoop to search, the lane being infamous as the haunt of petty thieves and drabs who brought customers to conduct their business amongst the shadows. Before my eyes could adjust, I flung myself headlong down the twisting alley, desperate to shake off my pursuer.

Recklessness proved my undoing. I bumped into a group of crouching figures sharing the objects of their recent pilfering, lost my balance, and tumbled, sprawling in the dirt. I managed to retrieve my basket but as I staggered to my feet a greasy hand encircled my ankle. Instinctively, I kicked out. My cursing assailant loosed his grip, but wrenched at my skirt to maintain a hold. With an alarming ripping sound, I fled amid a roar of ribald laughter. Voices slurred with ale called lewd remarks.

"Stop that woman!" A refined, youthful voice rang with authority.

"Has the wench cheated you, sir?" Another voice cackled with mirth. "She's a lively one. Sim can vouch for that, can't you, lad?"

Attacked from behind by another pair of exploring hands, I elbowed and wrestled using basket and contents as weapons. Picking eggs from my basket, I ground them into a face, aiming for the eyes. From the furious yelping, I guessed they'd found their mark.

There followed a mad scramble amongst lurching shapes and angry, screeching noises. I registered vividly the shocked face of a girl entwined with a wrinkled goat of a man against a wall.

By some miracle, I finally escaped into daylight at the end of this evil-smelling tunnel. Filthy and dishevelled, my kirtle torn and my bodice spattered with egg and grease, I hurled myself among the crowds. From the look of disdain a stout tradesman's wife gave me, I guessed she mistook me for a whore. Clutching my empty basket like a talisman I raced back to Dowgate.

Just outside the house a jangle of raised voices caught my attention, and once in the kitchen I encountered a scene of utter confusion.

"My purse has been stolen!" I fumbled in my sleeve, conscious of my soiled gown with its torn skirt. "I was attacked—"

"She's gone!" Kate shouted above the roar of voices, jumping up and down with excitement. "Oh there's been such a to-do! You should've seen. And you'll never guess who she was!"

Dorothy tried to speak but I couldn't catch her words. Fat Rosamund pushed towards me, gabbling and gesticulating, her enormous bosom heaving.

"Too bad you missed it," Jennet said. She thrust Rosamund aside.

"—some noblemen came to fetch her."

I caught the tail-end of Dorothy's explanation as the room fell silent and Master Rowland ushered in our illustrious patron. "Sir Robert wishes to acquaint you with the truth of the unusual events which took place this morning," he said. His fishy eyes flicked a warning.

"Where's Anne?"

Dorothy nudged me with her elbow, nodding towards Sir Robert.

"Lady Anne Neville was here at the request of her brother-in-law, George, Duke of Clarence—a particular friend of mine." The refined, nasal voice finally caught my attention.

Lady Anne Neville! Anne Neville! The Kingmaker's daughter! She'd stayed here among us, disguised as a cook-maid and I'd spoken to her as an equal! I barely heard the rest of Sir Robert's speech.

"Imagine! Her father was the Earl of Warwick." Kate's excitement trembled in her shrill tones.

"Who was killed at Barnet." Grim-faced Jennet glared a challenge at Rosamund. "And good riddance."

"Oh Jennet, that's unkind," gentle Dorothy said.

"He was an arrogant, ambitious knave—and deserved to die for the way he treated the queen."

"How can you be so heartless, Jennet? He was Anne's father." Cecily looked plainly dismayed. "And her husband was killed at Tewkesbury."

"Husband?" Rosamund stammered, goggle-eyed. "Was she married, then?"

"To daft King Henry's son." Kate's enthusiastic prattle engaged us all. "He hid in an abbey during the battle. A woman in the Chepe said King Edward dragged him out and killed him in revenge for the murder of his own young brother who was hacked to pieces years ago—"

"But why was she here? What's going to happen to her now?"

"She's been taken to St Martin's Sanctuary." Cecily's expression grew dreamy. "The Duke of Gloucester means to marry her. Isn't it romantic?"

"Well, I don't suppose she'll be inviting us to her wedding," said laughing Kate. "She'll have forgotten us already."

The Duke of Gloucester! Hadn't Harry told me my black-haired man wore Gloucester's device? But why had Anne Neville lived in disguise at Dowgate? If the Lancastrian prince had become king, she'd have been his queen. Hadn't I promised her a crown? But now she'd wed a mere duke—and youngest brother to the king at that—

"Nan told her fortune." Jennet's dark eyes fixed on mine like those of an adder. "She's certain to remember that."

When Master Rowland sent for me after breakfast the next morning I swallowed nervously. *No doubt he means to chastise me for the loss of purse and purchases,* I thought, drying my hands on my coarse apron. *How can I explain?*

"You've to get all your things," said the serving-lad who'd been instructed to find me. "Hurry up! Roly's in one of his bad moods."

This didn't presage well. I wondered what Margaret Mercer would say.

"Well, Nan." Master Rowland's shrewd, pale eyes perused me. He pressed his index finger to the corner of his lower lip. "Mistress Mercer, whose opinion is much prized, commended you to me. But now you seem to have found favour with Lady Anne. So much so she's desirous to make you her maid-servant—a more pleasing prospect than being a cook-maid, I think, even in such an illustrious house as this?"

"Lady Anne Neville desires me to be her maid, sir?" I couldn't believe my ears.

"Indeed she does." Master Rowland looked equally surprised. "She's sent this gentleman to bring you to her without delay."

Bewildered by my summons, I failed to notice the other occupant of the room. Leaning with his elbow against the casement, half-hidden by the shadows, stood a tall, broad man dressed in livery. My heart skipped a beat when I recognised the emblem of the white boar. My escort stepped into the light and then I saw his face clearly.

"Lady Anne's instructed me to guard you with my life." He spoke courteously but his piercing blue eyes moved hotly over me. His mouth twisted in a sly smile. "Will you go with me, mistress?"

Like one under a spell, I joined him by the hearth, my heart hammering with a curious mix of delight and apprehension.

"I'd the devil's own job to find this place." He turned to Master Rowland. "I'll be glad to quit London for the clean air of the north. Fortunately my master's keen to conclude his business and get back to Middleham without delay." Pride and mockery rang in his voice.

Somehow I found myself out in the street.

"Miles Forrest at your service," said my escort. He performed an insolent bow. "I've been waiting for you for a long time. But you know that already."

Shock kept me tongue-tied. Amused by my evident embarrassment, the black-haired rogue leaned nonchalantly against the wall. "Do you believe in fate, mistress?"

For a heart's-beat I pressed a hand to the bundle of cards hidden in my bodice as if it burned into my flesh. "Without a doubt." I raised my eyes to meet his, my face aflame at the delicious memory of a kiss in Silver Street and a score of wanton dreams.

"Then you and I are fated to be together." The pleasing, sensual mouth grinned; the blue eyes devoured me. "Everywhere I go, you turn up. I'll swear you put some spell on me. But why didn't you keep your promise?"

"Promise?"

"To meet me at the Boar's Head. I waited for you. Even in dreams I've been looking for you ever since."

Taking my bundle with a possessive air, he turned towards the city.

"Perhaps we'll have time to better our acquaintance now." He awarded me a secretive, knowing smile, driving a delicious flutter through my belly.

"Where are we going?" I asked, trotting along at his side like a dog who's found its master.

"St Martin-le-Grand," he answered in the curt manner of the north. "Lady Anne's lodging there until arrangements can be made for her marriage."

He took my hand with a boldness I ought to have dismissed. "You must be a special wench to have found favour with the Neville maid. They say she's proud like her father—but I can't fault her choice." He smiled so winningly the hot blood rushed into my cheeks. "I look forward to our onward journey together." The saucy glint in his blue eyes set a flood of delightful anticipation coursing through me.

So I found myself in attendance on the Kingmaker's daughter in the sanctuary apartments of the church where I'd prayed as a child and lit candles for my beloved father. But this time the promise of freedom and fulfilment beckoned.

Miles Forrest and I were bound to go to Middleham together.

Part five

Middleham
1471

Chapter Forty-One
Middleham Castle

The broad hand clamped across my mouth, stifling a giggle.

"Ssh!" A voice, husky with desire, whispered by my ear. "Christ, girl, do you want me dismissed?"

We struggled together, hands busy with laces and buckles, tongues probing, breaths gasping, hungry for consummation. Staggering back into the dark, I heard the stamp and snort of horses in their stalls, smelled leather harness and warm animal flesh, the mingled scents of hay and dung.

He forced me back, my nails raking the tight fabric of his doublet as we fell into soft straw. We rolled and clung while fingers squeezed and caressed, wrenched at garments, hoisted heavy skirts, and mouths tasted new delights. I clung to the hard, muscular body while it heaved and twisted above me and the strong hands explored the soft, wet core that betrayed my need.

"Now you can laugh all you like," he said, as he thrust inside me, but I didn't want to anymore. Instead I fastened my mouth on his and drew him deeper until we panted for air and broke asunder. At the last, I threw back my head and opening my eyes, saw the triumph in the shocking blue of his.

Scrambling out of the stable, I fretted and tugged at my dishevelled clothes all the way back to the painted chamber in the west tower.

"You're in a hurry." An impudent young manservant accosted me on the stairs. He plucked a piece of straw from my hair. "Been out riding?"

I snapped my skirts around me and flounced away, my cheeks burning at the sound of his ribald chuckles.

Mistress Collins looked up from the bed she was making. "Tha's late." She eyed me up and down with flinty, disapproving eyes. "Give Emma a hand with those bolsters."

The little duchess, married only a few months ago, expected a child in January. Under the auspices of Jane Collins, a skilled midwife, I assumed various duties in preparing for the birth of the noble child, mainly by helping her to organise the lying-in chamber and the nursery. Though brusque in manner, Mistress Collins struck me as a fair-minded, industrious matron, and her down-to earth speech reminded me of Margaret Mercer.

Emma smiled at me. "The priest's saying special Masses for Lady Anne in the chapel," she said.

Jane Collins snorted. "She'll need them." She unfolded an exquisite embroidered coverlet. "Here, take that end—" Dried sprigs of lavender scattered to the floor as we smoothed out the creases and tugged edges into place. "The duke may crave a son, but that wench'll not go full term, mark my words."

"She's very pale and slender," I answered. The midwife possessed a practised eye and Lady Anne's constant sickness and growing fatigue dismayed me. The duke watched her constantly with a vigilance I thought suspicious rather than tender, although the servants assured me he was devoted to her.

"Is that bad?" Emma's girlish face gazed appealingly at Mistress Collins.

"It doesn't bode well." The stout Yorkshire woman looked grim.

When Lady Anne's pregnancy proved so difficult the physician ordered her to bed, Emma wept.

"No use shedding tears, lass." Mistress Collins bustled about the nursery, heaving blankets from the press. "We mun do what we can. These noble wenches need cosseting. Tha can take her some wine and honey. Get one of the kitchen-maids to make some up."

The girl scuttled away and Jane Collins gave me a sharp glance. "I fancy I'll need thee shortly," she said. "Tha'd best sleep in the nursery from now on."

I nodded, but the import of her words didn't strike me until a freezing night not long after when she roused me suddenly from sleep.

"Tha'd best come and help, lass. I hope tha's a strong stomach."

Flinging on my gown, still half asleep, I followed her in a daze, my feet stumbling on the steps, my hands buried under my armpits for warmth. An icy draught whipped smoke from the flickering torches and I flinched at an eerie, animal scream from somewhere above.

The stench of blood and pain corroded the lying-in chamber. Several shadowy figures scuttled to and fro, parting before Mistress Collins to reveal the full horror of the huge tester bed where the little duchess writhed and grunted.

The heifer-hipped midwife stooped, blotting out the sight of Lady Anne's tortured mouth gaping cavern-wide. Her skilful hands probed among the mound of soiled and tangled sheets. "Here, Nan, hold her hands." I glimpsed a pale, flailing limb and gritted my teeth against the next uncanny scream.

At last the plain-faced woman handed me a bowl and a bundle of bloody cloths, wiping her hands on her coarse apron. "Well done, lass." She steered me from the bed. "Tha'll like as not have this to do again." She nodded at the spent white figure around which the serving maids hovered with basins of water and clean towels. "They've no strength for bearing children, these women. Her sister were just the same. Miscarriage after miscarriage— But they go on and on wi' it."

Listening to the drone of the flat northern sounds, I thrust the cloths into a basket and carried the bowl to where Emma, the little nursery-maid, crouched against the door.

"Can you take this away?" I asked.

She shuddered, averting her face.

"Thou'll have to get used to such sights, lass," Mistress Collins called, not unkindly, "if thou wants to wait on my lady."

The girl grimaced as she took the bowl.

"Empty it down the sluice quickly," I said. I nudged her through the door.

Mistress Collins' broad, capable hands heaped more rugs on the bed against the icy blast that blew through all the castle chambers during the winter months. "She'll sleep now." The serving wenches fluttered away in a murmuring chorus.

I looked at the delicate face and closed eyes, wondering how much Lady Anne heard of Mistress Collin's blunt speech.

"Tha need to be strong as a horse to bear healthy children," the midwife said. She shook her head at the occupant of the bed. "She may have her father's spirit, but she's not built to carry bairns."

247

The slender hands gripped the coverlet.

"She's barely sixteen," I said in a low voice. "She's plenty of time to have other children."

Mistress Collins gathered together her implements and gave me a searching look.

"There's some as wants children and can't have them, and others who find they can, as shouldn't."

Under her scrutiny heat flooded my face. I stooped to pick up the basket so she couldn't read my expression.

"Tha wants to watch theesen, lass." She went on relentlessly while I lifted my sad burden. "Miles Forrest has something of a name in the village for the wenches. And there's one or two bairns around and about the country might call him father if he passed by their houses some day. A handsome face and a pair of bonny blue eyes isn't all he's famous for, mark my words."

"I will, Mistress Collins." I answered without turning my head. "I'll bear what you say in mind."

My heart hammered as I crossed the bed-chamber. Just how much did the shrewd Yorkshire-woman know? Pausing a moment, I hoisted the basket higher to pass through the doorway.

"Burn it," she said.

I swallowed hard. The stench of blood in my nostrils, I fought back a wave of nausea. Behind me I heard the midwife picking up her things and moving around the chamber purposefully. "Tha's done well this day, lass. Don't go throw it all away for nowt. Forrest's the Duke's man and knows how to look after hissen. First and foremost he's his own interests at heart. Make sure tha'rt one of them. A woman who yields too readily never makes a wife. Remember that."

She nudged *me* through the door then. I stumbled down the steps feeling bewildered, guilty and ashamed, like a child who's been caught out in a piece of mischief.

Barely a year had passed since I'd come to Middleham. Finding myself alone at last with Miles Forrest, I felt awkward and embarrassed. The memory of my wanton dreams kept me tongue-tied. What did I really know of this man? The reality of the black-haired stranger who teased and pursued me, muddled and confused. Flattered and frightened by turns I allowed him too much intimacy. We should have taken time to forge a friendship, taken time to grow into affection. Hadn't I warned Philippa to be careful of her affair with Ralph Fowler? And hadn't I begged

Eleanor to be more sparing of her favours with the king? With Miles I acted as foolishly, perhaps more so, for wasn't I already enamoured of his image before we met? In truth I knew nothing of the man, yet couldn't say no to his demands. Was I then as wicked as the tavern wenches I'd been taught to despise? I deserved to be called a fool and a jade. Nevertheless, I bore Jane Collins' advice in my head, determined to be more temperate the next time I met Master Forrest.

⌘

"Don't play the virgin." He thrust me against the wall, his hands busy at my bodice. "It's not a part that becomes you. Let's not waste time pretending what we're not."

He twisted me towards him, grinding his hips against me, his intentions plainly obvious. His mouth brushed against my neck and I gasped at the sharp edge of teeth on my flesh. I struggled in the ferocity of this embrace, heard the low laugh in his throat as his lips sought mine and fastened on them hungrily. For a moment I resisted, then returned the kiss, thrilling with the urgency I could arouse in him, conscious of my own increasing need. Feverishly, we clung together, bodies craving sweet proximity, until, deliberately, reluctantly, I snatched my mouth away.

"I must go to my Lady."

"Later."

Miles' voice grew husky with desire. He drew me close against him, trying to drag me towards the bed-chamber.

"I shouldn't have come here." I pushed away the exploring hands, resisting the greedy mouth, sensing the traitorous weakening in my limbs. "I remember now—" His face pressed so close to mine I saw the sparks of lightning in the fierce blue of his eyes.

"I remember too." His breath panted raggedly. "I remember last Wednesday eve and what we did and I would savour such moments again." A spasm of pleasure coursed through me as he bent his head to nuzzle at my breasts. It filled me with such an ache, I knew I must tear myself away or drown in its deliciousness.

"No!" I pressed my hands against his chest. "No more—"

An angry hand grabbed deep into my hair, spilling loose tendrils over my neck. He wrenched my head around to face him. With his other hand he attempted to lift my skirt.

"Please—"

"Oh I'll please you, be sure of that." His mouth worried at my throat.

"Miles, don't—"

"What's the matter with you?" he snarled. I strained against him. "This isn't like you—I'd have you as you were last Wednesday eve—"

Tears stung my eyes. I whimpered as the powerful hands continued to move, seeking out the most intimate parts of my body. The brutality of this behaviour overwhelmed me. Miles' face became a blur.

"I shall faint—"

Something in my voice halted him. Supporting my weight, he held me in his arms. My hands clutched at the fabric of his jerkin. With my head drooping upon his shoulder, he lowered me gently until we huddled together on the stone steps like two lost children.

"What is it?" The eyes that looked into mine expressed concern. He kissed my brow. "I'd never harm you, Nan" he said, his dark voice grown tender. "I thought you meant to tease me and I don't like such games."

He helped me to my feet and we stood looking at one another in uncomfortable silence.

"I shouldn't have come here. It was very wrong of me." I hung my head. In my mind I pictured Jane Collins' warning face—heard her disapproving tone.

"Not so wrong on Wednesday last nor all the months before." A sting of anger lingered.

"I'm ashamed of my wantonness."

I couldn't meet his eyes. Already I regretted what I might have thrown away. It hurt to think Miles considered me only as a moment's pleasure.

Laughing harshly, he asked, "Why all this trickery? If you no longer wish for my company I'm sure I can find another to cheer my solitude." The barb of those words made me wince.

"I heard such tales in the village—" I said between my tears.

"I'm not ashamed of anything I've done." A hint of genuine amusement softened this admission. "The lasses were willing enough. I'll wager that's not all you've heard, either. Well, let me tell you more. There were others at Barnard Castle and there's one or two wenches in Burgundy dallied with me for an hour or so, some maybe for a few days, but I've never tried to hide it from the world. I don't regret any of them. The hours I spent were pleasant enough, but no more than that. But I thought—"

He paused and waited, the silence growing upon us. My sobs and sniffs subsided.

"They say you have children."

"The Duke himself has bastards," answered Miles. He shrugged. "It's no uncommon thing."

Suddenly he snatched a breath, a gasp of understanding. "Is that it?" Laughter bubbled in his voice. "Is that what you're trying to tell me? That you're—"

"No!" A cry of horror halted him. "No! I don't know—I mean—"

He seized me in his arms. "Why, lass," he said, kissing me hard on the mouth, "I see I must make an honest woman of you." He folded me into his arms then and I laid my head against his chest, comforted and spent.

"I told you we were fated to be together." He stroked stray curls from my face. "There's no denying fate, lass. You've said it often enough yourself. In truth, I never meant to marry, but I see it must be so." He dropped another kiss upon my brow. "I'll speak to the Duke immediately."

Chapter forty-Two

The scent of dried rose-petals will always remind me of our wedding. Jane Collins and some of the other women scattered them in our bed. All night long, as I lay in Miles' arms, their perfume haunted me.

The Duke and his Lady proved generous. Our marriage was celebrated with all due ceremony. Afterwards we shared a festive meal prepared by His Grace's own cook, at which the Duke supplied both ale and wine. Later that evening, we retired to a sumptuous apartment in the castle. I couldn't believe my good fortune.

"How lucky we are," I said. "I've never lived in anything so fine!"

Miles swung me round until we were both dizzy, and we tumbled laughing upon the great bed, releasing clouds of dusty pink blossom.

"Let's enjoy its luxury while we can." His eyes burned hot with desire, his powerful hands already explored my body with practised intimacy.

Drunk with happiness, I yielded to his urgency, and so the night passed in a blur of passion and sleep.

When I woke to the delicate aroma of crushed roses, I lay wrapped in the warmth of him, wallowing in the knowledge of being safely wed to a man who enjoyed some standing in the Duke's entourage. I should never want.

Watching Miles sleeping, his dark head buried in the crook of his arm, I felt a strange responsibility—as if I'd taken on an enormous task. Hadn't this man for years haunted my dreams? Yet I seemed no nearer solving the mystery of the visions. What connected him to the boys whose lives I must somehow save? And what did I really know about him? Now he was mine—but what did that mean? Something ominous jarred this marriage— So strong were my feelings, that, involuntarily, I reached out as if to protect him from an unexpected blow.

My sudden movement woke him. He turned towards me with a groan, his eyes still closed, his face contorted, his fists clenched. For a moment, I thought myself a watcher by a sick-bed, and found myself stroking his forehead as a mother might tend an ailing child.

When his lids flickered open, understanding dawned in the fierce, ice- blue of his eyes. "What's wrong sweetheart?" he asked sleepily. "Is it day already?"

"The birds are singing in the dawn."

He ran his hands through thick, black hair, arching his neck. "Time, then, to prepare for our journey."

"Journey? What journey?"

"The Duke's ordered me to Barnard Castle." Miles hauled himself out of the bed. "We must make haste. The roads are foul at this time of year and the light soon fails."

"You said nothing of this." I clutched the coverlet to me, loath to quit the rapidly cooling shelter of the bed.

"I thought you knew." Miles struggled into his clothes.

"What must we do at Barnard Castle?" My voice sounded querulous. I felt betrayed.

"His Grace has appointed me Keeper of the Wardrobe." Miles smirked proudly. "Come, dress yourself, my lady." He wrenched the coverlet from my hands, laughing at my protests. "There'll be plenty for you to do at Barnard, never fear. You'll find a welcome there amongst the womenfolk. And you'll have me to keep you warm at nights." He chafed my shoulders, his eyes straying longingly over the swelling curves of my breasts. "Let's be gone before you catch the ague or I'm tempted to teach you other pleasures."

❧

A wretched journey spoiled my happiness. A raw wind and freezing drizzle pounded us all the way we rode north, dispelling the previous day's delights. Muffled by a thick hood, my grumbles fell on stony ears. Miles chose to ignore me for the main part, preferring to ride ahead with someone he addressed as "John". Two taciturn servants rode behind, and their silence, combined with the general gloom of the day, grew steadily oppressive.

Presently, the aching cramp tormenting me for the last few miles ripened into a searing pain. Leaning low over the horse's damp neck, clutching at my belly, I breathed in sharply as each spasm took me in its grip. Recalling Lady Anne's recent travail, I squeezed my eyes tight shut, as if to extinguish the agony. Sweat soaked my body. Just as I feared I must cry out, Miles and his companion drew their horses to a halt.

"We'll stop at the inn to water the horses," said the stalwart John. "It's just around the next bend in the road. The food's good and will cheer us on the next part of our journey."

Never had the sight of a tavern been so welcome.

Dismounting, Miles handed his horse's reins to John in order to assist me.

As I slid from the saddle I felt the gush of wetness between my thighs. With a sense of dread I leaned against Miles for support. He slipped his arms about me.

"Art thou weary, lass? We'll have you warm and snug in no time." His cheeriness threatened to reduce me to tears. Averting my face, I pressed my lips together.

Once inside the inn, however, I alerted him to my situation. The frown between his black brows deepened. A flash of sudden fear glinted in his eyes.

"Find the landlady or some serving woman who can help me." I whispered to him, unwilling to arouse the attention of the others drinking ale by a roaring fire and shouting for food.

After a brief exchange, the bald-pated landlord called a stout woman from the kitchen.

"Come with me, hinny," said this ruddy-faced wench in grey woollen gown and coarse linen apron. I followed her gratefully. "We'll have to go upstairs. Can tha' manage?"

Clasping my hands across my belly, I plodded after her broad back, up the twisted, narrow stairs into a small, bright bed-chamber.

"Is it thi first?"

Another nod, and a gasp of pain.

She took my cloak and gently helped me remove my gown sodden with rain and blood. A wave of nausea set me staggering and I grasped the bed-post to steady myself.

"Thou must lie down, hinny. Best take off thi shift. I'll fetch some water so thou canst cleanse theesen."

Trembling, I stripped off my shift, and using it to prevent soiling the bedding, crawled under the blankets shivering like a wounded animal.

Her hands were capable and kind. She spoke of practical matters as I surrendered to the pain, and consoled me when the ordeal came to a bitter end.

So I lost my baby in the landlord's bed-chamber at the The Greyhound. The emptiness of such grief remains indescribable.

"We'll make another child." Miles enfolded me into the warmth of his embrace. I couldn't speak. Even the benison of tears eluded me. The landlord's wife hadn't offered me such easy comfort.

Chapter Forty-Three

Barnard Castle

Barnard Castle perched like an eagle on a high bank across the River Tees. In the rain-washed light of a February morning, it appeared to me both terrible and imposing. With a heavy heart, I entered its portals.

The responsibility of his new post hung heavy on Miles. He promptly handed me over into the care of Mistress Moore, a woman of generous curves, a florid complexion, and abundant brown hair.

"I've been in service at Barnard since I were fifteen," she said warmly. She guided me through a warren of corridors and steep steps. "You'll find us one big family here." She paused to exchange pleasantries with a pair of hefty wenches. "This is Mistress Forrest." They nodded an enthusiastic greeting making no secret of their curiosity. "I'm telling her we're a friendly lot up here and she'll soon adapt to our ways." Stopping outside a stout door, she gave me an appraising look. "Ee, but you're not what I expected."

I smiled wanly. "What did you expect?"

"Well, you're a bonny lass but there's not much of you. You're a dainty, little thing. I expected summat a bit more substantial." She smiled broadly, giving me a nudge as if to share a jest as she pushed open the door. "The men round here tend to favour buxom wenches— Ee, lass, forgive me, I'm an old fool. You must be fair spent. I'll have Lizzie bring you something to eat. No need bothering to come down to the Hall. There's a fine fire lit here already."

Lizzie, a slatternly wench with a voluptuous bosom, brought me some kind of pottage. But exhaustion overwhelmed me. I'd no time to appreciate the comforts of the chamber. Instead I nodded off before the fire.

In my dream I climbed an endless winding staircase. Dark shapes danced upon walls and moisture oozed from the stones. Closed doors mocked me with secrets.

Presently I heard a child singing. The clear, boyish treble soared and swooped and I stopped to listen to the melody. The words spoke of lost love and betrayal, the cadences rising and falling with such yearning, tears pricked my eyes.

When a door swung open of its own accord, I dropped my taper and darkness rushed at me like a slavering beast. I tried to scream but no noise came. Instead, a hand fell heavy across my mouth. I kicked out, flailing clenched fists—

"Ssh!" A voice called out of the darkness. "I'm here."

Sweating, panting, tears wet on my cheeks, I struck at something solid and woke suddenly.

Daylight filtered through heavy drapes. Beside the bed Miles nursed his cheekbone with mock injury. "I think you've had a nightmare," he said. "At least I hope so for I've done nothing to merit such violent treatment."

"It was horrible." The appalling images loomed so vivid in my mind I couldn't dismiss them. "I can't think what such a dream might mean."

"Must dreams mean something?" Miles leaned close. The blue of his eyes seemed to smoulder. He smoothed some wisps of hair from my forehead, his fingers lingering on the strands. "Or may they be just a muddle of nonsense from our daily lives?"

"Sometimes they're important." I clasped his hand, finding comfort in the solidity of his presence.

"You're a strange lass." He kissed my fingertips. "There's some witchcraft in you. You've a way of saying things that startle, as if you know more than you tell."

"It's not the first time I've been called a witch."

"You've bewitched me."

The statement was made without jest and my heart skipped a beat. I stared into the enigmatic eyes as if to read a reason for this unexpected remark but their expression remained unfathomable.

"I can't think how."

"I knew I must have you from the first moment I saw you. And as for dreams—Why, yes, I dreamt of you before we met. But I've told you that already. And you say you dreamt of me."

"I didn't know you believed in such things," I said, holding his gaze.

"I've good reason to believe in them. Our fates are intertwined, lass. I knew it in my bones the day I saw you at that house in Silver Street. Maybe I'm not such a churl as you think."

"I never thought you that."

Miles wrapped an arm around me, kissed me on the brow. "And I never thought to take you for a wife. I'll not deny I wanted you in my bed. And I'd never met a lass so eager for bed-sport. When we first came to Middleham I thought myself a lucky knave and heard others envy me my prize! But what began as sport has grown more serious." He looked deep into my eyes so I might see his confusion. "What spell have you used? How did you invade my dreams to make me yearn for you so desperately?"

"No spell, Miles." I returned his kiss, moved by his tender regard. "If I'd such skills I'd have snared you earlier!" I leaned into the comfort of his embrace. "You've always played an important part in my dreaming. Since childhood the same dream's plagued me over and over. I knew I must find you to prevent a great wrong —"

"Not now, lass." His voice soothed, gentle as a caress. "Be easy and rest. Time enough to talk of such things when you're recovered—" He rocked me in his arms. "I'm truly sorry about the babe. I told Agnes Moore you'd had a hard time. You'll find her understanding of such matters. In a while, when spring comes, you'll see Barnard at its best. Then you'll feel you're not among strangers anymore."

"The people here seem friendly enough," I answered drowsily. "Was it you put me to bed?" I noticed my stained gown cast carelessly upon a wooden coffer.

"I did. And you were so exhausted I had a hard time undressing you!" His eyes twinkled with mischief. Swinging down from the bed, he gathered up his cloak. "I must ride over to Staindrop now, but Agnes promised to send some wench to wait on you. I dare say you'll find her a better maidservant than me." He chucked me under the chin. "The duke's honoured me with this appointment and I mustn't fail him. I'll be back before nightfall and we'll go down to supper together in the Hall. How will that suit you?"

When he'd gone, I crept out of bed and drew back the drapes. Glancing down into a windswept courtyard, I spied a gardener lopping dead branches from a tree. Leaning on the sill, I watched a pair of crows swoop back and forth over his head, evidently much displeased by his handiwork. Finally, unable to resist any longer, I explored all the rooms in my new apartment, admiring the ornately carved oak furniture, the fine tapestries, the silken hangings patterned with blue and gold fleur de lis. My garments, scattered with sprigs of lavender, lay folded neatly in a heavy, polished chest in the bedchamber and my little jewel casket, wooden trinket box, brush, comb and pins sat together upon a shelf above. Miles wouldn't have arranged things so carefully. Whoever put them away must have moved as silently as a cat while I dozed before the fire.

Finding a ewer of water and a bowl, I shed my ruined shift and washed swiftly. Dressed in clean clothes and standing before a fine looking-glass, I brushed my tangled hair, combing it loosely about my face in the way Miles loved so well. Then I opened the trinket box and took out my precious cloth-wrapped bundle tied with green ribbon. Kneeling before a vast stone hearth decorated with leaping stags, I laid out the pattern of Mara's wondrous picture cards just as a plump little wench with bright auburn hair opened the door.

"Who are you?" I scooped up the cards with shaking hands, my heart racing.

"Amy Sadler, Mistress Forrest. I've been appointed to wait on you." Her face burned scarlet with embarrassment. Her interlaced fingers twisted nervously. "I didn't mean to startle you."

"Was it you who put my garments in the chest?" I fumbled the cloth about the cards, hardly daring to meet her eyes.

"I didn't like to wake you." Her breathy voice sounded hesitant, apologetic. Curiosity burning in her eyes, she watched me tie the ribbon. "Is it a new game, Mistress Forrest?"

"Yes," I lied, averting my face, remembering how Harry told me once what a poor dissembler I made. "Just a game. But I didn't expect—you made me jump."

"I'm sorry—"

"No matter. I flung the bundle in the press. "Thank you, Amy, for being so considerate. You've done well."

She smiled shyly. Under the fading blush a smattering of freckles painted her nose and cheeks. Tawny eyes shone with flecks of gold. "Aunt Agnes—I mean, Mistress Moore, said I should see if you needed anything."

Amy Sadler proved an energetic little wench. Like a sparrow she flitted about her tasks and entertained me with local gossip. She ran errands for everyone and her bright chatter spread sunshine about the castle. As Miles had promised, the close-knit clan of Barnard's womenfolk quickly drew me into their circle.

"Ee, th'art a miracle of knowledge, Nan," said Agnes. She and the other women rifled through my herbal remedies. "And this infusion will cure the headache?"

"Or you could try some thyme vinegar."

"Ee, what a canny lass! My grandmother swore a sprig of thyme under a child's pillow would drive away nightmares."

Lucy sniffed at one of the lotions. "What's in this?"

"Lovage. It's good for removing blemishes and spots."

"Try some, Amy," said Lucy with a giggle. She pointed to the angry red pustule on the girl's chin. "Let's see if it works." She smeared a daub upon it while the maid blushed to the roots of her hair and the other women laughed.

"Well, my mother always said there's a herb to cure everything —"

"Aye, but there's others to kill an' all—"

"If you've some poison for a lazy lump of a rogue—"

So the banter continued, but I didn't mention Mara.

Miles proved right about Barnard. In spring the meadows bloomed bright with flowers. The rolling heather-scattered valleys lay fragrant and warm. How I loved the times we wandered on the heath, when he caught me in his arms and carried me easily upon his shoulder like a child, or chased me under the trees until we fell into a tickling embrace. Entwined among the long grass we shared kisses and secrets, while jubilant birds filled the branches with song and bees hummed drowsy lullabies. I relished this taste of purest happiness.

"There's a fine colour in your cheeks, hinny," said Agnes Moore. "And there's a sparkle in your eye! I'll wager that man of yours has been showing you the delights of the countryside hereabouts!"

Her teasing always brought the blushes to my cheeks.

One sun-drenched day in April, Miles took me walking amongst the most dramatic landscape I'd ever seen. Scrambling over fells and cliffs, through gorse-clad rocks and across ancient boulders, we climbed high into the hills until the distant splash of water became a nearby roar. Taking my hand, he lifted me over a stile to view the hurtling cascade that fell like shattering crystals on to the rocks far below. In the brilliant sunlight, every droplet became a jewel, so I might have been watching a miser scatter his precious hoard.

"This is the highest waterfall in the land, they tell me," said Miles, shouting above the force of the water. Drawing me close, he kissed me on the mouth. Around us the spray fell like rain, sprinkling our hair and garments while the torrent rolled. "The stones are slippery. Hold on to me as we go down the slope."

Under the shadow of the trees away from the thunderous noise we stretched luxuriously, sharing the bread and cheese and ale we'd brought with us. Never had a banquet tasted as delicious as that humble feast.

"So tell me about this dream." Miles brushed away crumbs from his doublet and wrapped me in strong arms.

Leaning against his chest so close I could hear the steady beat of his heart, I shared the visions that had haunted me since childhood. As I spoke, Mistress Evans's melodious voice returned to remind me of her prophecies—"Saddles and horses for you, and a long road to travel"—and here I was in the north—

"You're an uncommon wench." His hand stroked my unpinned hair. "But I knew that from the first." He paused, and turning me to face him looked deep into my eyes as if to read a mystery. "But these dreams are too dangerous for other ears."

"I've told no one save the priest—and a wise woman I met in Norwich." Something prevented me from mentioning Harry.

"You must be careful. The wenches here delight in gossip and have loose tongues—you understand me? Our duke's very pious and witchcraft's a hanging matter. I know, I know—You told Lady Anne her fortune! But dreams and visions—That's something else —" He sat upright. "I'm unlikely to have any business at the Tower, nor are we likely to return to London. The duke's not easy at court —he's no love for the Wydeville wench or her ambitious family.

No, we'll stay either here or at Middleham. Don't look so disappointed, lass. I know you miss your family in London but you must content yourself with sending messages." He kissed me softly on the lips, his eyes beginning to smoulder with languorous promise. "Besides, I thought you were so happy with me you needed no other pleasures—"

"I am! I am!" I flung myself upon him so that he slithered down the tree-trunk he was leaning against and bumped his head.

"Why is it then, you're always beating me?" He rubbed his head with mock agony.

The sheltered privacy of the trees guarded our nakedness as we unlaced our garments to tangle upon a soft, leafy bed, stroking each other's bodies into a frenzy of delight. Groaning with ecstasy, Miles turned me in his arms to straddle him so that the dark, luxuriant cascade of my unloosed hair fell across his face. Twisting his fingers among its curls he pulled me gently towards him, so our mouths might touch and drink in each other's moisture.

As my tongue traced the black hair that threaded down the muscled contours of his chest towards his hardening manhood, he groaned and wrenched back my head. Drawing me down astride him again, he reached to squeeze my breasts, his eyes a furious blue blaze beneath me.

"Forget what those cold-blooded priests have taught you," he breathed, suddenly clasping his hands under the curve of my buttocks to lift and enter me with a swift, fierce, delicious thrust. "Rules made for monks deny the woman's right to lie on top, yet I avow a wench may please a man any way she chooses. These holy men know nothing of pleasure," he murmured, as he urged me to move above him, his gasps growing harsh and ragged. "You may ride me now to paradise."

Dizzied with kisses, his mouth now at my breasts, sucking and teasing the taut nipples, Miles pressed me closer, thrusting up to meet me with mounting urgency and vigour. Writhing sinuously in the power of new-discovered sensation I abandoned myself to this surely forbidden pleasure, flinging back my hair, enticing him with rapturous cries, revelling in the strength, the heat of him, as we strove together towards a powerful, shuddering release.

Spent and satiated, we fell apart at last to lie in the drowsy aftermath of love. Lazily entwined, we watched the sunlight flicker through the branches and Miles covered me with little kisses.

As we strolled back through bracken and heather, his arm about my waist, he told me how he returned from Burgundy to take up soldiering for Warwick, and after the Earl's disgrace, he joined the Duke of Gloucester's men.

"I've pledged my allegiance, Nan, and nothing will make me change. Gloucester's bound by loyalty to his brother, the King, as am I to him. He's a good man and we're fortunate in his patronage." He stopped to look me in the eye. "But no more fortune-telling—"

"But what about the dream?"

Guilt bloomed in my cheeks, for hadn't I read the cards for Agnes Moore already? Little Amy tattled of the new game she'd caught me playing, intriguing Agnes. Before long she persuaded me to share my secret. Miles' warning caused a sharp stab of anxiety. Could I trust Amy? Agnes called her a "canny" lass. I wondered how many others she told about my skill with the cards?

"Put it aside, lass," he said. "I'll not go chasing after a pair of mysterious brothers, however noble! Don't look so serious. If fate will have us find them, then let it be so—until then, let's enjoy life while we can!"

Somehow Miles made my fears evaporate like morning mist. Anxious to please him, I immersed myself in my new life. Love makes fools of all of us. Hadn't I learned that lesson from Eleanor? But Mara's wisdom and Brother Brian's advice faded into insignificance while I plunged recklessly into passion. I think I was delirious that summer. I spent my days with Agnes and her friends and wallowed in Miles' love-making by night. Never had I felt so young or happy.

This feverish existence couldn't last. Presently I noticed things that intruded on my perfect contentment. Miles disappeared on a number of puzzling errands. Amy evaded my questions but her sly smile vexed. Agnes pretended ignorance and Lucy eyed me suspiciously. When I questioned Miles he grew tetchy. I realised my adored husband had secrets of his own that he wouldn't share. They say Love's blind. But how long can his foolish blindness keep us in thrall? I had welcomed Miles as the passionate lover of my dreams. Now I found him flawed. What was everyone hiding from me?

Chapter forty-four

"Who is she?"

Agnes plucked me by the sleeve, trying to divert my attention to a fine display of fabrics. I'd never seen such pure dyes and several women, including fat Lucy from the buttery, exclaimed over the quality of the wool. But the flaxen-haired wench with the bold stare demanded my notice. I couldn't stop myself from looking at her.

"Look at this, Nan." Agnes lifted a heather-coloured worsted. "Have you ever seen the like?"

"It's not the first time I've noticed her in the market." I ran the cloth between my finger and my thumb. "But I'll swear today she wants me to pay her heed. And you're equally determined to avoid my questions. Now tell me, who is she? If you don't tell me, I'll ask someone else."

I looked pointedly at Lucy but she pretended to be engrossed in examining a length of green wool, so I turned again to eye the buxom figure leaning against the wall. "Or better still, I'll go myself to ask her what she wants of me."

"Nay, don't do that!" Agnes seized my arm. "Pay her no mind. She's bent on making mischief."

"What cause has she to single me out? Until I came to Barnard, I never clapped eyes on her before. There's some secret here."

"No secret." Agnes smoothed her calloused hand over a plum coloured velvet. "Her name's Chrissie Burnham and her father's a tapster in Staindrop. Her mother'll likely be hereabout somewhere for they're often here on market days."

The woman by the wall rewarded me with an insolent smile as if she sought to challenge my presence at the market. Something in the jut of her hips and careless fold of her arms implied self-assurance. The saucy curl of her red lips suggested she knew a good deal more than I did about certain matters. An instinctive prickle of dislike roused in me an irrational desire to box her ears. When I confided this to Agnes, she sniggered and whispered something to Lucy that made her cackle like a hen after laying an egg.

"Ee, but thou art a canny wench," she said.

"Aye, you've got the measure of Chrissie Burnham and no mistake," said Agnes.

Our laughter disturbed the handsome figure by the wall, for she pulled herself upright and thrust out her elbows as if ready to counter some offence. I couldn't help but admire the brazen courage of her.

"I daresay she's many admirers. She's comely enough in a kind of shameless manner, but I can't see what quarrel she might have with me."

The quick exchange of glances between Agnes and Lucy and the uncomfortable shuffling of the other women suddenly enlightened me, as clear as if a voice spoke in my head.

"This has something to do with Miles."

The words scarce fell from my lips when an older, plumper woman carrying a black-haired child joined the wench. They huddled into conversation, and then, taking the child from her mother, for I'd no doubt this older woman was she, the fair-haired wench turned deliberately so I might see the child quite clearly. It was like a slap in the face.

Agnes squeezed my arm. "It was a long time ago. No one can be sure about it. Chrissie Burnham's so free with her favours hereabouts I doubt she's sure herself who fathered the brat. Pay her no mind. She just wants to make trouble. She can't bear to see someone else's got him for a husband. No one in the dale could swear who that bairn's father is."

I loved Agnes for the comfort of her bluster but I'd no doubt who'd sired the black-haired boy.

I nodded at the wench in acknowledgement, and holding my head high, turned back toward the castle. "I think I've seen enough of the market today," I said.

Approaching our apartment in the Headlam Tower above the old gate-house, I heard a stifled squeal. Thrusting open the door, I came face to face with a giggling, pink-cheeked Amy. The smile fell from her mouth. Nevertheless, her eyes darted sly backward glances as she adjusted her bodice and smoothed her dishevelled hair.

"What's going on?" I asked a sheepish-looking Miles.

"A jest—nothing more." He feigned a grin and gave Amy a quick tap on the bottom. "Off with you now and no more nonsense. What would your aunt say if she knew you were tangling with such a rogue?"

Amy's flush deepened but the saucy pout didn't deceive me. She looked out from under veiled eyelids, nostrils flaring, like a pretty little filly who knows she's admired. With a bob of a curtsey she sidled out through the open door, casting a quick, furtive glance over her shoulder.

"Nan," said Miles smoothly, taking my basket. "I thought you'd gone to the market. Didn't you find anything to suit your fancy?"

I turned on him immediately, berating him for his lechery with the fury of an ale-wife until at last I could speak no more and dissolved into violent sobs. He let me weep myself into snivelling silence and then, wrapping an arm around my shoulders, drew me to the settle.

"Have you finished with me now?" He grimaced. "Or is there more? I can't think this outburst was caused just by my teasing a foolish serving-wench. I think you've something else in mind."

"Chrissie Burnham is on my mind," I said. I spat the words into his face as a snake does its venom and saw the sudden recoil in his eyes.

"Ah," he said and turned his glance aside.

"Is that all you have to say?" My voice shrilled with spite.

"I wondered how long it would be before she showed up. Well, now you've seen her. What's there to say? I never lied to you about my past and I've no doubt you heard some pretty tales of me at Middleham. But Chrissie Burnham has no more claim on me than any other man."

"She has your child."

"Perhaps, perhaps not." He shrugged his shoulders. "She couldn't swear to it."

"You would deny your own son?" I asked bitterly. Envious tears filled my eyes.

"I can't be certain he's mine." He gathered me to him with a sigh. "But I've seen she doesn't want for anything. The lad's better off than most."

"And then I find you dallying with Amy."

Miles laughed. "By the Rood, tell me you don't believe I'd seriously tangle with Amy Sadler? I teased the wench—nothing more."

He held me at arm's length so he could look into my face the better, then kissed me soundly, assuring me of his continued affection, cosseting me with tender words and soft caresses until I ached to believe him.

"I know what you need."

He picked me up and carried me to bed. His hands were busy at my laces even before we'd fallen backward. I didn't try to struggle.

Chapter forty-five

Standing by the casement one fine July evening, engrossed in watching the young horses paraded to and fro in the courtyard, I didn't hear Miles slip into the chamber. A prickle of disquiet finally turned me.

I ran towards him then laughing with surprise and pleasure. "Oh, Miles, I didn't realise you'd—"

His furious roar halted me in my tracks. I opened my mouth to form a question but a blow knocked me off my feet. Brutal knuckles grazed my teeth, splitting my lip. Shocked beyond reason, I clung against the wall, shielding my head and face, while Miles spewed invective. A warm, salty taste flooded my mouth.

"I'll not endure foul sorcery in my household, do you hear? There'll be no taint of witchcraft on my name! By Christ's Wounds, I'll beat the wickedness out of your skull if I catch you conjuring again!"

He seized a jug from the shelf, shattering it against the hearth. Other articles followed, and I flinched from each splintering crash until the room finally stilled. In the pulsing silence, I inhaled the smell of mildew from the stonework, my heart's panicked thud echoing in my ears. Tensed for the next assault, I listened to the fury of his breathing as he crouched over me, sensed the heat off him and willed myself not to scream.

I knew in an instant Lucy'd betrayed me. She could never keep quiet about anything. Learning from Amy about my strange picture cards, she badgered me to read her fortune. How I cursed the sly little serving-wench with the pretty face. Lucy had, as they say in the north, "a tongue that wags." Garrulous by nature, she spilled confidences with no more thought than a hen that takes corn from the butcher's hand.

"Get up." A hiss of contempt accompanied this command.

Face shielded, I rose clumsily, clutching the wall for support. Miles spun me round by the shoulder forcing me to confront him.

In the flickering candle-light his face gleamed wolfish. The wild black hair, the unshaven flesh stretched across high cheekbones, the lips pulled back from the sharp teeth, and the fierce eyes like blue flames, resembled the features of a savage beast.

"I've never trafficked with evil spirits," I said, flinching again as he raised his other fist. "You may ask my village priest."

"But you told fortunes. And I told you not to!" Seizing a handful of my hair he wrenched me closer, flecks of spittle flying from his lips. "I had it from Si Henshaw in the tavern."

"A fitting place to hear such gossip," I dared to answer, though I trembled in every limb.

"Just gossip, is it?" Ale tainted his breath. His thumb pressed cruelly against my throat.

For a heartbeat I stared into the pitiless, bloodshot eyes of a stranger, but I held my nerve.

"I'm not wed to a witch, then?" He wavered in the face of my defiance, the storm of his anger evaporating.

Knowing the ale fuddled his reason, I answered carefully. "I've never conjured the devil nor harmed anyone. But I told you, since childhood, I've had an ability to see what others can't. I made no secret of it."

"But you told Lucy Henshaw's fortune." In his eyes a spark of danger reignited.

"It was no more than a game. Everyone plays such games on feast-days. You told me yourself your mother took advice from the local wise-woman."

"But witches are more than tricksters. It was a witch did for my mate, Rob, at Barnet. And now she wears a crown."

"You mean the queen?" An appalling image of a dagger slicing through a taut throat brought bile into my mouth.

"Aye, the king's Grey mare!" He laughed bitterly. "She did for Warwick and his army. All those brave lads died at Barnet with her conjuring. I'll never forget or forgive her for that damned fog."

Tears welled in his eyes. When I reached out a hand, he crushed it to his lips. "Sweet Jesu," he whispered, kissing each finger-tip in turn, "I never meant to hurt you, Nan." He touched his own trembling fingers to my cut lip, smearing the blood away with his thumb. His bewildered expression suggested he'd only just noticed what he'd done.

"It was when Si spoke of your fortune-telling." From his bluster he evidently sensed something of my hurt. "It reminded me of that Wydeville bitch and what she did." He slipped an arm about me as if to win my confidence.

I didn't shake him off but neither did I respond. Hadn't I confided in him and shared my closely guarded secrets? How could he destroy this trust in a single, drunken moment? Would he turn on me now as Johanna and Philippa had done? Wary as a wounded creature, I shrank into myself.

"Surely it was the king who quarrelled with Warwick."

"Aye, but who is it has the king in thrall?" Miles snapped his teeth. "She hated Warwick from the first. She knew she must crush him if she were to keep Edward's soul clenched in the hollow of her white hand. Warwick loved his men, but more than all he loved Ned Plantagenet."

"If Warwick loved the king why did he abandon him and swear allegiance to Lancaster?" I grew sick of all this war talk. Would it never end? "People say Warwick was the victim of his own ambition because he realised he couldn't rule Edward any more."

Miles' face grew grimmer. "If you see a fly entwined in a spider's web, what would you do? For charity's sake you'd kill it, not watch its life-blood slowly sucked away. So Warwick knew what he must do to save the king. That Wydeville bitch cozened Edward with her black sorcery. Warwick knew her for what she was. I tell you Nan, because I knew him—Never mind what people say! I was there! He may have fought for Daft Harry but his heart still belonged to York. Even when he knew he was damned he wouldn't quit the field. They'd a horse waiting for him in Wrotham Wood, but he'd vowed to fight beside the men on foot and share their danger. And by the Rood, he kept his promise. That devil's whore had him stabbed through the eye, you know. She's no pity or remorse. No man I ever met possesses such cruelty."

Moved by his passion, I wrapped my arms about him, trying to lay aside my own sense of injustice. We swayed together, sinking before the hearth, tearful as two children who've just mended a quarrel.

"You should have seen that fog creep in—Like an animal, a grey twisting thing that blotted out the light. It wasn't natural. The men said it was a spell. A prophecy foretold Warwick would be undone by a wizard. It had us all frightened."

"Tell me about Rob." Alarmed by this talk of prophecy, I cradled his head in my lap, stroking the dishevelled hair. An unpleasant memory stirred.

"I met him in Burgundy. Rob was a deserter. He abandoned the Lancastrian army when Margaret let her mercenaries run mad. He couldn't stomach such atrocities. He told me he'd only taken to soldiering to mend a heart-ache for they'd wed the maid he coveted to another."

My hand froze in mid-gesture. A chill enveloped me. "Robin Arrowsmith."

Miles raised his head, blinking in disbelief. His eyes rolled vaguely. The ale would shortly bring a drowning sleep. "Have I told you this before?"

"Never. I knew it must be Robin. His sweetheart was my friend —Alys. My village priest told me of their separation."

"He died with her name upon his lips. They wed her to the reeve."

"And broke her heart. I've dreamed of Robin many times. It's hard to think he's dead. He was such a lively, mischievous boy. Alys adored him. Even Brother Brian knew that. It was wrong to separate them. I had an awful dream about a foggy battlefield—I called your name and woke the household—"

"Your dreams are dangerous. I'm afraid of them and afraid for you." He fixed his eyes on mine, their expression steely. "You must keep this strange gift of yours a secret. I daren't think what our Duke would do if he were to find out. He abhors witchcraft."

"But Lady Anne—"

Miles pressed brutal fingers on my mouth. I felt again the pulse and throb of pain.

"I don't want to hear any more." There was no mistaking the warning. The shadows fell across his face, lending it an ominous expression. I shivered in spite of the heat in the room, conscious of Mara's cards hidden in the little wooden box Harry had made me for trinkets lying but a span from where we sat together. Suppose Amy had told others about them?

"I forbid you to dabble in such practices again." Miles crushed me to him possessively, jealously, as if he feared I might leave him. "A child may plead innocence, but no priest will save a woman from the accusation of witch-craft. By Christ's bones, Nan, I wouldn't have you burn."

Chapter forty-Six

"Aunt Agnes says wolfsbane's good for bruises." Amy smiled, but her eyes narrowed slyly.

Morning sunlight filtered through the chamber as she brushed the shards of pottery from the hearth. "My uncle had a vicious temper. He was always breaking things."

"It was an accident," I lied. "I fell."

She didn't answer. Humming a merry snatch of a tune, she gathered up Miles' discarded cloak and folded it neatly. She rearranged the hangings, straightened furniture, picked up scattered cushions. I clenched my fists, sickened by her bright, quick movements, the confident lift of her head, the mischievous gleam in her eyes. How well did she know Miles?

"My sister-in-law asked me if you'd tell her fortune."

The import of her words pricked me like a dagger's point.

"It's not something I want to circulate—"

"Oh!" Dropping a cushion on the settle, she looked at me with a wide, clear gaze. "I didn't realise it was a secret."

"The duke dislikes such practices."

"But I thought it was just a game." She looked at me coyly, stooping to retrieve a broken candle from the rushes. "It's witchcraft the duke hates."

"Well, I wouldn't want him to misconstrue such games." I turned back to my glass dabbing some ointment on the bruise, my heart beating fast.

"She'll be disappointed."

I ignored the remark.

"I suppose Master Forrest doesn't like fortune-telling either." She moved closer. I smelled the scent of lavender on her amethyst gown. The sly insinuation made me pause. I touched a finger to my raw lip.

"It'll be hard to stop the womenfolk talking about it."

I turned on her at once, confronting the power of her bold stare. "Then you must make sure you don't encourage them anymore," I said.

She shrugged. "I'll do my best." She awarded me an almost insolent smile. "I wouldn't want to make Master Forrest angry."

"You can go now, Amy." Trying to keep my voice steady, I fumbled in my purse. "Here, buy yourself some sweetmeats. You've done well."

She snatched the coins greedily.

Better to buy her silence, I thought as she skipped out of the chamber. She could prove dangerous.

⁂

When the leaves hung scorched gold and brittle, a messenger arrived from Middleham ordering us to return. Relief flooded me. Miles had grown restless and moody, subject to frequent ill-humours. More and more, he frequented the ale-house and came home surly and intractable. I couldn't understand this change in him, but I blamed the drink. Though he never raised his hand to me again, I lived on a knife-edge and learned to dread the storm of violence which tore down hangings and shattered trinkets.

Pert little Amy pretended solicitude on these occasions, skittering after me and making a great fuss of setting the chambers to rights. Inwardly I fumed at the cloying sympathy. Increasingly she managed to raise the subject of fortune-telling when we were alone, reminding me of how Lucy prattled to others about my astounding skill in such matters. It was like picking at a scab. The bright-eyed innocence of her face roused a shameful animosity in me. My glass revealed the reason. How drawn I looked—how heavy and lumpish in my loose gown. Her insidious gaze slid over my figure.

"Would you like me to fetch anything from the market?" The flirtatious way she tossed her pretty, auburn curls annoyed me. "I don't expect you want to go out in this heat." As always, she managed to cozen some coins out of me.

The especially hot summer brought bouts of sickness and townswomen reported outbreaks of the bloody flux all over the dale. Everyone seemed on edge.

◦⧸ℭ◦

One humid evening at the beginning of August, Amy burst in, breathless with excitement.

"Oh Mistress Forrest, there's been some trouble in the tavern. A man's been killed in a brawl." Her eyes flicked around the chamber. "Is Master Forrest not home yet?"

"He went on some errand for the duke." I tried to answer calmly, but the implication of her question frightened me.

"Perhaps he's ridden over to Staindrop," she said. This seemingly innocent remark stung me like a barb.

"Perhaps." I lumbered to the casement, drawn by the sound of voices in the courtyard. "Who are all these people?"

Amy craned her neck to peer over my shoulder. "That's the landlord," she said, pointing to a stocky fellow in a padded leather jerkin. "And those are some of the men who were in the tavern. There's Colin Waters who told me about it and that's John who found the body—"

"So no one knows who killed him?" I turned to face the girl.

"No, but some names were mentioned—"

Did I detect the glint of accusation in her eyes?

"Thank you, Amy, for letting me know the news." Though my heart hammered, I turned back to the settle and picked up my sewing. "But there's no need to wait with me," I said cool as frost. "I'm sure Master Forrest will be home soon."

Gossip raged for days after but no one was brought to account. Miles dismissed my questions though I suspected his involvement even before I heard Lucy chattering in the buttery, for from that night he stopped going to the village and drank over-much at home instead.

◦⧸ℭ◦

"Found lying on the steps with his skull broke," Lucy said with relish. The buttery maid's little mouth formed a perfect O of horror. She leaned forward like a butterfly lured by the sweet taste of nectar.

"Oh he's an evil temper, that one. I wouldn't want to cross him."

"Si told me Dawkins was a spy." Lucy gabbled with excitement. "Forrest had the Duke of Gloucester's instruction to silence him. It's not the first time. They say he's undertaken such commissions before. Why, I heard, he even had a hand in poor King Henry's death!"

"But they say King Harry died of melancholy."

Lucy snorted at the wench's gasp. "Everyone knows that sainted idiot was murdered. Five years they kept him a prisoner in the Tower and everyone knew King Edward wanted him dead." She lowered her voice and leaned toward the maid. "They say his corpse bled on the pavement at St Paul's in London. Folk who saw the body say his skull was crushed— the hair all matted with blood. Does that sound like melancholy? No, our duke recommended some reliable skull-breaker to rid his brother of a nuisance—"

"Forrest?"

"Who else? He was with the duke in London that May. It's what he's hired to do—why, everyone knows that. The rest is wind — And I'll wager this business with Dawkins—" She looked up suddenly and spotted me.

"But was Dawkins a spy?" persisted the buttery-maid.

"Why, hinny, how would I know?" Lucy chuckled nervously. She nodded at me to alert the girl's attention. "Why, Mistress Forrest, how are you? Amy tells me you'll shortly be returning to Middleham. You'll happen find the journey something of a trial." She smiled sympathetically at my swollen belly.

"No more than when I came here, I hope." Her broad face flushed with embarrassment. I think she could have bitten out her tongue, recalling my earlier miscarriage.

"Ee, I've never known a hotter summer," she said to cover her embarrassment.

I clung to the door post, my mind still whirling. Lucy's suggestion that Miles had been hired to murder King Henry horrified me. Yet Miles *had* accompanied the duke to London in

May. "It's what he's hired to do..." Those words gnawed at me. My queasy stomach lurched threateningly.

"You've gone very pale, hinny," Lucy's voice echoed from afar. I sank down on the stool she brought. And suddenly, unbidden, I glimpsed a broken cage and a forlorn black bird hopping to and fro upon a simple altar, a spattering of blood before the cross—

"It's a fair way from here to Yorkshire," said the buttery-maid.

"Miles has promised I'll ride in a litter like a grand lady," I replied.

Lucy handed me a pewter mug and, forcing down nausea, I swallowed a mouthful of weak ale. She squeezed my hand.

"We'll miss you here at Barnard." Her eyes shone with sincerity. "It's no light matter having a child. I should know, for I've had six." She snatched a look at the buttery-wench and winked. "Remember that when you're strolling in the dark with that lad of yours!"

The babe would be born at the end of November, that dark mysterious time of year. Already the thought of its creeping fogs oppressed my spirits. I daren't say anything to Miles. He'd grown more sensitive about what he termed my "odd fancies" even though he showed a tender regard for my condition that quickly drew us back into our old intimacy.

Relieved to be back in Yorkshire and to glimpse the towers of Middleham with their painted gargoyles like powerful sentinels hove into view, I tried to blot out the implication of Miles' secret errands.

Chapter Forty-Seven
Middleham Castle

"Your Grace!"

Nicholas Headlam, pale face scalded by fierce sunlight, panted across the green, rudely interrupting the game of bowls Lady Anne was playing with Meg Huddleston, Grace Pullan and her clever cousin Elizabeth Parre.

Lady Anne shouted with delight as Grace Pullan's ball swerved, striking against Meg Huddleston's with a loud crack and driving it further off target. Then laughing because she was winning, she snatched the scroll from the messenger's hands and scanned its contents.

A fierce frown swiftly replaced the smiles. Throwing down the letter and abandoning her ball with a thud, she stormed into the castle. Mouths dropped open. Grace and Meg exchanged wide-eyed looks, while quick-witted Elizabeth snatched up her yellow skirts and ran lightly across the grass in pursuit. The stifling August heat crackled with tension. Clumsily, I stooped to retrieve the letter.

"What's displeased Lady Anne so much? Read it, Nan. What does it say?"

"It says Her Grace, Queen Elizabeth, has been safely delivered of a son," I answered, dizzy with the effort of rising too swiftly. "And he's to be named Richard."

How many messages passed in their quick, furtive glances!

Ignoring an embarrassed Nicholas Headlam, brushing aside the excited gaggle of women, I plodded heavily after the duchess. I'd a fierce headache from lingering in the sun and this news stirred old anxieties.

In the corridor I stumbled into Miles returning from the stables. He slipped a supportive arm about me, his face alight with impertinent humour.

"So the Wydeville bitch has whelped another brat!"

"That's unfair, Miles. Childbirth's as difficult for a queen as it is for the lowliest spinner. Besides, she's overcome misfortune and endured poverty to achieve her present status. With the king in exile, she waited alone in the Westminster Sanctuary—"

"Hardly alone, sweeting. She had her witch of a mother with her—"

"And no idea whether she'd ever see her husband again."

"You're too generous, my love." Miles squeezed me close and dropped a kiss on my cheek. "But it's the queen's family the barons really hate, isn't it, Guy?" He appealed to the little lad he'd hired to attend on us. "They're like greedy geese, always following her to court, and begging favours of the king. Popinjays is what folk call them, for they're nothing but petty country squires who don't deserve advancement. Besides," he added, with a wink, patting my jutting belly, "they breed like conies!"

"Suppose these two princes are the ones I dream about—the ones in danger?"

Throwing back his head, he roared with laughter. Taking his lead, snub-nosed Guy, dancing at his heels, grinned up at me, roguish face brimming with mischief.

"What nonsense passes through your pretty head!" Miles kissed me indulgently. "I suppose you'll have me galloping off to London now and vowing to guard these Wydeville princes with my life?"

Impatiently I shook him off, pressing a hand to my throbbing temples.

This sudden gesture erased his mirth. Halting my steps, he turned me toward him. "You look pale, Nan. Never mind Lady Anne—Let me have Guy fetch you some spiced wine." Frowning, he touched my brow. "As I guessed! Standing in the sun's made you feverish. Lady Anne's thoughtless keeping you outside so long."

Having dispatched the lad to the kitchens, he steered me towards our chamber, and in spite of my protestations that I could prepare myself a hot infusion of sweet marjoram, carried me to the settle. He made me lie back while he stroked my temples—his strong hands amazingly soothing. "You worry over-much, lass. Put these wild thoughts out of your mind and let me take care of you. We must be specially careful of you now."

But I miscarried at the end of September. Though Jane Collins comforted my distress, Miles suffered most. He blamed himself for the shock of my encountering Chrissie Burnham at Barnard, the accusations he'd levelled at me in July, and the discomfort of the journey back to Middleham.

I lay on the couch in the hazy, purple twilight, still weak and defeated by my loss, too preoccupied to heed him. Only Jane Collins witnessed my rage. She listened without censure as I railed bitterly against the fate that had robbed me of my child, yet favoured the rude health of the bastard boy being raised in the north.

"Forgive me Nan." Miles knelt beside me, cursing his neglect. "I've been too hard on you—but by the Rood, I was afraid someone would tell the duke about the fortune-telling—" He bowed his head like a sinner seeking absolution. "If you'd stayed at Barnard you might have kept this babe—" With a sob he laid his head on my hands.

Absentmindedly, I stroked the unruly black hair, too bruised to answer. He *had* hurt me that last summer. I'd seen a side of him I never imagined, and the shock of it still burned. Could I forgive him? Vaguely I wondered if we'd ever recapture that tempestuous rush of feeling that had driven us to seek out one another for so long.

Would I ever hold a child of my own in my arms? Leaning over the cradles of the babes in the nursery, I ached with longing. I was twenty years old. Was I destined to remain barren like Lady Anne?

The little duchess had miscarried several times. Hearing of my loss, she called upon me at once and, scattering sweetmeats into my lap, urged me to make a speedy recovery. But her merry humour couldn't hide her own anguish and I took her hand in mine. For a moment we shared a wordless sympathy.

"You must join my ladies." Her false cheer stung me to tears. "Nursery duties are too burdensome for you. I missed you while you were at Barnard." She turned to leave, a bird-boned figure in a hyacinth-blue gown, then paused as if remembering something. "We've much to discuss."

The import of those words struck me like a blow.

During the next months, she kept me constantly at her side, introducing me to her circle of well-born waiting women in the bower-chamber as her dearest friend in an hour of great need.

"Without Nan, I might still be languishing in that awful kitchen in Dowgate." Her proud manner clearly invited all to look at me, causing me much embarrassment. Under the sharp scrutiny of their curious, aristocratic gaze, I felt small and insignificant, a common creature among thoroughbreds. Amused by my bashful manner, she recounted the fantastical tale of her disguise.

"I've at least one thing for which I may thank my cousin, George," she said. A coquettish tilt of her head lent amusement to her expression. "If he'd not hidden me in Dowgate, I'd never have met Nan. She showed me my destiny."

A rustle of interest stirred amongst the keen-eyed ladies. Guiltily I flinched, aware of the fortune telling cards hidden behind a loose brick in the fireplace in our apartment.

"Ah, but that's a secret not for your ears," she said teasingly. "Your busy tongues would tattle to the whole of Middleham if I told you all. Suffice to say Nan helped me find my destiny in my husband, the Duke of Gloucester."

She urged them out into the gardens, retaining me to stroll with her through the draughty avenues of fluttering trees. Watery October sunshine sent the ladies scampering like a flock of unruly hens. The shrill tones of their animated gossip floated on the wind. No doubt they prattled of Lady Anne's latest whim—me. But few were privy to her thoughts.

She proved a skilled dissembler. I watched her play the dutiful wife at banquets. Eyes downcast, she feigned humility. Noble guests thought her meek, demure as a maid, timid like her mother, but I knew this to be a sham, a mask that hid a scheming, clever mind. Mild-faced Isabelle, her elder sister, was the humble wife, but Lady Anne favoured her father. How well she deceived— especially her husband, whose own ambition she fed drop by drop, sweetly urging him to extend his power in the north.

"Did you ever see King Henry's French Queen?"

We sat in her bower-chamber a little apart from the others while Katherine Scrope read aloud from some book of romance. The rainy late autumn afternoon seemed to quiet us. In the mellow candle-light the elegant ladies drooped over discarded needlework, their rapt faces caught up in the tale of chivalry.

"Only as she rode by in a procession."

Lady Anne's eyes glittered with sly remembrance. "Now there was a woman." I noted her grudging admiration with curiosity. "Marguerite d'Anjou—a woman of strongest mettle. How she chastised my father! I saw him on his knees before her, saw him kiss the hem of her gown and beg forgiveness, then heard him swear allegiance to Lancaster." She laughed harshly, causing Katherine to pause. The ladies swivelled their heads.

"Go on, go on." She waved a careless hand. "Of course, it was all lies and they knew it. Both of them were greedy. They needed each other to fulfil their desires. He craved to rule England, and she would have sold her soul to see her son crowned."

"Did you love Prince Edward?"

Shocked by my audacity, Lady Anne turned the full, penetrating stare of her green cat eyes on me. "I was barely fourteen, Nan, and had been educated to detest the entire Lancastrian herd. What did I know of love?" She grimaced. "In the country I think girls may wed their sweethearts, but for those of noble blood matches are made for advancement or gain, to mend a quarrel or seal an allegiance. If love should follow, why then so much the better—but if not—" she shrugged. "A man may get children on a woman without love and still be happy to see his son carry on his name. And a woman may become a wealthy chatelaine protected by her husband's strength without love."

I thought of Alys and the reeve, but didn't say how even the poorest of us would sell a maid's happiness for security. Fat Marion doubtless welcomed the reeve's generosity in taking her pretty, dowerless daughter to wife. I knew Alys' tears and Robin's heartbreak counted for nothing when measured against the promise of a prosperous future.

"You may have found love in Master Forrest," Lady Anne said, "but others are neither so fortunate nor reckless in their choices." Her face assumed a sudden grave expression. "A noble wife's duty is to provide an heir and so far I've failed."

She clapped her hands suddenly and Kate looked up from her book. "Enough for now." Ignoring the groans of protest she executed her sweetest smile. "You read well, Kate. You may continue the tale tomorrow."

I wondered then if Lady Anne loved her duke. The servants still whispered of his devotion, but I saw no answering sign in her.

Chapter Forty-Eight

In early spring, on the pretext of teaching me to play chess, Lady Anne began to share her most secret ambitions. Though I dreaded the responsibility of these secrets, I knew the real strategy was to get me to read her fortune. Since Barnard, Miles had counselled me to avoid anything that smacked of sorcery. But how could I refuse a duchess?

Picking up a pawn, she snorted with contempt. "When my father quarrelled with King Edward, I was nothing to him—no more than this lowly piece which may be sacrificed to win a game. From being his treasured daughter, I was reduced to a mere bargaining point. If he could marry me to the Lancastrian heir then he might grasp the greatest prize in England." Smiling bitterly, she replaced the pawn. "Through me he thought to rule. And I hated him then. I vowed when I wed Prince Edward, I'd be ruled by no man—father or husband. I'd follow Marguerite's example. They married her against her will to that simpleton, Henry, but she exerted her own power—and she never wavered in her purpose. When she bore her son she fought for his inheritance —even to the last."

"But the talk of his parentage—?"

"He talked of nothing but fighting, you know—her brave Prince Edward." She ignored my interruption. "His mother made a god of him and he thought himself invincible." She uttered a tiny, melodious laugh as if at the recollection of this folly. "A fine way to begin a marriage—but, young as I was, I'd no reason to expect romance." She paused as if to remember clearly. "King Edward dragged him from Tewkesbury Abbey where he hid after the battle." Her smiles grew melancholy. "When he confronted the king he spoke with such arrogance, demanding back his throne, the king struck him on the cheek with his gauntlet. I can well believe it. There's another story of how the king, himself, put the prince to death—stabbed him with his dagger. Perhaps it's true— Ned has a fierce temper— but it matters nothing now."

Her words stirred an old dream and I winced at the bleak remembrance.

"You dared to ask me, Nan, if I loved him—Marguerite's son. I wept when I heard of his death, but more for myself than his loss. I'd been a wife for five months. All I could think was: Who will want me now?" Her tongue flicked over the tiny pointed cat's teeth. "And I know you're thinking— why did I marry my cousin, Richard?"

Several of the ladies *were* listening now. Their muttering petered into silence. Undeterred, Lady Anne continued her revelation. "Richard wanted my fortune. He and brother George worried like terriers over the Neville and Beauchamp inheritance." Her laughter rattled through the chamber, dry and brittle as bone. Deliberately, she turned to address all the listeners, her eyes hard as shards of green glass. "It's why dear George hid me in the Dowgate house—you all know the story—so Richard couldn't have me. And what could I do? Fatherless, widowed, alone? What better offer would I get?" Her face assumed a fierce, hunting aspect. "Besides, I knew Richard from childhood—He was sent to train under my father's tutelage at Middleham. I saw in him something of myself—the younger, less necessary child—Perhaps that drew us together—" She stopped suddenly. Gazing round at the astonished circle of faces, she tossed her head defiantly. "My, my, how shocked you all look! Yet you know as well as I do that such is the way of marriage among our families. Which one of you would prefer to wed a tradesman and live in a hut with a tribe of unruly brats?"

I couldn't join in the laughter which followed. While she and her ladies gossiped of the various noble matches being made that year, I slipped away to seek Miles.

"To what do I owe this honour?" he asked, when I found him in the mews. The falconer, who gave me a curt nod of acknowledgement, was showing him a fine peregrine.

"The duke will fly this bird soon," he said. "Young Jonas caught it as a brancher—a young bird just about to leave the nest— aye, it's the makings of a swift hunter, this un." Gripping the bird firmly in wiry, scarred fingers, he fanned out the broad wing feathers skilfully with his other hand so we might admire the power in them.

286

"Jonas said you've acquired some eyasses from Sheriff Hutton."

Stroking the peregrine's barred breast tenderly with his gnarled knuckles, the falconer gave Miles a shrewd glance.

"Aye, I may have done. But they're not for every knave to gawk at."

He put the peregrine back on its perch.

It watched us fiercely, yellow eyes gleaming in the white face with its distinctive black markings. The sheen on its blue-grey plumage lay like liquid honey-glaze. Tiny bells on its jesses tinkled. I stretched out a finger to touch the sleek black head before the falconer slipped on its hood.

Clearing his throat noisily, the narrow-shouldered fellow turned to address Miles. "If thou wait a piece, I'll mebbe let thee see 'em. I can see thi wife has a gentle way with her."

Proudly he displayed the hatchlings with their scrawny, writhing necks and wide-stretched beaks.

"Happen the duke'll raise some of these for hissen," he said. "Or mebbe give one or two to his friends. He's taken thee hawking with him afore, I tek it?" He fixed me then with his agate gaze and gave me another grudging nod. "Some wenches mek a fuss and frighten the birds. I can see thou hast more sense. I like a quiet lass."

All the way back to our chambers, Miles jested about how I'd stolen the taciturn Yorkshire-man's heart.

"I like a quiet lass." Miles mimicked the falconer's grumbling voice and caught me in his arms. "I'll warrant the poor fellow will pine away in the mews for love of the little witch who's charmed him today."

I hated to be called a witch but didn't want to dispel Miles' good humour.

"Has the duke no duties for you?"

"When we left off hawking he dismissed us. He's had letters from London." Miles eased off his boots. "He seemed distracted— even out on the moors. Tom Metcalf told me there's been talk of the king reclaiming lands in France and he's raising money for some expedition or other."

"More war!" I grimaced, pouring a mug of ale.

"But why has Lady Anne dismissed you so soon, dear wife?" Miles mocked me as he accepted the proffered drink. "I thought she couldn't bear to part with you these days."

"I sneaked away." I grinned up at him mischievously, settling by the hearth. "She and her ladies are busy arranging matches for every single heiress in the county."

"Aye, she's an acquisitive head on her shoulders." Miles loosened his cornflower-blue doublet, exposing the lawn shirt beneath, and looked thoughtfully into the fire. "She certainly urged Gloucester to bring her mother to Middleham but was it just for the old lady's protection?"

"What do you mean?" It was the first time I'd heard Miles make a disparaging remark about the duchess.

"The Countess of Warwick possesses a fair fortune. Perhaps Lady Anne feels it safer in her husband's hands? After all, rich, elderly widows may still find suitors—" He gave me a saucy wink. "Remember John Wydeville and the Duchess of Norfolk?"

In light-hearted manner, I reproved this insinuation as I sipped my ale. The queen's young brother had married the ancient Norfolk dowager while still a stripling. I leaned against the warm stonework imagining how Maud would have entertained her listeners with some lewd tale of the old woman waiting in her bed while her youthful husband fondled her fortune.

"The whole of the country laughed at that match," I said. "Even Lady Anne giggled at the bawdy jests. But our duchess isn't above scheming herself. She may not be as avaricious as Elizabeth Wydeville but she's very ambitious—especially for her husband. Perhaps she wanted to please him by bringing her mother's fortune to Middleham? Nevertheless without a son she surely has little influence?"

Miles didn't answer. Our own childlessness was something we didn't discuss. But I could see he was considering my words very seriously.

Chapter forty-Nine

"Did you bring the cards?"

Ever since I'd miscarried, Lady Anne plagued me to look into the cards for answers. Both of us grew frantic for a child. Though she quickened twice, I remained barren since returning from Barnard—until now.

The fruitless French expedition took both our husbands away. During their absence we spent more time together. I'd not told Miles about my pregnancy, fearing to raise his hopes too soon. Now, flaunting my swelling belly, my heart singing with excitement, I longed for his return.

"It's so hot—" Lady Anne flapped her wide, jade sleeves. "I'll be glad when August's over. Did I tell you the troops are on their way home? You'll be able to tell your husband the good news—although he may see it for himself now!"

Clumsily, I drew the cards from my bodice. They spilled across the little table, The Lovers falling into Lady Anne's lap.

"Sit down, Nan." She giggled. "You've grown as fat as a sow and block out the light." Spite spoiled the jest. Lowering myself to the settle, I sensed the strength of envy that roused such malice and pitied her. Perhaps she felt it too for she threw me a cushion.

"Forgive my ill-manners." She picked up the scattered cards. "I wish I carried such a burden. My Lord grows anxious about my health, but I tell him I'm well and strong." Her laughter rang false. Turning desperate, tear-filled eyes on me, she shuffled the cards feverishly. "Suppose he puts me aside?"

Before I could respond she began to babble. "I married him in defiance of the priests without even waiting for the papal dispensation. I knew him, Nan, I knew how he stood in the shadows like me. No one dreamt of our ambitions but I believed our union would bring us great power—"

Something in this hysteria reminded me fleetingly of Eleanor.

"But without a son I'm nothing to him. I must have a son, Nan. I must!" She thrust out her chin defiantly. "And *you* must look into the cards and tell me I *will* bear my Lord an heir—and soon!" Imperiously she thrust them at me. "There!"

I laid them out in the familiar pattern Mara had taught, the heat of Lady Anne's passion scalding me like steam.

"You should beware the woman who holds the greatest power." The Empress' grave visage confronted me. "She stands between you and your desire."

"The Wydeville bitch." A sneer distorted her lovely mouth. "She has two sons now."

Flinching, I shut my eyes against her malicious outburst. As I turned the next card, two little boys with bright hair seemed to stare out at me from a barred window.

"No!"

Her cry returned me to the present. Beneath my fingers, the Hanged Man dangled from a leafy gibbet.

"Delay." My voice rang hollow with disappointment. I lifted my head to offer comfort just as a shaft of sunlight pierced the chamber. "Spring time." This ray of hope uplifted me. "We must wait until next spring."

"So many months—" Her anguish pierced me like a blade. "Why is she so fortunate and I must wait and wait—?" She lowered her voice, fixing her green eyes on me so fiercely I shivered. "They say her mother's a witch—Can't you help me, Nan? I know you have the skill—"

Thrusting the cards into my bosom, I sketched a curtsey. "Such skill is death, Your Grace." My hand before my mouth I ran clumsily from the chamber, retching with horror.

❧

I bore Dickon on a dark November night just before my own birthday. Watching streaks of lightning sear the black skies—for I demanded the shutters be opened—I held him fiercely. Gloating, I recalled Mara's words as I realised this child would walk under the sign of the powerful Scorpion and secretly promised I should cast his fortune to see what lay in store for him. Beside me, Jane Collins crowed with admiration and Miles wept for joy.

Nothing can ever destroy this happiness, I vowed. *Like a vixen with her cub I'll guard this child with my life.*

❦

The sound of his mother's weeping followed him from the abbey. He drew himself upright, smoothing his velvet doublet, anxious to appear adult in front of his escort, shamed by the display of female emotion they'd witnessed. His sisters clung to his clothes and hands, his mother clasped him in her arms—a thing most unusual—and all the time he could think only of escape. The gloom and confinement depressed him.

Outside, the air smelled fresh. Lifting his face to the sun, he revelled in his new freedom. But where were the adoring crowds to greet him? Instead of riding in splendour to the palace, someone bundled him in a sable cloak, the stifling hood drawn over his face, and carried him through winding alley-ways. Were they afraid someone might recognise him?

Somewhere along the way the elderly prelate into whose care his mother entrusted him, disappeared, and a new guardian was appointed—a stripling with a sly face who sported a white boar badge.

The lofty palace walls filled him with alarm. No guards and no courtiers? Surely this dark, spiralling staircase couldn't lead to the royal apartments?

Thrust into a fire-lit chamber where a bishop in splendid robes stretched out a welcoming hand, he stood on his own feet at last. Kissing the ruby ring in homage, he looked up into a hawk face whose yellow eyes gleamed fierce and predatory.

"Your brother will be glad to see you." Something so sinister in the silky voice frightened him. He turned to run but the door slammed with a resolute thud. "Now both of you will be safe together—"

I woke in darkness sweating with fear. Beside me, Miles lay far away in dreaming of his own, his mouth curved in a smile, one hand thrown careless on the pillow. Heart still racing, I slipped from the bed.

"Mistress Forrest—"

The little wench appointed to wait on me rose from her pallet by the cradle, like a ghost. I gasped, snatching at the bed-post for support.

"The babe?"

"Sleeping, Mistress." The girl held my arm while I stooped to peer at the swaddled bundle. "You should rest, too. You're still weak. Will I pour you some wine?"

"I had a bad dream. I was frightened. I wanted to save the boy —"

"He's quite safe, Mistress." She helped me back into bed and held a goblet of wine to my lips. "New mothers often have nightmares. It's normal to be anxious. Try to sleep while you can." She waited as I swallowed a mouthful and leaned back with exhaustion. "The babe will wake you soon enough."

She proved right. Startled by fretful wails, I sat up. For an instant, I looked round bewildered. Then the girl laid the babe into my arms. My heart melted at the sight of the soft mouth, the down of black hair, the huge unfocussed eyes, but even as I gazed in adoration the dream persisted, prickling my nerves.

The boy I'd seen before. A merry little knave, Miles would have called him. He'd the kind of face adults call pleasing. The sparkling eyes and red-gold hair would conquer hearts. His dress and manners suggested wealth and breeding. He and the older boy looked so alike— surely brothers? Miles laughed when I suggested they might be the Wydeville princes but somehow this made sense. The white boar badge intrigued, for it was Gloucester's personal device. Those spiralling stairs seemed familiar too. Surely the palace must be the Tower? But what was happening and why all the secrecy? And what was Stillington's purpose? The eager look in his eyes taunted me with its duplicity. He meant to harm those boys.

Filled with terror, I looked down at my own babe nestled close in my arms and remembered the pledge I'd made to guard him with my life. But didn't those other boys need my protection too? If I couldn't persuade Miles to help me find them, I must devise another way. Too long I'd revelled in my own preoccupations. "Perhaps the time hasn't yet come." Brother Brian's voice reminded me of the purpose that had set my childhood dreams in motion. "Perhaps the time is now," I whispered to the child in my arms.

Chapter fifty

In late March, Lady Anne summoned me back to her bower-chamber.

"I've missed you, Nan."

Sunlight bathed the blue and gold floor tiles, gilded the oaken panels. From the casement where her sewing women bent over their embroidery came the gentle cooing of doves. But the little duchess paced restlessly before the hearth, her book and chess pieces discarded, needlework crumpled like rag.

"I'm afraid."

Her slanting green eyes fixed upon me. Tension gripped the slender body. "My husband needs this son. I can't fail him again—"

"You're young, my lady." My eyes travelled over the almost flat belly. I attempted levity. "No need to fear. Why, even Queen Elizabeth had three daughters before she bore the king a son."

Her pretty features twisted. "Aye, but all the wenches lived. The Wydeville women have no trouble bearing children."

"All women fear childbirth." I placed my hand over hers in an impulsive gesture of affection. "Why, when Dickon was born you were with the Duke in London so you didn't see how frightened I was."

"You never seem afraid. Dickon's such a lusty little boy."

The envy in her tone, the involuntary tremble of her lips, made me ache with pity.

"Such fear is natural among women of every class, believe me. But afterwards it's all worthwhile." With pride, I recalled the healthy, squirming body I held in my arms each day. I hated leaving him in the nursery. "You'll see—This time it'll be different."

"Will it?" She bruised me with a searching stare, gripping my hand. How strong her grasp seemed for one so seemingly frail.

"Will you look into the cards to see if this time I'll bear a healthy, living son?"

I pulled my hand away, glancing at the other end of the chamber where the sewing women chattered and the doves' croon continued undisturbed.

"Your Grace, I told you last time to be patient until spring. And now spring's upon us." I indicated the huddled women. "My husband's warned me not to indulge in fortune telling. It's not safe —"

"*My* lord goes hawking in the afternoon," she said. Lightly she disregarded my excuses. "We'll not be disturbed by men-folk then. Come to my private chamber so we may speak freely." She smiled like a conspirator. "A secret," she whispered. The green eyes danced. Why did Lady Anne keep secrets from her lord?

I sought solace in the nursery.

"What's put the storm-clouds in your face?" Jane Collins gave me one of her sharp looks.

I shook my head.

"Tha'll not stop him drinking in the tavern." She assumed Miles and I had quarrelled and I didn't disabuse her. "And tha'll not stop him chasing after lasses." She folded blankets with a practised hand. "A full belly and a willing wench is all men want out of life. Oh, and a fight now and then to give them summat to shout about. I remember the Cade Riots and all the men swearing they'd follow him to the death. A lot of foolish bluster—"

"Cade?"

"Aye, Jack Cade—a rogue who thought he could put the world to rights. Raised up poor folk to disobey their masters and brought nowt but trouble. My husband and his cronies made a deal of noise but when Cade came to a bad end they shut their gobs and ran home with their tails between their legs—"

I laughed along with her. I'd no illusions about Miles' violent temper. Too much ale made him argumentative and turned him into a braggart. But it didn't stop me loving him. He handled a sick horse and delivered a foal with such tenderness I wept. At such times my misgivings evaporated. In the privacy of our chambers I saw a softness, an affection he kept from others. I didn't doubt the nature of his love.

"The Duchess will soon have her own babe to put in the nursery."

Jane Collins shook her head, plain face sombre, mouth down-turned. "It's still a way till June. Let's hope she'll carry this one to full term." She crossed herself.

"Do you believe in prayer?"

"I don't know, lass." Weary resignation marred her face. "I've said enough in my time, but few were answered."

I leaned over the cradle where Dickon slept, chubby arms outstretched. I couldn't resist touching the soft dark hair upon his brow. How beautiful he was! I longed to scoop him up into my arms and hug him to my breast. No love, not even my powerful feelings for Miles, burned as strong as this fierce maternal affection.

"Don't wake him, lass." An indulgent smile softened Jane Collins's coarse features. "Emma's had a troublesome time with yonder rogue."

"I think he's a tooth coming," the nursery-maid said. "He's such a lovely babe. I hope the duchess will have one just like him!"

"I wonder why some women bear as easily as farm-cats and others struggle," I said. Lady Anne's panicked eyes still seared my mind.

"These gently born ladies are too delicate. They've no strength or stamina. Look at Lady Anne's sister, poor Isabelle—one miscarriage after another and dead before Christmas."

"But the queen's borne many children."

Mistress Collins shuffled uncomfortably, her eyes shifting away from mine. Her hesitancy made me bold. "I've heard say she uses sorcery to ensure their well-being. Her mother's supposed to be a powerful witch."

Pursing her lips, Jane Collins looked at Emma tending one of the stirring Metcalf babes. "I've heard that too. I know nowt about witchcraft, lass, but if I did I'd be the first to use it for our little Duchess, and that's the truth. For all his so-called devotion, the Duke grows impatient. No man'll keep a barren wife. She needs all the help she can get."

And I needed no other answer.

I hid the cards in my bodice when I went to seek Lady Anne that afternoon.

*

"What is it? What do you see?"

She leaned so close over the little table her breath fanned my cheeks. Her eyes darted back and forth, restless, famished.

"A successful enterprise." I touched the painted images with the tips of my fingers. "The Sun signifies happiness, and the Chariot overcomes all obstacles, brings the realisation of your hopes—"

Two hectic spots bloomed in her cheeks like rosebuds, her breathing grew rapid, her eyes glittered with excitement.

"You must be careful of your health." I picked up the Six of Swords, overwhelmed by her trust in me. Suppose I'd been mistaken? Meeting her gaze, I marked the dark hollows beneath her eyes, the pallor of her lips. She looked too sickly for childbirth.

"Though you've powerful friends, you must be wary. Many seek their own preferment." I explained each card in turn. "There's danger round you—"

"But I'll have my son!" She whirled about the chamber, hugging her arms about herself, heedless of all else, while I cringed from a shower of blood and watched a wasted hand reach for a fallen crown beneath the twisted spikes of a hawthorn bush.

Chapter Fifty-One

"It's too soon." Jane Collins wrung her hands. "A seven month child won't live."

I tore my hair in a frenzy of urgency, finally dragging her from the safety of the nursery.

"We must save him!" Desperation made me savage. "Lady Anne's in great distress. She's set such store by this child, I can't see her disappointed."

I forced Mistress Collins down the steps, cursing the cruel April morning, the bane of women, the injustice of life—anything I thought might rouse her from despair. "You can't just give up! She needs us!"

In the lying-in chamber an ivory-faced wench, wincing under the whip of Lady Anne's screams, made hurried preparations.

"I sent the others away." I glanced at the midwife, emptying out the herbs I'd collected. "They were more trouble than help. This one at least has some sense."

I brewed a wallflower posset and afterward a tisane of lady's mantle and ergot to speed the birth. The tight-lipped serving wench fetched and carried without complaint while Jane Collins probed and pressed and murmured encouraging lies. Hour crawled after hour, Lady Anne's cries turning from screams to groans. I wiped sweat from her brow and held her hands, reminding her over and over again of the success I'd seen in the cards.

At noon, fearing for the lives of both mother and child, I dispatched the wench to find the duke. But Lady Anne showed herself stronger than anyone could have imagined. She didn't complain once throughout the long ordeal. And she refused the henbane I promised would bring her a half-sleep.

"I must bear my son in the customary fashion of all women." She spoke through gritted teeth. "And I must be awake to see his face."

The marks of her nails left crescent wounds on my arms, but when she held the tiny, mewling babe, I witnessed her triumph.

All the bells in Coverdale rang to mark the birth of her son. At Middleham, the household drank his health and wine and ale flowed freely. Even the lowliest scullion grew tipsy with the cheer. A time of singing and laughter enveloped the household. Lady Anne had given them an heir.

The duke, refusing to consider the child's frailty, named him Edward, in honour of his brother, the king. No one knew how his duchess suffered to bear this precious child. Yet three months later he still lived.

Lady Anne, gathering us together in her bower-chamber one afternoon, showed him off to all her ladies.

"Isn't he perfect?" Her green eyes sparkled with pride. At her elbow, Isabel Burgh, the wet-nurse, hovered nervously.

"He's beautiful, Your Grace." I answered with complete honesty, for the babe I held in my arms was truly angelic in form. Gazing upon the tiny, delicate features, Durga's words returned to me from long ago: "Such children are precious gifts, given to us to cherish for a little space so that we may glimpse perfection." A stab of terror set me shaking.

Lady Anne snatched the babe from me with the greedy possessiveness of the new mother.

"Nan predicted his birth," she said, a mysterious, gloating smile on her lips.

A ripple of unspoken conjecture stirred amongst the ladies and I tried to ignore the furtive glances, sly nudges, and complicit understanding which passed between them. How long before someone accused me outright of practising sorcery?

"My Lord is delirious with our good fortune."

I found it hard to imagine the Duke delirious about anything. The little I'd seen of him hadn't impressed. The pinched, starved-looking face betrayed no emotion save watchfulness and that always made me feel uneasy. Although Miles spoke warmly of Gloucester's courage and agility in battle, I saw no charm or wonder in him. He lacked his royal brother's fascination.

"I wish my father had lived to see this moment." Lady Anne said. "In this child, the glory of the Nevilles will live again."

She looked so happy and so vulnerable tears pricked my eyes.

"Why, Nan, how tender-hearted you are." She squeezed my arm affectionately.

I dashed away the drops with my fingertips. "I know how much this babe means to you."

"You must train your Dickon to be his trusty companion and playmate."

Again I sensed that rustle of suspicion amongst her ladies. Laughing, she held up the beautiful child, turning with him in a dancing circle of delight.

"He'll have need of loyal servants when he's grown."

"You may depend upon it, Madam."

How sturdy Dickon seemed against this frail infant.

She stopped at once and turned the child toward me, green eyes grown so grave I cowered with sudden foreboding. "You must tell me, Nan, what future you see for my son."

For a moment, I felt like a prisoner facing condemnation. The clutch of waiting women leaned forward, all attention. Every eye accused. Already these ladies talked openly of Lady Anne's curious "fostering" of me, and speculated regarding the herbal remedies I brewed—though several of them spoke highly of their efficacy. But fortune-telling raised other matters. How could she place me in such danger?

"Don't you predict a long and happy life for him?" She gave a coquettish toss of her honey–coloured hair. Did she extract pleasure from my torment? "What do you think?" Inclining her head to include the other women, they gathered round babbling nonsense, breaking the tension.

"He'll be a brave warrior, your Grace." Margaret Huddleston, always bolder than the rest, smiled enigmatically. "Already he has a look of your noble father."

"He's so beautiful, Your Grace," said giddy Genevieve Mountford. Eyes shining with genuine wonder, she reached out a white hand to touch the tiny fingers, gasping in awe as they curled about hers.

"You may go now, Nan." The little duchess awarded me a secretive smile. "Isobel will bring him back to the nursery." Holding the babe with the protective pride of a lioness, she swept into the throng of admiring gentlewomen. They swallowed her up in a mass of rustling taffeta and silk, shunning me as a flock of elegant birds abandons the bedraggled outsider. I wondered how long I'd wait before she summoned me to read the child's future.

Chapter Fifty-Two

"This feast will rival Prince Richard's." Meg Huddleston looked up from lacing the duchess's elaborate silver-tissue gown.

A magnificent summer banquet announced Middleham's public joy in the Gloucester heir.

"You flatter me, Meg. But the queen likes to flaunt her power." Lady Anne's mouth twisted in the faintest hint of a sneer. "I suppose it's still a novelty for her." She turned, allowing Elizabeth Parre to fasten the clasp of her pearl and topaz necklace, and laughed disparagingly. "Her mother may have been a duchess, but her father's nothing but a low-born opportunist with a handsome face. And how long before her beauty no longer bewitches? The king indulges her, but they say Shore's wife enjoys more favours."

Lips twitching with amusement, Alice knelt to adjust the gown's shimmering folds, while Meg Huddleston flashed Elizabeth Parre an impudent look behind the duchess's back, and Grace Pullen winked at me. Didn't our little duchess demand similar indulgences from her husband?

"One day Meg will go too far," Alice whispered, as our little party tripped down the steps to the great hall.

Genevieve nudged her. "I don't think Nan knows—"

"Knows what?"

"Ssh!" Alice raised her brows and widened her eyes in warning for Lady Anne missed little. "Meg loves to goad Lady Anne." She murmured in my ear. "It's because she's her sister—"

"Half sister." Genevieve stifled a giggle. "She's the Earl of Warwick's bastard."

"And Lady Anne's rival for his affections, so they say. He married her into the wealthy Huddleston family—"

"Well, it's dangerous to get too close to these great ones."

Listening to their mischievous prattle, everything fell suddenly into place—Meg's pert remarks and saucy answers, her cleverness and pride. No wonder these noble households nurtured such hotbeds of intrigue.

A resounding flourish of music urged us to our places. Scrope, Lovell, Radcliffe and Greystoke, Metcalf, Parre, and Tyrell— the north's influential families, gathered to dine in the sumptuously decorated banqueting hall. Welcomed with a wonderful show of courtesy from Lady Anne, they raised brimming goblets to Edward, the new Prince of Middleham. The vast chamber rang with their praises.

Dressed in my finest gown, I joined Miles amidst this illustrious throng, listening to the stirring music of shawms and rebecks, the lilting ballads of sweet-voiced minstrels, supping fine wines from Burgundy and France. Roasting meats basted in delicious sauces, pungent with spices and herbs scented the air. Martyn the Fool juggled and capered, the vast stone walls echoed with shouts and laughter, and afterward, we gasped in awe as tumblers executed amazing balancing feats.

When the servers carried in a magnificent subtlety in the shape of a swan with a babe lying in a gilded cradle between its wings loud acclaims filled the hall. At the high table the little duchess clapped her hands with delight and the tight-faced duke stood to pledge allegiance to the king. Rising noisily the men-folk echoed his words, but their clamorous voices rang hollow in my ears. In an instant, all the glamour of the occasion faded. My mind filled with the image of my merry-faced knave and his brother peering out at me through the windows of their turret chamber while armed guards paraded below. An eerie sense of foreboding unfurled like a huge dark wing, spoiling the rest of my evening.

Vainly I threw myself into Miles' arms for the farandole, scampered among the other ladies in foolish games, and exchanged gossip and jests with my tipsy neighbours. But only a surfeit of sweet hippocras could blot out my fear. That night I sank into a heavy, drowning sleep, only to be roused in the black, early hours by a voice which called: "Beware the archbishop!"

Teeming darkness pressed about me. I crouched against the bolster, aware of the familiar crawling sensation tingling through my limbs, a sheen of sweat bathing my brow. An unquiet spirit walked. Stillington's cruel, yellow eyes seemed to stare at me from out of that pulsing dark. But the voice appalled. I knew it to be in great pain. It was a voice I knew well, although I'd not heard it in a long time. It was Brother Brian's.

Despite frequent attempts to discover his whereabouts I discerned nothing of the priest. Many times I wrote to Harry, but the monks at St John's grew plainly hostile when subjected to questioning. What connected Brother Brian to the wily Stillington? What had become of that letter I'd penned from the Convent of the Carmelites? Mara promised its safe delivery, but I recalled her prediction saying it would pass through many hands. Suppose it fell into the wrong ones?

❧

Little Ned of Middleham proved an ailing child whose welfare occupied all my time. Vigilant as a mother-cat, Lady Anne watched his every quiver. The merest tremor sent her flying to me for remedies. Patiently, I brewed herbal possets for coughs and colic, massaged his tender skin with soothing unguents, wrapped him in softest sheepskin, and showered him with every remedy I knew. Mara's teachings served me well during this unlucky time for the nursery became my day-time prison. Here Jane Collins bustled to and fro with warm poultices, harrying the serving boys for wood to keep the fire a-flame, and young Emma, instructed to shield this precious child from draughts, sudden noises or disturbances, rocked his cradle, singing him softly into sleep.

Meanwhile, my own boy grew swift and sturdy. His impish smile set my heart leaping. His presence in the nursery eased away the tension of my confinement. Watching a proud Miles lift him on his shoulder or jog him on his lap, I tried to shake aside all my old misgivings concerning his link with the boys in the Tower. How could such a loving father ever harm a child?

❧

Sitting by the casement in our apartments one early evening, warm sunlight bathing my shoulders, I savoured a rare moment of solitude.

"Not in the nursery?"

Miles' voice startled me.

303

"The children are asleep." Putting down my pen, I turned to welcome him with a smile. "So Jane doesn't need me. You're back early from the hunt."

He stood in the doorway the warm smell of horse-flesh wafting from his clothes, filling the chamber with that oddly comforting odour of the stable.

"And you're writing another letter?"

"To Harry." I stretched voluptuously, flexing my cramped, ink-stained fingers. "Did you have good sport?"

"Aye, the duke caught a fine stag. There'll be venison at supper."

Miles' good humour pervaded the chamber. He heaved off his boots to lean back against the settle, flexing his feet with a sigh of satisfaction. "I'd be jealous of this Harry, if I didn't know you better."

"Harry's like a brother to me. Without him I'd have been lost in London."

"Ah, yes, I forget how important London is to you."

"I spent a good deal of my childhood there," I answered evenly, wondering what he inferred. "My village priest took me to live with my aunt after my father died."

He sauntered behind me to watch the loops of my letters unfold, and for an instant I recalled how I'd once watched Brother Brian's scholars in the chapel with such avid curiosity. Although Miles could write, he'd no regard for this expertise —having once told me at Barnard, clerks performed such craftsmanship as he needed.

"I suppose the priest taught you?"

"No." I answered without thinking, my mind flooded with memories of Alan Palmer and the letters I'd penned to him in Ely.

"Then where?"

Conscious of his scrutiny, I turned my head away to dip my pen into the little bowl of ink. "I learned at Norwich."

"Ah, from the Butler widow."

Something sinister in the way Miles pronounced this remark made me wary. My shoulders tensed. We'd spoken little of my time with Eleanor and I often wondered what Miles knew about her. I didn't mention Sister Absalom.

"I'm a poor scholar." Surveying my work, I attempted lightness. "I fear Harry will have a hard time with all these blots."

"I wonder you find so much to say to him and that a baker's son should have learned such skills. He must find little use for them." Stung by his surly tone, I swung round to face him with a bold, teasing smile.

"Why I do believe you *are* jealous, Miles! If you must know, poor Harry was *made* to go to school. The Mercers are quite well-to-do and wanted the best for him—but by his own report he got little pleasure though many beatings from his expensive education. Still, it's proved useful in keeping accounts, and now we live so far apart, we can share news." I squeezed his hand. "You've no cause to worry," I said mischievously. "I like to tell Harry about you and Dickon and life here in the north. One day I hope you'll meet."

Pressing my palm to his lips Miles fixed his blue eyes on mine with a fierce intensity that made me tremble. "London has no lure for me. My world's here with you and Dickon. I need nothing else."

Folding my letter I prayed he'd never return to the city, but in my heart of hearts I knew an important task remained unfulfilled. Both Mara and Mistress Evans taught me that destiny may not be escaped—only postponed. One day I must save those boys.

"Where's Guy?"

"In the stable, grooming the horses." Miles fiddled idly with my pen. "The roan mare's in foal. I said I'd go and take a look. The duke's anxious about her."

"I'll come with you." I wiped his inky fingers with the rag I kept for the purpose. "Let's look in the nursery afterward. Dickon sometimes wakes about this time. I'll make sure Jane Collins needs nothing more for the prince tonight."

I knelt to help Miles put on his boots again and he wound a shawl around my shoulders, reminding me of the wind blowing cold off the moors.

"The duke's ambitious for that lad of his." We shivered our way down the narrow steps. "He speaks of the honours the king'll surely heap on the boy when he's grown. But I think your Lady Anne's keen to raise a new Neville hero and it's she who pesters to get the king's recognition for the lad. You wenches are all the same!"

I thought then of Lady Anne's greedy cat-eyes and the possessive way she watched her delicate prince. Only yesterday she'd extracted a promise of me to bring the cards to her bower-chamber so I might cast his fortune. She couldn't forget the crown I'd seen in hers.

"Little Lord Ned will need to grow stronger if he's to be another Warwick."

"Aye, but doesn't she rely on you to perform some spell upon him to make it so?" Miles widened his eyes knowingly. I looked up in astonishment. Unsure of his intention, I chose to brush aside the remark.

"Of course," I answered with a pert smile. "Am I not able to bewitch all men?"

Chapter Fifty-Three

"Why can't it always be like this?"

We sprawled on a tumbling hillside by a stream. Snatching a rare opportunity to escape the confines of the castle and the restrictions of duty, we sought the freedom of the moors. Exhilarated by the brilliant April sunshine, we splashed with Dickon in the shallow water or chased him among the furze and harebells. Worn out at last, he rolled like a young pony in the long grass to fall asleep by an outcrop of rough stone, one fat cheek pillowed on a tussock, chubby arms flung carelessly above his head.

For a blissful moment, Miles and I lay side by side on our backs gazing up at the sweeping blue dome of sky, soaking up the sun's warmth.

"I wish we could keep this moment forever."

Miles laughed. "There's nowhere better than these moors in spring."

Leaning on one elbow, I followed his gaze. Hills and dales swathed in luscious greenery stretched out before us like a mariner's chart. The heady scents and bees' drone lulled me. I yawned and stretched, contented as a cat, so that Miles caught me in his arms and twined around me in drowsy, murmuring comfort.

Startled by a kestrel's shriek we woke to the urgent drum of horse-hooves. Miles sprang up at once.

"Someone's in a hurry." Shielding his eyes against the light he squinted back towards the castle.

Finding himself in an unaccustomed place, Dickon whimpered. Snuggling him close, I pressed his grubby cheek against my neck, watching his eyes grow round with wonder.

"What is it?" Foreboding strangled my voice.

Miles shrugged but when Walt's surly, weather-beaten face appeared over the brow of the hill, I groaned.

"Trouble," he said tersely. He wiped sweat from his bald pate with a grubby rag. "Thou'd best come quick, Master Forrest. The Duke's asking for thee, and he's in no mood for sluggards."

"What's happened?" I hoisted a gurgling Dickon on to my hip.

Walt's eyes slid over me with unconcealed contempt. He treated his own wife with churlish indifference and made no attempt at courtesy towards others of a species he considered both inferior and intractable.

"Thou'd best make ready to travel." He addressed his remark solely to Miles.

"Back to Barnard?" Miles picked up his discarded jerkin. His muscles tensed. "Is there rioting in the north again?"

"Nay," growled Walt. His impatient lolloping gait carried him away from us. He shouted over his shoulder. "I reckon he means thee to go with him to London to sort out summat with Clarence."

"Clarence?"

Miles's question conveyed surprise. I strained to hear the answer, but Walt created a fair distance between us. Carrying Dickon, I soon trailed behind. The child called out to his father although Miles paid no heed. By the time we reached our apartments, Dickon set up a fearful howling. While I bathed him, told tales I'd had from my father and sang old lullabies, he waged a desperate struggle in my arms until a fretful sleep finally overwhelmed him.

"What's happening?" I flung myself upon Miles as soon as he opened the door.

"I'll need some clothes." He thrust me aside impatiently. "Walt's right. The Duke wants me to leave with him for London at first light."

"But why? He hates going to Westminster."

"I know. Only a serious matter would lure him away from Middleham in such a hurry—"

"But why does he need you? You're his Keeper of the Wardrobe, not—"

Memories of other secret undertakings rose up alarmingly— the brawl in which Dawkins, the so-called spy, had been killed at Barnard and Lucy's terrible words: "It's what he's hired to do."

I knelt beside Miles at the cedar-wood chest where he kept his garments. He raised the lid, filling the room with the scent of lavender.

"His brother's the cause." He waved a dismissive hand at the scarlet doublet I held up. "It seems he's accused the queen of murdering his wife."

"What!"

I dropped a jerkin. My sudden yelp woke Dickon. Before I could ask more, I must soothe the child.

Dickon finally yielded to our combined efforts to quiet him. Afterward we shared a cheerless meal brought to our chamber by a sullen serving-man. In the mellow candle-light Miles brooded, his swarthy features wolfish in the red-glow of the fire.

Spurred into nervous action, I gathered up discarded dishes. "What does the duke want you to do in London? Clarence is nothing to us. Surely the king will deal with him?"

Miles leaned back against the settle staring at me with stoat-like intensity. At once my festering unease burst into full-blown fear. A spare figure with wispy brown hair knelt at an altar. A bird squawked and an ominous shadow raised a fist—I reeled at the sudden flood of violent images filling my head.

"What are these secret errands all about? What is it Gloucester wants from you?"

"You ask too many questions, Nan. Be content to stay in ignorance like other women." Menace lurked in this mild delivery.

"I can't live with secrets! People are saying terrible things about you—What am I to believe?"

The blue eyes flashed a warning, but I ignored the danger. My ears rang with the frightful sound of crushed bone, the grunt and thud of a falling body. "Ever since we heard those riders this afternoon and Walt came to spoil everything I can't rest. Why won't you tell me about the duke and these mysterious errands? If it were for some good purpose you'd surely—"

"You're too clever for your own good." Miles leapt forward snatching my face in so fierce a grip I cried out and the images fled. "Do you think the Duke's favour comes cheap?" He took a sweeping glance around the opulent wood-panelled chamber hung with rich tapestries, and then with deliberate violence dashed the platters to the floor with his other hand. "Do you think we live like this for nothing? Don't pretend you know nothing of my obligations to the Duke."

The pressure on my jaw grew so strong I feared the bone would break. "Lady Anne—" I endeavoured to say in spite of the pain.

Miles released his hold, laughing without humour. The coldness in his eyes terrified.

"Lady Anne may hold you in some regard but she doesn't control the reins of power. Gloucester puts a high price on loyalty and rewards those who do his bidding. After Barnet I swore I wouldn't stay a common soldier and sell my life cheaply for any man. As you say, dear wife, Gloucester doesn't have his brother's easy nature, but his ambition burns brighter and will lead him far."

"It'll lead you into danger." I nursed my bruised jaw and eyed him boldly.

"No venture is without risk. I decided long ago I'd make myself his henchman so I might share some of the spoils he'll surely reap."

"Loyalty's an admirable virtue. Isn't it the Duke's own device: Loyalty binds me?" I bent to pick up the battered pewter dishes, thankful Dickon hadn't woken. "It may earn a man honour and respect in the eyes of his fellows, but—"

"But it demands unswerving obedience," Miles finished for me.

I couldn't answer. I set the platters down. For what seemed an eternity, we crouched in uncomfortable silence.

"You're no fool, Nan," Miles said at last. "You must have guessed."

His penetrating stare unnerved me.

"I heard talk at Barnard. They said Gloucester held you in high esteem. And Jane Collins always says you're the Duke's man." I glanced at my hands. For a moment I thought them bathed in blood. Resolutely I looked up into the unflinching blue eyes. "But what does that mean, Miles?"

"It means I must do everything he asks of me. I'm bound by my allegiance."

"*Anything* he asks of you?"

Miles shrugged. "It's no hardship to ask a few questions or stop the mouths of a few knaves. Soldiers can't afford to be squeamish."

I thought again of Dawkins on the tavern steps with his skull crushed, and then of poor, mad King Henry murdered in the Tower. "But you're not a soldier now."

"Don't trouble yourself with men's matters," he said. He pulled me close. "I don't like it when you grow fanciful." His hands began the slow purposeful caresses that were always a prelude to rough love-making. "A woman should be soft and tender when her husband's about to set out on a dangerous journey. She should think only of his comfort."

He kissed me long and hard. "Tell me, what shall I bring you back from London?" A smile curved his lips, cruel as a blade.

⁐

He left at dawn. Peering down into the narrow, shadow-blurred courtyard I saw the duke mount his favourite stallion while Miles and others lurked in attendance. With a heavy heart, I watched the hooded figures turn like a snare of conspirators towards the gate. It marked the end of any certainty or quiet.

During the endless, nervous weeks which followed I nibbled on unsatisfactory snippets of news gleaned from passing travellers. I joined a knot of women in the market listening to a glib-tongued peddler.

"The Duke of Clarence's caused a mighty quarrel in the royal family. He blames a household servant for his wife's death. This wench once worked for Queen Elizabeth, so the queen accuses Clarence of insulting her. Will the king intervene? Oh, it's a very sordid matter, ladies. There's even talk of sorcery—"

But in the twilight of the nursery, Jane Collins spoke of Clarence with some sympathy. "That poor man's been fair demented since his wife's death. Lady Isabelle were never strong and that last babe killed her. Nothing to do with servants and poison— That Wydeville wench has allus been a vicious piece of work." She gave me a sharp look. "I've no high opinion of a wench without compassion so don't stare at me like that, Nan. Did tha never mind the tale of the Desmond boys?"

"What Desmond boys?" This cryptic remark piqued my curiosity.

"Why, King Edward and the Earl of Desmond were best friends from boyhood. When he married the queen, Desmond called her "the grey mare" for she were John Grey's widow. It were a jest—nothing more than any coarse remark the men-folk might laugh over, but she were that angry—took it as personal slight, folk say. So, when the king were absent on business, she took his ring and sealed a warrant for Desmond's arrest. His two little lads were murdered by that wicked John Tiptoft. Struck down in their beds, God rest them—" She crossed herself. "It's unnatural for a mother to harm a bairn. I can't forgive it. She's much to answer for—"

Her vehemence unnerved me as much as the wicked tale. Mara had warned against the danger of revenge. "An ill wind will turn back to blow upon the sender. Retribution belongs to other than ourselves."

"The queen must think about those murdered boys now she has two of her own." Vividly I recalled the mischievous face of the child who haunted my dreams.

"Aye, well let's hope the king'll realise Clarence is grieving for his wife, and make allowances. He's allus been fond of his younger brothers."

But I'd seen another side of Edward Plantagenet in Silver Street. The golden knight silenced those who threatened his stability. He forgot past favours when he chose. Even favourite brothers could be discarded.

Chapter Fifty-four

Miles sent no messages. The green April days lost their charm and inauspicious dreams of malodorous dungeons and baleful fires racked my sleep. Fatigued and fretful, I snapped at Dickon and quarrelled with the serving-wenches. My head pounded with a dull, perpetual ache. What detained Miles so long in London?

The traditional May Day Fair briefly distracted Middleham from court intrigue.

"Emma's pestering me to go," Jane Collins said. She watched me spoon some honey into the prince's mouth. "I've no desire to be pushed and shoved amongst crowds these days. I'm too old and the place'll be thick with rogues looking for easy pickings. Mind you, I'd relish some cheese from the white monks of Jervaulx Abbey. They're allus at the market."

I kissed the babe and laid him gently into her lap. "I'll ask Lady Anne if I can take her." I licked the spoon. "We need more honey. I'm sure the monks will have some and I'll get you your cheese. Leave it to me."

I ran to the duchess's apartments and found a team of servants engaged in rigorous cleaning. The air hung heavy with the smell of lye and lavender. Too busy with her steward to pay me much attention, Lady Anne nodded a brusque consent and I delighted the nursery maid with the news.

✥

In spite of a damp, grey start, the following day proved mild. We found the village thronged with people milling about a muddle of stalls in search of bargains. Watching the men-folk roistering together, spilling in and out of the taverns in increasingly merry mood, I thought of Miles when the ale made him lazy and good-humoured. But it brought no comfort. What dark undertaking lured him back to London? I dismissed an inner sight of the Tower circled by ominous black birds and the sinister oily waters of the Thames, throwing myself into the fair's activities with reckless abandon.

Stilt-walkers, jugglers and tumblers enthralled; painted players in fantastical costumes shouted for attention; beggars crawled under stalls to filch fallen fruit, sweet cakes and morsels of roasted meat; dancers wove in and out the crowds urging them to join their boisterous revels; and troops of ragged children shrieked their way through a rabble of spectators.

Dizzied by noise, we paused at last to wonder at the antics of a dancing bear.

"Look at its great teeth." Emma pointed with gleeful horror at the poor beast lumbering upon shaggy paws.

"There's to be a bear-baiting in the tavern yard tonight." A bold-looking stripling eyed Emma hotly. "I could take you, if you've a mind to it." He lounged against a post, displaying his fine parti-coloured hose, his mouth puckered in an insolent smirk.

"Such sport isn't for ladies." I hurried a pink-cheeked Emma towards the busy booths selling pastries. A fleeting, ominous memory of Philippa confiding her love for Ralph Fowler crossed my mind. I vowed then to shield Emma from such flattering rogues. Blowing on hot pies filled with savoury minced meat, we discovered stalls heaped with fabrics, gloves, and kerchiefs.

"Look at these!" Emma rifled amongst a heap of ribbons and woven purses, jesting with the roguish stall holder. Dusting pastry flakes from my fingers, I helped her bargain with him for some lengths of lace.

A raucous crier announced the beginning of the jousting tournament.

"Oh do let's go." Emma seized my arm.

"I promised Mistress Collins some cheese. And if you want to watch the dancing—"

Rosy faced maids garlanded with blossom, skipped around the maypole, weaving the bright-coloured ribbons in intricate patterns. They ducked and dodged, turned and twisted to the rhythmic beat of the music, open-mouthed and sparkling-eyed, bringing pretty Alys into mind.

"In my village, the fair used to be the highlight of our summer," I told Emma. "And the crowning of the May Queen caused the wildest merriment of all. It seemed like something from a folk tale then and we were so excited we couldn't sleep for days after. On May Evening it was the custom for the village boys and girls to sleep under the stars. It was also a time for choosing sweethearts and plighting troths."

"Did you have a sweetheart, Nan?"

"I was too young," I answered, laughing. "But I often wonder who might have chosen me had I stayed there."

We laughed our way back to the cluster of booths where strident voices proclaimed their wares with growing desperation. The sultry turn in the weather threatened to spoil the perishable goods and a carrion stink of putrefaction wafted from the meat stalls. We followed the bustle to where the White Brothers kept their store of cheeses and preserves, almost knocked down by a jeering hubbub of grimy, wild-haired boys and tattered girls pelting a little hunchback with clods and stones.

"What harm has that poor creature done?" Emma said. She fumed with outrage as the unruly mob upset barrels and bottles, spilled jugs, trampled pies into the dirt, and shouted insults at the stall-holders. "Why must people be so unkind?"

I didn't answer. Wide-eyed and speechless, I watched a white-robed monk at the cheese stall smiling gently on the herd of matrons clamouring for service. When he glanced up at me, his mouth dropped open. I couldn't take my eyes off him.

"I wrote to you."

"And I to you. I had your letter from the convent—but many months after it was written. The seal was broken so I'm after thinking other eyes read it before mine. And one pair in particular —but we must speak more of that in private. I answered at once, but having no more news, I followed with another letter and another—"

Brother Brian's blue eyes spoke such affection, tears filled my own.

"Are you well?" The lines in his gaunt face had deepened, but the familiar lilt of his speech and sweetness of his smile warmed me as ever. "How have you travelled to Yorkshire—so far from Norwich? What strange adventures are you after having since you left Dame Butler's service? I thought you lost."

"Oh, I've travelled far indeed." I laughed through my tears. "And many strange adventures brought me to this place." I squeezed his hands affectionately. "I'm so glad to see you! I'm married now. My husband serves the Duke of Gloucester—we have a little boy and live at the castle. After Norwich, I returned to London. By chance, I met the Duke's wife and won her favour. So much has happened—" I glanced at Emma, clearly listening to the breathless tumble of our conversation. "But how long have you been at the abbey?"

Brother Brian read the warning in my eyes. "I think we're after needing more leisure to tell our tales." He rewarded me with a complicit smile. "I've been at Jervaulx these fifteen years—"

"And always in my mind." I slotted my arm through his as I walked him a few paces from the curious listeners. "We've purchases to make from your stall—Emma, the honey—and don't forget the cheese." The maid took my purse, allowing us a few delicious moments of privacy. "We must meet again—and soon."

"Come to the abbey. I must speak to you about Bishop Stillington—but this is not the place or time to air our history. I'll send a message—Mistress—?"

"Forrest." I answered with a genuine laugh, although the mention of Stillington set my heart racing. I hugged the monk close, both of us weeping. "I'll wait impatiently for your summons."

A sudden commotion diverted our attention. A breathless, red-faced matron panted into the press of women by the stall.

"They say she'll be tried at the assizes—as a vagrant if not a witch."

The woman's words produced a cacophony of shrieks.

"A black-haired wench she is—a foreigner by the sound of the curses she gave the guards who arrested her—"

"But who sent for them?"

"Did you say witchcraft?"

The priest and I exchanged fearful glances.

"Emma!" I all but dragged the reluctant maid back to the castle, the word "witch" ringing in my ears.

"And in all the revelry, I'll wager tha forgot about my cheese," said Mistress Collins, having listened to Emma's lively account of the dancing bear.

"No, but we've so much to tell you—"

"Th'art very pale, Nan." Jane Collins took my basket. Inadvertently her broad hand brushed my fingers. "Th'art chilled to the bone!" She chafed my hands between her own rough palms, her worried expression fixed on my face.

"Emma, leave that." The girl rummaged through ribbons, lace and sweetmeats to retrieve the cloth-wrapped cheese. "Fetch Nan a mug of warm ale and honey." Her shrewd eyes assessed me swiftly. "I hope tha's not taken a fever. These hot, damp days can be unwholesome. Who knows what pestilence vagabonds may have brought to the fair!"

"I met my old village priest." I wanted to quell her anxiety. "It was such a shock after all these years, I still can't believe it's true! I never thought to find him in Yorkshire, let alone meet him at the fair!"

"Oh, it was lovely to see them together." Breathless Emma planted a mug of ale on the trestle. "I'd never thought I'd see a monk weep, but he was quite overcome. He's been at Jervaulx for years and years. He and Nan were laughing and crying and hugging like old friends. It made me cry too."

"Fifteen years he's been our neighbour," I told a bewildered Jane Collins. "And I never knew it. Brother Brian took care of me when I first went to London—after my father died. I owe him so much."

"They said a witch had been caught—" Emma interrupted, her face rosy with excitement. "I wanted to find out more but Nan wouldn't let me. She said we must come home. But perhaps the monk'll tell her when she sees him again. He wants to talk about Bishop Stillington—"

"Stillington?" Jane Collins interrupted. "Does tha mean the king's chancellor?" Her puzzled face accused me.

"I met him once— in London." Inwardly, I cursed Emma's innocent remark. "Perhaps it's something to do with that—" My thoughts flew to poor deluded Eleanor and faithless King Edward, gorgeous as a peacock amongst his fawning courtiers at Westminster.

"And what's all this about a witch?" Jane Collins stared from me to Emma and back again.

"Oh, a woman came to the cheese stall, and she said—"

I let Emma tell a rambling tale, pretending amused indifference.

⌇

An uneasy sensation roused me from sleep the next morning. Eerie grey light seeped through the lancet window. Thick silence enveloped the castle. Shivering at the unexpected chill I snatched up my robe and ran across the damp rushes to peep outside.

Fog tumbled over the moors. Fascinated, I watched this ethereal tide swallow trees and buildings so fast they faded in a moment.

Behind me, Dickon stirred. In spite of Jane Collin's disapproval, sometimes I let him sleep in our chamber instead of the nursery. I carried him to the window.

"Look!" I pointed to the unseasonal spectacle. "Dragon's breath."

He blinked, stretching out his little arms. Laughing, I jogged him up and down, nuzzling his soft dark hair. He smelled of spring grass and I pressed my face against his baby-plump cheeks. "You won't be able to go out today. We must watch out for dragons!" I tweaked his nose setting him gurgling with laughter and then made a growling noise as I ran back to the bed where I threw him amongst the blankets and bolsters, romping and shrieking, pretending to be a dragon threatening to devour him—a game my father played with me in the far-off days of childhood.

A hammering at the door made me jump so fiercely Dickon giggled until Jane Collins burst in, dishevelled and florid. Never had I seen her so flustered or untidy.

"Is the prince sick?" I leapt from the bed grabbing clothes.

Her bosom heaved with the effort of running. "That foreign woman's confessed to practising witchcraft. She's to be burned for it."

"Burned—"

Dickon stood up on the bed shouting for attention.

"A foreign woman, you say?"

Jane Collins picked up Dickon, jogging him in her arms while I clapped on my garments, clammy hands fumbling with strings and laces. My stomach lurched at the vivid memory of Mara.

"She roamed the fair all morning. It's a wonder tha didn't see her. They arrested her in Sheriff Hutton. She's a beggar or traveller of some kind. She accosted folk in the market and outside the tavern, saying she could read the future. Old Walt says she's confessed to conjuring spirits."

Panicked by Jane's stammering tale, I dressed a chuckling Dickon with some difficulty.

"Walt says women who dabble in black arts should be burned. Oh Nan, does tha still have them cards?"

When I opened my mouth to speak no sound came.

"Lady Anne's not allus careful about what she says." Jane's broad features twisted into a grimace. "I tried to warn thee several times, lass. When little Lord Ned were sick with fever—Remember how we sat up wi' him night after night? When thou were brewing that coltsfoot remedy, Lady Anne told me tha'd cast her fortune with cards. She said he couldn't die because tha' said he'd a long and happy life."

"I didn't say that."

"But tha did tell her fortune?"

"A long time ago before the prince was born—when we were at Dowgate together." Guiltily, I recalled the many times since I'd read the cards. "I only told her she'd bear a living baby boy."

"And the cards?"

For the first time I noticed tears in Jane's eyes.

"Hidden away. But they're nothing. An old woman gave them to me—The one who taught me how to use the herbs for healing draughts. I meant no harm."

"Tha mun destroy them! Oh Nan, dost tha know what danger tha's in? When Emma came back from the May Fair and mentioned Bishop Stillington, I knew it mun come to this. Tha art playing a dangerous game and if the Duke should find out—"

These words twisted like a knife in my belly. Everyone knew about the Duke's piety, his abhorrence of ungodly practices. Hadn't Miles warned me often enough? I could expect no mercy there. And what of Miles himself? During his long absence I trusted in Lady Anne's protection, wallowing in ignorance like a pig being fattened for the butcher's knife.

"The whole country's gone mad with talk of witchcraft. The Duke of Clarence accused that serving woman—Ankaret summat— And now Walt's ranting about the Bible's commands for burning witches. Oh Nan, I wouldn't want to see thee—"

Tears drowned the rest. Ignoring Dickon's fretful wail, I clasped her to me. She held me with the ferocity of a mother animal protecting her cub. For a moment I yielded to the comfort of this embrace. But nothing could assuage my terrible premonition, relentless and annihilating as the fog on the moors.

Chapter Fifty-five

Although not an enclosed order, the White Brothers of Jervaulx kept silence for much of the day, and received few guests save passing pilgrims. Strict rules governed visits. Badly frightened by the prospect of a witch trial, I determined to see Brother Brian without delay. Seeking Lady Anne's assistance, I found her in the solar reading a letter with Meg Huddleston and Grace Pullen in attendance.

"Of course you must visit your old priest," she said. "Don't look so worried, Nan. Doesn't she look serious?" She flashed her waiting women a teasing smile. "I'll write to the Abbot on your behalf. He won't refuse." She giggled conspiratorially, evidently in a good humour, and I couldn't help glancing at the letter in her hand.

"Perhaps Master Forrest will be home soon." She arched her brows mischievously. "And perhaps our dear brother, George of Clarence, has done us a great service after all." Laughing, she hid the letter in her sleeve and skipped away.

Meg Huddleston darted a sly look at Grace which made me feel uncomfortable. Since the rumours of witchcraft at Middleham Fair, I noticed more of these covert looks, and a storm of whispers in the bower chamber. But perhaps a strange mixture of guilt and imagination provoked these feelings? Meg, in particular, delighted in stirring dangerous tittle-tattle. Eyes sparkling with mischief she drew attention to my skill at making remedies from curious plants, hinting about strange country crafts and pretending fear of my powers.

"Is it true you saw a witch at the Fair?"

Seeing Grace hide a smirk behind her sleeve, I forced a smile. Linking an arm in Meg's, I drew her with me to the settle.

"Do you know," I said, adopting such a friendly manner she was plainly startled. "I was there all day with the little nursery-maid but we missed all the excitement. Is it true she's a foreign woman?"

My feigned ignorance clearly surprised her but she retained her composure.

"I believe so. But there are so many rumours it's difficult to know what to think." Flashing Grace an appeal for rescue she rose gracefully. "Forgive me, Nan, but we have an appointment with Master Giacomo concerning music lessons."

Alone in the solar, I sat haunted by memories of Mara. Suppose the woman arrested at the Fair was one of the Rom I knew? In spite of the brilliant May sunshine, I shuddered. Perhaps Brother Brian could supply an answer to this mystery.

Strolling among the abbey herb gardens with my erstwhile priest some days later, I recalled Lady Anne's unexpected behaviour. Thanks to her, the Abbot granted Brother Brian the quiet hours for private prayer and spiritual readings till Vespers to spend with me. Sister Ursula of the grudging, gargoyle face would never have approved this dispensation.

The aromatic scent of flowers wafted on the breeze; bees hummed lazy lullabies amongst the carefully tended plants; birds chirruped in the leaves—but my thoughts ran restless, goaded by fears of discovery and denouncement.

"Stillington came to Jervaulx some three or four months ago," said the priest, when we were out of earshot of the infirmary building. His voice trembled, tightened by extreme anxiety. "He acquired my letters to you of a Sister Absalom at Norwich. Discovering you'd escaped from the convent, he sent his people searching for you—but without success. By the time he reached the abbey a fume of ill-temper shook him. He questioned me about your present whereabouts several times." Fear lurked in his eyes. "What is it he seeks of you so urgently?"

Twisting my fingers in a fever of apprehension, I surveyed the dusty tracks beside the neatly planted rows of lavender. How should I answer? To reveal my secret would burden him. Yet he was the one person I trusted.

"I met Stillington at Westminster." I halted, weighing each word carefully. "It was when Dame Eleanor pressed her petition to King Edward. I believe he suspected something irregular in their relationship—When you were at St John's I told you about her infatuation, if you remember—"

The mention of the priory clearly stirred a different memory. Anguish flickered in the priest's eyes.

"I do recall it." Pausing as if to consider the matter deeper he sighed and shook his head. "But how can this be of interest to the bishop—unless—" A sudden stab of understanding seemed to pierce him. "Is this then the reason for his recent association with Clarence?"

"Clarence?"

"There's some tale about Clarence questioning the validity of the king's marriage—"

"Then Stillington *has* told him!"

My sharp cry startled the priest. He drew me to a bench. Several novice monks tending the gardens stared in our direction.

"What is it, Nan? I'm thinking you have something heavy on your mind—something you need to tell me."

How well the priest knew me. Wistfully, I smiled up at him. Like the little girl who'd travelled with him to London all those years ago, I put a trusting hand in his.

"King Edward promised Eleanor Butler marriage," I said. "I witnessed his pledge."

The priest's eyes widened.

"Only I and Brother Thomas—Dame Eleanor's chaplain—knew of it. I don't know what became of Brother Thomas, although Eleanor's scullion said Stillington's man took him away—and me, Stillington locked up in the Norwich convent, as you know. He seemed very anxious then to scotch any gossip. My escape must have shocked him. Once he sought my silence, but now he seeks me out to further a different purpose. No doubt Clarence promised him great honours if he attains the crown." I squeezed Brother Brian's tremulous hand. "It's a secret I've guarded a long time. And now I've placed you in grave danger by sharing it. Forgive me."

Withdrawing my hand, I bent my head like a penitent. Around us the birdsong continued to flow harmoniously, the soft breeze fanned the trees, the insects droned. All remained the same. Yet in a single moment I had destroyed the old monk's peace entirely.

"There's nothing to forgive, Nan." His low, melodious voice proved comforting. "Haven't we shared our troubles through the years? And once again I'm after fearing for your safety. But where can I hide you now?"

"No need," I answered. I met his troubled gaze without blinking. "Stillington will find me soon enough. But first he'll wait for the opportunity that suits him best." I laughed suddenly, recalling the prelate's shrewd, predatory eyes. The discordant sound startled Brother Brian. He touched my hand, his gaunt face twisted with anxiety. I shook my head. "Don't worry. I'm valuable to Stillington now. Though once he desired to stop my tongue, now he may require me to speak out. All depends on Clarence and the king. They say at Middleham the queen's angry and the king will do anything to soothe her. And even Lady Anne—Oh, these royal cousins are devious in their desires. Your presence is my greatest comfort. All we can do is wait."

I rose as if to continue our walk, my confidence too fragile a disguise to pursue conversation. Nor dare I mention the witchcraft arrest or the cards. Instead, I spoke of Lady Anne and how she'd brought me to Middleham, of Dickon, and the little Gloucester prince. Yet all the time my mind ran upon Miles and his secret errand in the city. What scheme had Gloucester devised concerning his reckless brother, Clarence? Could it be Lady Anne pursued her own ambitious purposes? Miles was wrong about her influence. She knew well how to manipulate her husband. I reeled at the magnitude of my own suspicions.

"The light's fading." Brother Brian drew my attention to the dappled shadows gathering round us like curious watchers. "You've a long walk back to the castle."

By a honeysuckle hedge, its sultry fragrance heavy and languorous in the evening heat, we faced each other uneasily.

"Will I see you again?"

"Of course." He laid a resolute hand on my arm. "In the meantime I shall pray for your safety."

The bells tolled for Vespers. Looking back, I saw one of the young novices engage Brother Brian in conversation—a delicate looking lad with pale blonde hair. For a moment as the setting sun flickered through the leaves, I thought him Alan Palmer.

Chapter Fifty-Six

The priest and I met infrequently—a situation which troubled us—sometimes on market days when it proved difficult to speak freely and occasionally at the abbey where too many listeners lurked. So we wrote to one another instead. Letters at least enabled us to share something of our concerns.

One warm afternoon the following month the clatter of horse-hooves mingled with hearty cries of welcome drew me from the latest letter I was penning. Peering through the casement, I glimpsed the Duke of Gloucester dismounting from his huge grey stallion and spotted Miles among his entourage. Rubbing ink from my fingers, I flew down the steps out into the courtyard. By the time I got there Gloucester had gone. I pushed my way through a mass of people clustered about the horses, heedless of the grinning men-folk.

"Well, lass, have you missed me?" Miles seized me in his arms and kissed me. His teeth drew blood.

Someone snorted disapprovingly and I noted the grind of Walt's surly muttering. Behind Miles I spied a youthful face painted with an insolent grin.

"See to the horses, Jack." Miles turned towards its owner. "Walt'll show you where. I've business to attend to with my wife." The low laugh and sly wink amused the watchers and their answering sniggers and coarse jests made my face burn like a brand. Grinning wider as he returned the wink, the bold-faced lad took the horses. Something vaguely familiar in the angles of his face disconcerted me, but Miles urged me indoors. All the way up the stairs to our chambers his mouth worried at my neck. Between kisses and muttered endearments his eager hands fumbled at my breasts.

∽

"Is it true the Duke of Clarence is arrested?"

We lay spent in the hazy June twilight.

"Aye." Miles twisted a strand of my hair between his fingers. "And will remain in prison until he regains his reason. He shouldn't make such wild accusations against the Wydeville bitch."

"What's he said?"

"That she's a witch and the king's a bastard. But that's nothing new." Miles' laugh drawled, lazy with satisfaction. He rolled to face me, leaning on his elbow, the shadows falling across his brooding face. "More shocking is his accusation their marriage is invalid."

I sat up at once. "Why would he say that?" My mouth seemed dry as bone, though sweat pricked my palms. Had Stillington truly spoken to Clarence of Eleanor?

Miles' lips curled in a curious smile and I cursed my hasty behaviour. His eyes surveyed me keenly as he might a horse he thought to purchase.

"He said tradition doesn't allow kings to marry widows."

A pause quivered with tension while Miles waited for my reply. Instead I averted my eyes and began picking at a loose thread in the coverlet.

"The tale of the king's bastardy is an old one." I feigned thoughtfulness. "But fancy Clarence accusing his mother! Lady Anne says she's very pious."

"Pious and proud." Miles stilled my hand with his own. "I was once part of her household, lass, and I should know." He paused again to study my expression. "But perhaps Clarence knows more than any realise."

Deliberately I looked him full in the face. "Surely you don't think that tale of the archer and Cicely Neville is true?" I widened my eyes in pretended amazement.

The swarthy face loomed over me, predatory and watchful. "I wasn't alluding to that. I was thinking more about the secret marriage."

Gooseflesh rose on my arms. "How could he know?"

No sooner did the words pass my lips than I regretted them.

"Why, everyone knows the King married the Wydeville widow in secret." His eyes narrowed menacingly. "But there are whispers." He tugged a hank of my hair, gently drawing my face close to his. "Secrets have been whispered behind doors." He spoke so low I had to strain to hear. "Bishop Stillington and Clarence are thick as thieves—"

"Stillington! What's he to do with Clarence?"

"Rumour has it the chancellor's some secret knowledge of the king's youthful indiscretions—a rumour that's roused Clarence's special interest." Miles scanned my face intently. "The queen's vexed such an eminent churchman should ally himself with Clarence. She says it's tantamount to treason. Since then Stillington's been out of favour with King Edward. There are those who predict his imminent fall—"

"Stillington's a dangerous enemy." My heart thudded and my mind busied itself fashioning a plausible tale of deception. "He tried to prevent Dame Eleanor from petitioning the king for the return of her estates. His avarice is legendary, as is his cunning. Be sure you keep away from him, Miles. For all his supposed piety he's an untrustworthy knave without compassion or conscience. The king would be very wise to dismiss him from court."

"My, my, what a passion the bishop raises in you, wife!" Miles' words rang with teasing contempt. "I never thought you vindictive but young Jack Green told me—"

"Jack Green!" I gasped. "Of course!"

The bold-faced lad was Lady Eleanor's scullion grown into a gangling youth; little Jack who'd wept at slights and begged me help him get a place at Sudeley; little Jack who'd worked at the Mercer's bakery; little Jack Green who'd fallen in with bad company. How the threads of fate interweave like spider webs to bind us in their sticky fibres!

"He remembered you." Miles spoke without astonishment, his eyes searching my face scrupulously. "He said you worked together at the Butler household in London. He's some interesting tales to tell."

"We ought to visit Dickon—" I wriggled free of his restraining arms. "The daylight's going fast. Mistress Collins'll have him asleep if you don't hurry."

Throwing on my garments and conscious of Miles' eyes upon me, I kept my face turned lest he should read my thoughts.

"Jack Green told me an odd story about Lady Butler's priest."

Miles hadn't moved. I made much of stooping to retrieve our discarded shoes.

"Brother Thomas was a fervent young chaplain. I remember the sermon he once gave us about King Edward miraculously seeing three suns in the sky."

Miles ignored this attempted distraction. "Jack says he was arrested on Stillington's orders and no one saw him again after that."

"Oh, he told me that story when we left for Norfolk." I answered, carelessly. "He was just a child then. I'm sure he made it up or he misheard some tittle-tattle amongst the servants. The whole household was rife with gossip."

Leaning out the bed Miles grasped my arm suddenly, spinning me round to face him. "You've told me little about Norfolk or how you came to be in London when I found you."

"There's little to tell." The heat of treacherous blood coloured my cheeks.

He drew me down to sit upon the bed beside him. Touching my burning face with one finger his lips twisted into the familiar wolfish smile.

"You're full of secrets, wife. See how the wanton blood blooms. What tales could you tell me of secret lovers, I wonder?"

"What folly is this?" I looked at him feigning boldness. "I'm ashamed to think you listen to the half-remembered stories of a scullion. Jack Green knows nothing about me. And as for secrets, why, you're full of them yourself. You tell me nothing of your mysterious errands."

It was a daring challenge. Shaking myself free, I laughed as lightly as I could, for Miles' moods could change as quickly as an April day. As I ran from the chamber, I turned to smile impishly over my shoulder. "Perhaps I'll tell you something of my many past lovers if you can catch me!"

Giggling and panting we reached the nursery, but I evaded his grasp and burst in upon a stone-faced Jane Collins mending hose before the hearth.

"It's a pity tha didn't turn up earlier." Her sharp glance took in Miles' unlaced sleeve and dishevelled hair. "He were excited as a new puppy hearing his father were home, but he soon wore hisself out." She looked up at me with disapproval, her eyes like spikes of ice. "Best let him sleep now."

Chastened by this blunt scolding, I returned to conclude my discarded letter. Writing materials littered the table, but finding the little pot of ink overturned and my pen fallen to the floor, I knelt to search, assuming a sudden draught had dislodged the letter too.

"What are you looking for?" Miles squatted on his haunches.

I continued to rummage among ink-stained rushes. "A letter I was writing to Brother Brian. I'd almost finished it when I heard the duke's arrival and came to welcome you home."

"Is it so important that you must roll about the floor like a dog looking for titbits?" Miles laughed. "Can't you write another?"

"Of course I can, but where can it have gone? I left it on the table and no one else has been to our chamber—unless someone came in while we were sleeping—"

"Or busy with other matters—" he said, roguishly. Noticing my gravity, he stooped to help me up. "It was probably taken while we were in the nursery. But who would want such a letter?"

Who indeed? I didn't dare voice my suspicions. My letters to the priest concerned private matters. How I cursed my stupidity in leaving one unguarded. Pretending exasperation I sat down to pen another, my mind spinning. What had I said that might be misinterpreted? Had I revealed anything that might invite suspicion? The yellow hawk eyes of Bishop Stillington returned to taunt me. What might he pay for such a letter?

Chapter Fifty-Seven

The following day, I met Jack Green by the herb garden. I assumed he'd been to the stables, for he carried a bridle.

"Do you remember how the king called on us when we lived in London?" We crossed the courtyard together. "I've often wondered why he spent so much time in Dame Butler's company."

"He promised the restoration of her husband's estates." Eager to be rid of him, I quickened my pace. Something insidious in his manner of speech provoked me. "He was always courteous to those in need."

"There were some thought his interest more than courtesy. I remember the chaplain being anxious about his visits."

"Brother Thomas was overzealous," I answered, curtly. Jack's desire to raise these old matters irritated me—particularly since Miles mentioned Stillington in connection with the king's youthful indiscretions. What might Jack, the scullion, remember of those days in Silver Street? And why now did he seem so interested?

"Why the haste?" Jack seized my arm. "Have you no time for old friends?"

"I've work to do." I glanced at the bridle. "And doubtless you've errands of your own. Gossip belongs to grandmothers dozing by the fire or idle mischief makers. If you've something to say to me, Jack, then say it quickly and have done with subterfuge."

He laughed then showing sharp teeth. "Why Mistress Forrest, what a shrew you've become. I wonder Dame Butler shared her secrets with you."

"What secrets?"

The weasel smile goaded.

"Bishop Stillington's most anxious to speak to you." His slitted eyes bored into mine. The quiet insinuation struck cold terror into me. Catching my breath, I twisted my fingers into the bunched fabric of the shawl against my breast.

"He sent out spies in search of you in London but you weren't easy to catch. Remember Cutter's Lane?"

"You!"

"It was as well we didn't catch you then, for I think the good bishop might have dealt with you quite differently from what he now intends."

"I've no business with Bishop Stillington, either then or now."

"You'd best tread carefully, Mistress Forrest, for you've sorely tried his patience. You can't hide so easily in Middleham."

I pressed a hand against a wall to steady myself. "Why should I want to hide?" Anger fuelled my query.

"What did Brother Thomas know? What secret is worth dying for?"

"I don't understand. What became of Brother Thomas?"

"Times are changing, Nan." Jack's eyes shone cold as stones though his lips still smiled. "Those who've risen to high estate may soon find themselves cast down. I tell you, you'd be best to follow the new order if you treasure all you hold dear." He turned his head meaningfully towards our apartments. "The Duke of Gloucester's an ambitious man. Your husband's chosen wisely in his allegiance."

"You're Stillington's spy." I took no pains to conceal my fury and contempt. "How can you speak of Gloucester when you imply that Stillington's in league with Clarence?"

The lad's mouth twisted into a gloating smirk that brought bile into my throat.

"Clarence lies in prison, Nan. A prisoner can't wear a crown. A captive can't dispense favours. Only fools follow lost causes. Stillington puts himself in danger if he persists in his dealings with a traitor. But some of us have seen a different future. As I understand, your secret might change a dynasty. You'd do well to foster those whose favour can be useful to you and yours."

He leaned so close, I smelled the scent of sandalwood about him and wondered vaguely how he could afford such costly spice.

"You'd betray your master for such advantage?" The venom in my speech caused him to draw back sharply. "Bishop Stillington doesn't know what a viper he has in his employ. For one so young you've learned much, Master Green."

"Indeed, I have," he said, recovering himself and looking smug. "I've much to thank the bishop for. He, more than any other, taught me the art of self-preservation. What can a scullion expect from life but constant servitude? A clever man sees which way the wind will blow and seizes every opportunity to advance his cause."

"What does Miles know of this affair with Stillington?"

He shrugged, thrusting out his nether lip. "Miles seems surprisingly ignorant about some things. But then it's difficult to know what he's thinking. I'm never sure what's true or what's dissembling. He's plainly Gloucester's man, but he doesn't share confidences easily."

He tugged at the pearl earring in his left lobe and his eyes glazed over as if considering something. Caught by the green stone in the silver ring upon his little finger, I gasped. Where had I seen such a ring before?

"You've told Miles little of Dame Butler and the king." Jack lifted an eyebrow slyly. "And I see now you're reluctant to place your trust in one who desires to help you. Perhaps you need more time to consider your situation." He executed a mocking bow. "I mustn't delay you further, for you have *work* to do."

I watched him stride away wondering just how much he knew of Eleanor's relationship with King Edward. What secrets had Stillington unleashed? Unbidden, the ascetic face of Brother Thomas rose before me bruised and badged with blood. Around its neck, it wore a hempen noose. Far away I heard the voice of Mistress Evans reminding me: You will be a keeper of secrets. Was I then the only one left who knew the exact truth about Eleanor? The tortured face blurred and became that of Miles lit by candle-light. As I watched, his hands reached up all bathed in blood and I shook with the horror of the image.

Suddenly, raindrops struck me. Huge, black, clouds swelled overhead. *How apt*, I thought, as I turned inside. Just as Jack Green turns up unexpectedly, so the weather changes. Other storms threatened our peace now. I must warn Miles about Jack Green. And I must speak to Brother Brian immediately.

⁕

"Mistress Forrest."

The curvaceous little wench on the stairs smiled up at me.

"Amy!"

"My aunt secured me a place at Middleham," she answered. The impertinent gleam in her eyes made my heart leap. "It's good to see old friends again. I'd hoped to be a nursery maid, but for now I must be content with the dairy." She paused to award me a wide smile of feigned admiration. "They tell me you have the duchess's special favour."

"Lady Anne's generous." I brushed aside the sly insinuation. "She approves my skill with herbs—"

"Your skills are still spoken of at Barnard," the wench replied. The smile remained pinned to her generous mouth. "But I'm sent to bring you to the duchess. She attends you in her bower-chamber."

As I picked up my skirts to run up the steps she touched me on the arm.

"I hope we may swiftly resume our acquaintance, Mistress Forrest," she said.

⁂

Bathed in candle-light, the duchess sat by her chessboard. She hummed under her breath, her hand hovering over an ivory pawn.

"You sent for me, Your Grace?"

She glanced up, eyes narrowed. "Would you like to play?"

I shook my head. "I've no skill in such games."

She gestured into the shadows. Two ladies rose like spectres and melted away.

"Come sit by me, Nan. I'm anxious to have your opinion on a delicate matter, knowing I can rely upon your loyalty."

Obediently I sat, my eyes drawn to the intricacies of the game while my mind still drummed with the shock of Amy's arrival.

"You've doubtless heard about my lord's brother?"

"Miles told me he'd been imprisoned, Your Grace."

She studied me a few moments, sitting so still in the flickering light I was minded of the way a cat will watch a hapless mouse which has wandered into its territory.

"A prophecy tells how G will one day rule the kingdom." Her eyes glowed, hard and unblinking. "The Duke of Clarence is named

George." It seemed a matter-of-fact statement, but I knew better. She reached a delicate hand across the chess-board to pick up the queen. Examining the piece carefully as if searching for something in its design, she spoke again, her words coldly imperious. "You've no skill with games, you say, but you have other skills." Her little, pointed tongue flicked across her lips. The green eyes blazed. "I want you to use your *special skill* to tell me if this prophecy is true."

"My lady," I answered, my tongue stiff in my mouth. "I'm afraid to use such tricks. A woman was arrested in Sheriff Hutton for telling fortunes last May."

"Tricks? I never heard you call it that before. Indeed, I remember at Dowgate how the wenches dismissed the idea of chicanery because your prophecies proved so accurate."

I fumed against such keen intelligence, noting how cleverly she'd chosen to ignore my mention of the woman arrested for sorcery. I hadn't dared take the cards from their hiding-place since. Now, with Amy Sadler's sly implications fresh in mind, the reality of discovery preyed upon me.

"Conjuring's against the law. The church condemns those who practice it. How can I take such a foolish risk?"

Smiling, though her eyes gleamed murderous, she held up her hand so the little queen thrust right into my face. "I know you can do it," she said. "And I've some authority myself. Don't you trust my protection, Nan?" Her voice softened. "No one need know." A sly gleam lit the feline features. "Besides you and I are old in secrets, are we not?"

In the hearth, dancing flames mocked me with their pointing fingers. The smell of burning made me sweat. I thought of the foreign woman in prison. *Please let it not be Mara,* I prayed.

"It's dangerous to meddle with fortune-telling. Even noble ladies are subject to the church's commands. No one's safe from the fire."

"Trust me." Her whisper became a serpent's hiss.

I bowed my head, wondering how I might extricate myself from this latest intrigue, Brother Brian's troubled smile vivid in my mind.

Chapter Fifty-Eight

Wild rumours about Clarence enlivened a dank, dismal November.

"He's plotting with the French." Genevieve murmured nonsense among the little huddle of maids in the bower-chamber. "They're going to help King Henry's old queen to invade England."

"But why would Queen Margaret want to come back here?" Meg Huddleston flashed me an indiscreet glance, tossing back her head with exasperation. "Her husband and son are dead. I don't know who told you—"

"Anyway Clarence is in the Tower," interrupted Grace, eyes still on her book. "He can't plan an invasion from there, can he?"

"But that little wench, Amy Sadler, said she heard Master Metcalf discussing it with our Duke." Peevishly Genevieve threw down her sewing.

"Amy Sadler's a mischievous inventor of spurious gossip," said Meg. She turned to me. "Nan knows her of old, don't you?" I smarted under her artful words. "Do you know what the servants are saying about Clarence, Nan? I'm sure you must have heard something on your frequent visits to the nursery."

"Mistress Collins hates gossip," I answered. My cheeks reddened with suppressed rage.

"Well, I'm sure Lady Anne will be glad her brother-in-law's incarcerated after the way he –"

"Treated her so unkindly?" Lady Anne's sudden arrival silenced us and left Meg flushing with discomfort. "I must send you to the nursery at once, Nan," she said. "My son's complaining of a headache. No one else has your healing touch."

I rose under the deliberate approval of her smile.

"Now, Genevieve, what gossip have you to amuse us?" she asked pointedly, as I quit the chamber.

❧

Dining in the great hall amidst choking smoke from the wayward fire, the evening's conversation buzzed with news. Clarence had slandered Edward's birth, criticised his government and made outrageous accusations against the queen.

Old Walt, pompous with too much ale, spoke up a touch too loud. "He's allus been trouble. It's time the king put an end to all traitors, brother or no brother. Leniency is weakness." He raised a belligerent arm. "A king mun punish if he means to have respect."

Gripped by this vitriolic outburst, the other diners froze.

"The queen'll see Clarence punished." Jane Collins shifted uncomfortably in her seat, her expression severe. "He'll happen find no mercy in that wench."

Old Walt threw her a scowl. "Aye, but it's not for wenches to rule," he said caustically. "It's a man's business. And the king'll happen summon Parliament to put Clarence on trial in a week or two." With a grim smirk of satisfaction, the curmudgeon surveyed his audience. "Then we'll see justice done."

Someone dropped a knife, breaking the tension.

"Not at Christmas." Jane muttered just loud enough for all to hear.

"Nor before the royal wedding," added Tom Metcalf, with quiet amusement. He quickly engaged the company. "The king won't miss the opportunity to see his youngest son claim the Mowbray inheritance. He plans a huge affair to celebrate this event, and even Clarence won't spoil his pleasure in it. I have this from our duke himself!"

More than willing to be distracted from Walt's harangue I listened to Tom Metcalf's garrulous wife chattering of this royal marriage set to take place in the new year.

"It'll be a glorious occasion." Plump Elizabeth Metcalf's eyes sparkled. "I'd love to see it."

"And so should I." A plan began to form in my mind. "I went to Westminster once. The king keeps a magnificent court there."

"Well I never! Is it true all the chambers are hung with cloth of gold?"

Even as I recounted the magnificence of the royal palace I resolved to write to Harry and arrange to meet him in London. Somehow I must persuade Lady Anne to take me with her to her nephew's wedding.

✍

Through the last week of the month the road to Jervaulx lay bleak with frost.

Though Miles advised against the journey I pleaded to see Brother Brian before winter marooned him across the moorland until the spring thaw.

How desolate and forbidding the abbey appeared against the iron-grey sky. Sheep huddled in the fields, the skirling cry of curlews filled the air with lamentation, and a biting wind whined amongst the granite hills. I wondered how the monks could bear such bitter solitude.

At the guest-house, the young novice monk with the pale hair awaited me.

"Brother Brian's in the infirmary," he said, flushing crimson. "I'm to take you there."

Introducing himself as Edwin, he explained he was a native of the county sent by his family to further his education. Like Alan Palmer, he seemed a shy, sensitive youth.

"Come in, come in," called Brother Brian. He stooped before the hearth, his face reddened by steam, ladling liquid into a bowl. "I'm after helping Brother Silas with his infusion for the winter cough. Several of the brothers have taken sick with it already. Bring Mistress Forrest a stool, Edwin, so she can sit by the fire."

I settled close to the heat watching Brother Brian pour hot liquid into an earthen cup. Smiling at my hesitancy he handed it to me. "Taste this. It'll warm you and chase away any ill-humours hanging about the place. Is it sweet enough?"

Sipping the brew I marvelled at its delicious honey flavour.

"Our own bees," nodded the priest.

"And are there cloves in it, too?"

"And ginger and nutmeg. It's one of Silas' own recipes."

"Did someone mention me?"

An elderly monk carrying a basket of russet apples appeared in the doorway. In spite of his advanced years, a wiry, sprightly quality hung about him and an impish expression lit his rheumy eyes.

"Brother Silas, this is Mistress Forrest." Brother Brian turned to introduce me. "I mentioned her proposed visit if you remember. The guest-house's a draughty old place at the best of times and Edwin tells me there's no fire lit—"

"No matter—I've a guest myself as you see."

A lithe figure I knew well slipped into the chamber.

"Master Green's something of a scholar. He's recently joined the Duke of Gloucester's entourage and expressed a wish to see our library. He tells me he's interested in the making of our herbal remedies. The Abbot's granted him permission to further his studies among us."

Smiling broadly, Jack Green leaned nonchalantly against the fireplace, arms folded across his chest, a picture of calculated insolence.

"What an unexpected pleasure to meet you here, Mistress Forrest." His glib words and over-confident posturing made me want to slap his face.

"I'd no idea you were such a scholar," I answered. Both Brother Brian and Brother Silas flinched at my derisive tone but Jack laughed although his eyes remained wintry. "Jack and I are old companions," I explained to the elderly monk with the basket. "He and I worked together in the kitchens of a fine house in London—"

"Indeed." Brother Silas darted a meaningful glance at Brother Brian.

"I'm thinking Mistress Forrest and I might be better in the guest-house after all," Brother Brian said, gathering up his cloak. "Edwin will make up the fire. And then you can show Master Green the workings of the infirmary without interruption."

Edwin, observing all from a nook by the huge press, sprang to his feet. I noted how Jack Green's lip curled as the delicate youth hurried to the door.

"Thank you, Brian." Brother Silas turned his astute gaze upon me. "I'm glad to make your acquaintance, Mistress Forrest."

I felt the weight of Jack Green's ill-concealed animosity as we took our leave.

"That young man," said Brother Brian, as we shivered before a meagre, smoking fire, "is the source of much unease, I fear."

"He's Stillington's spy. Already he's made threats against me, but I never thought to see him here at Jervaulx. Before he alerts his master of my whereabouts there's something I must do—"

"Concerning the children in the Tower?"

Looking into the troubled depths of his blue eyes I seized his hands in mine. "I must warn their mother before it's too late. And I've found a way at last. Pray for me."

Chapter Fifty-Nine

"Hurry Nan!" Emma burst into the nursery and stood dancing from one foot to the other with impatience and cold. "We've been called to help the Duchess's ladies with the packing."

Jane Collins held out her arms to take Dickon from me. We watched the fluttering dance of the snowflakes as they drifted by the little lancet window.

December brought a whirl of winter storms and overnight the moors turned into a hostile wilderness. Already deep drifts blocked some roads. Brother Brian would be snow-bound at austere Jervaulx Abbey now.

"Ssh Emma!" Mistress Collins frowned. "Tha'll wake the prince. He hardly slept a wink last night. Did tha get that milk? Wherever hast tha been all this time?"

The girl's already frost-reddened cheeks darkened guiltily.

"Gossiping, I'll wager." An exasperated Jane Collins gently uncurled Dickon's fingers from her hair and tried to restrain his struggles to escape from her lap. "What's all this about packing?"

"On my way to the buttery I met Amy Sadler. She said the Gloucesters are going to spend Christmas in York, and—"

"Well that's no surprise." Jane chuckled at Dickon's loud demands for "snow."

"But straight after they're going to London." Emma looked as if she was about to burst with excitement. "King Edward's invited them to Prince Richard's wedding!"

"Ee, what a pother over a couple of bairns," said the stout Yorkshire-woman. "Prince Richard's still nobbut a babe. King Edward's after that Mowbray lass's inheritance before anyone else offers her marriage. Tom Metcalf knew as much."

I couldn't help laughing at her blunt reproof. The king's avarice was legendary and little Anne Mowbray reputed the richest heiress in the country.

"When's this grand occasion to be?" I followed Emma from the nursery.

"The fifteenth of January. Oh Nan, wouldn't it be wonderful to be there? Amy said—"

"This way, this way!" A strident voice already issued commands. We climbed the stairs to the ducal apartments. Jostled by sweating servants doubled over with the weight of boxes and furnishings, we did our best to avoid the mischievous attentions of Master John, Lady Anne's fool, who revelled in all the chaos. Crouching like a little ape, he thrust his bauble under the feet of the unwary— antics which earned cuffs and curses from the men-folk and outraged squeaks from women who tripped over their skirts.

"Watch out!" called Emma.

Master John reached out to pinch me. Laughing, I twisted away from the snatching fingers and leapt up two steps at a time.

"Oh, see how the little mice scamper when the cat's invited them to a great feast!" The fool began capering on the steps until one of the bolder lads gave him a kick in the buttocks that sent him tumbling down. Even then he seemed unrepentant, curling up like a ball and bouncing and yowling until he reached the bottom where he scuttled about like a spider, endeavouring to creep beneath the skirts of an empty-headed scullery-wench. This trick provoked wild shrieks, especially from the matrons, but much bawdy laughter from the men.

When we reached Lady Anne's chambers, we faced a storm of flung garments— velvet gowns trimmed with miniver, silken hose, hoods, kerchiefs, silver girdles, golden collars, fustian kirtles, lawn under-gowns and soft leather shoes. Staggering underneath a load of winter robes like a pack-horse, I found myself nudged into a line of similarly burdened bodies and bullied down the stairs.

"Do you think I'll go to London?" A pile of mantles tucked under her nose muffled Emma's speech.

"I doubt it." I sneezed, spitting tufts of fur. "Only a few of the duchess's noble ladies will be chosen. Be thankful for the Christmas festivities in York. That journey in the snow will be bad enough, but travelling to London will be particularly unpleasant in this raw season."

"But Amy said you're to be part of Lady Anne's entourage." Emma paused to stab me with a sharp look.

I hoisted my bundle of sliding furs higher inwardly cursing Amy Sadler's clacking tongue. That wench seemed to know everything. "I'd rather huddle by the fire than shiver in an open litter in the driving sleet," I answered, feigning reluctance. "I don't relish the long journey, or the separation from Dickon."

"But you'll have new gowns." She pouted with envy. "Alice Skelton's telling Meg Huddleston the duchess has ordered splendid clothes for all her attendants. You're so lucky, Nan."

I laughed off her resentment, conscious that many of Middleham's servants wondered how I'd managed to gain a place in the inner circle of favoured ladies. In spite of my lowly birth, the duchess's intimates treated me respectfully. Several times, clever Elizabeth Parre asked my opinion of village wise women and I noted how intently the others listened to my answers.

"You're quite the wise-woman yourself, Nan." Meg Huddleston examined a flask of valerian root from the basket of herbals I brought into the bower-chamber to show them. "What's this for?"

"It brings calm, refreshing sleep. And this one is thyme-vinegar which is good for headaches."

"I'll vouch for its efficacy." Lady Anne made a wry face. "You should try it, Alice, for those headaches which have plagued you recently."

"And I swear by Nan's infusion of frumitory to fade freckles," said Grace. Sheepishly she confessed her regular patronage for my remedies. "Haven't you noticed how mine have almost disappeared? That little dairy-wench, Amy, recommended it. She knows a lot about Nan's expertise. She said at Barnard—"

"I've others for blemishes and troublesome spots," I said quickly, "and a wonderfully soothing skin lotion made from lovage and daisies—Here, smell it."

They clustered around me, tasting, sniffing, touching—but also passing secret smiles as if daring one another to ask more. Did they know something about my fortune-telling skills? Whenever I heard someone mention Amy's name I squirmed. The wench seemed to have inveigled herself into everyone's confidence.

"Take me with you to London, my Lady."

I lingered when the duchess dismissed the others and offered to let her try my newest skin lotion. She lay on the settle so I might massage it into her forehead, smoothing away anxious lines with gentle outward strokes. Tension seized her in its vice as soon as I made my request, but I maintained the sweeping rhythm of my fingers quite unperturbed.

"I've often heard you express concern about your family's welfare, and I know you're anxious for your son's future. You told me there are several dangerous *factions* at court. Perhaps if I witness these at work I'll better be equipped to advise you."

She sat up suddenly. "You're very determined, Mistress Nan." Her restless hands toyed with the phials and bundles in my basket, her shoulders rigid. "I think you've something very particular in mind."

"It's always best to see one's rivals face to face, Your Grace." Mischievously, I added, "But you're right, of course. I'm hopeless at pretending. I'd like to visit family in the city. So I beg a favour for a favour."

She caught my eye and at once the tension ebbed away. "How can I refuse such a charming request?" She sniffed the flask of valerian with a sly smile. "Besides, my husband needs your husband's services, so what could be more appropriate than you travel with us?"

Part Six

London
1478

Chapter Sixty

The magnificent Christmas Feast at York drew all the duke's northern friends to his table. Wearing a fine blue damask gown made from fabric Miles brought from London, I sat down to dine in the great hall lit by the flames of a hundred flambeaux conscious of many admiring glances. Fleetingly I wondered what my mother and Fat Marion would have said if they'd seen me among such affluent company.

"The duke's noted for his generosity," Miles murmured in my ear. "There's already a flock of peasants and supposed pilgrims at the kitchen door waiting for the seasonal offerings of food and wine."

"I suspect His Grace imitates the late Earl of Warwick," said Tom Metcalf, from beside me. "Warwick's hospitality's legendary in these parts, and I daresay Lady Anne encourages her husband to follow in her father's ways."

I leaned to question Master Metcalf further about Warwick when an ear-splitting fanfare of trumpets announced the arrival of the boar's head. A troupe of serving men in white lawn shirts and scarlet hose carried it in on a silver platter. How we cheered this opening signal of the traditional Christmas Banquet! Miles filled my goblet to the brim, ogling a vast peacock pie, garnished with magnificent tail feathers, as it passed amongst us. While hasty servers distributed platters the Duke of Gloucester gave the toast, urging us to enjoy this sumptuous repast in honour of Our Lord's Birth.

Piety forgotten, we fell upon the food, cramming our greedy bellies while merry music issued from the gallery. Momentarily I forgot the bitter wind whining about the castle and the harsh journeys to come.

After Twelfth Night, Miles and I would ride south in the Gloucesters' entourage. Though awed by the thought of sharing chambers with Lady Anne's high-born ladies at Westminster, I shook with excitement. I'd see King Edward again. I'd see the queen and her mysterious French mother reputed to be a witch, and perhaps glimpse her handsome father, the unfortunate object of the old nobility's greatest disdain. And, at last, I'd see the boy I believed to haunt my visions. I trembled at the thought of the daring plan I'd devised to alert their mother of the danger which threatened her sons.

Miles eluded questions concerning his duties at the wedding, but Lady Anne's words roused misgivings. What services did Gloucester require of Miles? All through the Christmas revels my mind fermented with anxiety.

Emma, on the other hand, forgot her disappointment, elegant in a new gown of fine pearl-grey worsted trimmed with crimson, and absorbed by all the lively festivities. Giggling and sharing confidences, she played at ninepins with the other maids and delighted in the dancing, quickly learning to execute the steps of the pavanne and the farandole. Several young swains courted her favours and whenever they swept her into the revelry, I smiled fondly—until Jack Green joined their number.

"Don't allow Master Green too much licence," I said. "He's something of a reputation among the ladies."

She blushed, lowering her gaze, so pretty and vulnerable, I trembled for her. Smug Jack, flaunting an amber journade with long, padded, gold sleeves edged in dark fur, winked at me. Uneasily I watched the dancers glide by.

"Well, lass," Miles seized me around the waist, "have you no time for your husband?"

Before I could answer he kissed me heartily on the mouth, rousing a roar of approving male voices. He whirled me into a wild dance, spinning and lifting me at tremendous speed until my ears and eyes stung with noise and brilliance. Clinging to him as the music faded, I reeled like a drunkard, glad to sit on his lap while an impudent-faced minstrel and his accomplices entertained us with a score of ribald ballads.

By Twelfth Night most of the men lay slumped across the tables, too fuddled with ale to stay awake. That evening nimble dancers leaped and jingled about the great hall, and women ran shrieking from the lewd attentions of the Holly Man, a capering fellow in green hose, crowned and covered in a bushy disguise of twisted ever-greens and prickly holly boughs.

"Who's won the bean?"

Everyone asked the question while we crumbled our fruit-laden portions of the rich Twelfth Night Cake.

"It's Master Snowdon!" Genevieve Mountford shrieked and pointed at Lady Anne's yeoman of the chamber sitting opposite. He seized her by the wrist, flaunting the bean he'd found in his cake with his other hand.

"I'm your Lord of Misrule for this night." He rose with a loud guffaw. "Now, what task shall I appoint Mistress Genevieve?"

Several mischievous young men called out lewd suggestions while Master Snowdon pounced upon other victims. Some abandoned their places in an attempt to avoid his notice, scattering crumbs and spilling wine, but once chosen, no one dared disobey his commands. The luxuriously decorated chamber soon echoed with roars of outrage and delight as these unfortunates executed ridiculous penalties.

"Oh no!" Emma squealed when Jack Green pulled a clove from his morsel of cake. Around them people shouted and gestured, faces puce with laughter.

"Villain of the evening Master Green!" Master Snowden executed an impudent bow in Jack's direction. "I congratulate you on your title."

Everyone cheered until a strident female voice called out in mocking tones, "Very apt for a faithless rogue!"

Though Jack feigned indifference, I knew such taunts annoyed him.

"I'm glad you're to come with me to London, Nan." Miles lurched through the draughty passage ways towards our chamber at the end of this last merriment. His words slurred. "I'd be lonely without you." He fumbled at my gown.

With pretended exasperation, I prevented him from falling against a door.

"The Duke's commanded me to ride with him. I can't disobey an order, can I?" He smiled at me stupidly. When I finally steered him into our chamber, he fell, fully clothed, on the bed into heavy, snoring sleep.

Restless, I paced up and down, my thoughts jangling. What could the Duke of Gloucester want with Miles at his royal nephew's wedding? What new secret, sinister errand had he in mind?

Next morning, fogged by a surfeit of spiced ale and lack of sleep, I took the cards from their hiding-place behind the loose brick in the hearth and thrust them into my bodice.

"Master Forrest's gone to the stables." Amy spoke from behind me. "I'm sorry, did I make you jump?"

"I didn't hear you come in." The blood burned in my face. "I didn't realise you were here—"

"Oh yes, I secured a place among the servants," she answered. A smile curved her plump lips. "Master Forrest sent me to help you dress, but I see you've managed already." She eyed my murrey gown with such insolence I could have struck her. "Let me fetch a warm cloak." She fastened the clasp and smoothed the folds, bowing her auburn head in the obsequious fashion of a lowly servant and then looked up with a calculating glint in her eye. "Master Forrest's risen high in the duke's favour. His friends in Staindrop will be pleased. And he promised to see me well rewarded for my assistance."

"Thank you, Amy." I snatched my hood over my head. How dare she remind me of that wanton wench who'd borne Miles a bastard child? My voice shook with suppressed fury. "I'm sure your worth will be appreciated."

Outside I dithered in the frosty morning watching the breath of men and horses rise like steam while men servants completed the preparations for our departure with annoying slowness. Still smarting from Amy's ingratiating manner, my mind turned suddenly to Brother Brian.

"This journey will test your strength," he said. "Trust no one. These great ones have no conscience. They trample over one another without a qualm, intent only on furthering their own purposes. Be especially careful of the king. He won't have forgotten Dame Eleanor Butler or the promises he made."

Would Edward of York recognise me after all these years?

"Mistress Forrest."

Insolent Jack Green tipped his fur-trimmed hat as he trotted by on a fine dappled gelding, his frozen smile driving a bolt of terror through me. So, Jack would be riding among the duke's men after all. Fists-clenched, I cursed his inclusion in the retinue. What schemes simmered in that cunning brain of his? Jack Green threatened our safety.

Emma, wan and sleepy, turned out to bid me farewell. While I fretted at the delay she huddled against me for warmth, her gaze following Jack Green's strutting posture.

"I hope you're not so smitten with Master Green as to weep for his departure," I said. "Or is it just the cold that makes your eyes water so?"

"Why do you dislike Jack so much?"

"Take care he doesn't break your heart." I could have bitten out my tongue when her face twisted into the ugliness of grief.

Chastened, I hugged her, recalling my own foolishness where Miles was concerned. "I don't want to see you get hurt, Emma. Now promise me you'll take special care of Dickon while I'm away."

Leaving my boy sleeping in the nursery gave me a heart-wrenching moment. How small and innocent he seemed, his fists lying upon the pillow, his lips parted, the soft whisper of his breath gently stirring the pile of the velvet coverlet.

Stomach churning with sudden dread, I climbed up into the cart amidst a jabber of female voices. Suppose I met Bishop Stillington in London? The servants cheered as we set off, doffing their caps with exaggerated courtesy. Disconcertingly, I glimpsed Amy Sadler's pert face among the crowd. I turned away to wave a hand at an ashen-faced Miles as he rode by on his snorting steed towards the head of the company. He made no gesture of acknowledgement and I shuddered. It seemed an ominous farewell.

Chapter Sixty-One

At Westminster I shared a chamber with Genevieve Mountford and Alice Skelton—a luxurious room, oak-panelled and draped with velvet hangings. The enormous carved beds, canopied and curtained in embroidered damask, were furnished with warm feather quilts and silken counterpanes. Two oak settles scattered with gold woven cushions, a carved chest and a press for garments, a large looking-glass, a stool, several pewter candlesticks, and a woollen tapestry depicting a hunting scene completed our comfort. Fresh rushes on the tiled floor lay fragrant with sprinkled meadowsweet.

Chattering like magpies, we helped each other dress in the cherry-coloured gowns Lady Anne had chosen.

"That colour suits you, Nan." Genevieve spoke with genuine admiration.

"It brings out the brilliance of your eyes," agreed Alice. She smoothed her rippling skirts.

Touched by the sisterly way she and Alice treated me, I paused to smile at my reflection in the glass.

"Don't you think it makes me look pale?" Genevieve came to stand behind me, frowning and twisting her head this way and that.

"You need some colour on your cheeks, that's all." Alice produced a casket in which she kept scented lotions, perfumes and little pots of coloured powder. "Send the girl to the kitchen for eggs," she said.

Puzzled, I dispatched the little serving-maid assigned to us upon this errand. When she returned, Alice showed us how to mix an egg yolk with finely ground red powder to make a paste. This she smoothed over Genevieve's cheeks and lips. The dramatic change astounded me.

"You look lovely," I said. I stood back to survey Alice's skilful painting. "Like a flower in bloom!"

Yielding to Alice's persuasion I allowed her to decorate my face, too. How we giggled as she applied a silvery-blue powder to our eye-lids, and then, with a little, pointed stick drew a smudgy charcoal line above and below our eyes to accentuate them.

"Don't we look beautiful?" Alice laughed. Eagerly, we peered into the glass.

"I fear men will swoon when they see us!" said Genevieve.

"How did you come by such stuff?" Pleased by my own startling transformation, my eyes staring huge and full of light, I examined the pots of colour, sniffing at the various creams and lotions.

"The dyer in Middleham has all kinds of things. They're not all costly, though some are made from crushed gems. Mistress Glover, the chandler's wife makes herbal remedies too. But you're skilled at making skin lotions yourself, Nan, so those will be no secret to you. The older matrons disapprove of painting, but why look jaded when one can look rosy? Anyway, Lady Anne herself has been known to use such artifice."

Certainly we drew admiring glances when we joined the duchess's entourage. Following her slight figure in its emerald velvet encrusted with pearls, we entered the Chapel of St Stephen for the wedding ceremony.

The walls of St Stephen's hung with tapestries of azure and golden fleur de lis. Dressed in crimson cloth-of-gold, little Prince Richard waited under a golden canopy for his bride. A sturdy boy with thick red-gold hair, he stood with his back towards us as we edged into our places. Beside him, slender and stately in silver tissue, the queen turned her haughty gaze upon the congregation. Glancing about surreptitiously I noted the slight, crimson-clad figure of the Duke of Gloucester but caught no sign of Miles among his attendants.

"Oh look!" Alice turned, breathless with wonder. Anne Mowbray, copper-red hair streaming down her back, progressed solemnly down the aisle led by a tall, lithe, gentleman with hair of palest gold.

The royal children in their wedding finery, pledging their vows in piping voices, earned indulgent smiles and tear-bright glances.

Turning at last, the prince rewarded our loud acclaims with a broad grin as if caught out in some mischief. I gulped at the sight of his bright, impish face. While others cheered I watched this merry-faced boy of my dreams walk toward me, clasping his pretty bride by the hand. Her fine-boned features reminded me of that other little prince at Middleham whose fragile health gave us sleepless nights. Instantly I realised Anne Mowbray wouldn't make old bones. But the boy beside her seemed full of promise. My heart ached to snatch him up and run to some place of safety where evil, ambitious men couldn't find him.

"Did you see the king?" Genevieve giggled her way back to our chamber. Hurriedly, we cast off our garments.

"How fat he's grown," I said, standing in my shift before the glass. I mourned the loss of the lean, muscular giant who'd visited Eleanor at Silver Street. The golden youth with the easy charm whose friendly arm had once draped around Lionel's shoulder had gone forever. In his stead loomed a huge, corpulent figure with a bloated face and piggy eyes that disappeared into ridges of mottled flesh. Magnificent clothes studded with precious gems couldn't conceal the swollen neck, the massive thighs and enormous belly straining at the seams.

Alice sighed folding away her cherry-coloured sleeves. "He was once so handsome women swooned with desire as he passed."

Genevieve smirked. "Well, they say certain ladies still battle for his favours. Can you imagine what it must be like to bed with such a mountain?"

"The queen must be made of strong stuff!"

Alice rolled on her bed weeping with laughter.

"I heard Mistress Shore's mad with love for him." Genevieve mopped her eyes on the hangings.

"Perhaps she appreciates his hidden qualities," I said.

"Bawdy talk will make us late." Alice dragged the blue and gold gowns Lady Anne instructed us to wear for the feast and jousting at Greenwich from the oak chest. "Make haste and I'll fix your hair and faces. Nan, you must let me pluck back your hairline to broaden the sweep of your brow."

Scented with rose-water, we finally tip-toed down the steps, necks strained under the weight of piled up hair, stretching up our heads like swans—hoping to hide the effort of balancing the elaborate gauzy butterfly headdresses.

"Our king fashions his court on that of Duke Philip of Burgundy." Alice pointed out the luxurious furnishings as we entered the hall in the wake of Lady Anne, who bloomed like an exotic flower in a shimmering purple gown edged with marten fur.

Exquisitely decorated, Greenwich's palace walls hung rich with vivid tapestries and cloth-of-gold. By the great carved doors the king stood to welcome his guests, a towering figure in scarlet doublet flashing huge diamonds. His engaging laughter boomed with warmth. None could resist the magic of his presence. The household gentlemen, wearing collars of suns and white roses, directed us to our places, while our duke plunged his hands into golden basins filled with gold and silver coins, casting them to all the people present. I felt sure this extravagance would enrage the worthy London merchants whose wages were subject to the king's new, exorbitant taxes but like my companions I was carried along by the enchantment of the spectacle.

From her seat at the high table, the queen, in gold silk and ermine and wearing the tallest hennin I'd ever seen, clapped her slender hands, smiling upon us graciously. Around her thronged her numerous family members, and while the servers plied us with yet more sumptuous delicacies, Alice and Genevieve pointed them out to me by name.

That night I slept badly. Perhaps the rich food and the strange bed contributed in part to my discomfort, but long after Genevieve and Alice succumbed to sleep, I lay restless. Learning the victorious knight of the magnificent tournament was the queen's brother, Anthony Wydeville, the pale-haired gentleman who'd escorted the little bride into the chapel, I grew doubly anxious for the safety of the princes. Hadn't the older boy asked for this uncle in my vision? And hadn't Bishop Stillington held up his severed head? Clearly the distinguished nobleman, famous for his learning as well as his jousting, stood in grave danger. But my priority remained to save the little boys. Eventually my feverish plotting as to how I might seize a moment to speak to the queen dulled my brain. I sank into a troubled, unsatisfactory sleep.

Waking the following morning from muddled dreams I gritted my teeth under giddy Genevieve's relentless prattle. Pleading a headache, I lay with the curtains drawn about my bed, relieved when she and Alice took themselves off to breakfast.

Later, wrapped in my warmest cloak, I strolled outside in the frosty gardens to clear my head. The parklands shimmered with ice and by the lake I paused to watch the swans gliding gracefully under the willow trees. Several young children stood feeding titbits to a herd of fallow deer and men and women in thick fur mantles nodded to me as they passed.

Inside I met Genevieve weaving her way through a rowdy mass of elegantly dressed courtiers parading in the opposite direction towards the great hall. She held out a small wooden box and a sealed note.

"Lady Anne's asked me to take this to the queen." She wrinkled her brow with impatience, glancing at the passing hubbub. "I'll probably miss supper."

"I'll take it." Rejoicing in this piece of luck, I snatched the note from her hesitant fingers. "If you hurry, you might just catch the eye of that young squire in Lord Hastings' retinue you danced with last night."

Thrusting the box into my hands, she scampered away in a moment leaving me to navigate the winding passageways towards the queen's apartments. Twice I got lost and had to ask directions of men in livery, but the music finally steered me to her. Drums and tabors marked out foot-tapping rhythms, and outside a pair of vast oaken doors towered armed men wearing the sun-ray blazon of York.

By then my heart beat its own rapid tune. What should I say? For days I'd rehearsed my speech but now the moment had come, the words seemed weak and futile.

A riot of colour and sound assailed me as those great doors swung open. The inner chamber sparkled in a dazzle of torches and blazing candles. I glimpsed a swirling troupe of golden-haired maids executing an intricate figure to the musicians' beat. These silver clad girls with garlands of silk blossoms about their unbound hair, I took to be the princesses.

Servants carrying dishes of sweetmeats stepped aside as I edged towards the high dais where the queen reclined on one elbow among a heap of jewelled cushions. The eyes of a score of burly guards followed me intently.

Gracious matrons in elegant gowns of varying shades of blue, embroidered about the hem and sleeves with silver rose emblems, surrounded the Wydeville queen. In cloth-of-gold the bright colour of a jay's feathers, her wondrous, silver-gilt hair bound up in an elaborate pearl-encrusted net, she nestled upon silver-grey cushions embroidered with seed-pearls, like a mermaid upon rocks.

Nervously I sank into a deep curtsy to announce the purpose of my errand. A blue-liveried page took my offerings, kneeling wordlessly before the queen. Ignoring us, she scanned the message. Around the chamber the buzz of conversation continued without falter; the chink of pewter and the ring of glass mingled with light laughter; the dance progressed. She kept us kneeling a long time. Limbs trembling, I held my breath, summoning up courage to speak out.

"Return my thanks to the duchess for her gift." She looked up at last. Her voice drawled, languid with boredom. The box remained unopened.

I raised my eyes to the exquisite features, taking in the pure white forehead, the finely arched brows, the petal blush of colour across the sculpted cheek-bones, the perfect coral of her lips. She sat so still she might have been a marble statue.

"Your Grace."

Her eyes widened with surprise. I caught the rustle of fabric as she drew upright, smelled the subtle fragrance of lilies. "You've some other message to deliver?" The tone whipped, sharp with annoyance. The eyes gleamed winter-cold.

"I must speak out, Your Grace. I must warn you."

There, it was done. I pressed my nails against the soft flesh of my palms, conscious of the quiver in my calves and the cruel press of the marble tiles against my knees. The silence crackled with tension.

"Who are you?"

The white heat of her anger scalded.

"Waiting-woman to the Duchess of Gloucester, Your Grace," I replied. My heart's drum accelerated. "But my duty to the crown bids me speak. Your Grace, I come to remind you of Astwith Gorse."

The shock of her gasp sparked a flutter among the matrons. She lifted a slender hand. The music died. Conversation ceased.

"Be gone." Her command exploded like the snap of ice. "The entertainment is at an end."

A clatter and a scrambled removal of platters and instruments fractured the silence. Whispers of protest travelled among the princesses. The chamber emptied. About the queen, the matrons hovered uncertainly while the guards froze at their posts, pikes crossed.

"Now," she said, fingers caressing the delicate necklace about her throat, "tell me what you know of Astwith Gorse."

My gaze arrowed to the milky stones winking bright colours. I watched them turn to drops of water.

"I bring you tears without number, Your Grace." Unbidden, the words spilled from my lips. "Remember the Egyptian woman on Astwith Gorse who promised you lasting fame? I travelled with her twelve years ago. She spoke of you and the prophecy she made."

The queen leaned forward, hands gripping the sides of her chair, eyes fixed on mine. Staring into those black pupils, I travelled a dark corridor pulsing with menace.

"You're no Egyptian."

"No, but Mara taught me her skills. She sends me to you now— to remind you of the future she promised. 'Bone of your bone will join three great houses in one.' Isn't that part of the prophecy?"

The hiss struck like a snake's bite, but I didn't flinch.

"Destiny chose you for greatness, Your Grace. You've wed the royal prince she promised. Your beauty and fame will continue beyond death, as predicted, but first—"

"What? "She spat the word at me, the venom in her voice unmistakable. "Tell me your worst, wench, whoever you are!"

"Grief beyond all imagining." I saw again Mara's dark lips speaking these words. "Troubles dire will fall upon your head. The time approaches, Your Grace. I come to warn you."

"There *is* hope?" The voice executed a rising scale. The eyes raked my face.

"The boys, Your Grace. They must be saved. Don't send them to the Tower."

Brittle laughter trembled on the edge of hysteria.

"The Tower—Do you mean my sons? I can't save the others— They're dead these ten years—Tell me what you mean—enough of riddles and rhymes—I must know more—"

"Don't part with the youngest. Don't let them persuade you to it. Keep him close by you. All the knights in Christendom can't save them if you yield." Suddenly, alarmingly, I saw a red dragon fly through the sky. "Beware the dragon from the west. It will swallow up the sun and pluck the rose to wear upon its sleeve. It has no mercy."

"I told you, no more riddles!" Her voice shrilled with anger. "Tell me truthfully, will my son one day wear the crown?"

I bowed my head. The pictures raced, leaping like stags across my inner vision. "I see the crown raised high and hear the triumphant anthem as the bishop lowers it—"

"And? Spit it out, wench. Don't toy with me."

"Your eldest daughter must be cherished, Your Grace. Destiny chooses her for a great marriage." I heard her groan and rose at once, moving away like one in a trance.

"Wait!" The command halted me. The guards about the door clashed their pikes.

"Do you know I could have you burned for this fortune-telling?"

"I merely repeat the message I'm sent to deliver." I didn't turn my head. "Sooth-sayers must speak freely, Your Grace. Mara taught me that. I think you may have learned something of this from your lady mother—"

An angry growl curdled my blood. Attendants raced to draw me back but I couldn't move. I'd chanced my riskiest remark, for the Duchess Jacquetta, Elizabeth Wydeville's French mother, was reputed to be a powerful witch. Knowing this, would the queen dare accuse me of sorcery?

"Let her go."

The thwarted attendants sighed.

"Does the Duchess of Gloucester know of your skills, Mistress?"

Turning to acknowledge her authority with a deep curtsey, I answered boldly. "I have the duchess's protection, Your Grace."

Chapter Sixty-Two

No one sent for me. Obedient and quiet, I fulfilled my duties to Lady Anne. In my leisure time I gossiped with the other waiting women, played at cards as if I'd no cares. Just for amusement, Alice, Genevieve and I flounced about our bed-chamber in our shifts, tried on each other's clothes, washed our hair and combed it different ways, leaned out of the window to jest with bold-eyed swains we lured to flatter us, or lay upon our beds nibbling sweetmeats.

But my daring act constantly occupied my thoughts. Had the queen spoken of me to her husband? Had she commanded her attendants to keep silent? Would someone tell Lady Anne of my indiscretion? And why did I feel such a sense of failure? More and more the futility of my warning oppressed me. Hideous dreams of the Tower chamber troubled my dreams. Every night the assassins prowled the darkness and every morning I denied the familiar figure whose northern voice I recognised so cruelly.

"I saw your husband with the duke this morning," said Alice. Seizing me eagerly from amongst a group of the queen's ladies chattering on the stairs, she drew me into our chamber. "No one looks as well in blue as he does, do they? But he was with that rogue, Jack Green. They were heading towards the council chamber. There's a rumour Bishop Stillington's being interrogated by the king's inquisitors."

"Stillington?" The name was a stab of fear. "I didn't know he was at Westminster."

"He's involved somehow with that scandal about the Duke of Clarence." Alice gave me a sharp look. "I thought you and he were old acquaintances. I'm sure Meg Huddleston said—"

"Jocelyn says Clarence will be hanged." Genevieve's high-pitched laughter interrupted us. She lay on her bed reading a letter but she sat up immediately she heard us come in, ready to share news she'd had of her latest admirer.

"I don't think the king would harm his own brother," reproved Alice.

"The queen's ladies say he'll be kept in prison a while," I said.

Genevieve chattered of Clarence's misdemeanours while I fretted over Alice's words. What could that weasel Jack Green want with Miles? *No one looks as well in blue, do they?* The words taunted me. Vividly I saw Miles' eyes full of apprehension. What mischief had the duke sent them upon? And what did people know of my relationship with Stillington? I agonised on how I might get to Harry. Dare I remind the duchess of our bargain?

Towards the end of the month, heavy snow fell on the city. The lake at Greenwich froze. Some of the more adventurous of us went skating and boisterous youths pelted us with snow balls. This activity recalled the days of village childhood, with races on the ice and Fat Marion ladling out bowls of steaming broth. Red-nosed and laughing, we ran inside eager to sup warm wine and huddle by the fire.

"I'll be first!" I hurtled along the corridor straight into the path of the king!

A gasp of horror and a falling back of my confused companions left me confronting this giant figure. Swathed in an enormous sable cloak, the hood drawn over his head, and with but a smatter of attendants about him, I assumed he intended to step outside for a moment of private entertainment.

Flustered, I sank into a curtsey, blurting apologies. Hearty laughter flowed over me like a cascade of warm water. The king drew me to my feet, his enormous, jewelled fingers crushing my hands.

"Have I seen you before, Mistress?"

I shook my head though my heart pounded with alarm. "I think not, Your Grace. I'm one of the Duchess of Gloucester's waiting-women."

"Ah, Gloucester's people—from Middleham?" He surveyed me keenly, his hazel eyes flickering over my face and figure with practised appraisal. "And yet, I could have sworn I'd seen you somewhere else—a long time ago perhaps. Your eyes are most striking, Mistress—"

"Forrest, Sire—Johann Forrest."

"So," he cocked his head, his eyes glinting, calculating, "you're Forrest's wife. My brother speaks most highly of your husband, Madam. A loyal servant is a jewel. You're fortunate, indeed, to have my brother's favour—He's sparing in his approbation. But you're so like—" He smiled again, and in the ruin of his red-veined, bloated face, I glimpsed some vestige of the beauty he'd once worn so carelessly. "Did you never work in London?"

The question terrified. Something in the insistent way he stared at me and the insinuating manner in which he searched his memory for clues, flooded my face with guilty colour. Did he remember me after all these years?

"I worked in Mercer's pie shop in the Chepe when I was a girl."

The spectators laughed, an infectious sound that forced the smiles into my own features and much amused the king.

"Nay, though I've been over-fond of pies these recent years!" He clapped his belly, his own mirth mellow as liquid honey. "I was remembering an occasion many years ago—when I was a rash youth somewhat enamoured of a charming lady who lived in Silver Street or thereabouts—I fear I made some foolish promises she misinterpreted. I saw someone very like you in her house—I've often wondered what became of the lady and her household."

"I'm sure she could never have forgotten you, Sire," I answered boldly, looking him in the eye. "But sometimes it's best to keep quiet about youthful memories lest those bent on mischief trouble us with needless questions." I tried to keep the teasing note in my voice.

"You're wise, Mistress Forrest." He kissed my hand graciously, his hazel eyes flashing green fire. "I understand you offered my wife some words of wisdom recently." He laughed seeing me flinch. "Oh, she believes such stuff, Mistress, and takes your advice to heart. Rest assured, you'll not suffer by it—" He put an arm about my shoulder steering me away from the watchers and stooped to whisper in my ear, his lips brushing my hair. "But such dangerous dealings shouldn't be pursued further—As you infer so cleverly, sleeping dogs should lie in peace, lest, being disturbed, they rise up to bite us all."

I stumbled away, conscious of his laughter spilling uproariously as if he'd told a marvellous jest, but I shook like a storm-wracked sapling all the way back to my chamber.

"Nan, what are these cards?"

Genevieve and Alice crouched by the oak chest amidst a tumble of garments.

"Lady Anne told us to pack after a messenger came to say Prince Edward's sick. She wants to leave tomorrow—" Alice attempted a confused explanation for the rifled coffer, the scattered clothes, and the discovery of my secret. Her darting eyes avoided mine.

"Can you tell fortunes with them?" Genevieve's curiosity made her bold. Her eyes sparkled, bright as innocence. "Meg Huddleston said Amy Sadler told her about them and that you—"

"Amy Sadler's an unscrupulous chatter-box," I said. I clenched my fists. "She delights in stirring up trouble. I'm surprised Meg listens to her lies."

"Meg says the wench has a talent for rooting out secrets." Genevieve cast me a wounded expression. "So she asked Lady Anne if you'd told her fortune—"

So, it had finally come to this. Clever Meg had wheedled the information from the duchess just as I'd suspected. No doubt all the ladies knew.

"They're just picture cards. An old woman gave me them." My voice croaked as I trotted out my old excuse. "It's just a game."

"But what strange pictures they are—Look at this one of the devil, and this of death—I should have nightmares if I played with these—and what does this one mean?"

Eyes wide, mouth open in pretended horror, Genevieve held the Hanged Man towards me.

"Nan does have nightmares." Alice pinched Genevieve's thigh in warning.

"It's a game," I pleaded, alarmed by the eagerness in their up-turned faces. Who'd told them about my nightmares? "I showed them to Lady Anne when we were in Dowgate together, and she's —"

"Never forgotten what you told her." Alice finished for me. "Meg told us. But what *did* you see for her? Will she really be queen one day?"

"No, no." I crossed myself as if to stave off ill fortune. "Meg's mistaken. You mustn't say such things. It was a foolish game—no more than that—I'm sure you've played such games yourselves on holidays—"

"But Lady Anne says you have second sight." Alice refused to be deflected. "You must read the cards for us, Nan." Giggling, Genevieve thrust the pack toward me. "Tell me what you see for me."

I stretched out my hands but the cards spilled like a cascade to the stone floor, their painted images swirling into a pattern which terrified.

"What is it, Nan?" Alice asked.

"The tower—and death—death by water—" Looking up I glimpsed the blaze of their white faces before the chamber filled with beating wings. "Crows," I whispered, my ears scraped by the harsh crawk-crawk of their calls, "a murder of crows—" and fainted, striking my head against the stone.

When I came round, Alice was pressing a soft, damp cloth to my forehead, and our little serving wench stood holding a basin. "You'll have a fine bruise, but I don't think there'll be a scar," Alice said. "I expect you've some salve of your own making to speed the healing—No, don't try to get up yet." Someone laid a palm against my shoulder. "Genevieve has some wine and honey for you to drink."

Leaning back against the cushions on which they'd propped me, I sipped the warm liquid, conscious of Genevieve kneeling on one side and the little maid's frightened gaze on the other. Alice's capable hands dipped the cloth into the basin, blotted the wound again and rinsed away a smear of blood.

"I wrapped the cards for you." Genevieve bent to pass me the bundle when someone tapped at the door.

The serving wench jumped, almost dropping the basin, but Alice signalled to her to discover our caller.

"The Duchess of Gloucester wants to see you all now."

Swiftly, I stuffed the cards into my bodice and allowed Alice and Genevieve to help me rise.

"Are you sure you're strong enough to walk?" Genevieve asked.

The serving wench stared inquisitively.

"Clear this away, Joyce." Alice's command jolted her into action. "We mustn't keep the duchess waiting."

Lady Anne's sumptuous chamber, though clustered with waiting women, seemed still and subdued. Wrapped in an emerald mantle with a furred hood, the duchess brooded by the casement, her pretty cat-face face grave and thoughtful. The sun's bright glare dazzled, melting the lacy ice patterns on the glass lozenges, shedding its rays across her folded hands and gilding the elaborate furnishings. A qualm of apprehension stabbed me as we joined this silent tableau. How sick was the precious Gloucester prince?

"I've arranged for us to leave for Middleham at first light," she said. Her fingers twisted nervously. "My son's ailing, and I need to be with him." A slight catch in her voice betrayed anxiety. "Because His Grace has business to complete in the city, our party will go on ahead while the weather favours us. Have your baggage ready for the men to remove before supper."

Murmuring assent, the ladies turned in a milling crowd.

"Nan! Wait! I want to speak to you in private."

Only a fool could have missed the sudden fever of interest. The pack of women exchanged furtive glances. Some lingered as long as they dared.

"What have you done?" Lady Anne touched a finger to my brow as the door finally closed behind them.

"A foolish stumble, my Lady. We'd been ice-skating and I was hurrying back—"

"My boy's taken another fever." She interrupted me, her voice trembling toward tears. "I need your help, Nan. You've more skill than any physician. Stay by me this night."

The burden of Lady Anne's words lay heavy on me, but how could I refuse?

Snuggled together in thick cloaks and draped in furs, our party dozed its way back to the north. The snow was melting. Already spikes of green pushed through the earth. Drowsily, the women murmured of spring and pleasant days upon the moors while the wagons rumbled over rutted tracks, the men cursing the mud that clogged the wheels and the dripping trees soaking their garments. Lady Anne insisted I travel with her in her litter beside Meg Huddleston and Elizabeth Parre. While they twittered like starlings, my own thoughts ran raggedly on unfinished business in the city. Harry would wonder at my broken promise.

Part Seven

Middleham
1478

Chapter Sixty-Three
Middleham Castle

Fleet as a deer, the duchess entered Middleham's portals. Without stopping to remove her damp cloak, she rushed to the nursery, dragging me behind her like a bond-slave, questions flying from her anxious lips, servants dancing at her heels.

"How is he?"

"He slept well last night, Your Grace." The stout Yorkshire-woman, flustered by the sudden interruption, left off lifting blankets from the press to dip a curtsey. "The physician gave him a tincture for the fever. It seems to have settled him."

"Tell me what you think, Nan."

We leaned over the flushed face lying on the pillow. Conscious of my own boy struggling and calling to me in Emma's arms, I laid a hand on the prince's brow.

"He still seems a little feverish, Your Grace. Perhaps I should give him some of my mulberry and honey syrup?"

Satisfied, she made a hasty departure, but not before scattering orders among the waiting servants which sent them scrambling in all directions.

"Bring me news when the prince wakes," she called.

I hugged Dickon then, listened to his excited prattle and exclaimed over his growth.

"Aye, he's strong as an ox, but it's been a hard winter for yon lad." Jane Collins nodded to the Gloucester prince. "Last night were so raw we couldn't sleep for shaking. My bones ached like toothache." She grimaced, rubbing her back.

"London's still thick ice," I said, holding my tingling hands before the blaze of the nursery fire.

"Tha looks pale, after the journey. I've brewed a posset that'll put the colour into thi cheeks. We'll all take a sup to bring some warmth into us bones."

She stooped to lift a pot from off the fire and ladled steaming liquid into pewter tankards. "Drink it as hot as you can."

I clasped my tankard in both hands letting the steam bathe my face. A sour smell of wine and pungent herbs made me gag. Startled, Emma lifted her head from the rim of her own cup, her lips ruby with moisture and Mistress Collins cried out.

"What is it, lass?"

I must have fainted. When I opened my eyes again she was chafing my hands and Emma knelt, mopping up spilled wine. Their voices rang hollow and distant—full of questions.

"Tha's a nasty bruise on thi forehead. What hast tha been doing?"

The frantic beating of wings still bruised my ears. As I raised my tankard a sudden shocking premonition overwhelmed me like a great cacophonous swoop of black birds. Somewhere in the Tower a murder was being committed. But it wasn't a murder by water as I'd told Genevieve and Alice. It was far more sinister, and one of the assassins was my own husband.

"Here's a health to your Lordship!" A mocking voice called from far away. He heard the clang and skitter of a fallen goblet.

Licking the last, sweet drops from his lips, he tried to turn, but someone seized his arms and shoulders in a forceful, compelling grip. Suddenly, sickeningly, his world turned upside-down. He glimpsed red-spattered rushes and a blur of stone. Struggling, he cried out, but a heavy hand thrust into his hair and pressed him downward.

A glow of golden liquid rose to meet him. In its swirling depths he saw his own reflection, a white, staring face that seemed to swim in blood. Behind this awful image, two shadowy shapes loomed huge and menacing. He heard the rich echo of male laughter. The flowery scent of wine mingled with the stench of sweat and fear.

"Grab his legs, John," a deeper voice said. "He's changed his mind." The northern vowels confounded him as he plunged into the darkness.

Just before the liquid slapped against his face he drew a breath to shriek. But the darkness swallowed him whole. His hapless fingers scrabbled against the wood, like the claws of a cornered rat. His legs seemed caught, as in a trap. Twist and writhe as he might, he couldn't free them.

Again and again he swallowed cloying sweetness as if he sought to drain the barrel dry. At last his throat rebelled. He might have spewed had he found air, but a great light seared his eyeballs. The roar in his ears stilled as his lungs burst in an explosion of pain. Down, down he dived, wine-wrapped and drifting, and somewhere in his fading mind called "Mama!"

Somehow my mind performed a curious trick, linking it with another's so that I saw through his eyes, tasted through his lips, heard through his ears and shared his suffering. I recognised Jack Green as the caller of the jeering toast. Miles laughed and ordered some knave named John to hold the victim's legs. Never before had I seen a vision so strange. Events were surely catching up with me. What next?

Slipping early from my bed in the nursery next morning, I dressed in shivering anxiety. The grey, rain-lashed sky lightened as I made my way down to the Hall for breakfast. How I longed in that moment for Miles to draw me into the reassurance of his embrace, to tell me all was well, that his service to the duke demanded nothing but the carrying of messages and relaying of orders. But doubts, like a great flock of carrion birds feasted upon my thoughts.

I found Grace Pullan entertaining Lady FitzHugh with tales of Westminster and old Walt, spooning pottage into his surly mouth, making disgruntled comments. "A mighty expense for two little children." He wiped dribble off his chin with the back of his hand. "I expect the king'll be asking us to pay more taxes to pay for all this fol-de-rol."

Genevieve, sitting opposite, turned up her aristocratic little nose and sniffed.

"Only a miser would put a price upon such an occasion," she said. She toyed with her bread and meat as Walt hawked and spat and went off muttering about the foolishness of women-kind. She stuck out her tongue at his retreating figure. "Yon niggardy-breeches would've had a fit if he'd seen all we did in London."

"You're dressed very finely."

Genevieve smiled, stroking elegant purple sleeves edged with coney fur. "I believe a certain gentleman may call upon me this day."

"You're a mischievous jade, Genevieve," I teased. Grace Pullan laughed and Lady FitzHugh turned her attention on us with an indulgent smile. "Not satisfied with breaking hearts in London, you now seek to do the same in Yorkshire! But is there any news of Clarence?"

"Still in prison and set to lose all his titles and estates." Genevieve pouted, looking pleased and smug. "Our little Lord Edward will be made Earl of Salisbury in his stead and the Duke will be Chamberlain of England. Lady Anne said it herself."

"Well, we'll see." Lady FitzHugh seemed unconvinced.

Lady Anne has more power than any of you realise, I thought, listening to their chatter, *but she won't be satisfied until she wears a crown.*

❧

Three days of hectic preparations followed. Servants scrubbed and polished, swept and scoured, plumped up cushions and scattered sweet herbs among the rushes against the duke's arrival. Lady Anne troubled her steward with endless instructions and sent us all on countless errands, so that I escaped to the nursery where the children proved less demanding.

During the afternoon of the fourth day she summoned us to the solar to listen to a harpist she'd hired to entertain her husband, knowing his fondness for music. A bleak sun streaked across the chamber like a sword, accentuating faces and eyes made pallid and hollow by winter's absence of light. Melancholy brooded in the harps flowing arpeggios, lulling the mind into lost places and old memories, and I found myself thinking of Mara.

A sudden, harsh rap at the door destroyed the melody.

"A courier from London, Your Grace." The steward's brusque interruption provoked a rustle of curiosity. His familiar face seemed oddly strained and grim. "He brought this letter."

Impatiently the duchess broke the seal. The chamber juddered into chilling silence. As if enchanted her features assumed a marble rigidity, her fingers curled like claws about the vellum. In a voice which shook and soared she read to us—

"The Duke of Clarence has been executed."

"God have mercy." Grace Pullan gasped and crossed herself—an action repeated on all sides. Even the harpist sketched a blessing.

"How could the king have his own brother put to death?" Meg Huddleston's blanched face turned accusingly upon the duchess.

A terrible, cold sensation crawled through my limbs. Afraid I might faint again, I leaned against a trestle for support.

"No doubt the queen will be glad to have Clarence out of the way." Lady Anne's expression remained impassive but in her eyes a diamond-hard glitter ignited. "They say she'd good reason to fear him."

No one spoke. Too many ugly rumours circulated. The king's removal of Clarence meant Stillington would remain out of favour —an asset for my own safety—but Miles' involvement bound him irrevocably to Gloucester. What other murderous schemes were being hatched in secret? This death would fuel Lady Anne's ambitions for her precious son. An earldom beckoned but I knew she craved a loftier title.

Sure enough, Miles rode home in the duke's entourage. Watching the familiar way the muscles moved in his shoulders as he dismounted in the courtyard, my heart lurched with that same passion as when I first saw him. I rushed headlong down the stairs. As always he swung me round in his arms, laughing and showering me with kisses. While he hugged me close, shaking snow-flakes from his hair, I found it hard to imagine he could ever hurt another. But when I took his hand in mine I trembled at its strength.

Chapter Sixty-four

February's snow showers quickly melted but little Ned of Middleham's recovery proved equally brief. Struck down by a sudden fever that shook his frail body and addled his wits, the child took to his bed. While he rambled in a cruel delirium Lady Anne badgered Jane Collins with visits to the nursery and the duke consulted daily with his physician.

"The prince must be kept apart from the other children," the duchess commanded. "His food and drink must be prepared separately. Nan, you must watch over him at all times. There's no one else I can trust."

I daresay many envied me this esteem but it caused more gossip. Perhaps she saw Dickon's rude health as a testimony of my craft but I think she attributed more to my art as a seer.

"Can't you look into his future?"

"I've already cast his horoscope, Your Grace. Destiny can't be altered to fit our own desires." I recalled Mara's teaching with a heavy heart.

The stars predicted intelligence, quick wit and tenacity for Lord Ned, as well as affection and adulation—but a child born into a powerful family could surely expect such qualities. He didn't lack courage and possessed a capacity for greatness, but poor health marred his fortunes. Unsurprisingly, the little duchess refused to accept the implications of this unwelcome augury.

"I know you can save him." Her vehemence frightened me.

The following night as I sat by the child's bed, the duke himself arrived.

"Will he recover?"

A pair of haunted eyes stared into mine. In the tumbling shadows cast by nervous candle-light I couldn't tell whether they were blue or grey. Fear surrounded the duke like a miasma. I smelled it in his sweat.

"I believe so." I kept my gaze steady although my hands trembled. "The fever's finally abated and he's sleeping calmly now. Sleep is the great healer, Your Grace."

Together we looked at the child. The fine, corn-coloured hair lay limp and sweat-darkened upon the bolster, and the delicate, heart-shaped face gleamed waxen, but the breathing sounded more natural.

"If anything should happen to him—"

The voice cracked with emotion. This revelation of masculine suffering stung me to tears.

"I understand, Your Grace. There's no one at Middleham who doesn't love Lord Ned. He's the sweetest child I ever nursed."

"You've done well. Lady Anne's always spoken highly of you. She's never forgotten your kindness." He touched my arm. "Now I, too, am in your debt. I'll not let this pass unnoticed."

The pinched face might have been carved out of wood. I couldn't remember ever having seen such anguish. *How will it be,* I thought, *when there's no more aid for this child?* In my heart I knew Lord Ned's frequent fevers were not a passing phase. Hadn't I seen the possibility of an early death in his birth chart? Though I'd tried to broach this subject with Lady Anne, she wouldn't hear of it.

"My wife places much store by you." He might have read my thoughts.

"I'm honoured, Your Grace," I replied. I wished I could find the courage to speak honestly. I drew a breath. "My husband—"

"Is a loyal servant." The troubled eyes fixed on mine. "I've trusted him with those things most dear to me."

I'd never been so close to the duke before. I wanted to ask him to release Miles from servitude, to allow us to live freely far away from here, but now I had the chance I couldn't speak of it. Fine lines like spider-webs etched his face. Stubble bruised his tightened jaw. His spirit burned as fierce as fire and I understood then why Miles pledged himself to follow this man. But Lady Anne nurtured his ambition. In spite of his tenderness for the child, a ruthless quality made me I shudder.

"You're exhausted by your labours. You should rest. I'll watch with the child now." Strangely, compassion lurked in the enigmatic eyes.

"Your Grace should call me if there's a need. I've given a herbal posset to Meg Huddleston for my Lady. She's weary with watching and it'll restore her strength."

I longed to find some word of comfort to soothe away the twisted grimace of his mouth and ease his mind but my own inner eye filled with shocking images.

"My Lord—" I caught at the murrey velvet of his sleeve as he turned from me. "Sometimes we're the victims of a fate more powerful than we realise. The moth drawn to the flame follows his desire even though the heat alerts him of danger. Sometimes we choose to follow a perilous pathway against the promptings of conscience or the heart."

"You speak in riddles," he said. But horror flooded into his eyes, and I knew I'd touched a nerve.

"You've many enemies about you, Your Grace," I said daringly. "Forgive me for my presumption. I speak out of concern for you and yours."

I made a curtsey, swiftly turned to leave, afraid he might see in my eyes the torn bodies and the bloodshed, the plunging hooves and tattered banners, the sinewy stranger's hand grasping the fallen crown.

Back in the quiet of my own quarters where Miles slept deep, I fell upon my knees and prayed. I'd not prayed for a long time. I prayed for the child and the mother, but most of all I prayed for the consolation and absolution of the duke.

⁂

"Stillington's arrested."

Jack Green's voice gloated. I halted by the half open door of our chamber and signalled Dickon to be quiet.

"So Ned Plantagenet grows more cautious." Miles snorted with contempt. "I doubt the bishop will sing the information he seeks."

"Oh, Stillington's cunning. He'll say as much as keeps him comfortable. But the king will stop his mouth once and for all if he thinks he knows too much."

"What, after Clarence? I think not. He'd qualms enough about murdering his own brother, but when it comes to priests, these Plantagenets are squeamish."

"Well, I'll wager Stillington will wriggle free. Not because the king's squeamish, but because the bishop has the luck of the devil."

"And you should know all about that." Miles laughed. "I've never known anyone as glib as you in a tight corner. Why when that gaoler asked us what we were doing—"

Dickon, tired of waiting, squirmed free and toddled into the chamber.

"Here's my brave little knave." Miles scooped the child up on to his knee and tweaked his nose.

I nodded to Jack, standing by the hearth with a tankard in his hand. Inwardly trembling, I set my basket on the trestle.

"We had a fine walk to the market, didn't we, Dickon?" I spoke in matter-of-fact tones. "And we saw Mistress Metcalf, didn't we?"

"Monks," said Dickon. He struggled to escape his father's clutches. "Mama—"

"Yes, we saw the monks—"

"And was there a good crowd in the town today?" Jack fixed his weasel smile on me.

"There was. And plenty of gossip, too." I emptied my basket. "Elizabeth Metcalf says Bishop Stillington's been sent to the Tower." I returned Jack's smile with deliberate ease.

"It's true enough." Miles released the gurgling child. "The king grows tetchy with those whose tongues wag carelessly." He grinned at me. "Take care, wife, you and that gaggle of the duchess's wenches don't offend him with your tittle-tattle."

"Oh, Nan knows how to deal with the king," said Jack airily. He set down his tankard and sat down, crossing his shapely legs, admiring his violet hose. How I longed to swipe the smirk from his face! "She'd plenty of practice when he came to see Dame Butler in London."

The good humour vanished from Miles' face and the frown between his black brows deepened.

"What's this?" he asked, half-rising. Dickon, crouched before the fire playing with a little wooden horse, turned his head in alarm. No mistaking the menace in his father's voice. "I didn't know you were on intimate terms with the king."

"Hardly intimate." Inwardly I cursed Jack Green. "I was sometimes in attendance when he called on Dame Butler about her estates. I exchanged but a few words with him. I doubt he'd remember me."

"I was jesting, Miles." Jack's insolent smile fixed on me. "I thought Nan would've told you about the king's visits to the Butler household, that's all."

Miles said nothing but his eyes clouded.

"Will you join us for supper?" I smiled through gritted teeth.

"You must excuse me." He rose and sketched a bow. "I've another appointment. It would be cruel to disappoint the pretty little wench who waits for me, wouldn't it?" He threw Miles a knowing smirk that sickened me and retrieved his elegant cloak. "I thank you, though, for the offer of hospitality, Mistress Forrest." He nodded obsequiously.

I didn't press him.

"Mind what I said, Miles." Jack's eyes flashed warning sparks. "Our fortunes depend upon Stillington's fate." With a jaunty flourish of his feathered cap, he quit the chamber.

Miles winced as from a blow. I wondered how a stripling like Jack Green should have the power to frighten him.

"I saw my old priest again at the market," I said, gathering up discarded tankards. "The brothers at the abbey were shocked by the news from London."

Miles sat brooding as if he hadn't heard me.

"He said the Duke of Clarence's estates will pass to Gloucester and that's probably why our Duke didn't intercede."

"Enough! I'm sick of all this talk. Clarence was a traitor and deserved to die." Miles turned away with his head in his hands.

Dickon crept into the corner watching with frightened eyes.

"Do you really believe that? Mistress Metcalf says he was driven mad by the loss of his poor wife."

"Elizabeth Metcalf's a prattling fool!"

Two loping strides brought Miles to tower over me. He raised his fists and I cowered, knocking a tankard to the floor. Dickon whimpered.

"Why do you torment me?" Miles roared, but the expected blow didn't land.

"You torment yourself."

Silence stretched taut as a bow-string.

Daring to look up at last, I noticed the ugliness of suffering in his expression, his arms hanging loose at his sides.

Impulsively I clasped my own around him, drawing him close. Tremors wracked his body.

"You'd leave me if you knew the things I've done." When I didn't answer, he tipped up my chin to face him. "Do you know what I've done?"

I looked full into his eyes. "You've become a hired assassin," I said, spilling the words I'd so long avoided at last.

"A soldier's expected to silence enemies."

"That's an old excuse, and one you no longer believe in yourself. You haven't been a soldier for a long time."

"The Duke of Gloucester—"

"Requires your loyalty. I know, I know, you told me that before, but Richard of Gloucester will demand your heart and soul to satisfy his ambition."

"He's a good man."

"And may not a good man be mistaken?"

"He seeks to do what's right for England."

"And is it right to kill one's brother?"

Miles shook his head as if to expel some confusion.

"Oh I know what part you played in Clarence's murder." I seethed with anger then, watching his eyes widen in surprise. "Your unswerving loyalty to Gloucester has brought you to a pretty pass. Gloucester may have many virtues, but he'll ride rough-shod over anyone who stands between him and his desire. Thanks to Lady Anne he's developed his own vision for England. You've always underestimated her power. She's her father's daughter and she'll follow Gloucester to perdition if it suits her."

"I carried out orders, I gave my word, but I've been a fool. You knew—you always knew it was a trap, but I wouldn't listen. You warned me—but now I've so much blood on my hands there's no way out." He sank on the bench, exhausted by the weight of despair. "Jack Green's a fiend and Deighton thinks of nothing but profit—Oh, Nan, what hope is there for me? Tell me what to do!" His fingers twisted in his hair as if he could tear the guilt out his mind.

"We must get away from here." Ignoring the nagging voice that reminded me how I'd wasted time at Barnard and at Middleham when I should have spoken out, I threw myself down, grabbing at his hands. "We could find a place easily enough. We've money to buy a farm with what I've saved these last years. You could breed horses and Dickon could grow up without fear of reprisal. We could be free of all this plotting and intrigue—"

"Would you have me be a horse-keeper like Deighton? Do you think the duke would let me just slip away? After what I know he'd sooner kill me than let me out of his sight!" A painful gash appeared between his brows. "And you're no safer than I am! Haven't you pledged yourself to the duchess with your accursed fortune-telling? That Sadler wench has a poisonous tongue for all her pretty promises. Do you think the men don't taunt me about my wife, the sorceress?"

I sank beside him, the words of Mistress Evans echoing over the years to remind me—"Beware the man with blood upon his hands." Only now did I truly understand their meaning.

Chapter Sixty-five

In April Gloucester rode north to inspect his garrisons on the Scottish borderland, taking Miles in his company. Though I fretted at this new separation, I knew it would keep him away from London.

"The duke's the king's Lord of the North. Edward trusts him to keep the region in order," Miles said as we parted. "When Lord Ned's grown he'll take over this appointment, so keep him friendly with our Dickon. A prince's esteem's a jewel. He'll not have to go soldiering in Burgundy as I did. He'll enjoy wealth and ease."

"Is that so important?" I laced my arms about his neck. "Doesn't this former soldier enjoy the duke's favour and live in some comfort—not to mention having the devotion of a loving wife?"

Miles kissed me lightly on the mouth. "I wouldn't want Dickon to live as we do." He stroked back my hair and looked deep into my eyes. "But my wife's a clever little witch who can worm her way into anyone's affections."

These farewell words put me on edge. That same evening when Lady Anne sent for me, they returned to torment me in a most sinister fashion.

In the duchess's apartment, the little chamber-maid sat drowsing by the hearth. She hadn't lit the candles and thick silence wrapped the twilit chamber in secrecy. Lady Anne, dressed in a ghostly grey mantle, put a finger to her lips, indicating for me to sit by her on a settle. A languid atmosphere like the fragrance of poppies seemed to envelop me as I joined her beneath the window. In the dusty corners, sinister shadows gathered, sly as thieves who wait on opportunity.

"When will I have that crown you promised?"

Her whispered words drove a crawling prickle of unease through me. Gooseflesh rose on my arms as if an unquiet spirit stalked the chamber.

"You're no fool, Nan. You understand more of court intrigues than anyone." She clenched my fingers, forcing me to look into her face. "Don't pretend you know nothing about the secret Clarence sought to uncover. My Lord's had some interesting information from your old acquaintance, Master Green." Her eyes compelled. "Tell me now what lies in store for my Lord of Gloucester and for me. Do you have your cards?"

I shook my head, speechless with fear. The gathering dusk blurred her features, but I sensed the power that possessed her. Its vibrant energy filled the chamber. Closing my eyes, I allowed my mind to immerse in its rolling waves, expanding inner sight. Pictures uncoiled, startling me with the magnificence of their colour and resonance of sound.

"Lady, a great fanfare of trumpets fills the cathedral," I said. "A churchman in a shimmering gold-encrusted cope processes towards the high altar—A bare-headed knight kneels before you, his sword upon his palms—and then a hungry shadow crosses the sky. It creeps slowly—so slowly—swallowing up the sun, blotting out the light. The wail of many women fills the air and then—"

"Your Grace!" The chamber-maid sprang up suddenly in a flutter of consternation. Blinking and rubbing her eyes, she fell into a low curtsey, stammering apologies.

"Enough, enough!" Lady Anne's fury sent her prowling the chamber while the perplexed girl fumbled with the candles. Though the chamber flooded with their dancing brightness, I couldn't move. The scattered fragments of my vision still fell about me. My heart raced with excitement.

⁓

Ned of Middleham proved more resilient than expected that summer. Daily he and Dickon rode out on the moors together.

Jane Collins chuckled, watching the prince struggling into his riding boots. "The duke were a sickly infant hissel," she said. "He vows his survival were due to the firm training his cousin Warwick gave him. So tha can see why he wants yon lad to learn the knightly skills."

The fragile little boy with the pale hair and the heart-shaped face sprang up with a heart-melting smile. "May I go now?"

"You must take your medicine first," I said.

He tried to stand tall like a man-at-arms while I dosed him with coltsfoot and honey for his cough. "One day I shall be a knight and Dickon shall be my liege-man."

Miles' parting words returned to haunt me in this poignant remark.

"Master Metcalf's waiting, Mama." Dickon tugged my sleeve, jumping up and down with impatience. Being an energetic, restless child, he excelled in outdoor activities and couldn't wait to be gone.

"You must keep warm." I addressed both boys, although my main concern was the prince's health. "It's still windy out on the moors." I wrapped the prince in a thick woollen cloak and marvelled at my own boy's sturdy figure at his side. Barely six months older than the prince, he stood a head taller, with a thick mop of unruly black curls.

"Master Metcalf says we can ride to the rocks today." His eyes blazed as they raced down the nursery steps together.

"That lad of thine's horse-crazed," Mistress Collins said with an indulgent shake of her head. "Aye, and the prince thinks the world of him."

I wondered if she guessed Miles' ambitions concerning this childhood friendship.

"The prince loves his riding lessons, too."

"Aye, he's a determined soul for all his ailments." She helped me on with my cloak. "Did tha know he can read and write already?"

"I know he can beat Dickon at chess."

I followed the boys out into the courtyard. Already they were walking their mounts up and down under the watchful eyes of their tutor and I smiled at their expertise. I thought how proudly Miles and I had first watched Dickon leap up fearlessly into the saddle and take the reins with the assurance of a seasoned horseman.

"He rides well."

Jack Green's smooth tones grated but I wouldn't let him spoil my pleasure.

Dickon trotted by on his barrel-bellied pony, the morning sunlight dancing on its harness. Behind him Edward of Middleham, dressed in green and sporting a goose feather in his cap, bestowed a beaming smile upon the watchers. Master Metcalf, proud and upright in the saddle, inclined his head as he followed closely in the wake of his two young charges. I waved after the little entourage as it made its way towards the gates.

"He loves the horses," I said. "Just like his father."

"Who is presently engaged upon some further business with the Duke, I believe." Jack Green arched an impudent eyebrow. "The Scottish Borders can be troublesome, and doubtless lonely, too."

I turned aside, determined to ignore this taunt. Why did Jack Green's presence make me feel so uncomfortable? A knowing watchfulness hung about him like a cloak. He'd acquired a silent step, an unnerving manner of appearing suddenly. The sly humour in his remarks rankled. Too often he goaded me with sneering remarks about Brother Brian, or probed me about poor Eleanor's fate. I wondered if he still spied for the disgraced Stillington or if he worked solely to further Gloucester's influence. Certainly the duke favoured him over-much. Jack possessed some charm that allowed him licence to travel freely between Middleham and London, and he was often seen at Jervaulx, at Sheriff Hutton and at Pontefract. I puzzled over Gloucester's motives.

"Miles's fond of his boy," Jack said, at my elbow.

Once again I caught a whiff of danger.

"Your cousin, Harry, too, is very much the family man." His eyes glittered with menace. "I couldn't resist going back to the shop when I was last in London. Of course, Harry didn't recognise me, but I remembered him. The Mercers are well-meaning folk, but I was never meant to be a baker's errand boy." A vicious smile lifted the corners of his perfectly sculpted mouth. "No, I was fortunate to profit from the kindly offer of an education—I had my own priestly mentor too, Nan." Again that malicious smile scoured me. "Though there was a certain price to pay for his assistance, I learned to snatch what opportunities life handed. A scullion's born to face adversity—but I think even you'll admit, I've made a pretty pass of my fortune so far. I'm not a family man myself but I can appreciate the charm of children—Harry's son seems sturdy—just like your boy, and the little maid's very pretty—"

"I envy you your glimpse of them." Disgust lodged like a hard stone in my gullet.

"Ah, of course, you miss your London friends. Do you remember Maud Attemore, too?" He spoke mischievously but his eyes hardened like chips of brown pebble. "She still commands the best gossip in the Chepe. Her tales are marvellous entertainments. Is it true Dame Eleanor bore a child at Norwich?"

This question almost knocked me off my feet.

"You seem astounded. I'd thought you, of all people, would know the truth of it. Some say the Duke of Norfolk took the child in but perhaps it remained with the nuns?"

The feigned innocence of his inquiry infuriated me, but I stared at him with a bland expression.

"You'd better ask someone other than me." I pretended a careless shrug. "I've no answers that can satisfy you."

But I woke in the early hours in a cold sweat of terror. Jack's words about Nancy revived an alarming memory. Hadn't the child discovered the cards hidden in my clothes' chest while playing with Margaret Mercer? Suppose Jack questioned the little maid about me? Like an incubus, the thought sat upon my heart, devouring sleep.

Chapter Sixty-Six

Towards the end of the year Miles returned from the Borders, morose and edgy. He seemed leaner, full of dark silences and given to riding out alone in the early hours as if something preyed on his mind.

"Master Forrest rode off like a demon this morning. He almost ran me down." Startled, I glanced up. Amy Sadler appeared on the steps above me as if from nowhere. "I suppose you're wondering why I'm here." She trilled laughter, her bright eyes sly with secrets. "I sneaked into the nursery to chat to Emma while Mistress Collins was at breakfast."

"Well, you'd better disappear quickly," I answered, "because she's on her way back. I saw her leaving the Hall just now—"

"Oh, she won't mind." Amy tucked an auburn wisp under her cap and patted it into place. "I think she likes me. I keep trying to persuade her she needs another nursery-maid."

"The Duchess is the one you need to convince," I said. Her pert manner irked me. "And you'd better hurry back to the dairy before you're missed."

"Oh, they're too busy talking about the plague to notice," she answered. She skipped by me with a knowing look.

"Plague?"

"Oh yes," she called. "One of the Duke's messengers told me about it." She preened and simpered, flirting her eyelashes. "Ask Master Forrest—He was in the kitchen when the messenger arrived."

She didn't look back, but I knew instinctively she aimed to bait me.

391

Instead of going to the nursery, I ran to the stables and found Miles with Guy, rubbing down his sweat-soaked horse.

"I thought you'd be with Lady Anne," he said with a puzzled frown.

"And I thought you to be in the Wardrobe."

"Finish off here." Miles threw the goggle-eyed lad his cloth. "And put a blanket over him." He steered me away to the door. "What the devil brings you here to spy on me?"

"I'm not spying on you." I tried to lower my voice, aware of the grooms pretending industry whilst listening to our conversation. "You left so early and Amy said—"

"Amy Sadler will say and do anything to get attention." Miles laughed, but a storm brewed in his eyes. "The wench almost brought my horse down trying to lure me into conversation."

"She enjoys telling me she's seen you—"

"Aye, she would." He cupped my face in his hands. "Don't let her goad you, Nan. I was foolish enough to flirt with her once and now she's forever trying to cajole me into dallying with her—"

"She seems to know you well." I met his eyes boldly and saw him flinch from the implication.

"She means nothing to me." His glance burned. "But there's danger in her chatter. This morning she threatened to tell the duke of your fortune-telling if I continued to ignore her."

He laughed bitterly, then and turned me to look into the stable. "But ask the grooms here—there's not a man at Middleham she hasn't enticed with her pretty promises!"

The men grinned back and muttered among themselves.

"She said some messenger—"

"I know." Miles put a finger to his lips. "Don't spread such talk, Nan. The Duke has enough worries." His face grew grim and closed. What secrets was he hiding from me now?

But further rumours of plague in London blew in with the cold season. They cast a cloud over the Christmas festivities and shadowed us well into the next year. In March when the news of Prince George's death reached Middleham, Lady Anne ran mad with fear.

"Just two years old and struck down suddenly—Suppose Ned takes the sickness?"

"Your Grace, every precaution's been taken."

"But no one knows how to combat the plague. Wouldn't that youngest Wydeville child have had every comfort? And yet it took him—my Lord's just returned from Swansea. They say plague's rife there—"

Her fears exhausted me.

"George is an unlucky name." Genevieve sat down by me at supper.

"George of Clarence was executed and now little Prince George dies of plague—"

"It's divine punishment." Old Walt glowered at us. "Even kings must answer to the Almighty. No man should take up arms against his brother."

Although we all remembered how Walt had railed against Clarence, no one dared argue with the hypocritical curmudgeon.

"The duchess asked the monks at Jervaulx to pray for her boy," someone said.

"He's so frail he'd never survive the plague." Genevieve looked at me with tears in her eyes. "Oh Nan, can't you do something to save him?"

"Your brother, Sire."

The familiar, oily voice oozed courtesy, bubbled with underlying mirth.

The two noble boys confronted one another. The younger, as if recalling an oft-repeated lesson, knelt before the elder, head bowed in homage. A murmur of approving laughter rippled round the chamber.

The taller boy seemed clearly ill at ease. Two rosy blooms flowered in his cheeks. He coughed self-consciously.

"Please—Richard—stand up." He gestured awkwardly. "I'm glad you're to be with me."

"Our mother told me I must treat you as a king now." The younger lad's eyes danced with mischief. Back on his feet he grinned broadly, unable to suppress his high spirits. His eyes surveyed the sumptuous chamber in one wide sweep. "Are these the royal apartments?"

"They are, indeed, the chambers assigned to all kings before their coronations." The bishop opened his arms as if to encircle the vast walls hung with gilded tapestries, his great sleeves

spreading about the boys like enormous wings. "Now you'll have time to get to know one another before the formal ceremonies." His yellow eyes rested on the younger boy, possessive and predacious. "Better than being kept among women, I think?"

"Will Uncle Anthony come to us now?" asked the elder. His beautifully modulated voice trembled as if at its own audacity.

"Alas," answered the cleric, embracing all in his rich laughter, "I fear you must rely upon your Uncle Richard—"

"But I demand to see Uncle Anthony. I'm the king, and you must obey my commands."

Laughter drowned out the boy's protests. It grew in intensity and with it came the furious clap and whirl of huge black wings that conjured darkness.

Far away someone began to sing. The melancholy, discordant timbre of the voice echoed along distant corridors. The alien, outlandish words threaded through the darkness, filling the listeners with dread. Water dripped. A thin, sulphurous smell snaked through the twisting maze of stairs, as if towards the core of the building. And then a fog of filthy, stinking smoke billowed upward, pursued by flames that licked, and raced and roared—

"Sweet Jesu!"

Miles shook me awake.

I gulped and sobbed for breath, tears spilling from the corners of my eyes.

"What on earth?"

"A dream—a dream." I threw myself into his arms, clutching with cruel desperation, reassuring myself of his reality. "These last weeks have been so frantic. Lady Anne's talked of nothing but plague, I—"

"Ssh, ssh. The prince is safe enough, isn't he?"

Miles held me in uneasy silence while the sweat cooled on my body and my heartbeat steadied.

"Just one of your bad dreams," he said, at last.

The words reminded me suddenly and chillingly of my father and grief clogged my throat. How far away childhood seemed, and how very long I'd been running from my visions. Would I never find peace? I shook the hair from my face, rubbing my eyes and trying to laugh away fear. "Yes, yes, just another dream."

Miles watched me wary with apprehension. "What trouble comes upon us now?"

I swung myself out of bed and wrapped my night-robe round me.

"I'm afraid we haven't heard the last of Bishop Stillington." Hands still shaking, I poured us both some wine. "Does Gloucester ever speak of him at all?"

"Stillington no longer has any power." Confusion burned in his blue eyes. "Why would Gloucester have any business with his brother's disgraced chancellor? He's no fool like Clarence—"

"No, but he has the same ambition, if not more."

"What are you saying?"

"Lady Anne's spirit burns as bright as ever did her father's and she'll drive Gloucester to seize whatever power he can to promote their son's interests—"

Miles snatched me to him, spilling wine across the coverlet. He pressed his hand over my mouth. "What treason's this you're speaking?" His eyes rolled wild. "Haven't you warned me often enough to keep quiet? What madness has taken hold of you, Nan? You must discard these dreams. Do you want to see us both hanged?"

Shuddering, laughing, weeping, I lay against his chest, my eyes fixed on the scattered pattern of wine drops on the coverlet—like rose petals—like blood.

✍

Over the next weeks, a curious sense of waiting enveloped me, as if I stood upon the great rocks above Wensleydale far removed from the everyday world, a silent observer anticipating a great storm.

While Miles remained subject to the duke's commands, the duchess's needs ordered my days. Beneath the bird-chatter of the ladies, I sensed her vigilance. She waited too—I felt it in the simmering, impatient surveillance that kept her taut as a wildcat poised to strike.

London lay quiet. No squabbles soured the court. No feverish calls to battle troubled the country. Discord slept.

Tripping lightly down the steps from the solar one dew-sprinkled summer morning, my mind preoccupied with letters I had for the messenger, I didn't notice anyone.

A hand plucked my sleeve.

"Mistress Forrest?" The Duke of Gloucester held out a scroll. "I think you dropped this."

I sketched a flustered curtsey.

"No need for haste. The messenger's still eating breakfast in the servants' hall."

Confused, I hesitated.

"My wife speaks highly of you." The duke hesitated too, equally ill at ease.

"I'm glad to be of service, Your Grace," I answered lamely.

He gnawed his lip. No golden beauty shone in his care-worn face, but what intensity burned in his eyes. I sensed again the power that drew men to him. He lacked King Edward's charm—the boisterous laughter which conjured admiration, the brazen courage which earned men's fealty, the lazy, sensuous smiles which melted women's hearts—but Richard of Gloucester roused a different passion. A blunt honesty shone in his face—as if he said: *This is who I am. Follow me and I'll keep my word.* I realised how he'd won Miles' allegiance. He looked into me, as if he searched for something out of reach.

"One day I may ask you to speak up for me and mine, Mistress Forrest."

Though I bowed my head, I couldn't answer. Around him shadowy conspirators wearing smiles like scars gathered silently.

Chapter Sixty-Seven

Sunlight flooded the dale. Like a sentinel, the abbey building pointed defiantly toward the hot arch of sky. In the surrounding fields monks tended crops, watched over browsing sheep. Birdsong, bees' drone, plaintive bleating—earthy, living sounds— accompanied this daily toil. Gurgling water plashed over ancient stone. Plain-song drifted from the chapel.

At the gatehouse I enquired of Brother Brian. "I must apologise for my intrusion. A matter of grave importance brings me here unannounced."

My courteous manner impressed the kindly gate-keeper. Summoning one of the younger monks from stacking logs by the guest house, he directed him to take me to the infirmary.

A tiny monk with a sallow complexion raised mild eyes from the earthenware basin in which he was mixing crushed herbs and wine.

"Mistress Forrest."

My guide's announcement brought Brother Brian from behind a cluttered press with an armful of flasks and bottles. "We'll not disturb Brother Ignatius with our gossip," he said, depositing these on the trestle. "We can talk in the garden."

Hurriedly, he led me out of the infirmary kitchen.

"I'm sorry to alarm you. There was no time to send a message."

"No harm done." Brother Brian managed a wan smile. "I was only after assisting in mixing potions. Ignatius won't miss me, though I'm thinking he'll be asking questions. Now, what brings you here in such haste?"

"News of Bishop Stillington and recent conference with the Duke of Gloucester."

Brother Brian's trouble-haunted gaze swept over my face. "And so, daughter, we stand in danger."

"The king banished Stillington from court after the Clarence affair. I'd hoped never to hear of him again. Now he batters at our door. What are we to do?"

Brother Brian plucked a sprig of lavender. He rolled it to and fro between his fingers, inhaling its perfume. "Brother Silas is after praising the curative properties of this humble flower," he said thoughtfully. He snapped off another spike, offering it to me. "It brings a gentle sleep to all who breathe its odour, eases the troubles of the mind and restores heartache."

I savoured the pungent aroma emanating from the delicate flower-heads, remembering how Mara had similarly praised this lowly plant.

"We must be calm. We must trust our mightiest protector. The bishop won't want to be rousing the king's displeasure. And I can't think the Duke of Gloucester would harm his brother. Stillington's shrewd enough to lie low, and in the meantime we must make our own plans. Might you visit relatives in London?"

"London? Surely in London I'd be in most danger?"

"The bishop won't look for you there." Brother Brian resumed his gentle walk.

"But Jack Green would reveal everything! He's a spy for Stillington *and* for the Duke of Gloucester and will work for whoever offers him the fattest purse. Though he's thrown in his lot with Gloucester for now, I wouldn't trust him anymore than I'd trust a fox in the henhouse."

"Sadly, I must agree with you there. Already he's ingratiated himself with Brother Silas, and Brother Dominic, our librarian. Both speak highly of his scholarship, but I've been after wondering what reason he has to spend so much time at Jervaulx."

"Has he been here again?" Uneasily I glanced back towards the infirmary as if I expected to see Jack's lithe figure slide out from under the archway.

"Go home, daughter." Brother Brian's eyes were clouded pools. "Keep silence, carry out your duties. I must have leisure to ponder on this dilemma. I'll send a message—"

"But what if—"

Brother Brian took my hand in his own calloused fingers. "Be brave, daughter." His eyes penetrated mine with a reassuring gravity. "You're stronger than you know."

Daughter again. Three times that day Brother Brian called me daughter. I clung to the endearment as a talisman. Fate had thrown us together the day I ran to him for protection with a mob baying at my heels. I remembered his kindness as we travelled the London road. He'd never let me down. I kissed his cheek in filial obedience. From the trellis he watched my departure like a faithful guardian. Looking back, I wish I'd spent longer with the wise, old priest, and told him the depth of my affection.

⚜

The walk across the moor brought no pleasure. Once I'd have revelled in the rolling landscape with its sweet-scented grass, the rugged mystery of ancient stones, the drowsy summer scents, but now I cursed the heat and the uneven paths that made my journey a trial. Sweating under my cloak I hurried home fearful as the fox that smells the hounds closing in.

"Well, Nan, you're out early!"

A lean figure sat nonchalantly upon a rocky outcrop. Squinting against the sun, I tried to discern the features. "Who is it?"

"Why, Nan," the voice replied, sly and smooth, "don't you know an old friend?"

The figure executed a nimble leap from the rock and landed in front of me. With distaste I recognised the clever, weasel face of Jack Green.

"What do you want? Why are you spying on me?"

"Spying?" The silky tones assumed a mock air of offence. "Now why would I do that? I was up and about early myself and thought to take the air upon the moor. Then I saw you."

"I've been to Jervaulx, to visit my old village priest. What's wrong with that?"

"Why nothing at all." Jack smirked as he fell in step beside me. "Except that everyone is out looking for you."

"Everyone? Why?"

"Oh, there's been an accident." Jack's smile widened. "But, look, here comes Rob Metcalf. He'll tell you all about it."

Elizabeth Metcalf's eldest son, a tall, sturdy fellow with hair the colour of new rope, ran toward us, waving his arms.

"Is that thee, Mistress Forrest? Jesus be thanked! I've been looking all over. Thou mun come quick. Little Lord Ned's taken a bad fall. The Duchess is fair demented. Thou mun hurry!"

I'd barely entered the nursery before Lady Anne pounced on me like a hungry cat. "You must save him!"

Jane Collins and Emma hovered by the prince's bed. She flicked an impatient hand and they moved away.

I stooped to examine the angry bruises on the child's face. A swelling on his brow resembled a huge goose-egg. His eyes wandered.

"The fall's stunned him, Your Grace," I said. "He needs rest and quiet—that's all. I've seen other children with such injuries who were back at play in just a few hours."

"But Lord Ned isn't like other children," she answered, imperiously. Her green eyes glittered with passion. "You must understand how precious he is to me." She knelt beside me, the whisper of her breath warming my cheek. "He's the heir." Her eyes blazed with pride, the haughty Neville jaw jutted.

Tongue-tied, I winced as the enormous meaning of these words dawned on me.

"Remember you once offered me a crown?" Ambition illuminated her face. "I'm determined to have it now."

Among the shadows something stirred. Sudden cold tingled my flesh. In that instant I saw the future unfurl like a great, colourful tapestry. How could I tell Lady Anne I couldn't save her prince? Fate would favour but a few and then cast all away like broken flotsam.

"I've always found the cards to speak true," I said at last. "But sometimes the interpretation isn't right." My mind travelled back to a little dark chamber full of whispering, excited maids and a thin, quiet outsider. Even then, frail Anne Neville had astounded me with the strength and tenacity of her will. And hadn't I foreseen greatness for her?

"Once I might have scorned your cards for trickery, but time has taught me many lessons. Now I mean to have my way."

But many lie between your wish and its fulfilment, I might have answered, yet I knew better than to contradict her.

Chapter Sixty-Eight

The following morning I woke late, my head aching from an unpleasant dream of drowning. Finding myself alone and hearing shouts outside, I rose in haste. In the courtyard, I glimpsed Miles and several other men milling about, awaiting their mounts. Flinging on my night-robe, I ran out into the corridor.

"Where's Master Forrest going?" I caught Guy scuttling down the stairs. "Is the duke going hunting?"

"No, Mistress." The lad looked guilty. "Master Forrest told me you were sick. He told me to let you to sleep. He's going to London." He indicated the cloak he was carrying. "He asked me to fetch this."

Snatching it from the lad, I raced into the courtyard. "Take me with you!" I shouted to Miles.

"I think Master Potter would have a lot to say if I turned up with a woman in tow." He climbed into the saddle.

"But I'm not just any woman, I'm your wife." I clung to the pommel. "You promised you'd take me to London one day."

"And will do so—one day." He plucked the reins from Rob Metcalf's unwilling hands. "But not today."

Conscious of the attention we'd aroused, he continued in light-hearted manner.

"I've important messages to deliver and no time to take you sight-seeing in the city. Besides, who'll look after Dickon?"

"I could take him with me. The Mercers would be glad to see us."

Rob Metcalf waited uncomfortably, shifting from one foot to the other.

"No." Miles leaned down to plant a hearty kiss on my mouth, stopping my protests. "I'm on the duke's business and can't have you traipsing after me like a camp follower." His voice grew low and husky with desire as he stroked my dishevelled hair. Someone coughed discreetly. "Besides," he said, feigning laughter, "Master Potter has no means to entertain fair ladies. Nor can I allow you to go prancing to and fro all over the city by yourself. It's not safe for honest women."

"But my cousin Harry would take care of us."

"Hark at the wench!" The onlookers laughed.

"It's only for a few days." He set his cap straight. The silver boar badge glinted. "You'll not have time to miss me." He took the cloak from my unwilling hands. Stooping on the pretext of chucking me under the chin, he murmured, "Don't hound me, Nan. My duties are merely the ordering of provisions. You make me look a fool in front of the men." Although he spoke with the softness of a lover, his eyes gleamed flint.

"Avoid the Tower."

Furiously he shook off my grasp.

Full of misgivings I watched the horsemen depart. Spots of rain began to fall, blotching the delicate fabric of my robe.

"Mistress Forrest," said a detested voice by my elbow. "Are you so eager to see the sights of London? They say it's full of vice and intrigue since the king allowed his wife to lead him by the nose."

I shrugged without turning. "I know little of the queen."

"But something more of the king?"

"You're full of sly insinuations," I answered impatiently.

"Ah, Mistress Forrest, but I think you're full of secrets."

Rage spun me round to face him. "What is it you want of me, Jack Green? I'm tired of your insolent looks and your jarring voice. I can't believe I once felt sorry for you, even cared for you! Now you've become as sticky as a burr—as irritating as an itch no amount of scratching can soothe! Stop all this riddling and speak your mind. I'm sick of threats!"

"Why must you always be so angry with me, Nan?" He pretended injury. My outburst caught the attention of two stout matrons gossiping by the brew-house. He drew me by the elbow into a shadowed corridor leading to the Hall. "Let's be straight with one another. What do you know of an archer named Blayborne?"

"Blayborne?" I repeated stupidly. I tried to smooth my dishevelled hair. "What are you talking about?"

"Haven't you heard tales of the king's parentage? Surely you must have heard talk about how he bears no resemblance to the late Duke of York?"

"Oh, that old tale," I replied, still tetchy. "Of course, I've heard it. But what has that to do with me? The king's mother's still alive. You'd best ask her about it—if you dare. I'm sure Cicely Neville'll have you hanged if you so much as *breathe* scandal about her marriage."

"I have it on good authority the king's a bastard." Jack seemed unperturbed by my scorn. "He was conceived while the Duke of York was away campaigning and is the result of an adulterous affair between the Duchess and an archer in the garrison at Rouen. Moreover, there are documents can prove it."

"Be careful," I said, genuinely shocked. I pulled my robe tighter. "The Duke of Clarence was executed for speaking such treason."

"Indeed." Even in the dim light I couldn't mistake the leer on his face. "And I think you know something of that particular execution, don't you? Oh, Mistress Forrest, you're not always careful, are you? And you're so fond of your old priest. Your letters to him are most entertaining—"

My bones ran ice. I leaned against the wall.

"My noble master's anxious to spare the Duchess of York any embarrassment. He'd prefer to establish a legal claim to the throne by a less painful route. The king's marriage to the Wydeville widow has long been the subject of discussion. There are those who think its secrecy a ploy to hide a greater secret. Do you understand?"

"But the children—the little boys—"

"Bastards all," said Jack.

I turned towards the light, anxious to escape, but Jack gripped my arm. His fingers bruised my flesh.

"Come, Nan, be reasonable. Your husband's earned much honour by his loyalty. Would you see it thrown away? Would you see the kingdom given to the bastards of the Wydeville witch? Or would you rather see the triumph of the true nobility?"

"Your motive's not honour, but greed." My voice cracked with fury. "You care nothing about who sits on the throne as long as he keeps money in your purse. And your master, whoever he is, would have no need of such self-seekers, if his cause were honourable."

I wrenched my arm away and ran outside into the falling rain.

"Keeping your secret will cause you much pain," said Jack. His teeth gleamed in an extravagant smile. "Remember I tried to spare you that."

I took refuge in the beauty of the chapel, for its gilded, ornamental splendour was Middleham's greatest treasure. Before the statue of the Virgin, I knelt to admire the flickering jewels of flame lit by her many petitioners. The marble face reminded me of Eleanor. What had Eleanor's piety and devotion brought but suffering? Would it be so terrible to tell the world the secret she'd taken to the grave?

Somewhere, Eleanor's babe grew into sturdy boyhood in happy ignorance. Was it so important to wear a crown? I thought of my Dickon. I'd do anything to secure his comfort. Did someone cherish Eleanor's boy as tenderly as I did mine? My mind turned then to little Lord Ned and the Wydeville boys. Peasant or prince, children were precious, all worthy of the same protection.

Looking up, I thought Our Lady's face had assumed Lady Anne's proud features. I trembled at her determination to see her son wear the crown. Had Gloucester spoken to her of his brother's bigamous marriage? And if he knew of it, then Stillington had told him. Was Jack Green's "master" the Duke? If so, what plot were he and Bishop Stillington hatching? What part must Miles play in all this? And what role had they assigned to me?

My head swam with all these questions, my mind blurred with the subtle scent of melting beeswax, a fragrance laden with the elusive memory of summer-warmed wings. Brother Brian's face rose before me in the smoky darkness. Like a father, he'd protected me since childhood and taught me to follow my visions. "A promise made is binding," he said. Could I betray such a pledge? Brother Brian commended the power of prayer, and so I bent my head before the Virgin to enlist her aid.

Though no pious devotee, I begged her to have pity on me. I sat at her feet for a long time. No blinding flash of understanding struck me, no healing balm, nothing but the steady drum of rain on the roof, and the dawning certainty the gentle priest stood in mortal danger.

The guards found me kneeling at the Virgin's feet when they came to arrest me.

Chapter Sixty-Nine

In the murky glow of the torchlight the figure seated before me writhed like a demon in some hellish underworld. The tarry smoke of a brazier choked me with its stench. I twisted my hands in their restraints. The rope chafed against my wrist-bones. I licked cracked lips, but wouldn't ask for water. Nor would I ask after Dickon. They might do something dreadful to him. But surely a man of God wouldn't harm a child?

"Spare yourself this discomfort." The oily voice seemed genuinely concerned. "We know you guarded Dame Eleanor's secrets. You've only to admit witnessing the marriage contract made between her and King Edward and you'll be released."

"If you know her secrets, sir," I answered, drops of sweat stinging my eyes, "then why do I have to tell you anything?"

"Did the king promise marriage?"

"I can't say, sir."

"You mean you don't know or you won't say?"

Bishop Stillington grew impatient. A whip-like sharpness hastened the questioning.

How long had I stood here? Days passed in a haze—First the courteous inquiry at Middleham, then the threats and the hasty journey through the night, the bleak, solitary cell, the persistent, rigorous examination. I lost count of the times they brought me before the bishop. Was I at Sheriff Hutton or at Pontefract? They covered my head in a hood throughout the journey, and whilst I remembered constant drizzle, the smell of ale and damp wool, the sound of creaking leather and plodding hoof-beats, I'd no concept of the distance.

"Your priest has been more co-operative."

"What have you done to him?"

My stomach clenched with terror. I trusted Brother Brian wouldn't betray me however much they tortured him.

"Come, come, child," said the cleric, as if shocked. "Do you think I'd harm one of my own?"

I didn't answer. I knew he'd shrink from nothing to have his way.

He plucked some letters from his sleeve. "Your trust in the priest is touching." He opened out one of them. He toyed with another. "Your writing again, Mistress Forrest—but sadly Master Palmer has taken a vow of silence." He bared his teeth in a monstrous smile. "Brother Brian's saved you more than once from punishment, I think?"

"Punishment?"

"You were accused of witchcraft?"

The voice assumed its bland, smooth quality, but behind the deft control lurked bone-chilling menace.

"I was a child, sir."

"Ah, yes, of course. But where are the cards?"

"Cards?"

How I despised my foolish echo!

"The painted fortune telling-cards." Enmity hardened his voice.

"I threw them away." My heart pounded at the lie.

"So you don't deny possessing them?" He sensed my weakness.

"An old woman gave them to me." I began to babble. "I used them for amusement, nothing more."

"For amusement?" The cruel sneer taunted. "Since when was witchcraft deemed amusement?"

"I told fortunes for entertainment, sir. Never for wicked purposes."

Silence.

Sweat trickled from my armpits and between my breasts. I smelled my own terror.

"Do you know what happens to witches?"

"They're hanged, sir."

"Hanged or burned."

He uttered the words with a relish that turned my bowels to liquid. Surely he'd placed cruel emphasis upon the "burned"?

"Come, Mistress Forrest, let us speak frankly. Sister Absalom regretted your tendency to heresy while you were at Norwich. Your own husband was obliged to chastise you for fortune-telling, and yet you persisted in 'entertaining' your women friends with this conjuring."

"Not conjuring, sir."

"But I've talked to some of these friends of yours." The bishop looked pained. "Surely you remember Philippa Purseglove? She said you talked of nothing but spirits."

"That's a wicked lie, sir!" My voice shook with anger. How could Philippa betray me after all these years? "I was no more than a child when I knew Philippa."

"Indeed." The bishop lifted an eyebrow. He smiled as if bewildered, but his eyes were granite. "But what of Jennet Jackaman and Dorothy Bullinger? Did they lie too? I think you were not so young then—"

My mind skipped back to the girls giggling in the dark, fat Rosamund asking if she'd ever marry—to Agnes and Lucy at Barnard—how many of my old acquaintances had the bishop questioned? What of Alice and Genevieve? Meg Huddleston? Could it be even Lady Anne had betrayed me?

"It was just a game, sir, never conjuring."

"Well, then, call it what you will, but I think you need reminding of the gravity of such 'amusement.'"

"No, Miles warned me of the dangers. Because of this, I threw the cards away."

The bishop smiled as if amused. "And Amy Sadler? Did she warn you too?" He gave a signal.

Out the stinking smoke stepped a huge, hooded man holding what looked like a pair of metal pliers.

"Perhaps Master Raymond may persuade you to be more helpful. Show Mistress Forrest some of your toys, Raymond."

The giant threw something on to the brazier. At once the flames flared up ravenously. In the fierce roar of this fire I glimpsed the protruding stems of many metal objects. I watched in awful fascination as Raymond's gauntleted hand drew forth a pair of pincers heated to a scarlet glow.

407

"Applied to tender flesh these implements may make even the most stubborn spirit yield," the bishop said soothingly. "I've known strong men weep at the torment of their fiery pinching. And Raymond has others that can tear and burn, ones that rip as they scorch, some that probe and fry the secret places of the body in the most exquisite agony. Master Raymond's very proud of his skills, are you not, Raymond?"

As the ghastly hooded face turned to me I imagined its teeth fixed in a hungry grimace.

"Perhaps you would care to examine the pincers more closely?"

At the approach of the torturer, a cruel heat emanated from these claws.

"Ah, Raymond," said the bishop, as I swayed, "I fear the lady's frightened by your ardour. I don't think she's ready to make your intimate acquaintance yet." He addressed the guard standing at my elbow. "Let her spend a day or two in the company of the Welshwoman." He turned back to me, his voice caressing. "I think you'll enjoy meeting our foreign guest. She may advise you how to avoid meeting Master Raymond again."

In a rustle of scarlet robes the cleric departed as speedily as a spirit and guards dragged me along the dank underground corridors to evil-smelling darkness.

⁂

"Don't you fear the death?"

My eyes had grown accustomed to the black cell.

The little, pointed face turned upward as if towards a source of unseen light. A stifled gurgle akin to laughter shook the starved body.

"Who'd not fear pain? But to be free? I'd give much to feel the wind on my skin, to smell hay and hear the sheep bleating in my mother's pasture-land again."

"Your mother told me many things."

A cold hand, sinewy as a bird's claw, seized mine. "My mother's wisdom should've kept us both from this place. But I wouldn't listen. If I had, I'd be where Olwyn lies now, safe in the arms of Simon Halstead, listening to the cries of a babe in the cradle, and birds squabbling in the eaves. But I only laughed and said Olwyn could have him. I looked higher than to be a farmer's wife. Besides, I'd seen envy in Olwyn's face. I knew for the younger to wed before the elder would bring her shame. But I didn't spurn him just to please her. I wanted something more than that dull village for the rest of my life, and besides—"

"You have the Sight?"

"Oh, we both have that," she said. I tingled at this recognition until I realised she spoke of her sister. "Olwyn didn't want the gift, although we both had it from our mother and our grandmother before her. She wouldn't use it. She hankered after babes and housewifery." She brought her face close to mine. I smelled stale breath, the rank, sweet odour of sickness and unwashed flesh. Taloned fingers explored my face and hair. "I must have been very young. I don't remember you. I recall a fair wench who married the reeve." Her laughter rang eerily in the fetid blackness of the chamber.

"That was Alys Weaver."

"She was a lovely woman, the reeve's wife. I remember her hair. Like a river of gold it was falling over her shoulders. I thought she was a princess from a fairy-tale and he was a monster. She had to do everything for him. In the end he couldn't even wipe his own arse. He just sat drooling like a baby. I watched her growing old before her time, her beautiful hair fading until it was bleached white as bone, like an old woman's—her own boy gone—and she left with his ugly daughter—But I don't remember you."

"You were six or seven. I saw you winding wool in your mother's kitchen. I thought you a fairy child."

"Much good all this does us. We can't go back to those times. My mother's dead and the village as far away from both of us as paradise. You may walk un-scorched from this prison, mistress, but I must face the flames."

I opened my mouth to protest but she pressed her bony finger against my lips and laughed again. This time she wailed like the cry of a sea-bird. For a moment I thought I saw the beating of wings against bars.

"I'll be glad to escape. I've lain here forgotten for many seasons but now you bring me freedom. No, don't deny it, for you have the Sight yourself. He'll make you watch. Be brave, mistress. They say the pain is fierce but soon passes. I'll look for you out the fire. Watch for me and sing me to heaven."

She kissed me on the brow, a brush of dry skin against my own, and then she began to sing low and sweet in that strange language like rippling water. If it was a spell she wove I don't know but I drifted into dark, untroubled sleep.

✑

They burned Nerys on the next market day and the crowd roared at her death like hungry dogs over a morsel of meat. Bishop Stillington had me watch just as she predicted but I couldn't rejoice at her freedom. It was a cruel death. The crackle of the flames kept me from sleep many days.

I didn't need to see Master Raymond's toys again. The sight of that fire loosened my tongue. I longed then for absolution and thought it would come in death but the bishop oozed kindness. One morning he told me Miles had come to take me home.

"The Book of Leviticus is very clear about relationships between men." The sinister voice purred, slick with satisfaction. "I'm sure you understand how the Church grieves over unnatural vices among its brotherhood."

A single flame fluttered illuminating the ruby ring on an exquisitely groomed hand. Behind the light, locked in shadow, a hooded figure brooded, patient with menace.

A familiar, smoky aroma permeated the dank chamber.

"You are silent, Brother Brian. Perhaps you need time to consider the implications of these accusations?" The voice caressed, soft with solicitude. "Of course, if you could help us in another matter we might be persuaded to recognise this regrettable familiarity as mere kindness, a foolish fondness—"

Wax dripped from the candle. It congealed on the trestle in a tear-shaped puddle. The slender fingers began to tap and the ruby danced, a drop of blood in a circle of light.

"The matter grows urgent, Brother. Why delay?" The mellifluous tone vanished, its melody destroyed by pitiless, barely contained rage. "Must I call upon Master Raymond to assist you? Come, look upon his curious array of implements—A few easy words are all we require—After all, we know from your letters you share a close acquaintance with the woman. She revealed a secret to you, did she not? A secret that threatens the exercise of

justice in the kingdom. Surely you wouldn't have a lie perpetuated?"

Flames leaped upward. A sickening stench of scorched flesh tainted the air. Scream upon scream rang through the dark—

Choking and flailing, I woke in the small guest room where they kept me now—no longer a prisoner, but still guarded. Last night's embers glowed in the hearth lighting the curled form that slept before it. Nothing woke this lumpish waiting woman. Outside, in the corridor someone passed, keys jangling. No glimmer crept through the shutters. I huddled down into the blankets burying my face in my hands, trying to shut out the terrible knowledge that Brother Brian had been tortured.

Chapter Seventy

Miles locked me in so fierce an embrace I felt his heart thudding.

"I thought I'd lost you. Thank Christ we've powerful friends."

"And powerful enemies too." I buried my head against the comforting warmth of his shoulder.

Tilting my face so he could look into my eyes, he placed a warning finger on my lips.

A knock at the door announced a bold-eyed tavern wench carrying a tray laden with food. "Will I set this on table, sir?" She smiled at Miles, thrusting out her voluptuous bosom.

"Aye." He returned her smile, his eyes appraising the jutting curves. "It looks most appetising."

"It's pork, sir." Her hips wiggled as she stirred the pot and spooned the meat into two bowls. "Our Will's famous for his stews. There's bread here, sir." She gave him a saucy stare, pouting her lips mischievously. "Let me know if you want more."

Turning to the doorway to frown at the gawky girl clutching a pitcher and two tankards against her stained shift, she said, "Shift theesen, Nell. Set jug upon table. Folk don't want to be kept waiting while food gets cold."

How could we afford the best room in The Fox in Pontefract and dine in such extravagance? Who'd paid for all this? I looked at Miles' face for answers but his expression remained unfathomable.

"Eat, Nan." He steered me from the hearth where the landlord had provided a generous fire. "You're nearly as skinny as that simpleton. If it tastes as good as it smells, it'll put some flesh on your bones."

I swallowed a mouthful of tender meat stuffed with almonds and saffron, spiced with cinnamon and wild garlic, swimming in a gravy of onions, mushrooms, herbs and wine. Its unaccustomed richness quickly overwhelmed me.

"Don't slander Stillington." Miles spoke with his mouth full. "He and Gloucester hold the key to justice."

"Justice!"

"Aye, justice." Miles set down his knife. "What demon possessed you to withhold information about the Butler marriage?"

"I promised Dame Eleanor. And the king, himself, told me to keep it secret. Cecily Neville knows the truth but Gloucester daren't put her to the question. He's as much in awe of his mother as King Edward was. Stillington shut us up at Norwich to keep the rumour quiet but now he's eager to flaunt it to the world. I'm certain Dame Eleanor's chaplain was murdered for what he knew. Do you wonder then why I kept quiet?"

"Drink some mead." He poured the honey-scented brew, slipping an arm about me, drawing me close. "The landlord assures me of its medicinal properties. It might put some colour in your cheeks. You've a shocking prison pallor."

"Blame your precious Stillington for that."

"Stillington's an unscrupulous rogue." He resumed his meal. "But for the moment, Gloucester needs him." He gave me a searching look. "Did you say Stillington knew about the contract between the king and Eleanor Butler?"

"He suspected it. And he shared those suspicions with Clarence—" I flashed him an implicit glance. "And I'm sure you remember what happened to him. Don't you see? Stillington wants to set brother against brother. His actions will tip England into civil war again. Edward was just a stripling when he made that foolish promise to Eleanor. Hasn't he proved himself a good king all these years? We've had peace in the country. Do you want to see that destroyed for the sake of this so-called justice?"

"Would you let a bastard sit on the throne?" Miles threw down his spoon. Flint sparks lent his eyes added brilliance. "Do you think the Wydevilles will surrender power when Edward's gone and the witch's son inherits the kingdom?"

"Would you give your allegiance to a corrupt cleric intent only on feathering his nest and an ambitious younger son who seeks to seize his brother's crown?" I rose from my place, my voice shrill with exasperation.

"I've sworn my loyalty to Gloucester." His eyes blazed, steel-hard. "I'll not swerve. As for Stillington, I'm not afraid of him. Remember, Gloucester saved you from the fire and for that alone I'd follow him to death."

"Gloucester will demand your soul," I answered softly.

Miles didn't speak. He cradled me in his arms, holding me fast against his tense body. Silence grew between us. Below, the throb of the tavern with its raucous laughter, jeers, and stamping feet seemed a world far away.

"Gloucester abhors witchcraft but he spoke up for you. When he questioned me I told him you'd bewitched me long ago and that was the only witchcraft I knew you practised. He laughed at that. He said all women knew such spells to snare men, having learned them from the cradle. I swore I knew nothing of any fortune-telling." His hands gripped my shoulders forcing me to meet the steely eyes which intimated complicity. "Do you understand?"

I wondered then if he knew about the cards hidden behind the fireplace. What had Amy Sadler told him? Had Lady Anne spoken of them to her lord?

"Before you last went to London I begged you to leave the Duke's service—"

"Gloucester's a patient man," he said. He kissed the top of my head, his body relaxing as if his anxieties had evaporated like steam. "He won't squander his strength without cause. While Edward rules he'll play the loyal subject and you and I will profit by this forbearance." He poured more mead. "One day we'll laugh about all this. And I promise I *will* take you and Dickon somewhere safe when all's done."

Taking my chin in his hand, he turned my face to his. The tenderness in his brilliant blue eyes made my stomach lurch with that old passion that had first drawn me to him. He kissed me softly, his lips warm. "Those wenches at Middleham won't ask any questions. Everyone's been told your arrest was a mistake." He kissed me again and his eyes smouldered with the beginnings of desire. "Why, if the queen's mother can escape the taint of witchcraft, can't you do it too?" But no humour coloured his laughter then. I knew the reference contained a warning. Only the intervention of influential friends had saved the Duchess Jacquetta from trial for sorcery.

"Time to sleep. We've a long ride tomorrow." He closed the shutters against the wet March night. "Shall I call the lass to take the dishes away?"

Over the downstairs roar he shouted for service. "You can leave the mead." He gave the goggle-eyed kitchen maid a wink. "We've a mind to finish it in bed."

She dropped him a clumsy curtsy as if he were noble-born and after much fumbling, gathered up bowls and spoons, clutching them to her as if they were great treasure.

Once among the heap of blankets I surrendered to the fatigue which had haunted me since Pontefract. Sounds of the outer world drifted away.

"The priest betrayed you." Miles sat propped against the bolster, a tankard of mead in his fist.

"Brother Brian?"

"When I heard you were arrested, I rode from London like a mad man and Jack met me near Middleham. Stillington got his information from the priest, he said. So I rode straight to the abbey."

"Did you see Brother Brian?" A nail of fear tore me from sleep. "What had they done to him?"

"The Abbot tried to stop me. He said the priest was ill."

"You didn't hurt him?" Upright now, aware of the draught on my shoulders, I clawed at Miles my heart thudding with fright and fury.

"Hurt him?" Miles laughed harshly, stilling my hands. "I should've broken his skinny neck! But, by the Rood, when I saw him I hadn't the heart for it. He looked so puny, sick and old. He made no excuses, I'll give him that. He told Stillington all he knew. He couldn't take the torture. This cowardice was a worse punishment than any I could give. He begged my pardon but how could I forgive such treachery? His words condemned you to the flames! May he rot in hell!"

"No, don't say that! They hurt him terribly." I pressed my hands against my temples. The sudden image of a spiralling fall nauseated me. Clenching my teeth, I clawed at my belly, re-living the priest's suffering. Terrifying pictures unrolled. The fire-lit room grew distant. "The world's tumbling into darkness—" I yielded to the lure of hideous images, my voice unstoppable. "A great house is divided. Easter brings sorrow. A woman wails, tearing her hair. She beats her fists against the stones until they turn bloody but nothing will raise the children from their bed. Neighing horses summon to a monstrous battlefield—A great white steed rises above the masses. Its flanks run with blood. Nerys stands laughing out of the fire—and the flames turn into pennants—the red dragon of Wales leaps as if it means to devour the world. A crowd roars as the great horse stumbles on the bridge. I hear clanging metal, the rasp of spades on stone. Two shadowy figures prowl the dark—"

"Stop it! Stop it!" Miles shook me, his face a mask of terrified fury. The tankard skittered away. Opening my eyes wide, I clutched at him, sinking my nails into his flesh.

"I can't stop it!" I howled like an animal in pain. "I've never been able to stop it! Ever since I was a little girl I've been tormented like this! Do you think I want to see such sights?" I looked deep into his eyes where the old fear lurked like a rabbit deep in its warren. "Promise me, when you're in London you'll avoid the Tower."

Before he could speak the candle guttered out, plunging us into darkness. The fire sank low, the flames flickering blue. Like frightened children we clung together. It was the first and only time we spoke of these terrible events to come.

ɘ๑

"I must go to Jervaulx."

"Are you mad?" Miles' face whitened, his eyes panicked as an unbroken colt's. "We're back but a day and you talk of venturing out—and to such a place!"

"But I must see Brother Brian. I must speak to him."

"No!" Miles pressed me against the door. "I told you, the priest betrayed you. I marvel you can think of going to him after that."

"But it was because of me they tortured him." I clutched at his shoulders, desperate to convince him of the priest's innocence.

"And can you forgive his perfidy?" Miles spat at me. "Jack's no priest-lover but even he was stunned by the old fool's cowardice."

"Jack? What did he have to do with it?"

"He said some pretty boy monk named Edwin proved a useful source of information." Contempt curled his lip. "It seems the old priest doted on him. Jack gained the lad's friendship—though by what measures I don't care to think—and discovered the old man spent time in London before being sent to Jervaulx—"

"I know that." I grabbed at his arm. "I told you the priest visited me in the city—I made no secret of it."

"Aye, but did you know your priest enjoyed a secret relationship with a young monk at St John's Priory?"

"He visited Alan Palmer—a lad from my village." I shouted with exasperation, forcing Miles to confront me. "What nasty insinuations has Jack Green been nourishing now? And to what purpose?"

Miles shook his head with impatience. "Stillington showed particular interest in the priest's weakness, Jack said. The church condemns trafficking between men."

"So Jack Green used this hearsay to fuel the torture of an old man?" Tears of rage choked my voice. "What warped pleasure can he extract from such perverse pastimes? Or was it just a means to strike at me?"

Miles folded me in his arms and kissed the tears from my eyes. "Jack Green won't harm you, I'll see to that. But you must stay away from Jervaulx. I care for nothing except to have you safe. It would be foolish to annoy the duke now we have his special protection."

Reluctantly I yielded to his counsel, but the implications of the duke's protection nagged at my peace like toothache.

Chapter Seventy-One

All over Coverdale bells rang, their dark sonorous notes echoing through the hills, making the whole valley vibrate.

"What's happening?" Dickon started up from the stream where he'd been searching for trout. "Why are the bells ringing?"

Miles raised his head as if sniffing the air for clues.

"Something's wrong." I gathered up the discarded cloaks, the April day having proved warmer than expected. "We should go back to the castle."

Miles cast me a warning look. Ever since Pontefract he'd grown wary of anything that smacked of prophecy. He rose stiffly, hoisting the fishing pole over his shoulder. "Put your shoes on, Dickon. We've a good walk ahead of us."

At Coverham closed doors menaced us with their silence.

"What's happened?" Miles shouted to a lone villager by a gate.

"Don't tha know?" The elderly man scanned our faces in disbelief, his lips quivering. "King Edward's dead." He crossed himself. "Messenger brought news from London."

It seemed in that moment the false sunlight faded and the air chilled. I pulled my cloak around me, watching slate-rimmed clouds scudding across the heavens. As Miles stooped to pick up Dickon, I noticed threads of silver among his unruly black hair. A grim sense of our mortality struck me like a fist.

"We must hurry." Miles glanced up. "It'll rain soon."

Our eyes locked for a moment. I knew then that this day marked the end of our comfort. There'd be no more walks upon the moors; no more days spent together as a family; no more sweet privacy. Panting over the uneven landscape, even Dickon seemed subdued. Neither of us dared ask what would happen now peace had been destroyed by one untimely death.

At Middleham mourning had already begun. The guards stood sombre, the streets empty of life. We cheated the rain but a fretting messenger waited.

"His Grace requires your service, Master Forrest." An impatient lad in page's livery stood by our door.

Dickon, eying this messenger, demanded in a loud voice, "Will Ned be king now?"

The page's eyes took on an incredulous stare.

"Why, no," I said. I snatched Dickon's hand. "The king's son, Prince Edward, will take the crown. He's the heir to the throne, not our Lord Ned." I laughed to cover my embarrassment. "Lord Ned is the prince's cousin," I explained to Dickon. "Like us, he'll swear his fealty to the new king. If he's strong enough to travel, he'll probably go to the coronation." I hustled the puzzled child inside.

Grim-faced Miles followed. "This bodes ill." Alarmed by the ominous resignation in his eyes, I watched him brush his hair savagely. He ruffled Dickon's curls. "Look after your mother." Snatching up his cloak, he kissed me hard on the mouth and fled in a moment.

"Master Green said Lord Ned would be king one day and I might be his trusty henchman." Dickon stared after Miles. "Where's dada going?"

"Master Green was teasing you." I tried to keep my voice steady. "If anything happened to Prince Edward, his younger brother would be king. Ned may be made an earl someday, but he'll never be a king."

I found him a piece of marchpane. While he sat chewing the sticky sweetmeat I flung logs on the fire. "If you're good, I'm sure Ned will choose you for service in his household one day." I turned to plant a kiss upon the tip of his nose, smiling with a heartiness I didn't feel.

"But Master Green said Prince Edward and Prince Richard couldn't rule the land because they were base-born." His eyes shone bright with innocence but his face assumed a serious expression as if quoting a lesson carefully taught. "Mama, will our Duke be king? Master Green said the Duke will reward everyone who's loyal to him now. Are we loyal, Mama? I'd like to be rewarded."

"Master Green should be very careful what he says." My heart thumped with a mixture of fear and suppressed rage. "Such words are dangerous. Do you understand what a traitor is?"

Dickon frowned. "A bad person?"

"A very bad person." I wrapped him in my arms. "One who may be hanged."

He snuggled close as if considering this explanation, licking the last sweetness from his lips. "Will Master Green be hanged?" His grubby face shone with childish simplicity.

"He may if he speaks treason." But I knew Jack Green was far too clever to be caught. "Come now, it's time to wash your face and then we'll play knuckle-bones together."

Long after the child slept, Miles crept into the chamber. He stood by the hearth, his face grave. "The king's been dead above a week. The Wydevilles have sent to Ludlow for their prince. I'm to ride to London tomorrow."

"Why?" I looked up from the little shirt I was stitching to steady my shaking hands.

"Gloucester suspects some mischief." He crouched before the fire chewing at his thumbnail. "They're saying the king went fishing, took cold, and ate too heartily at dinner." He faced me then, his eyes bleak. "Apparently he was taken ill on Good Friday."

"Poison?" I had a distinct image of wily Jack Green grinding something in a mortar while Brother Silas' back was turned. Miles shrugged, but one eyebrow lifted questioningly. His eyes burned.

"Surely not?" I uttered an involuntary laugh. "That's the kind of tale Maud Attemore might spin." I stuttered nervously, eager to dismiss my intuition as fantasy.

"But it's hard to believe someone so strong and vigorous could die suddenly." Miles narrowed his eyes. "Don't pretend you believe these lies about catching a chill, Nan. You're no good at dissembling."

"He certainly wasn't sick when I saw him at Westminster." I recalled the huge, laughing figure in the scarlet doublet and how we'd jested about him.

"And he never ailed till now. This'll throw the lords into confusion. A child on the throne means trouble." Miles' expression became vicious, his tone iron-hard. "Think of addle-witted Henry. He was a babe when he inherited the crown and much good that did us."

Dropping my sewing on my lap, I stared into the flames, allowing my mind to recapture the melancholy lad of my visions. "They say the Prince of Wales is a scholarly boy."

Miles' scornful laugh growled in his throat. "Scholarly or not," he jabbed a finger for emphasis, "he'll be a puppet in the hands of the Wydevilles if we allow it."

"How can we prevent it?" I thought of Stillington holding up Antony Wydeville's severed head. "We've no say in the management of the kingdom."

In the firelight Miles' face assumed a wolfish leer. "Gloucester's named Protector. Some of us from the north are to go ahead to the capital and await instructions. The Duke intends to meet up with the Ludlow entourage. Hastings told him the Wydevilles plan an early coronation. I'll be lodging at Potter's house until needed."

"And so it begins. Don't you remember what I told you at Pontefract?"

Miles stormed toward me and, seizing me by the shoulders, dragged me to my feet. "Never speak your witch-craft at me, for I'll not listen to it." Spittle flecked his lips. "If we remember where our duty lies we stand to profit by this calamity. Hastings' man told us, when Potter heard the news he said, 'Then my master, the Duke of Gloucester, will be king!' He must know something more than we do."

"Be careful, Miles." I stroked his face, noting with dismay the glitter of excitement in his eyes. "Men have had their tongues cut out for speaking such treason."

He thrust me from him snarling with laughter. "Can you say that to me? Your words almost had you burned, or have you forgotten?"

"I warn you only *because* of that," I said. "I've learned my lesson well. But will you follow Gloucester blindly?" I seized his arms, forcing him to confront me, and daring to oppose him with a passion which shocked both of us. "There's no witchcraft in a woman's love for her husband, but there *is* danger in speaking out against the queen and her family. She's a ruthless enemy and never forgets an injury. You know what she did to—"

"The Wydeville witch has had her day," said Miles. "She'll shortly see what it is to spurn the old nobility." He squatted before the fire as if seeking some message in its heart while I gathered up my scattered needlework, my throat aching with tears of frustration.

"What's become of Jack Green?"

"I don't know. I've not seen him in days. Why?"

"Mistress Collins has been asking after him." A sudden impression of Jack slipping a vial into his doublet made me nauseous. I swallowed hard, resting a hand on the settle for support. "It's just—Emma's gone missing."

Chapter Seventy-Two

Miles' sudden departure provoked a storm of speculation. Throughout the following weeks, the duchess treated me with particular favour, sending me upon various personal errands, showering me with little gifts and inviting me to sit next to her. What did she know of Miles' errand? I anguished over this special preferment, conscious of her ladies now looking at me with pity in their eyes. I felt like an animal being prepared for sacrifice.

Stifled by the tense atmosphere of the bower-chamber, I begged to go into Middleham on the pretext of visiting Elizabeth Metcalf. "She's been sick with the quinsy," I lied. "I promised her husband I'd look in on her."

"A generous gesture, Nan. And one I approve whole-heartedly. Take her some honey from our kitchens and get one of the wenches to accompany you. It'll be busy today with the market." Lady Anne smiled so sweetly, I wondered if she'd seen through my poor deception. "Commend me to her. No doubt Master Rob will be at home?"

This last question produced a tremor of sniggers and sly glances amongst the ladies. The duchess smiled archly at Meg Huddleston.

I took the honey but no companion, being anxious to avoid sparking further gossip. Fortunately I found plump Elizabeth among the rowdy muddle of the market. She panted for breath with the exertion of pushing through crowds, but still had enough energy to examine the heaped vegetables on a stall with careful scrutiny. "These onions are going rotten." Her vehemence wiped the smile from the astonished stall-holder's face. "And I never saw such withered turnips."

She turned to me. "I hope you've not bought owt of this knave." Her wind-chapped jowls quivered with indignation.

"No, I was on my way to see you." I dragged her away. "I told Lady Anne you'd been sick. She sent you this honey."

Elizabeth chuckled. "I never thought you capable of such tricks —but the honey's most welcome. I suppose you're anxious for news. Rob's back from London. I believe he's a message for you."

All the way back to her house in Castle Street, she gossiped without pause. "Jane Collins talks of retiring—says she's too old for tending children now and plans to settle in Sheriff Hutton— she's some cousins there—And what about that pretty little nursery wench running off to meet some rogue in the village last week? Jane was out of her mind with worry. She says the lass came back very late and refused to say a word, but she's been sly and sullen ever since. She's an idea that knave Green's behind it. Sally Glover says he's led several maids astray." She looked at me speculatively but I'd no appetite for tittle-tattle. "Did you know the coronation's been postponed until June?" She puffed and panted through the muddy streets, her face turning the colour of her crimson kirtle. "I daresay Lady Anne's had wind of it but she's a devious one—just like her father. The Wydeville queen's refusing to come out of the Sanctuary. They say she took all her jewels and treasure with her. She's demanded our duke releases her brother, Antony before—"

"I'd no idea the queen had gone into Sanctuary," I said, astounded. "Nor that her brother was being held—"

Elizabeth's face bloated with excitement. "Didn't you know Lord Rivers is a prisoner at Sheriff Hutton? Aye, *and* that son of hers from her first marriage."

"But what have they done?" I asked, unnerved. "No one's told me anything of these events—not even Amy Sadler."

"You'll have to ask Rob. I don't understand the half of it. There's been that much coming and going this past month my head's fair mazzled with it all."

Being much favoured by the duke, the Metcalfs kept a comfortable house and I couldn't help admiring the luxury of its furnishings. The polished wood-panelled walls followed the latest fashion and must have cost a great deal. Wondrous embroidered cushions decorated the settle. One of them took my eye in particular— the colour of a kingfisher, it depicted a scene of damsels playing lutes.

"I saw a fine arras with that picture on it at the market in York." Elizabeth noticed my interest. "Tom wouldn't buy it me. He haggled with the fellow over a few angels, but neither would give in." She plumped down evidently glad to rest her ponderous bulk. "A thrifty husband's a blessing—" She groaned, easing her great hams upon the settle. "But there's thrifty and there's mean." She eased off her plum-coloured leather shoes. Stretching lumpy feet towards the hearth, she wiggled her misshapen toes and sighed with pleasure. "That's better." She leaned back. "Polly!" she called loudly. "Rob must be in the kitchen again—eating us out of house and home."

The little servant girl promptly appeared with a tray laden with goblets of sweet wine and a dish of comfits.

"Tell Master Rob Mistress Forrest's here." Elizabeth Metcalf gulped wine thirstily. "And fetch another goblet and a jug of this wine."

Polly nodded, pushing escaping corn-coloured hair under her cap.

"Sit down, sit down." Elizabeth Metcalf patted the cushions. "How's that boy of yours? Tom says he'll make a fine horseman. I hear he's very friendly with the duke's lad. Now there's a delicate piece of mischief." She rattled on at a great pace so I'd neither time nor need to answer. I sipped the wine, watching her cram comfits into her mouth by the dozen, and all this without pausing in her speech.

"Now, mother." Brawny, good-natured Rob entered the room smelling of leather and horse-flesh. He wiped his mouth with the back of his hand. "Mistress Forrest," he nodded, flushing to the roots of his pale hair.

Behind him Polly waited until he settled beside the hearth, then scuttled to set a goblet and jug before him.

"Nay, Polly," He gestured at these items, "I'll not want this. Bring me some ale. This is ladies' liquor." He grinned, his open, honest face suddenly reminding me of Harry. "Mother likes to impress her guests but she won't stop me from drinking good strong ale." He sprawled back in his seat, long, muscular legs jutting into the hearth.

"Leave the jug, Polly." Mistress Metcalf shook her head at Rob. "Some of us have refined tastes." She poured herself another measure and offered me the jug, but I'd no taste for such sweet stuff. "Well, Rob, are you going to sit there all day with your knees in the fire place or are you going to tell Mistress Forrest her message?"

Rob blushed with embarrassment, shuffling his legs awkwardly. "I met Master Forrest at Baynard's Castle—"

"Baynard's Castle? Isn't he in Redcross Street?"

"Nay," Rob drew a package from his sleeve. "He's lodging at Baynard's Castle alongside the rest of the duke's men. He won't be home for yet a while. There's been a change of plan about the coronation. He sent thee this as a token of his warmest affection."

As I unwrapped the contents, he coughed and cleared his throat. Awkwardly, he muttered something about Miles promising to bring Dickon something from London. A smoky, crystal tear-drop hung from a delicate silver chain in a web of filigree. At its milky heart lurked a faint wash of blue.

"To match your eyes, he said." Rob's tone clearly suggested embarrassment. He avoided looking at me.

Beneath this fragile item lay a bundle of bright ribbons, green, topaz, rose and aquamarine.

"That's a pretty piece." Elizabeth Metcalf reached out a plump finger to lift the links of the chain so the jewel winked in the light. She smiled knowingly. "A lover's keepsake, eh?"

"I'd rather have him home, pretty as it is."

Elizabeth wheezed with the effort of pouring more wine. "What's become of the Wydeville prince?"

"Lodged in the royal apartments in the Tower as tradition demands." Rob looked thoughtful, hands resting on his boot-tops. I noticed his badly bitten nails. "From what I saw as he rode into London, I'd say he resembles his mother. But I hear he's given to melancholy—not haughty like her."

"Well-a-day, the poor child's every reason to be melancholy with his father dead and all the burdens of kingship laid upon his shoulders."

"Nay, mother, he's his uncle and other barons to help him with matters of state." Rob patted her swollen hand. "But there's a lot of talk." He gnawed on his finger nails while she fumed for more details.

"What sort of talk? By Saint Peter, Rob, thou'rt a poor story-teller and no mistake. Can't tha see Mistress Forrest is anxious for all the news?"

Rob blushed again, grinning sheepishly. "Well, folk reckon our Duke's getting mighty powerful. He's gathered supporters including Lord Howard and Harry Buckingham. They say he's determined the Wydevilles'll have no part in running the country. In fact, some folk are of a mind Gloucester means to take the crown for himself."

"What!" Elizabeth Metcalf sat up so suddenly, drops of wine flew from her goblet on to her worsted kirtle. "Hast tha lost thy reason?" She squawked and brushed the liquid off with a furious hand. "How can the duke be king when King Edward's sons are alive?"

"I'm only telling you what folk say," said Rob, dogged as an old ox. "You asked me what was happening in the city. Some say Gloucester works only for the good of the young prince, but I'm sure our duke has his eyes on his own advancement."

I sat rigid, too stunned to speak. It was the first time I'd heard Gloucester's motives aired publicly. Perhaps more suspected the duke of calumny than I'd realised.

"Are you going back to London, Rob?"

"Aye, the duke commanded me to summon more troops."

"Troops?" echoed his mother, looking bewildered.

"He fears rebellion from the Wydeville faction. Lady Anne counselled him to take his northern troops."

So, I thought, my suspicions were right. Lady Anne followed the current situation. "Will you take some messages for me?"

"Aye, I'll be gone within the week. Don't look so worried, mother, I'd rather follow after Gloucester wherever he leads, than see the Wydevilles lording it over us ever more. Father shares my views. The Metcalfs have allus kept faith."

Chapter Seventy-Three

In the blackest part of the night, I woke lathered in sweat. Someone whispered my name. Senses heightened and alert, I lay taut, ears straining for the slightest sound. Something lingered in the shadows. My flesh crawled.

"Who's there?"

A faint smell of ink and dust wafted through that thick darkness; the merest sigh of cloth rustled over stone.

Brother Brian.

No answer came. But gradually the strange tension eased as if an unseen spectre had melted away like fog.

Slipping on a woollen robe, I tiptoed through the unfamiliar landscape of the midnight bed-chamber. From the little truckle bed Dickon's breathing continued uninterrupted. My hand found the door and I leaned against the wood inhaling its ancient musty scent. The reluctant iron lock grated. Beyond the opening, a darker chasm yawned. Wary as a blind beggar in a crowd, I groped into it.

Stumbling against a stool, I stifled a cry of pain. I nudged open the shutters, but no welcome glow of moonlight lit the chamber. Forced to find taper and flint—a feat accomplished with much difficulty and hard breathing—I finally banished the shadows. The feeble candle revealed the commonplace objects of our daily round. Gathering courage I fetched a shallow bowl in which I'd once collected acorns and filled it with water from the ewer by the hearth. Crouching in the soft halo of light, remembering how Mara made me gaze into the cloudy depths of a crystal, I focused my eyes on the shimmer of liquid. Gradually my vision swam beyond the surface, carrying me into pulsing obscurity where figures moved so fast and indistinct I couldn't even snatch at their purpose. I immersed myself in silence.

A white-clad figure turned, revealing Brother Brian's gaunt, ascetic face lit by a radiance I'd never seen before. He held his hands as if in supplication and I was filled with such an overwhelming sense of love, tears stung my eyes.

"There's nothing to forgive," I whispered.

His features dissolved and in their place another hooded head appeared. A younger, softer face materialised. The eyes widened, their dark centre rimmed with viridian that faded into palest brown, the colour of a sky-lark's wing. From a sleeve of bone-bleached linen, tapering fingers held out a roll of vellum—

A sword sliced through the air in a great arc, scattering bloody drops followed by a macabre dull thud. A crowd jeered. A woman's bare feet tripped over cobbles, the hem of a velvet kirtle dragging through filth. Transported to a richly decorated chamber with wondrous windows of stained glass depicting the lilies of France and walls where painted birds flew on fields of gold and vermilion, a boy's laughter trilled like harp-song. Across a tiled floor decorated with leopards and white harts leaping in regal splendour, a sprightly child executed a lively dance, his hair a golden nimbus around his merry face. I knew him instantly. A distant bell tolled. Then my Lady appeared dressed in purple velvet. A great fanfare of trumpets blasted my ear-drums with such a cacophony of sound I looked up—

Dickon stood in the doorway.

"How long have you been there?" I hustled him into the bed-chamber. "It's not day yet. Climb up into mama's bed and see if you can go back to sleep."

Snuggled in the downy heat of the blankets he whispered drowsily. "What were you doing, mama, kneeling on the floor?"

"Thinking and saying a prayer for your father."

The ease of this lie filled me with shame. I'd become a practised liar. The visions stormed and replayed in my head until a streak of pale sky pierced the dark. Since Pontefract, Miles had forbidden me to go to Jervaulx. Whenever I mentioned Brother Brian people shuffled uncomfortably. But I knew now he must be dead. He'd called to me out of that inky water. Mara told me the dead returned of their own volition but never before had I sought so willingly to unravel the secrets of the future. I knew it wouldn't be the last time I'd use the scrying bowl.

⁓

The duchess summoned me early to her bed-chamber that day.

A bird-twitter of excited female voices spilled into the passage. Curious, I sidled through the crack in the doorway and saw a tumult of figures milling about at the other end of the chamber.

"Your Grace—"

My greeting turned them and the chattering jangle fell silent. One by one the elegant ladies in their fine brocade gowns lifted their heads. As they dropped back, I saw the great, carved bed with its silken canopy and blue, embroidered curtains heaped with an array of garments of every hue like a cloth merchant's stall.

"Here," said Lady Anne. She flicked a jewelled hand.

I moved to join her at the bedside, baffled by this display. Impulsively, she snatched up a length of cloth-of-gold. "Take this."

"It's beautiful, Your Grace." I stood admiring the shimmer of its silken fall while she tossed aside a growing pile of garments. "But I couldn't wear—"

"Take it," she said impatiently. Her eyes flashed green sparks. "In memory of the coronation!" She laughed, two knots of hectic colour blooming in her cheeks. "Oh Nan, if only you could be there!"

She seized my wrists with quivering hands. The sensation struck me as something akin to the intensity before a storm. Her fingers felt dry and feverish. "My Lord wants me join him in London." Her eyes sparkled. "I'm packing." She indicated the pile of clothing with a wide flourish, the aquamarine silk of her sleeve rippling like water. "We're choosing only my most elegant clothes, for the London fashions are reputed to be exquisite. But first I must have some private speech with you." Glancing over her shoulder as she drew me away, she addressed the scattered ladies. "Katherine, take charge. Lay aside only the finest items. I'll have others made in London."

She led me into the solar where the sun streamed through the windows, casting claret and blue lozenges upon the furnishings. Two older ladies seated on the long bench with their tapestry work, stilled a maid's reading.

"Mother, this is Mistress Forrest of whom I spoke yesterday. She can be depended on to oversee the prince's health. And I've appointed Anne Idley Mistress of the Nursery so you've no need to worry while I'm away." The elder of the two nodded. "Mistress Collins is too old to take responsibility," the duchess said. "My husband advised Anne Idley as a suitable replacement. The Collins woman frets over-much—"

"She was worried about Emma running off with Jack Green—"

"Then she's more foolish than I thought. Master Green turns the heads of all the young wenches—These serving girls are just dizzy butterflies. Mistress Collins will be happier in retirement."

How could she dismiss years of loyal service so callously? I clenched my fists and opened my mouth to protest, but she continued without noticing. "Ned's too delicate for an arduous journey. I rely on *your skill* to care for him, Nan."

"Your Grace," I took a breath. Daringly, I brushed aside the implication of her words. "I would esteem it a great favour if I might accompany you to London."

She shook her head. "Impossible." Her eyes gleamed hard as agate now. "Though I value your loyalty and discretion, I can't take you this time. My son's safety is too important."

"My husband—"

"Will be well rewarded for his service to mine," she answered swiftly. She executed another imperious flick of her jewelled fingers. "I'll need you later. In the meantime, let my boy play with yours and continue their studies. Ned cherishes Dickon's companionship." She looked at me pointedly. "It'll prove worthwhile for Dickon to have Ned's patronage in the future. I've told Master Metcalf the riding lessons may continue, providing you consider the prince in good health." She took my hand. Through the hot, dry fingers I sensed the extraordinary strength of her will. Her pretty, pointed face flushed, animated to the point of exhilaration. "Extraordinary times are upon us." She drew me further away, halting before a brightly painted wall, where she pointed out maidens frolicking with nimble unicorns on green meadows spangled with flowers. I pretended interest in the pictures while she whispered in my ear, leaning so close I smelled the scent of vervain she favoured. "Didn't you tell me I would one day wear a crown? How proud my father would have been when that moment comes to pass!"

The import of this unguarded speech appalled me. But when I opened my mouth to speak, she placed a finger on her lips to signify a secret, her eyes dancing with merriment.

"Say nothing." She twisted the large, pear-shaped pearl hanging from her leather and gold hip-belt, as if considering some great matter. "Let's see how events shape our destinies." Her eyes grew grave but they challenged my disbelief. "I promise you, Nan, you'll not lose by our long friendship."

In that instant I recalled how her cunning father had manipulated the claimants to the crown. I recognised the same blaze of naked ambition I'd seen in Warwick's face as he rode through the streets of London. Anne Neville anticipated the coronation with such triumph, I trembled for Elizabeth Wydeville's boys.

"What do your think about this Henry Tudor?" She peered down into the courtyard as if searching for someone.

"I know little of him, Your Grace." I answered, puzzled by this abrupt change.

"People speak of him constantly. They say he waits in Brittany gathering forces to return to England. Will he ever become king?" The cruel, unexpected squeeze she gave my wrist made me wince. "Don't pretend you can't tell me. Before we leave for London I'd have you give me an answer." Flicking a glance at her mother bent over her tapestry she smiled mischievously. "My husband plans a great progress in the north after the coronation—through York, Lincoln and Nottingham—"

I cried out so sharply she sprang away as if confronted by an evil spirit.

"What is it?" She crossed herself, her face bleached white.

"Nottingham." I shook with dread, aware of her mother and the other lady now on their feet, faces also blanched in shock. "Oh my lady, don't go to Nottingham."

"Why should I avoid Nottingham?"

The chamber door burst open.

"Your Grace—" A flushed Meg Huddleston trembled on the threshold. "A messenger from London desires to speak to you. He's waiting in the Hall. He says it's urgent."

Without another word the duchess swept from the room.

Conscious of the stares and fearing questions, I dropped a swift curtsy and slipped by a puzzled Meg, out into the corridor. Nottingham had summoned a great black cloud about the duchess.

I saw her standing on the battlements of the great castle, wind whipping her unbound hair across her face. She wept and cursed, her nails raking empty space. And the duke knelt, arms wrapped about her knees, his shoulders shaking with grief.

Leaning against my chamber door, I realised I still held the cloth-of-gold. Though I could never wear such costly fabric, the gift symbolised a talisman of the Gloucesters' favour. I clutched it to me like a shield.

Chapter Seventy-four

With the Gloucesters gone and Jane Collins no longer in the nursery, Emma grew disturbingly truculent. Anne Idley showed no interest in my presence but chastised the girl like an impatient abbess. Of Lady Anne's ladies, only Alice and Genevieve remained at Middleham—but there was no comfort in their company, for they either complained about their exclusion or giggled incessantly.

Whenever Dickon and the prince studied with their tutor I roamed the castle, restless and tormented. Since no one would speak of the old priest, it was time to solve the mystery. Knowing I wouldn't be missed, I pulled a cloak over my head and fled towards Jervaulx.

How grim and silent the monastery brooded in the early morning. Against an eerie, ochre skyline, the sepulchral buildings rebuked me for intrusion. I felt a stranger, unwelcome, lonely.

"Mistress Forrest?"

Recognizing the tiny figure of Brother Ignatius, I requested a meeting with the Abbot. "The matter's a private one," I said, eager to dispel any attempt at questions. "I'd be grateful if you'd take me to him."

The Abbot's house astounded me with its plain, sparse furnishings. Though clearly disturbed, he greeted me with perfunctory courtesy.

"An unexpected visit, Mistress Forrest," he said. He blinked like an owl caught in sunlight. "With poor Brother Brian dead these three months—" He crossed himself. "I can't think what brings you here." He gestured to a bench.

"That business with Stillington—"

A grimace distorted the florid features. He pressed a finger to his plump lips. "Some things are best kept silent."

For an instant I imagined I was back at Norwich and listening to Eleanor's sister.

"But because of me, Brother Brian was put to the torture." My voice wavered, stricken by memories of the kindly priest.

The Abbot squirmed. "No! no! I'm grieved such wicked rumours should've come to your ears." His eyes blinked furiously. "Brother Brian took a bad fall, nothing else. The shock of it was too great for one of his years."

The fleshy face assumed an expression of genuine distress, but I knew how cleverly these churchmen could dissemble. Stillington had promised Eleanor assistance once.

"But the fall didn't kill him?"

My question goaded, kindling a spark of pure terror in the myopic eyes.

"He was sick. He'd been ailing for some time, you understand. And Brother Silas was overwrought. His words were perhaps hasty, over-critical. Master Green was always so careful of the old ones."

"Master Green found Brother Brian?"

"Yes, yes—at the foot of the bell tower. He tried to save him."

The Abbot's face quivered, cheeks puce-coloured. Tiny beads of sweat pimpled his upper lip.

Coward! my mind shrieked, outraged by this weak deception. *You know Jack Green hastened the priest to his death.* Even Brother Silas finally saw through his sycophantic pupil. I rose at once. A pair of yellow eyes mocked me yet. Stillington had sealed the Abbot's lips. No one would tell me the truth now.

"Are you sure you're ready to return to Middleham? Would you take some refreshment?" The Abbot quivered by my elbow peering anxiously. I stood stony-faced, unreadable.

"The walk will clear my thoughts." I strode to the door before he could prevent me. Clenching my teeth, I forced my features into a bland smile. "Please don't trouble anyone. You've answered all my questions, Father. Thank you."

Outside in the sunlight, the high call of a hawk startled me. In the infirmary gardens the herbs bloomed green and lush. How long ago had I stood in this place, overjoyed to have found Brother Brian again? My throat ached with unshed tears. Through a blur, a young monk stepped from behind a yew hedge into my path. I recognised him instantly. The soft eyes with their viridian core had gazed up at me from out the scrying bowl.

"I'm Brother Jude. May I speak to you?"

"I think you've something for me." I laid a gentle hand upon his white sleeve.

"Let's walk together in the herb garden." His singular eyes darted a warning for Brother Ignatius lingered by the infirmary door. Jude drew me towards the well-loved plot and we surveyed the neat rows with their fragrant leaves and flowers like old friends who need no speech to understand each other. Vividly I recalled how Brother Brian strolled here and called me "daughter." Inhaling the scent of lavender became too poignant a memory. I wept.

"I like to think of Brother Brian tending the plants here before his last illness." Brother Jude's words, warm with compassion, soothed and comforted. He touched my arm. "I believe you know Master Green from Middleham?"

"Jack Green had something to do with this?" Controlling my tears, I gave my suspicions voice.

"He spent time in our infirmary learning from Brother Silas skills in herbal preparations." The unique eyes stared deep into my own. "The duke procured him a dispensation from the Abbot. Master Green flattered Silas with a thousand questions concerning the secrets of his pharmacopoeia. To me he seemed a slippery fellow, though his lies were plausible enough."

"I tried to warn Brother Brian about his treachery."

"The Book of Leviticus is very specific concerning the relationships between men." Jude's eyes now fixed upon some distant point, a delicate flush staining his cheeks. "Bishop Stillington was fond of quoting it. His visits made Brother Brian the object of much speculation. Ugly rumours about his past circulated. Some said he had unnatural relations with young men in his parish when he was a village priest. In the light of this the Abbot instructed him to spend his days in the infirmary. It was here he suddenly took ill."

My mind reeled with the memory of Alan Palmer's white face— the scene I'd unwittingly witnessed at St John's. "What do you mean?"

"He was poisoned."

"Poisoned!"

"He fell into deepest melancholy after Bishop Stillington's last visit. Because he wouldn't eat, Brother Silas insisted on preparing special possets for him. Three days before his death, I found him in the latrines wracked with belly-cramps, vomiting profusely. Brother Silas was frightened. He said the symptoms suggested the ingestion of aconite."

"Jack Green!"

"The poison didn't kill him," Jude said swiftly. "It was the fall. But what induced him to climb the bell tower? Our Abbot says these old ones are sometimes seized with strange fancies." He looked at me expectantly.

"My husband mentioned a novice named Edwin who spoke to Master Green—" I looked back in the same expectant manner.

The flush in Brother Jude's cheeks deepened. "Edwin's repented of his indiscretion. But whether Master Green had anything to do with Brother Brian's fall, I can't be certain." His voice cracked with emotion. "He helped us carry Brian to the infirmary. Brian's wrists snapped as he reached out to save himself and one of his legs was broken. Worst of all his face— twisted into a black agony like the image of Our Lord on the Cross. To me this suggested something more sinister than a stumble."

"Was he conscious?"

"Yes, and in great pain— though he made no complaint. Our Lord Abbot counselled silence. He says nothing must bring the abbey into disrepute."

"But Master Green hasn't been seen since." I clenched my jaw. Understanding hardened my words.

Jude glanced nervously toward the infirmary. "Since I read the contents of the journal I found hidden among Brian's manuscripts in the library, I've grown more and more convinced he was the victim of foul play." He fumbled in his sleeve. "I think you should have it."

Swiftly, I hid the vellum-wrapped bundle in the folds of my gown.

"I sat with Brian in his final hours." Jude plucked a sprig of rosemary. "He spoke of you many times." The extraordinary eyes brimmed with tears. "He craved your forgiveness for his cowardice. He loved you very much. No one could condemn such love. And I truly believe he was received into the kingdom of heaven at the last."

I touched his hand in gratitude, the lump of anguish in my throat preventing speech.

Out on the moors I loitered in the vast, green spaces, savouring the smell of meadow-sweet, thinking back to my childhood. How long ago it seemed Brother Brian first brought me to London and listened to my troubles. His tales of Ireland and his gifted brother enthralled me. Never once had he doubted the truth of my Sight. Hadn't he always told me I was chosen to save the Wydeville boys? Now this unfinished task called to me more strongly than ever. I couldn't let him down. Somehow I must find a way back to the city.

Chapter Seventy-five

Three nights I dreamed of climbing stairs to a great tower. Serpent-like, the steps coiled upwards. Torch-light cast huge shadowy figures across sweating walls. A tapering, dizzying spiral led finally to a turret chamber. Beyond its door grim terror lurked. Yet there could be no turning back. Each night the heavy door gaped a little wider and on the last blackness lured me to the very thresh-hold. I woke sweating and gasping as in my old dreams of drowning.

A heavy pounding at my chamber rent the last fragments of sleep. I blundered from my bed, groping for garments.

"News! News from London!" A strident male voice roused the castle. Urgent footsteps clattered along corridors and down steps.

Opening the shutters, I observed men with torches roaming among black pools of dark. Horses snorted. Aware at once that something astounding was about to take place, I grabbed a shawl and stepped out my door into pandemonium.

"Assemble in the great hall!"

A storm of sound swelled from below.

Somehow, standing upon the high table at the top of the great hall, John Kendall managed to make himself heard above the hubbub. "King Richard!" He cheered, raising his right arm in salute.

Stunned, the people hung together upon a breath until the import of this announcement exploded. Suddenly, the world turned upside down.

"King Richard!" echoed the crowd.

They took up the cry with increasing fervour, seizing each other in celebratory fashion, clasping hands, thumping shoulders,

443

embracing and whirling in an ecstasy of rejoicing. The noise grew thunderous.

"King Richard!" shrieked those outside the castle gates. Servants and waiting-women, grooms and knights, washer-women and men-at-arms passed the message. The stones echoed with cries of triumph and disbelief.

In the nursery, kneeling by the young prince's feet, I tried to explain the astonishing events that had raised him to high office, while all around servants bowed in homage.

"Will my father be king?" asked the baffled child.

"Yes, my lord." The hectic spots of colour in his cheeks alarmed me. I remembered Fat Marion calling such marks "grave flowers".

"Too many people." A foreign voice sang by my elbow. The Gloucesters' physician appeared as if from the air. He waved a slender, brown hand dismissively. "The prince must rest."

"I told you Master Green said Ned would be a king one day!" Dickon crowed. "Dada will come home now—but what will happen to Prince Edward and Prince Richard?"

What indeed? I hushed his innocent prattle. "I'm sure they'll be treated with great courtesy." The words rang hollow and unconvincing. The euphoria of the duke's rise to greatness melted away. A vague memory of Jane Collins' tale of the murdered Desmond boys pecked at my brain.

"Genevieve, will you look after Dickon? I'm going to see if Master Metcalf's home. Tell Mistress Idley I won't be long."

"Of course." She smirked at Alice.

"What is it?" I snapped, irritated by their sly, covert looks.

"Oh Nan, don't you know what people are saying?" Genevieve giggled. "You tell her, Alice—"

"For goodness sake—" I wanted to slap her silly, pretty face.

"It's Master Metcalf," said Alice shame-faced. "Everyone says he's devoted to you and—" Her blush deepened. She pinched Genevieve, turning her gurgles of poorly suppressed laughter to squeals.

I snorted with exasperation, pushing my way out of the chamber, weaving through the knots of gossiping women jostling by the castle doors like pigeons searching for scattered grain. I ran all the way to plump Elizabeth's door in Castle Street.

"Come in, come in." She looked as if she expected me. "Miles is here."

My heart skipped a beat, but it was her brother-in-law, Miles Metcalf, who stood before the hearth.

"Forgive me for intruding." Embarrassed, I turned to Elizabeth. "I didn't know you had company."

The table stood ready for a meal. The rich smell of roasting meat churned my stomach. I'd not broken my fast since supper the previous day. "The news from London's addled my brain. I thought Rob might be here."

"Sit down, sit down." She waved podgy hands towards the settle. "Polly, fetch Mistress Forrest some wine."

"No, no, I won't disturb your meal—"

"Disturb nothing—Haven't we all been disturbed today? You must stay and dine. Rob told us of some shocking sermon a Ralph Shaw preached at Paul's Cross. I couldn't make head nor tail of it, but it seems it caused our Duke to take the crown. I still can't believe it but Miles knows more." She ushered me to a seat, chattering like a magpie until the meal was served.

"Will you try some of this eel pasty? It's our Martha's receipt."

A servant lad thrust food before me.

"Our cousin James of Nappa Hall said Shaw's sermon caused uproar." Miles Metcalf fastidiously cut his meat into small pieces with an ornate silver dagger. "It insulted the dowager Duchess of York by suggesting the late king was a bastard." He paused to chew a morsel of veal and stab at a dish of roast turnips.

"I think everyone's heard that tale." I toyed with my pasty, thinking of Jack Green's sly insinuations.

"But Stillington finally changed the succession." Miles Metcalf set down his knife to look me in the eye.

"Stillington!" I dropped my own knife with such a clatter Elizabeth Metcalf slopped wine on the table and began to choke. "What's he to do with it?"

"King Edward's fancy for the ladies is no secret." Metcalf, glanced anxiously at his sister-in-law mopping her eyes on her amber–coloured sleeve and making rasping sounds in her throat. He waited until she recovered her breath.

"Go on, go on," she said in a croak, her face reddened.

"It seems Stillington witnessed a marriage contract between the late king and Eleanor Butler, old Talbot's daughter."

"But that's impossible! Stillington was never there. I was a waiting-woman in Dame Eleanor's household." I spoke out heedless of the consequences, unable to believe the bishop dared to circulate this lie. "The king came to call on her about her estates. If any one could tell of a marriage between them it would be Brother Thomas, the chaplain, but he disappeared mysteriously on the day we set out for Norwich. I'm sure Bishop Stillington had him murdered."

Transfixed, both Metcalfs stared at me.

"You were at Norwich with Eleanor Butler?" Miles Metcalf's eyes glared gimlet-sharp.

I nodded, conscious of my racing heart-beat and dry mouth. I swallowed a hasty sip of wine. "Stillington had Dame Eleanor kept there. He would have kept me there too. He was desperate to conceal whatever relationship she may have had with the king."

The Metcalfs leaned toward me, greedy as hounds scenting prey. I tried to gather my wits.

"If Stillington knew of a marriage between Dame Eleanor and the king, why didn't he speak out before?" I asked, daringly.

Miles Metcalf leaned upon his elbow, his fingers stroking his fleshy lips as if reflecting upon my words. "Indeed," he said almost to himself.

"But if Bishop Stillington had spoken out before, perhaps Duke Clarence would have been king?" Mistress Metcalf looked puzzled.

"Elizabeth!" Her brother-in-law awarded her an ugly, sardonic grin. "You're right! Stillington's always been a master of intrigue. Remember how he nurtured Clarence's friendship until that foolish gentleman was put to silence? Aye, and endured a brief imprisonment himself for incurring the late king's displeasure—" He leaned toward me once more, a spark in his eye. "It looks as if Stillington's been biding his time to speak out. No doubt there are others who've similar secrets to reveal."

"Stillington wanted me to say I'd witnessed the betrothal between Dame Eleanor and King Edward. He had me taken to Pontefract for questioning."

Elizabeth spluttered something, but I fixed my gaze on the congealed mess on my trencher.

"And did you?" asked Miles Metcalf.

I took a breath before lifting my head to stare him full in the face.

"It doesn't matter what I said then or what I say today," I answered boldly. "My Lord of Gloucester's the king now."

Chapter Seventy-Six

If I'd been a man, I'd have ridden off to London to find Miles that night. The Metcalfs battered me with questions until I thought my head would burst. Though I warded them off with pretended ignorance, they weren't easily placated.

Back at the castle, filled with unease black and sinister as a storm-cloud, I wondered what Miles would say. In a fury of impotence I tried the scrying-bowl but the images blurred. Two children pressed their white faces against high windows as if to catch a glimpse of the world; a lean-faced, muttering physician wielded a pestle and mortar; and a giant of a man with shaggy black hair gnawed on a bone, wiping grease from his beard with a hand like a beast's paw. None of this made any sense except to remind me of the Wydeville boys and the danger they faced.

Had Elizabeth Wydeville taken steps to ensure their safety? Surely she couldn't have forgotten my warning?

With shaking hands, I laid out the cards. The Fool capered blindly, the Tower fell, the World hung topsy-turvy and the Knave of Swords turned upon his head as if taunting me. These inauspicious auguries further aggravated my forebodings. Taking up Brother Brian's journal, I began to read:

"When I dream, I dream of Ireland, of the rich smell of the black, crumbling soil, of the pungent smell of wood-smoke, of haunted glens and gloomy crags, of ancient mountains shrouded in clinging mists, of moss under my feet, dew-spangled leaves at day-break and soft feathers of rain upon my face. And I wake with such an ache in my throat and such emptiness in my heart that no amount of prayer can assuage."

My own throat ached with unshed tears. I remembered the priest telling me about his beloved homeland. How young and ignorant I'd been then, and how both of us had been shaped by exile and fear. The enigmatic entries concerning someone named Michael filled me with melancholy. The priest's affection for Alan Palmer drove him to solitude in Yorkshire, just as it seemed his earlier love for this Michael sent him from Ireland to be our priest. Mistress Evans's prophecy promised love and laughter for me, but I wished I'd shown more kindness to the priest. His care had lightened my burdens. Only torture forced him to betray me, and hadn't I revealed a similar cowardice when threatened by the sinister Raymond with the heated pincers? What would Brother Brian tell me to do now?

About dawn, my head throbbing with frustration, I drifted into a heavy sleep and dreamed Miles had come home. He smiled as I rushed to greet him, enfolding me in his arms. "I've so much to tell you," I said, but he pressed his hand over my mouth and nose until the roaring in my ears burst into a velvet bloom of darkness.

⁓

In Castle Street that afternoon I found Elizabeth Metcalf standing by her door.

"How many more men are needed for this coronation?" She pointed to the long lines of horsemen trotting down the road, the bright sunlight glinting off polished armour, sword and spur, vivid painted shield, jauntily caparisoned horse and fluttering pennant. All wore Gloucester's device of the white boar. Behind them came the rowdy foot-soldiers, the trundling supply-wagons, and the familiar draggle of bold-faced wenches that accompanies every army.

"I suppose it'll be a very grand affair."

She snorted so hard her heavy jowls shook. "Aye, but in whose honour? Our Rob says London's heaving with folk. Men will do owt for honour—even sail off the edge of the world if need be! Our noble duke, or should I say, the king, seems to think he can win folk's favour with costly banquets. But he's quick to silence any who speak against him. Even friends aren't safe."

I knew she meant William Hastings who'd been executed without even the formality of a trial. This news roused outrage at Middleham, where he'd been a favourite, and made me think of Joan laughing at his audacious flirting with Flemish Gerta in

Silver Street. For all his faults, Hastings' loyalty to York remained steadfast.

"What did Hastings do to merit such treatment? Why does our new king mistrust so many of his courtiers?"

Elizabeth shrugged. "Rob says there's been no end of trouble in the city." She drew me inside the door as if she feared eavesdroppers. "He told me the queen's eldest son by her first marriage escaped from the Sanctuary and was hunted through the streets by soldiers with dogs like an animal. And did tha know her youngest was hanged at Pontefract?"

"What!"

"Aye, they kept that quiet, didn't they?" Elizabeth's expression unnerved me. "Rob's always admired the duke, but all this plotting and killing—it doesn't seem right to me. I don't suppose thou's heard owt from Master Forrest?"

I shook my head.

"Aye, well that's men."

"But Lady Anne sends regular messages. She sent me a length of beautiful azure cloth for watching over the prince."

"Aye, she would. No one can accuse the Gloucesters of parsimony."

I thought then of Lady Anne lodging at Crosby Place, a sumptuous house in Bishopgate said to be the highest dwelling in London. How I wished I could be with her. Elizabeth's news offered no reassurance. Who was protecting those Wydeville boys now?

"Will tha take some refreshment?" Sensing my hesitation, she laughed. "No harm can come to the lad while he's with his tutor. Rob's out upon some errand but I expect him back at any moment. Come and see the arras Tom sent from London."

"A few minutes." I allowed her to lead me inside. "I've some shoes to collect—"

I admired the tapestry with its prancing hunting dogs and slender ladies riding jennets festooned with ribbons and silver baubles. Enthusiastically, she regaled me with the tale of its purchase.

"How's the little Gloucester prince?"

"He's the sweetest-natured child I've ever met. But I wish he'd grow robust like my Dickon. In spite of all the exercise they take together, he's frail as a kitten."

"His father was much the same as a child and both Neville girls were delicate."

"But as for scholarship I can't fault him. Master Bernall's forever singing his praises. It's a pity he doesn't say the same about Dickon."

We laughed together then, for when Lord Ned's tutor agreed to include Dickon in lessons, I encouraged him to learn to read and write. But Dickon showed little aptitude. Instead he proved wilful and inattentive, demonstrating how much he preferred to be outside riding upon the moors or shooting at the butts than pouring over books.

"They can't all be scholars." Elizabeth Metcalf chuckled. "But it's astonishing to think that yon frail lad is all the Gloucesters have when the Nevilles were once the most powerful family in the country. Why, old Ralph Neville had three and twenty children." She paused, shaking her head as if troubled by her thoughts. "But times change." She sank down upon one of the luxurious cushions. "Other families have waxed strong in their stead. Think of the Wydevilles. That witch, Jacquetta spawned sixteen children and her daughter's borne ten to the late king, God rest his soul." She gave me a sharp look. "Tell me, honestly what does tha make of that Wydeville marriage?"

The mere mention of the word witch made my heart jump. I grew even more uncomfortable under Elizabeth Metcalf's scrutiny. For all her gossiping, she possessed a shrewd brain.

"You mean that the king was bewitched?" I made an attempt at carelessness.

"Don't be so dismissive of the tale, for they were wed upon May morning—and in secrecy. The king spent the previous night under their roof. Everyone knows the last day of April is the great witches' Sabbath. What enchantments might have been practised upon him to bind him to their will?"

"It's just an old tale." I swallowed hard for Elizabeth Metcalf's face thrust close to mine and I caught the light of fanaticism in her eyes.

"I thought tha'd have something more to say about it than that," she said, disappointed. "Didn't tha have some dealings with witchcraft yourself? Wasn't there that nasty business with Stillington—"

"I was interrogated about a woman I knew, that's all." I pressed my nails into my palms. Would these accusations of witchcraft never end? The memory of Nerys and her fiery death still haunted me. "She was accused of witchcraft at Middleham's May Fair. Her mother was the local wise-woman in my village."

Elizabeth Metcalf leaned back as if considering this unlikely excuse. "Someone mentioned tha'd some fortune-telling cards." Her easy remark made me flinch.

"I used them to amuse my women friends but it was just a game. I told Bishop Stillington. In any case, I burned them a long time ago." What an adept liar I'd become.

"That's a pity. We might have used them to see what mischief's working in the kingdom." I wasn't sure whether she was serious. Her heavy face looked grave but a slight upward tilt to her mouth suggested amusement.

Rob's noisy arrival interrupted. Discovering me with his mother, his face lit up and I flushed at the memory of Genevieve's giggles.

"I've been looking for thee, Mistress Forrest. That sour-faced nursery wench, Widow Idley, told me thou'd gone to the shoemaker's." He handed me a bag heavy with coins, grinning at my amazement. "Master Forrest told me to give thee that. Aye, it's a goodly sum. He said to be sure and tell thee to get a fine gown made and buy something for the lad. Since his appointment as attendant to the late king's bastard, he's received an increase in his wages."

Something in my silence halted him. The cheerful grin faded. "I suppose thou art disappointed he can't come home?"

"Attendant to the prince?"

"No longer officially styled a prince but still treated with the courtesy due to base-born sons of kings." He chewed a ragged nail.

"Where are the Wydeville boys?"

"Lord Edward's still in the Tower but kept in all comfort. Besides Master Forrest, he's several servants and a physician. The other lad's with his mother in the Sanctuary. But there's plans to bring him to his brother so they—"

I didn't hear the rest. I fainted.

"This heat's terrible." Elizabeth pressed a damp cloth to my brow. "Rob's thoughtless delivering news so suddenly. When all this pother's over Master Forrest'll surely be recalled to Middleham."

Her words washed over me.

How many times had I warned Miles about his loyalty to Gloucester? Why had Gloucester chosen Miles for so great an office? The money bag lay heavy in my lap. What price would the new king exact for such a royal payment?

Chapter Seventy-Seven

Richard of Gloucester was crowned with all honour on the sixth day of July. Details of this magnificent event dribbled back to Middleham all through that hot, whirlwind summer. Rumour and gossip set us spinning like hapless dust motes. The snatching of the crown kindled such passion among the people of the north, it seemed as if a great torch had been lit and its sparks carried throughout the county.

"Did tha know the coronation banquet lasted more than five hours?" Elizabeth Metcalf revelled in telling tales she'd had from Rob. "Imagine, our little Lady Anne's queen now—I can hardly believe it." She leaned back on her settle, florid face lit by a satisfied smile. "She wore ells and ells of purple velvet for her crowning and the king wore an embroidered cloak of purple cloth-of-gold and ermine so long Harry Buckingham had to carry it. Eh, I'd have given anything to see that."

"It's a pity we weren't invited." I feigned a mischievous smile. "But we're much too important to fritter away our time at such grand occasions."

Elizabeth laughed. "Well, some have profited already. Francis Lovell and Rob Percy have been made king's officers—There'll be some envious southern faces at court now."

"Perhaps some of the king's favourite northern henchmen will win new honours too," I answered. "Maybe one will bear the name of Metcalf."

"Well, as our Rob says, the Metcalfs have allus been loyal to Richard of Gloucester. Sometimes I wish tha and he—" She sighed. "The king mun think very highly of Master Forrest to appoint him attendant to the Wydeville lad—"

Elizabeth's easy flattery awakened my anxiety.

453

"Imagine how the prince felt when he learned he couldn't be king," I said. My mind filled with a cruel image of his uncle parading through London's streets in his stolen crown.

"Aye, a terrible shock, that were. I thought there'd be trouble amongst the barons, but no one seems to have done owt on his behalf—" Elizabeth shuffled uncomfortably, shifting her great haunches on the cushions. "Still there's going to be a great northern progress."

"They're already preparing at the castle," I answered. "They've taken the hangings down for beating, the laundresses are washing all the linen, floors are being scrubbed, chambers swept, and every utensil in the kitchen's being scoured. It's all noise and bustle—I was glad to sneak away for an hour. But it'll be days before the king's here."

"Well if it's like that at Middleham now, imagine how it'll be in York." Elizabeth's eyes gleamed. "The Gloucesters have allus been popular there and everyone'll be out to get a look at them. There'll be pageants and musicians and all kinds of entertainments. Eh, it'll be a grand event, Nan, and I've no doubt tha'll be decking little Prince Ned out in his finery for it."

"I hope he's strong enough."

How helpless and alone I felt at the castle that season. Rumour and speculation spun around me in a tightening wad. The hard, envious glances and the spiteful whispers among the servants reminded me of my lowly status. Fear ignited like a bonfire, the greedy flames running toward me, driving away those I'd once trusted.

Emma kept strangely silent, quite unlike the artless maid who'd frolicked at the May-Day market. Something in this new behaviour roused my pity. Jack Green's flirtation had deeply wounded her, but when I mentioned him, she shied away like a nervous horse.

"I can't believe Mistress Collins spoke so highly of that wench." Anne Idley sniffed. "She's forever sneaking off on one mysterious errand after another. And if I scold her, she sulks. If the children weren't so fond of her, I'd ask her Grace to dismiss the petulant jade."

Perhaps I should have listened more carefully to Mistress Idley. Foolishly, I assumed Jack Green's desertion responsible for her ill humour. It proved a careless oversight.

Moonyeen Blakey

oʃo

Little Ned of Middleham, fevered by the news that had raised him to sudden greatness, succumbed to increasing bouts of sickness. Twice he fainted at Mass, sparking a delirium of anxiety and speculation. Vinegar-faced Anne Idley summoned the physician and the bronze-featured scholar in the flowing robes sent for me.

"The child chooses you." His vibrant, foreign voice swooped melodiously. "Let Nan sit by my bed—Nan brings me happy dreams. It is an excellent medicine."

His words brought tears to my eyes.

Without complaint, the child drank my tisanes in the firm belief they would restore his strength. Moved by his courage, the other ladies came frequently to the nursery bringing toys or dainties. But nothing could still the memory of Durga's warning. Never had Lord Ned seemed so precious.

My nightly vigil by his bed brought me little comfort. I dozed and drowsed, paced the chamber restlessly in the fevered dark, rose at dawn with a pounding head and eyes filled with splinters until exhaustion plunged me headfirst into a drowning impious dream.

Stairs snaked upward, pooled in shadow between each distant, guttering flambeau, the stone treads worn thin and smooth by long usage.

Clutching cloth-wrapped bundles, two boys in blue velvet doublets climbed reluctantly, their pallid features terrified.

"Why are we being moved?" The smaller one winced at the hollow echo. He shrank from the grim walls absent of tapestry. "Won't we be allowed to see the coronation?"

"Your uncle desires your safety." The unseen attendant's tone snarled with contempt.

A weighty door juddered. A lozenge of light streaked across a stone-flagged floor. An elusive scent of river water permeated a bleak chamber. The younger boy entered first, clambering nimbly up on to the ledge to peer through the narrow window down into a courtyard. Wrinkling his nose with distaste, he turned. "Why do we have to stay so far away from everyone?"

"Your new status requires protection of a different kind." The surly attendant made no attempt at courtesy. The boy flinched.

"But we are still a king's sons." The elder lad's remark betrayed a trace of hauteur, though he drooped exhausted on the great tester bed.

"And will be treated accordingly."

"Shan't we even see our uncle?" Unabashed by the hard voice, the boorish words, the younger boy spoke from his lofty perch.

"No need. Servants have been appointed."

"But—"

The door slammed. A key grated in the lock.

"We're prisoners!" The elder lad cried out after the retreating footsteps, despair wailing behind his words.

"No, our mother will send for us, Ned," A thin shaft of sunlight illuminated the red-gold hair, the bright intelligent face. *"They can't—"*

With a sinister thud, a ragged, black form fell on to the outside ledge. Fluttering stiff, rackety wing-feathers, it dropped an ugly gobbet of raw meat. A single eye gleaming dark malevolence inspected the young prisoners. Honing its wicked beak against the bars, the bird gloated at their discomfort. Sentry-wise, it strutted to and fro, opening its maw to emit a jubilant squawk. The jarring sound drove the boys together. Huddled on the bed they watched a thin streamer of blood curl down the inner wall.

"They mean to murder us," whispered the elder. *"Just like Lord Hastings—"*

"Mistress Forrest!" Anne Idley shook me awake. Her sharp, bird profile pecked at me in the grey dawn. "It's time to prepare the prince for his journey."

Stiff and bruised from sleeping on a hard bench, I rubbed my eyes, heaved the stifling blanket of the dream away.

"He'll never ride," I said. "He's too weak for such a journey."

"Master Metcalf's arranged for him to be carried in a chariot. His parents will meet him at Pontefract." She seemed all ice and hard edges—no sympathy in voice or eye. When the physician told me I should travel with the child, a weight lifted from me. At least he'd have someone he trusted.

Now styled Prince Edward of Middleham, he managed to walk through the streets of York with his parents, acquitting himself with such dignity and charm the sweating populace clamoured at every street corner to catch a glimpse of the tiny child in his heavy jewel-encrusted robes and crown. They little guessed what this ordeal cost his strength, though he smiled and nodded, his heart-shaped face and luminous eyes winning universal praise.

I watched this brave performance through a blur of tears. The child's spirit burned strong, but no one could hush the insidious whispers:

"Was there ever so delicate a boy?"

"Why are all the Neville children sickly?"

"How is it the Wydevilles breed like conies?"

"And where are King Edward's clever, handsome lads? What will become of them now?"

⌘

Back in the safety of Middleham we wrapped the frail boy against the early September storms whining across the moorland, cosseted him with warm, honey-flavoured wine, tempted his feeble appetite with morsels of venison dipped in rich gravy, soothed his restless sleep with gentle music. No prince earned more care or merited more affection.

The queen, briefly in residence at the castle before rejoining her husband's punishing northern progress, urged me to extra vigilance.

"My sister's son, Edward, must be dispatched to Sheriff Hutton at once," she said. Her tapping fingers betrayed urgency. "The king desires him to be trained in all the knightly accomplishments and has appointed his cousin John, Earl of Lincoln, to oversee this instruction."

Little Edward of Warwick, Clarence's ten-year old son, had been but newly placed at Middleham. He relished the lively companionship of the other children in the household. It grieved me to see him uprooted so soon.

"These boys are too boisterous for Ned," snapped the queen. Her green gaze confronted me with incredulity. "You, of all people, know the Prince of Wales must rest."

She plucked my sleeve, urging me away from the others. Close up, I noted the sheen of sweat on her brow, carved angles of her cheek-bones, haunted gleam in her eyes. She held herself taut as a bowstring. I sensed the scream quivering deep within, held back only by sheer strength of will. Never did I admire her more.

"Your Grace should rest too," I said.

Her hopeful smile cut me to the quick. "Time enough to rest when my Ned is safe and well. I have the crown you promised, Nan, and now you must save my son. You'll be well rewarded for it. Let your Dickon accompany young Warwick to Sheriff Hutton. He'll profit by such noble training and provide my poor orphaned nephew with a merry friend to cheer his days."

Though loath to part with my boy, I recognised the wisdom of this act. Besides, Miles would swell with pride at the generous opportunity it afforded. So I thanked the queen and checked my tears. Reassured by Emma's request to attend upon the two boys in their new home, I said a tremulous farewell to Dickon.

"It'll be only a temporary separation," I said, kissing his brow. "And Sheriff Hutton's just a step from Middleham. When Ned's well again I'm sure he'll send for you."

He hugged me close, hiding the tremble of his lip in my skirts, for Master Metcalf waited with the horses.

"Will he be well soon, Mama?"

How could I answer such a question except with hopeful prayers?

A frisson of fear shook me as I watched the little riders disappear under the archway and out through the gate. The pearl grey sky seemed strangely threatening and birds on ragged, black wings circled the castle.

⁂

A bleak Christmas-tide beckoned.

The king and queen remained in Westminster. Old Walt grumbled at the expense of lavish entertainments presented to impress royal guests, but he drank the cheer willingly enough at the Middleham feast joining the revels with familiar, grudging enthusiasm. As always the cooks served us with a variety of sumptuous courses, and minstrels, jugglers and dancers celebrated the season.

"All this to amuse a sickly lad." He growled, gesturing at the dwarfish tumblers in their exotic costumes. But he guffawed along with the rest at the Gloucesters' little fool, Martyn, capering for the prince's particular pleasure.

Fuelled by my reading out a letter I had of Dickon from Sheriff Hutton, Prince Edward spoke of riding on the moors in spring. It was a brief, formal thing, evidently guided by a careful tutor's hand but especially precious to me. It told me something of his training but best of all, his evident longing to return to Middleham —"I would I might spend the Christmas feast with you, my mother, and watch the revels with my dear friend, Ned." I think this last line pleased the prince most.

Chapter Seventy-Eight

"Mistress Idley said I might help in the nursery while Emma's at Sheriff Hutton." Amy Sadler smiled up at me from folding blankets when I entered the nursery one gloomy January morning. Her smug expression immediately aroused my animosity.

"Well, I daresay you'll supply us with plenty of gossip to while away these dark days." I returned her smile with forced cheer.

She sidled up to me. Looking from under her eyelashes, she spoke in a timid, breathy voice. "I'm so sorry about that affair with Bishop Stillington—I've wanted to talk to you about it—I never meant to—"

"No need." I cut her short. "It was foolish mistake, that's all. Besides, it was a long time ago."

"Master Forrest was distraught," she said with exaggerated sympathy. "We were so anxious for him. It's a shame he can't be here this Christmas, isn't it?"

"Master Forrest's duties are too important for him to leave London." I pretended interest in the pile of garments in the press so she couldn't see my face.

"I hear there's been ever so much trouble in the city." Her eyes stared round with horror. "The king's hanging all traitors now."

"Kings have to be careful." I thought back to the Duke of Buckingham's unexpected rebellion in October.

According to Elizabeth Metcalf, Buckingham mysteriously aligned himself with the Countess of Richmond's son, Henry Tudor. "And after the king heaped him with honours at the coronation! Some gratitude, eh?"

461

"Who is this Henry Tudor?" I asked old Walt at supper that night.

"His grandmother were old King Henry's French mother." Walt sneered at the assembled company in the Hall. "She let a butler named Owen Tudor warm her bed after she were widowed —and in the warming of it he got some children on her."

While the men at the table guffawed along with him, I thought myself back in Silver Street listening to Lionel telling the ghostly tale of Owen Tudor's execution.

"This Tudor," Walt gave me a surly glance, "thinks hissen part of the old nobility. His mother's a Beaufort and thinks herself summat of a scholar." He made a derisory noise which amused the menfolk.

"Aye, the Tudor's one to watch," he said, with a face like doom. "They say our Dick laughed when he heard the Tudor means to snatch the throne. But I wonder if he's still laughing now? Tudor swore an oath in some French cathedral on Christmas morning— to marry King Edward's eldest daughter when he's crowned King of England."

How strange, I thought, *if fate should choose a half-nephew of mad King Harry to undo the House of York.*

Talk turned then to the fate of the Wydeville boys.

"Those lads have been moved." Walt growled his disapproval. "To the Garden Tower or the White Tower or some such place—"

"I heard they'd been sent away from London," said Genevieve. She yawned behind her sleeve. "Some say they're gone to Flanders—"

"Who told you that?"

The conversation throbbed with speculation.

"They've not been seen since summer—"

Unnerved, I left the revels. The prince had fallen asleep and I asked Master Snowden to carry him to his bed-chamber. I didn't want him to hear such ugly talk. Since his father seized the crown too many disturbing tales festered and erupted like poisoned wounds.

Sitting with the cards in my lap that night, I prayed Miles watched over the Wydeville boys with all the care he might have lavished on Dickon. But the Hanged Man gazed up at me, his enigmatic face inscrutable.

❦

Storms and skirmishes at sea kept the proposed Tudor invasion at bay. While the king wooed his wavering countrymen with promises of peace and justice, we crouched at Middleham, buffeted by bitter weather.

In March, when the first green flags of spring began to flutter, I arranged to ride over to Sheriff Hutton with Rob Metcalf. Just about to climb into the saddle, I turned to see Mistress Idley running across the yard waving her arms.

"The prince is sick." Panting from her exertions, she dragged me away. "He's asking for you."

"Tell Dickon what's happened," I called to Rob.

My black woollen cloak streaming behind me, I followed at Anne Idley's heels, listening to her gasp out the sudden, shocking change in Ned's condition.

"He vomited blood and afterward he fainted. Now he speaks nothing but nonsense—though he called for you. Antoinette's gone for the physician—"

All day I watched by the child's bed. Around dusk, Rob brought me a message.

"Dickon were disappointed not to see thee," he said. He kept his voice low to avoid waking the prince. "But he sends affectionate greetings. I'll swear he's grown nigh as tall as the Warwick lad. He told me that young wench, Emma, disappeared a week or so ago, and no one's seen her since."

❦

The crisis came in April.

I'd watched by Lord Ned before, but this sickness was different. The child writhed and squirmed alarmingly throughout the warm spring night as if something gnawed at his vitals.

"Surely no child deserves such agony." Antoinette, the replacement nursery-maid, wiped beads of sweat from the white, elfin face.

Frightened, Anne Idley sent Roger Claxon for the physician.

"How long?" The foreign voice murmured soothingly. The dark, aquiline features inspired confidence.

"Since yesterday. He complained of stomach cramps and a headache. He fainted after dinner time. We put him to bed and I gave him some of the poppy juice. At daylight he began to vomit so copiously—"

The physician took the bowl and peered at the contents. His bronze face remained bland, enigmatic as a mask, but in the black eyes swam a grim resignation.

"I tried to get him to drink some wine this morning." Head inclined, the physician held the boy's slender wrist as if listening. "But he took little more than a sip. He asked if he might see his parents."

The poignancy of the request grieved me beyond measure.

Silently, the physician drew back the sheet and examined the enfeebled little body with a tenderness that made my throat ache. The child opened his beautiful aquamarine eyes, wincing under the gentle press of the exploring fingers.

"Is it hurting here, my lord?" The physician leaned close.

Lord Ned nodded, pressing his lips together. He was not a child given to complaining. Doubtless he'd been taught princes must bear all with fortitude.

"I am preparing a draught." The physician looked grave. "It is wise to send a messenger."

"It'll take days to reach them." Anne Idley's voice shook with fear. Bleakly, I recalled how I'd begged Lady Anne not to go to Nottingham.

"Then we must pray," replied the foreign voice. "There is much inflammation in the belly. Tell me now what he is eating since before yesterday."

Around noon the child became delirious, his wasted frame shaking violently. There followed more vomiting and purging. Antoinette, holding the basin and towel, regarded me with mute horror. Other servants began to arrive with pitiful excuses, anxious to be close to their little prince, adding their frantic, silent prayers for his recovery. The physician moved purposefully about the crowded chamber, his pale, swirling robes like shimmering clouds. Even Anne Idley hadn't the heart to chase the watchers away.

As morning crawled toward afternoon, sunlight gave way to rain. At last, Lord Ned raised himself upon one elbow and requested something to drink. He scarce moistened his mouth, but turned his eyes upon me with a piteous expression.

"I'd like—"

"What would you like, my love?" I bent to catch his words.

"I'd like to go and play with the children."

The yearning in the request made me catch my breath. Did he ask for Dickon? What children could he mean? "They have such a beautiful pony," he whispered. "I'd so like to ride it. Must I wait for my father's permission?"

Glancing at Antoinette, I saw the mute question in her lifted eye-brows. Someone pressed my hand. The physician sighed audibly. In my head I glimpsed the settling of a great carrion bird upon a battlement.

"May I go to the children? They're waiting for me."

"Why then," I said, without hesitation, "you must go to them."

Lord Ned gave me a brilliant, heart-breaking smile, closed his eyes, and died.

For a moment the room remained quite still. Time stopped. Then a shaft of sunlight like a long, sharp spear pierced the chamber. Gently I kissed the cooling forehead. Antoinette, recognizing the finality of this gesture, dropped the basin and fell to her knees, sobbing. One by one the anguished servants followed suit, crossing themselves, murmuring, weeping.

Dry-eyed, I moved to the casement, warm sunlight bathing my shoulders and face. I looked out beyond the castle to where the trees stood in their spring greenery spangled with raindrops. On the grass lay scattered blossoms like pale stars. A blackbird sang. Mara's words returned to me as out of far distance. The rosebud of York was dead. He would never fulfil the promise of his childhood; he would never wear a king's crown. My mind beat blindly at the injustice of it, but as the sun's rays flooded the landscape I remembered the two little Wydeville boys and my duty to them. Only then did I allow my tears to fall.

Chapter Seventy-Nine

"Prince Edward's to be buried at Sheriff Hutton." A grieving Anne Idley melted sufficiently to permit me to ride over with the group of attendants assigned to make preparations. Desperate to see Dickon, I punished my sturdy pony. I knew Ned's loss would break his heart.

A manservant directed me to the little chamber where Master Newton taught his pupils. Pressing my ear against the stout wooden door, I listened to the tutor's steady drone. When he paused, I tapped and entered.

The elderly man in the dusty black gown glanced up kindly. "Is there something you require, Mistress?"

"I'm Johann Forrest. I've come for my son, Dickon." I stared at the sea of alert young faces. Edward of Warwick smiled shyly. There was no sign of Dickon.

"But Mistress Emma collected him." Master Newton scratched his silver fuzz of hair, wayward brows raised in surprise.

"Emma?"

"Aye, the serving-maid from Middleham—Not long after the prince's death. She said she'd had instructions from you."

Boys began to mutter.

"But Emma's not been at Middleham since she came here with the boys last year." I shrieked, struck by a sudden, frightening possibility. "Sweet Jesu! Where's she taken my boy?"

The buzz of conversation grew louder. Someone dropped a book. Master Newton must have called for help for the room filled with people.

We searched the castle from top to bottom. Rob Metcalf arrived along with a dozen men or more. They scoured the barns and out-houses. Finding nothing, the search continued out into the town, leaving Master Newton and me to question the only servant who'd seen Emma and Dickon on the stairs.

"I thought nowt of it. I passed them on the stairs. I were taking summat to Master Skelton—aye, he wanted some twine—The lass smiled at me and the lad seemed happy enough. I never thought nowt was wrong—until—"

Frantic, I wept and raged. As the day darkened, they tell me I tore at my hair, screaming like a demented creature. I've no memory of these actions. Someone summoned a physician who prepared a sleeping draught. At first I wouldn't hear of it. When Rob returned and promised they'd begin searching again at first light, I grew hysterical.

"Without sleep tha'll never be able to look for him, Mistress Forrest," he said. His kindly face looked grey with fatigue. He held a goblet while I drank. The smell of the poppy infusion brought Lord Ned's face bright into my inner vision.

Someone must have carried me to a bed-chamber. I remembered nothing more until I woke at dawn.

Muddled by the effects of the draughts the physician gave me, I staggered through the following day—acquiescent, obedient, bewildered, while a search party explored everywhere between Sheriff Hutton and Middleham. Every scrap of gossip, every thread and fibre of a sighting was investigated. At night, sleep overwhelmed me like an enormous wave, carrying me through endless corridors and stairways where I wandered lost as in a maze. But no word of Dickon came.

Rob Metcalf swore he'd not give up the search. "Mother insists the wench has run off with Jack Green," he said.

At my bidding, he sent messages to London taking the news to Miles and a letter for Harry, though how I wrote it remains a puzzle. If Emma took Dickon to the city, I reasoned, Harry would surely discover him.

Wrapped in a long, hooded cloak like a felon, I rode out at last with stalwart Rob Metcalf toward London. No one dared to dissuade me.

Clear-headed now under the moonlight, I leaned over my mount's neck, watching his flying hooves eat up the miles, certain I would shortly find Dickon, discover Miles's whereabouts and rescue the Wydeville boys at last. The foolish simplicity of my faith kept me from madness.

"Your cousin Harry's made a hundred or more enquiries about Dickon." Rob tried to reassure me. "He spoke most confidently of a woman, he says, you know— a Maud Attemore. He says if anyone can find your boy, she can."

"I've no doubt of it." I answered through gritted teeth.

"And he says he can get you into the Tower, for he regularly delivers bread there. But there's no reply from Master Forrest."

I wouldn't meet the question in his eyes as he delivered this last part of his message. I didn't want to admit, even to myself, that Miles's silence boded ill. But the import of it festered and my dreams grew horrifying.

Trembling, I bent over the scrying bowl. Outside, the mournful winter wind whined like a hungry beggar, battering peevishly against the shutters. Lights swirled and colours tumbled, spinning the images into focus. A scroll lay unravelled across a table, the black script indecipherable. In the cresset a candle burned with a scarlet flame. Miles sat with his head in his hands, as if in grief or drunkenness. A great rooting boar encircled him. I knew then he was the king's thrall. And when the bowl began to fill with blood, I turned my eyes away.

At every inn along the London road we listened avidly to gossip. Intrigue and unrest simmered beneath cheerful banter. Under the shafts of sunlight that lent radiance to the blossom-scented air, the spectre of disillusionment stalked the country. King Richard's reign hadn't begun peaceably. Many disapproved of the way he took the crown. The nearer we approached the city, the more the rumours increased, and the tenor of them grew sinister. The death of the little prince of Middleham sparked a disturbing animosity. "A punishment for the foul deeds his father's done," said a surly wench who sold us bread.

Outside one small tavern where we stopped to water the horses, an ancient with a pot of ale accosted us cheerily, eager to impart his latest news.

"We shall have a new king by the end of this year," he said. He rubbed sleep from his rheumy eyes. "Aye, three kings in a year, a soothsayer said—and we've had two already—King Edward and now King Richard—"

"And who's to be the third?" asked Rob. He gave me a surreptitious wink, for the old man was well in his cups.

"Why, Henry Tudor." The fellow belched loudly and laughed at our incredulous responses. "Aye, just you wait." He slurred, pointing a grimy finger. "You don't believe me now, but you'll see."

Later that day, dining inside a populous place a few miles from the city gates, we discovered a grain of truth in this unlikely tale.

"That serving wench's full of support for this Henry Tudor who means to overthrow the kingdom," said Rob. He handed me a pot of small beer and indicated the woman mentioned. "When I asked her who he was, she laughed. 'What dark, country hole have you crawled out of?'" He nodded toward the boisterous group about the counter.

Rob rattled on but I merely half-listened. Again I saw Nerys laughing out of the flames and a red dragon swallowing the sun. A crown glinted under a hawthorn bush.

"Tha's dreaming," said Rob. He picked up the empty pots and grinned. "We'd best be on our way afore this Tudor comes."

Reaching the city in the early afternoon of a sweltering day, a wicked stench of rotting fish and bilge water overwhelmed us.

"I'd forgotten how bad London can smell. I must have grown used to it when I lived here as a child." I thought of Brother Brian bringing me to London. And here I was again, an adult now, but just as terrified.

We slaked our thirst in a respectable-looking tavern. Dusty and fatigued, we sat inside and engaged our portly landlord in conversation. He proved an amiable, talkative fellow, eager to share the city news.

"Have you travelled far?" He eyed our stained, shabby garments speculatively.

"From Yorkshire," answered Rob. He threw several coins on the table. "And we've healthy appetites from all this journeying. Hast thou any victuals to offer?"

Two generous platters of bread and meat arrived.

"The Wydeville witch's finally come out of the Westminster Sanctuary," said our garrulous landlord. "The new king offered her and her daughters his protection." He gave a knowing wink. "But I think she's other plans. She intends to spirit the wenches overseas to make wealthy matches." Lowering his voice, he invited us into his confidence. "Someday, folk reckon they'll be able to challenge the usurper."

"So you've no love for King Richard?" Rob stabbed a chunk of beef with his dagger.

"Nay." The landlord blustered with confusion, doubtless recalling we came from the loyal north. "I've nothing against him. I'm just telling you what people are saying."

"What about the princes? The Wydeville boys?"

"Now mistress— " He shook his head, assuming a lugubrious expression. "There's a mystery." He leaned so close I could trace the scarlet thread-work of veins across the wide expanse of his nose and cheeks. "After the coronation there were rumours about some plot to rescue them, then a yarn of how they'd been hidden away in some secret place—That was around August last year—or maybe September. But since Easter there's talk they've been done away with."

The landlord's face suffused with colour at my sudden anguished cry. "Well, I'm just telling you what's being said in the city," he said. "No one knows whether they're alive or dead. But I say, if any harm had come to them, why would the witch put herself in King Richard's protection? It makes no sense."

Part Eight

London
1484

Chapter Eighty

In Bread Street, the Mercers' affectionate welcome broke my control. Too long I'd held my fears in check. Now, like a bursting dam, they exploded. Sobbing without restraint, I fell into Margaret Mercer's arms.

"Maud Attemore's plied me regularly with information," a nervous Harry told us, "Aye, and sent me on several wild goose chases after some wench or other who might have been your Emma. Some of my experiences have been very peculiar!" He caught Meg's eye and they both laughed. "You'd never believe some of the places I've seen. In Southwark—" His mother coughed and raised her eyebrows at Nancy and Will smirking and nudging each another. "Ah, yes—" Harry looked contrite. "Only yesterday Maud told me the landlord at The Grapes in Stoney Street had taken on a new serving wench. She was rumoured to have a child so I went along and saw the lass myself—a thin little thing with pretty, blonde curls— not much older than Nancy—"

"That sounds like Emma. Did she have my Dickon?" I sat nursing Harry's youngest child, little Hal, on my lap, his wriggling body reminding me fiercely of my own boy—and tears threatened.

Harry and Meg exchanged glances. He gave my hand a squeeze. "No, I didn't see a child and I didn't get to talk to the wench. The landlord's a rough fellow and very protective of her—if you understand my meaning." He gave Rob a pertinent look. "I think he plans to keep her for the delight of certain wealthy customers—"

"We should go there now." I handed Hal to Meg.

"Not so fast. It might be best if Rob and I go alone. The area's hardly fitting for respectable women-folk—"

"No! You must take me with you. I'm not afraid of such places."

In the end they yielded, but not before Margaret Mercer had dressed me up like a doxy, and Rob and Harry sported villainous disguises to blend in with the rabble which generally frequented The Grapes.

This rowdy, old inn was one of many low looking taverns in Stoney Street. Mingling among an unsavoury assortment of ill-dressed ruffians who lurked about the dimly-lit Southwark lane, smells of sour ale, scorched meat, and unwashed flesh assailed our nostrils. I wondered how Jack Green could have brought Emma to such a place. Jack, with his fastidious, fashionable clothes scented with costly sandalwood would surely have been conspicuous here?

Shoving our way between jeering villains playing dice, drink-sodden ancients and whispering knaves huddled in corners, we followed the loud, coarse laughter to where a fire blazed in the hearth. Here, groups of affluent-looking men ate and drank among a herd of boisterous, gaudily clad wenches. All these wore tawdry gowns pulled low on their bosoms and shrieked and postured at every opportunity, while the landlord, a huge, pot-bellied knave with a villainous looking scar above his left eye and a vast, balding head like a boulder, barked orders to the scurrying serving girls. My eyes fell immediately upon the blonde.

An Emma, much altered and thinner than I remembered, moved with weary boldness amongst the leering men, her sweet features sadly coarsened, the curling ringlets lustreless. Her dainty hands bore soiled, broken nails. She smiled provocatively.

"Emma!"

For an instant she didn't recognise me, and then fear flooded her eyes. Panicked, she flung down her tray and would have run if Harry and Rob hadn't caught her.

"Come lass." Harry hustled her by the elbow toward me. "Your sister's been looking for you everywhere. Surely she deserves a moment of your time?"

Flinging a bag of coins to the scowling landlord, he winked and tapped his nose.

Once outside, we dragged the girl down a murky alley.

"Emma, where's Dickon?" Harry placed a hand over her mouth to stop her screaming and Rob in his black cloak, ragged hat shadowing his face, towered over her menacingly. "What have you done with him?"

"No one's going to hurt you, Emma. Just give Dickon to me or at least tell me where he is—"

The insolent girl turned her head to avoid me. "Jack Green has him," she answered, sullenly. "He told me he'd marry me if I got Dickon for him." She laughed then, a hard, mirthless laugh that spoke of painful disillusionment.

"You don't belong in this dreadful place." I seized her hand. "Come back to Middleham."

"Middleham! Me?" She laughed again, but tears welled in her eyes.

"At least let us take you somewhere more suitable. Somewhere we can talk freely."

Back in Bread Street, under Margaret Mercer's appalled eyes, the girl hunched by the parlour fire gulping sweet, warm wine while we questioned her. Once started, she ranted of nothing but Jack Green— how he'd promised to show her the sights of London, and she'd been bewitched by the pictures of the city he'd painted. "But it's a filthy place. I never saw such rotten houses and rubbish just lies stinking in the streets."

When he first brought her to London, Jack took her to city taverns where they dined on the finest food. He bought her trinkets and fashionable clothes, lavished her with entertainments and kept her like a lady in richly furnished lodgings with servants dancing in attendance.

"And Dickon?"

"Oh, he told me Dickon wouldn't be harmed." She laughed bitterly. "He said he'd promised to take Dickon to his father—"

"To his father? But why?"

"I don't know—I don't know." She grew petulant, and Harry gave me a warning glance.

He coaxed her gently. "Is Dickon still with Jack?"

"I think so." She flashed a quick, defiant look. "He was safe enough with me when we were first there. I took good care of him."

"And was Jack working in the city?"

"Oh yes." She seemed keen to share this information. "He always had plenty of money in his purse. He carried messages for King Richard—and for Bishop Stillington. One time he went to visit Sir James Tyrell, where he used to work as a groom, but he wouldn't take me—"

"But did you meet any of his friends?" Harry asked.

"Sometimes." She frowned as if attempting to recollect these occasions. "They were all surly fellows. One of them was called John Deighton. He's Tyrell's horse-keeper and often came to bring Jack messages. I didn't like him. Once he stayed with us for two days and did nothing but make coarse jests about me. There's something really nasty about him. He has the cruellest eyes."

Deighton—the name stirred a memory. I thought back to a journey to Barnard when Miles and I first married and our fateful halt at the Greyhound Tavern. A long history lay between Miles and this Deighton.

"Did Jack ever take messages to the Tower?"

"Oh yes. He had letters from the king for Sir Robert Brackenbury, the Constable."

"Do you remember my husband, Miles? He's at the Tower with the late king's son. Did you ever see him?"

"Ah, those poor boys!" Emma turned huge, frightened eyes upon me. "Jack said Lord Edward was sick with the toothache and was a miserable boy, always complaining—too lazy even to dress himself. But the other one—Lord Richard—he's a merry little lad."

"Lord Richard's with his brother?"

"Of course." Emma looked at me as if I were a simpleton. "Jack fetched him from the Sanctuary."

Jack Green again—How many cunning tricks had he played?

But how could Elizabeth Wydeville part with her boy? Hadn't I begged her not to send him to the Tower? Mara's words returned to taunt me—"The widow rejects your service." But why? Even the king said she believed me. What had Richard of Gloucester promised her? "She who sows tears will harvest sorrow." Mara told me that, too. Elizabeth Wydeville ordered the murder of the Desmond boys—I remembered her saying "They're dead these ten years." Would she now reap her own sorrow?

Harry crouched before Emma, speaking slowly as if addressing a child. "Did Jack take Dickon with him when he left you?"

She nodded, rubbing tears from her face.

"And do you know where Jack is now?"

"I've not seen him in weeks." She began to weep copiously. "But he'll be at Tyrell's."

Emma proved right. But Jack Green clearly expected us. The girl, though promised work and lodgings, had sneaked off during the night to warn her erstwhile lover. How could I blame her? Love made me weak and foolish, too.

"Mistress Forrest," Jack Green greeted me with an obsequious smile as we rode into the courtyard of Tyrell's fine manor-house. "What a pleasure to see you again."

"What have you done with Dickon?"

If Rob hadn't held me firmly, I think I'd have torn at Master Green's impudent face. As it was, Harry put a dagger to the knave's throat and gripped him firmly with the other hand.

"Tell us where the boy is and I won't harm you. But if you've hurt him, then by St Peter, I'll see you hanged."

"I think not, Master Mercer." Green raised his brow to indicate men in the king's livery. They appeared from the house to encircle us in silent menace. "You see, I have the king's protection. Besides, your fears are groundless." He gifted me his old, weasel-smile. "Where else would the lad be, but with his father?"

"With Miles?" Bewildered, I looked from Jack to Harry and then back to Rob.

"Aye," said the detested voice, with the merest chuckle of amusement. "The lad helped me persuade his father to perform a little service for the king. Miles can be difficult sometimes. As a reward, Miles now has Dickon in his keeping. I took him myself, early this morning."

With Rob's help, I leapt back into the saddle and turned my horse.

"What?" called Jack Green. "No thank you for my pains? Don't you want to hear how your old priest screamed and soiled himself when he was tortured, Mistress Forrest?"

He was laughing as we rode away.

Chapter Eighty-One

At Baynard's Castle they greeted us with open hostility.

"Miles Forrest hasn't been here in a long time." One of the officers wearing the badge of the dowager Duchess of York eyed me insolently. "King Richard made him rich—though what services he demanded for this favour I'm sure you can guess." He spat contempt. "Our Dick can be generous when it suits him! Forrest thought himself too grand for the likes of us. I've no idea where he's living now."

Leaving Rob to make enquiries in the nearby taverns, Harrry took me to Maud's shop in the Chepe.

Overwhelmed by her effusive welcome, we'd a hard time getting her to listen to our questions. Crushing me to her voluptuous bosom, she prattled admiringly of my changed fortunes, until Harry interrupted urging haste, and began interrogating her about the princes in the Tower.

As she related her store of news, her raddled handsome face grew graver. She assumed an awed voice, as if afraid to tell us the worst. Finally she leaned close. "Then last Easter, when we heard the little Middleham prince was dead, all the old stories started up —grimmer than ever, and by July a nasty rumour told how the king had decided to get rid of those Wydeville boys because he felt unsafe—"

"And did you hear anything of a Master Forrest?" Harry's homely face grew sombre.

"I heard the name once or twice." She gave me a wary look.

"My husband's disappeared."

Lowering her voice, she drew me aside, for a huddle of curious women had gathered in the street. "They said someone was hired to put those lads away—and the name Forrest was mentioned." The expression in her eyes shook me with horror. Was I already too late?

"I don't want to listen to crazy talk! I just need to find Miles and Dickon!"

My outburst shocked everyone. Stunned by the unexpected flood of tears which followed, Maud stretched out her arms, gasping in astonishment when I shook off this attempted embrace.

With a sympathetic nod to Maud, a patient Harry wrapped his arm about my shoulders and steered me away. "Don't let Maud's tittle-tattle disturb you. You know how she loves to exaggerate."

Turning briefly to where the bewildered gossip stood watching us, he waved a jaunty farewell. "Tomorrow, unless Rob has any other news, you must accompany me on my morning bread delivery to the Tower. I've a feeling your Miles may still be there—and where he is, we'll surely find Dickon." Although designed to cheer, his words didn't fool me. I knew Harry too well. His whole presence oozed anxiety. "We should have questioned that knave, Green, while we had a chance," he muttered. "By the Rood, Nan, I wish I'd cut that smirk from off his face!"

❧

In the steamy gloom just before dawn the huge, white-faced fortress of the Tower crouched like a beast waiting to devour the unwary. Its turrets rose tall and ominous against a cobalt skyline. Mist silenced the river traffic. Sultry heat clung about the fabric of the buildings, stifling the city's noise. Inside this terrible place, if my dreams spoke true, wicked shadows lurked and cries of pain echoed among its chill, damp passageways.

Time to confront the scene of my old nightmares, I thought, steeling myself to enter the notorious prison. Yet hadn't I travelled since childhood to seek it out? Brother Brian's haggard face flashed across my mind, his troubled eyes full of pity. What dreadful secrets did it hide? Did the Wydeville princes lie sleeping beyond those thick, stone walls? And was my own boy there with his father?

"Maud told me everyone watched the princes playing on the green in front of the Garden Tower," said Harry, his voice low and hushed. "They liked to shoot at the butts or fight mock battles—"

"But she told me by Christmas people saw them less and less, and in the new year not at all," I answered in a whisper.

Carrying a weighty basket of bread on my hip, I followed him across the great stone bridge towards the gates I'd studied as a child. Guards armed with pikes loomed ahead, and I recalled Aunt Grace telling me these men lived in the Tower buildings. How could they sleep in such a place?

"I always deliver here at first light." Harry feigned a cheery tone. He hoisted his basket higher on his shoulder. "It's brought us good business—this place. I've got to know some of the guards. They're a friendly bunch. They'll all know Master Forrest here."

Jesting about his new helper, the guards greeted Harry. "I prefer this dainty wench to that hulking rogue who normally accompanies you," said one, sparking a score of ribald comments.

"Colin's a sore head this morning," answered Harry. "I thought you'd appreciate meeting my cousin. Sadly, though she's spoken for, my lads! Her husband works here— you'll surely know him— attendant to the Lords Bastard."

"What name?" A bold-faced guard tore a chunk off one of the loaves and chewed it greedily, spitting crumbs.

"Forrest—Miles Forrest."

"Wasn't he in the Garden Tower?" asked the fellow of his companions, mouth full of new bread.

One pointed to the tall building, whose lofty walls featured in my worst visions. My heart quickened with foreboding.

"I'll take you," he said.

Relieved of our baskets, we followed him. Pushing open a heavy, timber door, he indicated a gloomy stairwell and gestured upward.

"Top floor." He tipped Harry a knowing wink. "If you plan on bringing the lads out for a bit of fresh air, I'll not disturb you. I've a desperate hunger on me and it's breakfast time." He looked at me with some sympathy then. "There's been a deal of noise up there since before light. Sounded as if they were moving furniture, but it's not my business to ask. I wish you success with your venture."

He closed the outer door and immediately, a stifling darkness dropped upon us like a mantle. Sconces on the walls belched oily vapour as we climbed.

Passing closed doors, I trembled at the memory of my dreams, wondering what secrets these locked chambers kept. A sour stench of urine and decay leached from the clammy walls. Slimy water swamped the stairs. Pressing my cloak over my mouth against the noxious reek, I recoiled from the scuttle and slither of scaly feet and tails. An evil miasma wreathed from the river and the ancient malevolence of the place gathered about us like great feathered wings. A penetrating cold gnawed my bones.

Further up, the serpentine steps narrowed ominously and the pall of darkness thickened. Choked by the weight of it, we moved laboriously, our footsteps the merest sigh upon the steps.

At the top a heavy silence brooded.

Gripped by a sickening spinning sensation, I recognised the timber and iron-bossed door which lay before me. It stood ajar, revealing a coil of inky black that smoked inward.

Clenching my teeth, I pushed it wide.

"Who's there?"

A torch flared suddenly, lighting up the chamber, stinging my eyes. Several liveried men, illuminated like imps in its flame, set down a heavy, carved chest. Beyond them, the chamber stood bare save for a bed stripped of its hangings and ashes in the fire-place.

"What do you want here?" asked the torch bearer, while the others squatted, panting from their exertions.

"We're looking for Master Forrest," Harry said from behind me. "He's attendant to the Lords Bastard."

"Gone," gasped one of the others.

"The boys were sent north to train as knights." A portly fellow with a broom offered this information while the others murmured and stretched their aching muscles.

"All the attendants were dismissed weeks ago," said the torch bearer.

"Black Will went last year," said another voice, choked by coughing.

"Forrest and Deighton were the last." The portly fellow sank down on the chest, wiping sweat from his brow with his sleeve.

"Could they have been sent with the lads?" asked Harry.

The portly fellow nodded gravely. "Very like—their uncle's sent them to Middleham where he trained under Warwick as a boy."

"Was there another little boy with them?"

All the men looked at me then with a mixture of curiosity and pity.

"Only the Wydeville lads were here," the portly fellow replied, his tone uneasy. "But sometimes visitors came—once a bishop—"

"Stillington?"

Bemused by my interruption, the men shrugged and began muttering together.

"Someone said the king came to see them," offered the torch-bearer.

The man on the chest laughed sardonically. "I doubt it. This part of the Tower's a forgotten place. And the king wanted to forget about those lads."

"Are you well, Mistress? You look pale." The torch-bearer grabbed Harry's arm. "Best get her outside, sir, into the air. She's probably heard some wicked tales of this place. The wenches are always fainting when they come here."

Outside, Rob waited with the horses as arranged. He showed no surprise when we told him the princes had gone. A grim expression distorted his usually pleasant face.

"There's a tale they've moved to Middleham," said Harry. "And Master Forrest with them."

With a brusque shake of his head, Rob urged us to mount. Harry glanced at his closed expression with curiosity. "Where to now?"

"Lombard Street," Rob answered curtly. "Master Forrest's lodging there. I had the information from that knave, Jack Green."

Chapter Eighty-Two

I never discovered how Rob got his information. He showed no inclination for talk either then or afterward. But tension made us all taciturn.

The fine house to which he took us stood in an area of the city where wealthy merchants lodged. Leaving Harry to hold the horses, Rob hammered on the door. A spindly lad of about thirteen, in a fine blue and murrey livery, opened it. He looked as if he was used to such rude summons.

"Master Forrest?"

"Aye, inside. Who—?"

"His wife and cousins." Harry pushed him aside. "Take our horses."

Inside candles blazed, gilding opulent furnishings. In spite of the warm day, a huge fire leaped within the hearth, and there, before it, sat Dickon, like a miser relishing the comfort of his gold.

I flung myself upon the child, pressing his body against mine, covering him with kisses and babbling endearments. He didn't respond. Stiff and unyielding in my arms, he stared at me with such cruel indifference I thought my heart would break.

"Sweet Jesu! What have they done to you?"

I noted then discarded bottles and goblets strewn amongst the rushes, but I didn't need these to tell me Miles was drunk. His tall, dishevelled figure wavered before us, clearly stunned by our unexpected arrival.

"Nan." His voice slurred, drowsy with ale and disbelief. "I prayed for you to find me." In the flickering candle-light his face gleamed gaunt and wolfish, the black hair standing in spikes like raised hackles. His eyes burned from dark hollows. Hugging me close, he murmured incoherent words into my hair.

"Miles, we must leave at once." I struggled from his ferocious grasp. "Harry and Rob have come to take us back to Bread Street."

Stupidly, Miles watched the servant lad collecting his belongings together.

"All's paid for, sir," said this youngling, when Harry offered money. But he gladly took the generous coins we left on parting.

Dickon rode with Harry. Stony-faced and silent, he kept his head turned from me though he drooped in the saddle.

"He's almost asleep," Harry said. "He's obviously had little rest in days. I'm sure he'll be a different boy when he's slept. It's the shock of seeing you again—God knows what he's been used to with that villain, Green—"

But to me it seemed an eternity before my child would even look in my direction.

❧

Early next day, Harry dispatched a reluctant Rob to Middleham. As rosy light painted the far horizon we watched him ride off through the city gates in a cloud of dust.

"There've been so many rumours about the Wydeville boys— that they've been sent to Sheriff Hutton with the king's bastard son, John, or shipped to Flanders—It's hard to know what to think —" Harry's voice trailed in embarrassment.

In silence we threaded our way back to the bake-house through the barely wakened streets, with the clatter of opening shutters, the roll of barrels, the creak of cart-wheels assaulting our ears. We passed a sleepy lad with a mangy cur on a rope, a drab in a frowsty kirtle, a stocky fellow carrying wood, as if we trod a dreamscape. An unspoken horror lay between us and at every step, the burden of it grew heavier on me.

As always, the house smelled fragrant with new bread. Down in the bake-house Will sang as he hauled a second batch of loaves from the ovens. In the shop, a yawning Marian drew up the shutters and Meg looked up from stacking pastries on the shelf to speak to Harry.

Entering the kitchen, I caught Margaret Mercer's eye and opened my mouth to spill the worst of my fears, but little Hal, his hair still rumpled from sleep, chose this moment to paddle in.

A relief, almost audible as a sigh, pervaded the kitchen.

Dickon, who'd slept in Hal's bed-chamber, followed warily, quite different from the lively, mischievous boy of Middleham.

"I suppose you boys want some oatmeal?" Margaret Mercer said, lifting Hal onto a stool by the table.

Ignoring me, Dickon's mouth widened in a smile and he ran to her at once.

Watching him playing chess with Hal and Nancy on the hearth while I washed dishes reminded me poignantly of Ned of Middleham whose skill at this game had so impressed his mother.

When Harry carried off Hal and Nancy went to help in the shop, Dickon climbed on the settle, swinging his legs back and forth, deliberately kicking over the chess pieces, his face a mask of sullen frustration.

"Stop that!" I cried, irked by this petulance and conscious of Mistress Mercer's reproving stare. "If you're tired of play, put away your toys."

Scowling, he gathered up the chessmen. When he began rearranging them in some private game of his own, Margaret Mercer, putting dishes in the press, turned to give me a nudge. Accepting this encouragement to win the child's confidence, I knelt to join him as he put some of the pieces into two little wooden carts Harry had made.

"That's the Duke of Buckingham going to his execution." He pointed to one of the carts which contained a single knight. "Here's the king and his henchmen coming to watch." The other cart held, indeed, the king and several pawns. This grisly example of the child's imagination sent shivers down my spine.

"And who's that?" I pointed to the bishop standing by the king's cart.

Dickon turned to look at me with a mischievous grin. For a moment I delighted in this return to his old behaviour—until he spoke.

"Why, that's Bishop Stillington, of course. Jack Green says Bishop Stillington is the most important person in England."

Margaret Mercer dropped a basin. It rolled and spun on the floor like a wheel, making a great clamour. Dickon and I bumped heads as we scrambled to retrieve it and for a few moments we crouched together making "oohing" noises and rubbing our foreheads ruefully.

"Mama, are you a witch?"

"Who said I was a witch?" Still kneeling on the floor, I flashed Mistress Mercer a swift glance. "Was that Master Green, too?"

He nodded, and then put out a hand to stroke my cheek. The gesture reminded me of his father and I smiled tearfully. Catching Dickon's hand in mine, I kissed it.

"And do you believe him?"

He hung his head.

"He said Bishop Stillington put you in the prison at Pontefract for being a witch."

The tremulous timbre of his voice grieved me.

"Indeed I was at Pontefract." I lifted his chin so I could look into his troubled face. "I went to answer some questions about King Edward, not about being a witch."

And may God forgive me for the lie, I thought.

"Now, does your Mama look like a witch?" asked Mistress Mercer.

Uncertain, Dickon looked up at her. When he turned back to me, I pulled a horrible face to make him laugh.

"Yes!" He shrieked, pretending to be frightened. I scooped him in my arms and tickled him then until he couldn't speak for giggles. While he laughed, I cursed Jack Green. What had that villain intended for my son?

I thought of Miles then, and leaving Dickon with Mistress Mercer, I carried a platter of bread and meat upstairs to the little attic room. I found him crouched on a stool with his head in his hands as if lost in a private nightmare.

Closing the door, I realised how dreadful silence saturated that room, separating us entirely from the busy shop below. Grey-faced but sober, Miles looked up and in my belly a knot of terror tautened.

"Is it true?" As if someone tightened a cord about my throat, my voice constricted.

The empty brilliance of his eyes frightened me but I refused to read its message, pleading instead.

"The Wydeville boys did go north to train as knights, didn't they, Miles?"

He rose then and laughed, an ugly, mocking sound that set my teeth on edge.

Hurling down the platter, I flew at him, beating my fists against his chest, clawing for his face. "Where are they, Miles? What did you do to them?"

Seizing my wrists, he held me off, his face granite-hard.

"The boys are dead."

As if he'd punched me in the belly, I crumpled.

Outside in the street the ordinary sounds—the uneven rolling wheels of a cart, the steady clop of hooves—continued inexorably.

"Surely you didn't believe those lies?" He stooped to draw me to my feet and I swayed, trembling in his arms. "You of all people?" Our eyes linked cruelly. "Of course you knew. Didn't you warn me often enough to abandon Gloucester?"

Mute with horror, I listened to the increasing bitterness in his voice, the awful self-mockery.

"He's made me wealthy, Nan. But just as you predicted, the coins are the price of my damnation. They hang like weights about my neck. But they can't buy back my soul, can they?"

He flinched suddenly, his eye caught by something just beyond my vision. The expression on his face terrified. Turning, I glimpsed a flash of colour, an elusive movement. Imperceptibly a freezing chill invaded the airless chamber. Gooseflesh rose on my arms.

"I'd never killed a child—" An unsteady note entered his voice, driving shivers through me. "The dead don't rest, Nan." He laughed again. "But you've always known that, haven't you?" He turned the full horror of his shockingly blue eyes upon me. "He follows after me now, the little knave. Deighton's a fiend. He did it without a quiver. It's one thing to kill a man but—Now I see them everywhere. Even when I try to close my eyes they're there." Again the awful laughter set me shaking. "Your precious cousins should tear me limb from limb for what I've done."

Releasing me, he sank heavily on the stool as if exhausted and I crouched on the edge of the bed, my eyes drawn to Miles' ragged nails, crusted with earth or blood. Those hands had caressed me, carried Dickon—I didn't want to think what else they'd done.

A profound silence settled over us.

At some point, Dickon slipped into the room and climbed into my lap. Leaning his head against my breast, he fixed his gaze on his father's brooding face. Something in the solemnity of our stillness affected him deeply. He didn't speak, but the warmth of his body pressed close to mine comforted.

"Ask Jack Green if you want the truth of it," said Miles suddenly looking up. I ached at the sight of his wasted beauty—his face all angles and umber shadows. "The little lads were no trouble. The youngest was no older than our own boy—such a merry little knave—" The catch in his voice wounded me worse than a blade. "He used to sing and tell such tales—Aye, and he'd dance for us too. He was so bold, so full of life—he climbed right up on to the parapet once. I carried him down on my shoulders—" Again that piteous catch in his voice. "The elder was sick. Too sick to care for anything in the end, God rest him." His voice hardened. "But they were a trouble to the king—Jack said they must be *eliminated*—and Deighton urged me to it. He's an evil piece of villainy—but when Jack threatened me with Dickon's life what could I do? 'Finish the business,' he said, 'and in return I'll bring your boy to you. Deighton can't manage it on his own. The Wydeville brats or your boy—which is it to be?' But he didn't keep his word—Even though I damned myself, he kept my boy—Not till the day before you came to Lombard Street, did I have one glimpse of him and then—" The bitter laughter stuttered into dry, wrenching sobs that shook his frame. I sat immobile, unable to offer any solace.

How had I believed I could save those children? I kissed Dickon's soft curls savouring the animal warmth of his body, the living weight of him—grateful for this at least.

Chapter Eighty-Three

August burned with rumour and intrigue. The stinking city streets seethed with treachery as more and more people fled to join the Tudor. The ferment of rebellion flavoured the air.

In Bread Street, Miles withdrew more and more into a shadowy half-existence that appalled everyone. Steeped in silent agony, he shivered by the hearth as if with ague or refused to quit the stifling little room so kindly assigned to us. His frame grew skeletal as if some demon deep inside gnawed at his flesh, reminding me of a dreadful tale I'd once read in the library at Norwich of some ancient Greek whose liver was daily torn from his body as a punishment from the gods.

No one in the house spoke of our intentions. Instead they skirted round the subject which haunted us most. The disappearance of King Edward's sons peppered common talk in the city now the Tudor threatened the kingdom. Though the Mercers must have heard these awful speculations, they never questioned me. I suppose my silence provided answer enough.

They didn't urge us to leave either, although they must have desired it more than anything else that summer. Instead, Harry trained Dickon to make bread deliveries and sent the boy upon various errands. He came back from these excursions with cheeks glowing like berries on the hawthorn hedge, full of the marvellous things he'd seen, the tall buildings, the tottering houses, the gloomy churches with their twisted gargoyles, and the creaking, painted signs above the shops—poignant reminders of my own childhood wanderings. But when he told me he'd twice seen Jack Green in the Chepe, I shook as if with fever. Why did this knave continue to spy on us? I began to imagine him lurking at every street corner. For three days I daren't go out the door.

༄

"We can't stay here."

We'd hidden in Bread Street over two weeks.

A stifling dawn hauled me from bed. Hot daggers of sunlight gouged the glistering lapis of the horizon. Harry stooped by the open door of the bakery loading his deliveries into baskets. In the bake-house Will sang over his work.

"Where would you go?" Harry's bleak face confronted me.

"Would you shelter an assassin under your roof? No, don't be kind to me—" I brushed aside the friendly hand, clenching my jaw against tears. "It's what he is—though, God forgive me, I still love him. If you'd known him as I—" My voice cracked. "But I can't ask any more of you—" I bit my lip, swallowed grief, and fisted my hands.

Already heat shimmered off the cobbles. An acrid stench rose from the gutters. My stomach heaved. "We can't encroach on your charity any longer. Besides, our presence places you in danger. We must leave London."

His attempts to persuade me otherwise faltered into mere courtesy. I swept them aside as easily as dust. Poor Harry, I caught him off guard and he could think of no excuses.

"Let me organise something." He squeezed my hands, his honest face gleaming with sweat. "I'll speak to mother. Do you remember me mentioning Meg's sister, Judith, in Lincolnshire? I'm sure she'd take you in."

"No, he's sick. I can smell it off him. It would be wrong. Besides, my reputation as a witch is just as dangerous." I watched Harry flinch at the word, but before he could speak I stopped him. "Just get me some horses. We'll leave tomorrow."

"He'll never ride." Harry's face glimmered ashen with shock. Firmly, he set his hands on my shoulders. His eyes shone well-deep. "He'll never get to Lincolnshire, Nan. He's far too sick. We must take him to St Martin-le-Grand. Do you understand what I'm saying?"

"We must take your father to the monks," I told a frightened Dickon next morning. "He's very, very sick and needs their help. Harry's gone to hire us a cart."

When he saw the great heap of our possessions, the carter scowled.

"Is it the plague?" he asked, watching Harry lead Miles from the bake-house. He squinted at me, narrowing his eyes against the sun's glare. Then he crossed himself.

"It's not plague," Harry answered boldly. "My cousin's been sick of the sweat. Here, we've money enough to pay you for your pains—"

The surly fellow snatched the coins greedily, although his aversion prevented him helping Harry lift Miles into the cart.

"Go back to the bakery, Harry."

He hesitated by the horse's head, his kindly face flushed, clearly ill at ease. "Are you sure you can manage on your own?"

"If you can find us a place with Judith, I'll be more than grateful," I answered. Resolutely, I climbed into the cart.

"We'll speak tomorrow."

Heartsick, I watched Harry's figure grow small and distant as the horse clopped away.

Our carter drove as one who grudged assistance, nor did he help to unload our bundles when we reached the Sanctuary. For a few groats some ragged boys offered to carry our baggage, although I fear several items were pilfered in their handling. Between us, Dickon and I managed to guide Miles into the great church. As we entered, the bells tolled. I felt a sense of having done all this before, as if my whole life had led me to this one moment.

The good Brothers welcomed us with gentle courtesy. They asked no questions. They suggested cures, but didn't speak of miracles. Soothing herbal possets comforted every pain. Prayers pacified the troubled mind. They offered a sanctuary for all—rich or poor, good or ill.

I sent Dickon to scour the market for quinces since his father had a mind to them. I'd an old recipe from Mistress Mercer for a quince jelly I might make. Better the boy should run in the fresh air in the bright day than linger by a sickbed in a darkened chamber.

A young monk with apple cheeks tended Miles. As soon as I heard the soft cadence of his speech, Brother Brian came to mind. But there the resemblance ended. Brother Aidan's blue eyes, clear as rain-washed sky, held nothing of Brother Brian's sorrow in them.

"May we go back by the market?" Dickon tugged at my hand, having returned without quinces. "There are none to be had at this season," he told Brother Aiden. "But there's a tumbler there today…" His voice grew breathless with excitement. "And there's a troupe of Egyptians. One of them eats fire—"

"Jack!" Miles interrupted unexpectedly. He sat up, eyes blazing. "Jack! What have you done with my boy?"

Terrified, Dickon shrank from the bed.

Brother Aiden lured him away. "Help me make a special posset for your father."

They slipped aside like phantoms.

The vivid eyes locked on some unseen presence. Miles hadn't spoken in days—

"What are you doing up here? You might have fallen." He shook his head, his lips drawn back in a ghastly smile. "You're all questions, lad."

Stroking his wild, black hair, I knelt to calm him. Gently, I pressed him back to lie down on the pallet, grieved by the weakness of his emaciated body. Once he had carried me in his arms as easily as lifting a babe. Now no strength remained in him. I leaned over to kiss his brow—what other comfort had I to offer? But his eyes gazed far beyond me.

Something like a shadow settled at my back. The old, familiar tingling sensation crawled through my limbs. In their sconces the candles shivered, dwindled into tiny, bluish fingers of flame. A silence gathered, waited expectantly.

"They lie in secret. We hid them beneath the stairs."

"Miles?" I turned his face toward me, took his cold hand in mine. "What is it you want to tell me?"

"The boy— in Flanders—"

"The princes? The Wydeville boys?" I leaned close, his breath whispering across my face.

He smiled, touching his other hand to my cheek. "I dreamed of you." The tenderness in that look struck me deeper than a sword.

"You have my heart," I answered, stooping to kiss him.

A look of surprise entered his eyes, so that for the briefest of moments they flared with their old blue brilliance—then they grew wider and emptier than I'd ever seen and a new, strange quiet filled the chamber.

Distantly, as if from some long corridor, a gentle, lilting voice began the ancient liturgy for departing souls. The vast, cold solitude of the place embraced me, and I found myself alone holding a dead man's hand, carrying a dead man's secret.

496

Chapter Eighty-four

Where could we go but back to Bread Street? Harry promised to have us out of the city before autumn, but once again fate conspired against me.

In the black, early hours while Dickon still slept, I woke from a vivid dream of Mara. She sat in a cart drawn by a dun cob, a cluster of Roma children at her feet. Smiling, she pointed out the passing features of the countryside. At first the trees stood bare and skeletal, but when they began sprouting green shoots the dream changed. Suddenly, Mara turned her head to stare at me. She put her finger to her lips. Then, like a magician, she produced a bundle of painted cards from a crimson sleeve, just like the ones she'd given me. She spread them upon her lap, but just as she held up the Tower struck by lightning, I woke. Mara taught me this card predicted disaster. What new trouble threatened?

A messenger from the queen found me ready.

Anne Neville lay gravely ill. She much desired my company. To go to court was to risk danger, but how could I refuse such a plea?

"Dickon'll be safer here. Nancy can take care of him. He can help Will and me in the bake-house. The queen wouldn't send for you unless it was urgent. You must go." Harry's candid eyes offered sympathy.

So I found myself back at Westminster, but this time in very different circumstances. As the boat bore me up the river to the magnificent palace, I thought of Eleanor. I prayed I'd not encounter wily Bishop Stillington this time.

"Your Grace." I dropped to my knees before the day-bed where the queen lay surrounded by her flock of elegant ladies. A musician plucked the plaintive notes of a lute.

"Come close so I may see you better, Nan." Her voice croaked. The pointed little face wore a waxy sheen. She'd grown so thin her bones jutted visibly under her green robes. A skeletal hand reached for mine.

"It does me good to look on old friends again." Her cat-eyes gleamed fever-bright but she clasped me as firm as ever. "How fares your husband? We heard he'd been sick."

"Better now, Your Grace," I said, swallowing a lump of raw grief. The easy lie seemed to satisfy, but her penetrating gaze unnerved me. I turned away, pretending admiration in her luxurious apartments. I couldn't speak of Miles' last days at St Martin's. I wouldn't permit myself the luxury of thinking of him yet. Instead, the numbness of bereavement bound me and I clung to it like a mantle against frost-bite. If I once let go—

"And your son?"

Did I imagine the tremble in her voice?

"With my cousins, Your Grace."

"Sit by me, Nan. Let this gaggle of geese allow me some breathing space. They smother me with their vigilance."

The gorgeous, silken ladies scattered like flower petals. They flocked together in the corner of the chamber.

"Play something merry, Jacques." She turned to the swarthy lute-player. "These melancholy tunes are tedious."

The change of rhythm wrought its magic. The ladies began to tap their feet. The volume of their shrill bird-chatter increased.

"Did you know the Wydeville witch has sent her daughters from the Sanctuary?" Anne Neville's keen eyes searched my face with a scrutiny which alarmed. Had she sent for me to cast fortunes?

"We heard something, Your Grace," I said carefully. Recalling the garrulous landlord who'd told Rob and me, I wondered at the old queen's motives.

"But did you know my niece, Elizabeth, is enamoured of the king?" The green eyes sparked with hatred. Her nails raked the flesh of my arm.

Speechless, I stared at her, the idea too appalling to contemplate.

"Oh yes." She thrust out her chin in the old, arrogant manner I remembered well. "He lusts after her just as hotly with all the passion of a young lecher. He can't wait for me to die." She began to shake with silent laughter. "She's her mother's daughter, you see, and will stop at nothing to have him." I couldn't tell now if she laughed or wept. "You should have seen them dance together at Christmas," she said, the bitterness in her voice caustic as acid. "They hung together like lovers who can never have done with touching each other." She began to cough. The coughing turned to violent retching. Someone fetched a basin and a cloth. I held the queen while she vomited. The lute died into silence and the room grew still with horror.

"The doctor," someone said. A flutter of silk and velvet whisked through the door.

"My little boy—" The queen looked up at me, her eyes grown huge in the pallid face. Blood spattered her chin. "Did he suffer?"

"It was very peaceful." I thought of Ned's brilliant smile.

"Stay with me," she whispered, when the physician came.

"Till death."

※

Of course I saw her—the Wydeville princess. It was impossible to ignore such golden beauty. Her lovely face and hands owed much to her mother, but the voluptuous figure, the harvest-coloured hair and the sensuous nature were her father's legacy. Among the court ladies she stood out like a lily among a field of tares. Men flocked to her, drawn against their will as the moth to the flame. She turned toward them with such a powerful combination of innocence and ardour, they grew weak with desire.

She and the king danced around each other in that dangerous game lovers play to assert their power. Their mutual attraction both shocked and repelled, yet the court couldn't refrain from watching. We held our breath in anticipation of the next move.

In February, when the rumours crackled like lightning, the queen grew melancholy. One bleak morning as I helped her to dress, young Katherine Underwood rushed into the chamber, her face the colour of bleached linen.

"Your Grace," she panted for breath. "Forgive me." She sank into a curtsey. "I just heard a rumour you were dead!"

The queen swayed before me, a pale flower on a fragile stem. I held out my arms to catch her, but instead of swooning, she ran barefoot from the chamber, her honey-coloured hair unbound about her shoulders. She ran straight to the king's apartments. We rushed after, but the king caught her in his arms.

"Is it true, my lord," she said, clinging to the sable velvet of his doublet, "you desire my death so eagerly rumours of my demise are already circulating?"

"What heresy is this?" He smoothed her wild hair, but where was the tender regard he'd once lavished upon her? I saw only fear and guilt in him now. "You're overwrought," he said, patting her hands. "No need for such distress—"

Around him his gentlemen twitched with embarrassment. He made some jest to ease the tension, but the queen clutched at him with all the desperation of one condemned. I noticed how he struggled to hold her at arm's length as if afraid to breathe in infection.

"Your ladies are waiting." He fobbed her off with this feeblest of excuses, turning her gently towards us. I took her hand. A glimmer of recognition sparked in his eyes.

"Mistress Forrest, the healer." The thin-lipped smile appalled me. "You warned me once of many enemies. Do you remember?" Including his gentlemen, he added sardonically, "I think we have but one enemy to consider now, haven't we?"

Distracted by a crimson clad figure gliding towards the king's elbow I ignored the strained laughter. The figure laid a daring hand on the royal sleeve and the yellow hawk-eyes of Bishop Stillington locked on mine.

"Look after my wife." The king shared a conspiratorial smile with the prelate while I clenched my fists against the overpowering essence of evil. How could Gloucester have become such a monster? "She believes in your skills."

I urged the queen away but he called after us. "If you've some charm to rid me of this Tudor, Mistress Forrest, I wish you'd let me know of it."

The bishop's diabolical chuckle echoed down the corridor.

Like a sleepwalker the queen returned to her chamber. I left her there with Katherine and went to find her physician. On the steps outside I encountered Jack Green and reeled under the alarming sensation he'd been waiting for me. He stood, clad in the royal livery now, and seemed very much at ease.

"Good morrow, Mistress Forrest—" He awarded me a smile of such brilliance he might have been greeting an old friend. "Amy promised I'd see you again, but I didn't think to find you at court."

"The queen sent for me." I stared boldly into his impudent face.

"Of course. The queen still wields some influence, I believe." His gloating tone abraded me. "Poor lady, she clings too fast to lost causes. I doubt your skills can offer her much hope now."

"I'm bound to her by gratitude," I said. "She raised me up to be her waiting maid, and I won't forget such favours."

"Loyalty is admirable but sometimes it's necessary to forge new alliances to protect one's interests." His lips curved in the old weasel smile and his eyes gleamed menace. "Commend me to your husband."

I winced at this deliberate blow. But I held my nerve, thrusting out my chin and straightening my shoulders. "You've climbed high, Master Green." I steeled myself to smile. "But a fall from such great height might prove fatal." I hoped he thought of Brother Brian. "My husband learned that well."

Though the doctors plied the queen with their drugs, the sickness gnawed too deep. But it wasn't just sickness destroyed her but the king's absence which broke her heart. From then on he shunned her company and her bed, pleading the advice of the physicians and urgent matters of state. The truth was far more sinister.

Chapter Eighty-five

"How dark it grows!" Katherine chewed her lips nervously.

We clustered by the casement watching the March skies with bated breath. The astronomers predicted a great eclipse of the sun. Below in the noisy street, people gathered in horrified clusters. They pointed upward.

"A wise-woman foretold disaster would begin with a blotting out of the sun." Grace craned her neck for a better view. "And Master Penman says an eclipse is a mighty omen for he's made a study of the stars. What do you think, Nan?"

"It's not even noon but it's almost as black as night." Tremors shook Katherine's slender body. "I don't like Master Penman's eclipse, however important he thinks it."

She flitted away from the window, but her words awoke a memory. Hadn't Mara spoken of the noontime of the year? And hadn't I foretold the queen of this eclipse the last time I'd read the cards for her?

"The queen's awake," Katherine called.

I joined her by the great carved bed, wondering how long its occupant could endure such sickness. I'd made a promise but knew it was almost fulfilled.

The queen's wasted body prevented her from rising but the Neville spirit burned as strong as ever. She held my hand with a tenacity I wouldn't have believed possible.

"What month is it?"

"March, Your Grace."

"August," she said. Her voice had grown so weak, I leaned close to catch the words. "Take your boy back to the north, Nan, away from this cruel city."

I squeezed her hand but she made no more effort to speak.

Shadows plunged the room into awful darkness. The grip on my fingers loosened.

Katherine, already on her knees, shuddered at the strange heavenly phenomenon that hid the sun. Softly, I called the attention of the ladies by the casement and there began a rustling fall of bent knees and murmured orisons. I didn't pray. I thought of the little cook-maid whom I'd told would one day wear a crown, and Miles crouching by the hearth eaten away piecemeal by fear, just as surely as the queen had been eaten away by grief.

Chapter Eighty-Six

Under the Mercer's tutelage Dickon flourished. Looking at him, a mixture of aching love and dismay wrenched at my heart. Already he showed the promise of Miles' height and build. Full of new-found confidence, he greeted me, affectionately eager to relate his adventures. I ruffled the tousled black hair that so favoured his father, and the brilliant light in his eyes brought a lump into my throat. I was glad he hadn't inherited the Sight. His mind danced too feverishly for contemplation. Like his father, he joyed in the sheer animal pleasure of life, too firmly rooted in the things of this world to be a seer. Yet a wayward streak disturbed me. He talked of nothing but being a soldier in the Low Countries.

"He loves to watch the tradesmen at their work or the boats sail up and down the river. He's a powerful asset to me with the deliveries." Harry's words soothed my misgivings. "He's too quick-witted to waste his time on soldiering. Mark my words, Nan, he'll prove something better when he's grown. And for all his talk, he loves London well enough."

The next morning Dickon took me into the city.

"Look! He pointed at windows full of Flemish tapestries, shelves of silver necklaces, fine swords and daggers etched with patterns, cunningly carved wooden objects, bowls of sparkling Venetian glass, and costly ornaments cut from bleached bone. "I know all the best places to buy now."

Proudly, he led me through the streets, greeting acquaintances and doffing his cap at stout matrons.

Outside the cutler's shop we paused to speak to Maud Attemore, surrounded by a rowdy assortment of raucous wenches, clucking matrons, and disreputable fellows eager to jeer at her tales. Thrusting them all aside, the buxom gossip in the patterned ochre gown and embroidered, velvet cap, muttered to me in an undertone, her bold face stricken.

"Best keep your name a secret. There's a wicked rumour those Wydeville boys were killed by some knave named Forrest. You should get away from London as soon as you can." She kissed my cheek, squeezed me in a hug, and pressed several fat pennies into Dickon's palm.

Before I could respond, a portly matron with bright cheeks pushed in front of me, declaring, "Now, Maud, you old mischief-maker, what's this about that wanton wench in Littlewood Street? I heard she—"

Dickon caught my arm. "What's wrong, Mama?"

"Take me back to Bread Street, Dickon," I said, my attention caught by a shadowy figure sneaking apart from the loiterers and disappearing among a web of alleyways. "It's not safe here."

Without Anne Neville's protection I realised I stood now in gravest danger. Maud's warning reminded me that my old enemies wouldn't rest until they secured my silence.

⚜

"Will the Tudor be king?"

The question hung on everyone's lips.

I didn't need the cards or the scrying bowl to reveal this secret. Long ago I'd seen the bloody battle that would bring King Richard down. Already he moved towards his fate, having travelled to Nottingham to muster troops. Only when I heard the Tudor had landed in Wales did I summon the spirits.

"Nerys, Nerys," I called in the silent hours when the house slept. Recalling Mara's admonition about calling back the dead, I watched the water swirl with light as Nerys came to me holding high the standard of the red dragon. She beckoned. As I leaned toward the bowl, my unbound hair touching the surface of the water, Nerys commanded me to stand with her behind a line of soldiers looking up toward a hill.

Down the hill and across the plain a great white charger galloped, its hooves churning clods of earth into dust. The sun danced on the crest of its rider's helm, dazzling my eyes. Uncanny screams tore the air. The thunder of horses shook the earth so that it quaked as if in terror. Rider and retinue bore down, hacking their way through a forest of spears and pikes. The hot, familiar reek of horse breath scorched my face. Bloody rain blurred my vision. Glinting in the sunlight, a sword arced down. The red dragon plunged and wavered.

"Treason!" cried a voice. A black tide of soldiers swooped down like ravens upon the white horse, cutting it to ribbons. The rider fell, crushed amongst a hammering tumult. But someone held out a glittering object. When I realised it was the crown, I reached to snatch it—

"Will we go back to Middleham?"

"No, not to Middleham." I swallowed hard. "Somewhere new where no one knows us."

Dickon's voice quavered. "Shan't I see my cousins again?"

"Of course you will." Did he notice the traitorous wobble of my own voice? I forced a cheery note into my explanation. "We're going to Mistress Proudley's. She's Meg's oldest sister and our cousin, so we'll be among friends."

"Is Lincolnshire a long way from here?"

"Several days' journey," I answered, truthfully. "But with swift horses and a stout heart a man may be in London several times a year." I knew he didn't relish living among strangers. "Judith has a shop selling produce from her husband's farm. She needs help and has offered us work and lodgings. It's a piece of luck we can't spurn."

Memories tugged me back to the fortune-telling. Soon I'd see the landscape I'd described to Judith all those years ago. Dispassionately, I contemplated all the events that had brought me to this journey. I saw again the pattern and the shape of destiny unfold like a vast, vivid tapestry caught within the confines of a monstrous loom. Hadn't Mistress Evans warned me I'd a long road to travel?

King Richard paid me a generous pension for Miles's loyalty but I'd little hope the Tudor would continue. He showed no love for the usurper's henchmen, nor compassion for their widows. And Maud proved right about us not being safe in the city. Too many days I grew aware of a familiar figure watching me from dingy corners. Recently he dared to follow me into the market, taunting me with sly insinuations.

"The Tudor's averse to sorcery, Mistress Forrest."

"Have you nothing better to do than torment widows, Master Green?" I held my head high, the dull ache in my heart making my voice hard-edged. I knew he'd take any coins he could for whispering secrets. Before long, the Watch would come looking for me.

Besides, ever since the Tudor took the crown, new, wilder rumours circulated. People whispered the Wydeville boys had escaped the Tower. Some even swore they'd seen them. And lately someone dared to ask: Who gave the order for their murder? Was Gloucester truly to blame? Who else might profit from their deaths?

They say the Tudor's anxious to suppress such speculations. But suppose Jack Green could solve the gossips' newest mystery? What might that be worth? Perhaps, I thought, remembering Gloucester's vigil by his sick son's bedside and his desperate final courage, Master Green already served a new master?

"It'll be a great adventure." I tried to soothe a dubious Dickon, slipping my arm into his. "The Proudleys have several boys and one is near to you in age. You'll have a new friend to keep you company."

"I miss Ned."

Tears stung my eyes. "I know, but it wasn't to be. Ned was too good for this wicked world. You must be glad he's at peace now."

My voice shook dangerously but it wasn't Lord Ned's face which darted into my mind, but that of Miles. His guilt lay heavy on me. But I couldn't learn to regret my love for him. His last secret lay safe in my keeping. Fighting tears, I crossed myself and said a silent prayer for the comfort of his soul, wondering what Brother Brian would have thought of this new piety. And thinking of Miles, Mara's words came echoing back—*Yours is a thorny road, child, but love is never wasted or forgotten*—For a moment I was there, in the velvet blackness of her shelter all those years ago—

The rumble of cartwheels shook me from memories.

"Here's Harry. Carry our bundles, for you're the man of the house now."

But Rob Metcalf took them. "Harry sent word of your plans." He flushed with embarrassment. "I thought to guide you on the journey. I've a fancy for farming in Lincolnshire myself and I've found a place that might suit. Perhaps you'd consider visiting some time?"

Extraordinarily touched by Rob's devotion, I smiled at the memory of Genevieve's giggles. "Perhaps I might," I answered. I pressed his hand so the flush in his cheeks deepened. "I'd be glad to know someone trustworthy would watch over my son."

"Be sure and learn your letters so you can write to us," Harry told Dickon. "I'll warrant you'll be back in London sooner than you think."

Impulsively the lad flung himself into Harry's embrace, fighting tears.

As the cart bore us away through the twisted streets I thought how once I'd longed to leave the city and return to my village. Now I abandoned it with regret, thinking of those whose company I should miss. Unbidden, other loved faces returned—Jane Collins busy in the nursery; pretty, foolish Emma at the fair; Joan and Lionel boasting of Sudeley; Genevieve Mountford giggling at Westminster; Maud Attemore in flamboyant gown, stout arms upon her ample hips, head thrown back, mouth curving in a saucy grin, laughing at the latest scandal—Would I ever look on them again?

On my lap I held a precious bundle—Brother Brian's journal wrapped in the length of cloth-of-gold given to me by the late queen, and Mara's painted cards—all my treasures together. One day Dickon would have children and among them there'd be a new owner for the seer's tools.

Above the city gates a single bird like a hunchback in black rags crouched against the wind, draggled plumage fluttering. It cocked its head and winked an eye, flexed and fanned the wide, strong span of its wings. Momentarily, weak sunlight polished the feathers to an ebony gloss, transforming it into a thing of beauty. *Nothing is ever quite what it seems*, I mused, admiring the canny, handsome scavenger.

"The past is gone but the future waits. You have a promise to fulfil."

At last I recognised the timelessness of Mara's wisdom.

Hadn't I already seen the elder Wydeville boy? He sat on the Tower stairs, forlorn, unshriven, lost. Behind him crouched another, fainter, shadowy figure I took to be young Richard. But however hard I tried, I couldn't see his face, though I longed to glimpse again the impish smile that melted hearts. Could I soothe such unquiet spirits? There'd be time enough to consult the cards when we got to Lincolnshire. Mara would be pleased.

About the Author

~

Moonyeen Blakey

What do you know about Cleethorpes?

Although called a seaside, it's not strictly a sea which laps up its beach. The treacherous River Humber sweeps along this east coast and is known for trapping unwary "trippers" who go paddling and then suddenly find themselves cut off from the land. But each year, visitors are lured by the attractions of golden sands, donkey rides, arcades and amusements.

Anyway, I was born here.

East-coasters have a reputation for being tough — probably because the winds here are cruel. But it's worth walking the beach in winter, preferably at dawn or dusk, just to admire the windswept wonder of the scenery.

The Vikings settled on this coast. Grimsby — sister town to Cleethorpes - was founded by one Grim who is remembered in the tale "The Lay of Havelock the Dane" and the town became a famous fishing port.

I live in Lincolnshire.

My father, who was proud to be a Lincolnshire "Yellerbelly," brought me up to appreciate the treasures of the county Henry VIII once called "the most brute and beastly shire in England."

No doubt the king's opinion was soured by the memory of the Lincolnshire Rising of 1536. But dismiss Lincolnshire as just a vast swathe of flat, agricultural land, and you're making a big mistake. Walk the Wolds and you'll soon change your mind. Lincolnshire enjoys a few secrets...

I often refer to my region as "the forgotten county" because much of the country's population has decided it has nothing to offer by way of culture or history. Lincolnshire folk just smile when they hear this. They've grown accustomed to hiding their assets from strangers...

My Junior School was called Old Clee and I owe it a great debt of thanks. It was new when I started and its staff had an innovative approach to education. Under the auspices of genial Headmaster, Freddie Frost, I thrived.

There were 56 pupils in my class, but teachers encountered very few problems with unruly children. They captivated us with thrilling tales that stirred the imagination. Reg Lowis, himself a published author of children's stories and a wonderful painter, nurtured my creative writing skills and artistic talent. Olive Little inspired my life-long interest in theatre with her improvisation-based drama lessons. I still possess a copy of the book of plays she published and I like to think we inspired her to write them.

Books loomed large in my life from as long as I can remember and school reinforced my pleasure in them. Never will I forget Mr Harriman's rendering of Buchan's "The Thirty-Nine Steps"! These teachers influenced my developing talent as a writer as much with their personalities as their teaching methods from the mysterious Mr Tindall in his pinstriped suit and his catch-phrase "By Jingo!" to the gentle Mr Wright who moved us with tales of John Keats as a young doctor. All were striking characters.

From Old Clee I moved to Wintringham Girls' Grammar School. Here, feisty Miss Chalk continued to foster my love of literature as we studied for A levels. And walking back and forth to school each day, I entertained my friends with the most terrible serials I'd written!

But I wanted to act.

This passion for drama drove me to the Royal Scottish Academy in Glasgow.

After a long period of unemployment, however, I decided I must give up my dream of working in the theatre and start earning. Enrolling on a crash course in English at Bishop Grosseteste College in Lincoln led to a career in teaching where my theatrical experience proved invaluable.

But most of all, it coloured my writing.

✍

For the Finest in Nautical and Historical Fiction and Nonfiction

WWW.FireshipPress.com

Interesting • Informative • Authoritative

Lightning Source UK Ltd.
Milton Keynes UK
UKOW050707180912

199187UK00005B/26/P